WONDERING SIGHT

Book Two of The Extraordinaries

MELISSA MCSHANE

Night Harbor Publishing

Copyright © 2017 by Melissa McShane

All rights reserved.

ISBN-13 978-1-949663-14-3

ISBN-10 1-949663-14-0

No part of this book may be reproduced in any form or by any electronic or mechanical means, including information storage and retrieval systems, without written permission from the author, except for the use of brief quotations in a book review.

This book is a work of fiction. Names, characters, businesses, organizations, places, events, and incidents either are the product of the author's imagination or are used fictitiously. Any resemblance to actual persons living or dead, events, or locales is entirely coincidental.

Cover design by Eugene Teplitsky

To Jacob,
for always being willing to read just a little more

CONTENTS

CHAPTER 1

IN WHICH SOPHIA HAS AN
UNPLEASANT ENCOUNTER

L ondon at night looked nothing like Sophia remembered. The recently installed gas lamps lining the street shed an unwavering glow over the pavement, gilding the doors of the tall, winter-bleak houses. The light looked warm, but was unable to blunt the chill of the frigid November night that seeped through her cloak and numbed her cheeks.

Sophia nestled into the seat of Cecy's chaise and clenched her hands in her lap, shivering inside her fur-lined cloak and wishing her gloves were made of kid and not thin red silk. Not for the first time that evening she thought about raising the hood of her cloak. But that would disorder her auburn locks, so painstakingly arranged by her maid, and she did not want to look mussed for her first public appearance after returning to London.

She smoothed her gown over her knees; it was a modish emerald green that stood in vibrant contrast to the red gloves. She probably should have worn something that was not so eye-catching. Everyone would already be watching her tonight. That was something she was always certain of.

The lamps lining the streets of London were not the only things that had changed in the more than four years of Sophia's absence from the city. Despite the war, it seemed new construction, and the remodeling of old construction, was everywhere. New streets offered new routes to familiar old places; shops had vanished and were replaced by other shops. It was a testament to the irrepressible optimism of the English people.

The only thing that had not changed was the smell. The winter weather did little to dispel the odor of animal waste in the streets and the more distant but equally pervasive scent of the Thames. Sophia knew she would become accustomed to the smell with time, but only six weeks after her return to this great city, her nose still involuntarily wrinkled whenever she stepped outside. She remembered the brisk, damp breezes coming off the Tagus River, the soft rains that fell at this time of year, and experienced the familiar mix of longing and fury that rose in her whenever she thought of Lisbon and what had happened there.

"Whatever sour thoughts you are entertaining, I suggest you dismiss them soon," Cecy teased. "You will hurt Countess Lieven's feelings by implying you do not appreciate her generosity in providing you with a voucher." She seemed not at all discommoded by the chill in the air.

"It would be more accurate to say she pressed it upon me with great insistence," Sophia said. "The Countess's admiration of Extraordinaries is...rather overwhelming. I am grateful I was too young and insignificant to attract her attention when I was in London for my first season, because I would have found her terrifying. Besides, she may not even be at Almack's tonight."

"It is the first ball of the Season, and *you* will be there," Cecy said. "The Prince of Wales himself could not excite more—oh, my dear, I was thoughtless, wasn't I?"

Sophia realized she was clenching her fists more tightly together, and forced them to relax. "Hardly that," she said, but she knew Cecy could hear how false her reassurance was.

Her friend clasped her intertwined hands and squeezed lightly. "No one knows of the manner in which you left military service," she said in a low voice, though Sophia was certain Peter the coachman could not hear them in any case. "They know only of your exemplary record, that it was you who helped foil the Caribbean pirates by deducing how that foul man Rhys Evans was tracking our Navy's ships. Your reputation is secure. The War Office has seen to that."

"They also saw to my dismissal," Sophia said bitterly. "They may seem to care for the interests of the Extraordinaries whose actions they direct, but I know now they only maintain the public appearance of my reputation because it reflects well on them. They betrayed me, Cecy, betrayed me to keep the good will of a liar and an embezzler. Am I to be *grateful*, that they did not spread the word that my Visions are false?"

"Your Visions are not false!"

"As far as the War Office is concerned, they are."

"But you need not care about them any longer. You are free from your obligations, free to start a new life, and I insist you do so. I cannot bear to see you suffering."

Sophia smiled. "I might say the same of you."

"I feel very well tonight," Cecy said, pushing a lock of blond hair away from her thin face. "I have almost no pain, and I look forward to sitting and conversing with my friends while *you* dance the night away."

The smile fell away from Sophia's face. "I am not convinced this is not a mistake," she said. "It has been nearly three years since I danced with anyone."

"Did you and Richard not attend dances in Lisbon?"

"Richard was too often gone on his—he called them 'jaunts,' those intelligence-gathering journeys of his. I disliked dancing without him. And then he was killed, and I lost interest entirely." Her memories of her husband, dead these two and a half years, were distant and gave her only a little pain, unlike the far fresher stabs thoughts of her expulsion from the military gave her.

"Well, it is not as if you have forgotten how to dance," Cecy said in a mock-stern voice. "No one has introduced a new dance at Almack's in forty years. I doubt such a thing will happen again in our lifetimes. So you *will* dance, and you *will* enjoy yourself, because your isolation is beginning to cause comment."

"I know. The Duchess of Lenshire wrote to me again today on that very topic."

"She wishes you to give her a Vision?"

"In public, no less. I am invited to attend a dinner party at which I will be the entertainment. Not that even she would be so crass as to put it that way."

"I am afraid she sees you rather in the light of a performing bear."

"I know. I wish I did not have this talent."

"Sophy! Never say that! It is not true."

Sophia sighed. Her Extraordinary talent might be the proximate cause of her current anger and humiliation, but it gave her such joy she could not imagine giving it up. "I am in rather a mood tonight, aren't I?"

"Yes, you are. And if I can endure a little pain, you can endure a little social interaction. Even if the refreshments are bland and tepid."

The chaise was making the turn onto King Street, and in the distance Sophia could see the glow of their destination's many windows. She sighed again, but with a smile. "I will endeavor to be cheerful, and to enjoy myself," she said. "And perhaps no one will ask me to dance."

Cecy laughed. "You are an attractive, wealthy widow who is also a war hero and an Extraordinary. I probably should have found you a stick to beat the men away with."

The coachman assisted first Sophia, then Cecy out of the carriage; Sophia gave Cecy her arm and her friend leaned on her support only a little heavily. At least she was willing to accept Sophia's support instead of insisting there was nothing wrong with her. Cecy disliked being a burden and often lied about the amount of pain she was in, so Sophia and Lewis, Cecy's husband, had to watch her carefully for signs that her condition was beginning to trouble her. No doctor and no Extraordinary Shaper had been able to discover what it was that kept Cecy in near-constant pain, and Sophia had sought Dream after Dream with no more success. But tonight, at least, Cecy would be able to enjoy herself.

They passed through the famous doors of Almack's to find that although it was yet early in the evening, the place was thronged with people, all of them dressed in their finest and talking loudly enough that the noise spilled through the doors and washed over Sophia like a murmuring tide, warm and buoyant.

Sophia had never attended Almack's before tonight and was struck by how brightly lit it was, with the chandeliers that hung low over the gathering shedding their brilliance over the dancers and shining off the many large mirrors lining the walls. The mirrors, reflecting their own images, made the room seem larger than it was, as if they were windows opening on other, similar rooms filled with the dancers' doppelgangers who were enjoying themselves as much as their originals.

She caught a glimpse of herself in one, tall and gawky, with skin darkened from four years of the Mediterranean sun, and turned away, feeling some amusement that she would likely be considered a great beauty thanks to her talent when all the evidence showed her to be... well, *attractive* was the best she could hope for. Richard had thought her beautiful, but love did seem to alter the perceptions in unusual ways.

The room was surprisingly warm despite its size, with all those bodies in such close proximity, and it was comforting after the cold outside, though no doubt it would feel over warm soon enough. In the gallery, the musicians plowed through a reel with rather more energy than it probably required, and men and women filled the center of the room, passing and circling one another in time to the sprightly beat. The exertion of dancing would only make things hotter. She wished she had not forgotten her fan, though it was unlikely to do her much good, only moving the warm air from one place to another.

The thought of dancing made little tendrils of dread creep across her chest, chilly in a way that did not counteract the heat of the room. She might not have forgotten how to dance, but she felt as if she *had* forgotten how to converse easily with strangers who had nothing more in common with her than a mutual interest in dancing.

She pushed through the crowd, opening a path so Cecy would not have to endure the physical contact that so often caused her pain, ignoring the awed glances and whispered comments that spread through the crush as she passed. Her face might be as yet unknown, as she had rarely gone out in public since her return to London, but the red gloves, the outward sign of an Extraordinary Seer, were better than a calling card to advertise her identity.

Why they must be red was a tradition with origins lost to history, but she had donned them every morning for the last twelve years, ever since her Extraordinary talent had manifested, to avoid touching anything that might trigger a Vision. Not every object had enough history weighing it down to bear anything worth Seeing, but those that did could overwhelm her with the shifting, overlapping images of past and present and future connected to the object and the person most closely associated with it. Sophia had considered, more than once, wearing gloves of a different color, but although such an action would give her blessed anonymity, she was always uncomfortable at the idea, as if she were denying this fundamental part of herself in trying to conceal it.

She found them an unoccupied sofa and tried to appear serenely unconcerned at the discreet attention she was attracting. At least none of the guests here tonight would be so crass as to ask her for a Vision; more likely they would angle for an introduction that would allow them a few words with her that they could brag about later. Countess Lieven and her oppressive attention were nowhere in sight.

A woman sitting on a sofa about a foot away from theirs caught sight of Sophia and nudged her companion, a well-dressed man in yellow waistcoat and dark knee breeches. He began to raise his quizzing glass to examine her, then put it swiftly away and turned his head in such a deliberate manner that Sophia knew he was still watching her. *And so it begins.*

She straightened her gloves to conceal her discomfort at being stared at, even covertly. Most of her fellow Extraordinary Seers loved the attention they received, but Sophia had never quite been able to shed the feeling that the gloves made her an object, a living, breathing statue, instead of a person. It was a pity Lady Enderleigh, England's only Extraordinary Scorcher, was somewhere in the Caribbean; her entrance was likely the only thing that could eclipse Sophia's appearance at Almack's tonight.

"I do not see anyone I know," Cecy murmured. "Perhaps you will not have to dance after all, if you cannot secure an introduction."

"I am certain someone will find an excuse to speak to us. Until then, we will sit here and amuse ourselves by inventing histories for those who pass before us," Sophia said. "That young man speaking to the rather large woman, over there—does he not look like an insect? With that dull brown hair and his thin limbs?"

Cecy covered her mouth to hide a giggle. "He does! And—oh, no, Sophy, only see to whom he is speaking! Is it too late for us to hide?"

Sophia turned partly away. "Perhaps she does not see us. Quickly, turn your face."

"Mrs. Westlake!" A strident voice rose above the clamor of the crowd. "I'm surprised to see you here in London. And Mrs. Barham, good to see you out in public."

"Lady Daveril, what a pleasure," Sophia said. Lady Daveril, dressed in old gold silk with topazes around her neck and in her hair, loomed over them like an elegantly gowned battleship. "You look well."

"Fresh air and frequent walks, that's what keeps a body well. You should follow that regimen, Mrs. Barham," Lady Daveril said. Cecy's gaze dropped to her lap, and Sophia had to control the urge to rise and slap the tall, buxom woman across both her rosy cheeks. "But what brings you back to London so soon, Mrs. Westlake? I thought you had another eight months of service to go."

"How kind of you to take such an interest in me, Lady Daveril," Sophia said. Would she be ejected from Almack's if she took hold of the Countess's elegantly coiffed hair and yanked it out by the roots? "But after the pirates' decisive defeat, the War Office agreed I should be released early. As a reward, you see." It was the story the War Office had concocted, and she had no choice but to repeat it as they directed and pray no one realized how many months had passed between that event and her leaving the service.

"The more reward for us, that we enjoy your presence again," Lady Daveril said. "Pity about your husband, but you're well out of mourning and I imagine you're eager to remarry."

"I have chosen not to marry again, Lady Daveril," Sophia said. "I do not feel the lack of a husband."

"Nonsense," the tall woman said. "It's your duty to marry and produce talented children for England. And I intend to introduce as many eligible men as possible to you. Even someone as choosy as you can't reject all of them."

Can I not? Sophia thought, but said only, "I am very obliged to you, Lady Daveril, but we both know the law—"

"Oh, never mind the law," Lady Daveril said. "I'm talking about what's right. Never fear, Mrs. Westlake, no one's expecting you to marry where you don't feel an attachment. I'll speak with you later, shall I?" She sailed off into the crowd, unperturbed at forcing a few of the dancers at the bottom of the set to step out of her way.

Sophia and Cecy looked at one another. "This was a terrible idea," Sophia said.

"I know Lady Daveril is unpleasant, but you will have to find partners somehow, and at least she will provide an introduction," Cecy said.

"How is it you maintain such unrelenting optimism in the face of abject horror?"

"I will grant you horror, but it is hardly abject. Spine-chilling, perhaps."

Sophia laughed, and said, "I suppose I could always attempt to hide from her. But you are correct, and it would be ridiculous for me to come here and spend the entire evening *not* dancing."

"Mrs. Westlake!"

Sophia, startled by this high-pitched exclamation uttered in loud tones from only a few feet away, stood and turned to see who had spoken. A short, plump young woman with pale blond ringlets in some disorder around her face was looking directly at her, her mouth and hazel eyes as round as her cheeks.

"Mama, it's Mrs. Westlake! Mrs. Westlake, how good to see you—but I can see you don't remember me, I suppose it's been years since —I am Richard's cousin Daphne—oh, mama, Mrs. Westlake is *family*, don't make that face at me." The young woman approached Sophia despite the restraining hand an older woman with much neater blond hair placed on her shoulder. "Mrs. Westlake will want to speak to *us*."

"Daphne, contain yourself," the older woman said. "I beg your pardon, Mrs. Westlake. I am afraid Daphne has been sadly indulged all her life. But it is true, poor Richard was my nephew. I hope you received our family's condolences upon his death."

"Lady Claresby," Sophia said, dredging the name up from memory, "of course I remember you. Your kind letter was such a comfort to me. And Lady Daphne—it is good to see you again."

"I know I'm much changed since you saw me last, but I didn't realize you might not recognize—but then I was several inches shorter, I've grown much in the last four years—are you enjoying yourself? Because I have to say"—Lady Daphne's voice dropped to a whisper barely audible above the noise of the crowd—"I feel as if I'm on display, don't you? You know I'm an Extraordinary Bounder, yes? And I can tell everyone is looking at *you* as well—it's so uncomfortable, and they all know I'm determined not to marry until—you must tell me what the service is like! I tried to make them admit me two years ago, when I was eighteen, but no one would listen, and now I will be eligible in May and I'm in ecstasies!"

Sophia could not help smiling at the young woman's exuberance. "I am certain you will have many adventures, if your assignments are anything like Richard's were," she said.

Lady Daphne blushed. "I should not have reminded you of him, should I?" she said. "I beg your pardon. I forgot for a moment that Richard was a Bounder. I sometimes speak before I think—Mama is in complete despair over me—"

"Not *complete* despair," Lady Claresby said, "since you are trying so hard to learn self-control."

"I am, truly I am," Lady Daphne said. "I'm glad we met—may I call you Sophia? Or maybe you believe that's impertinent, since we are only cousins by marriage—but that's still family, don't you agree?"

"Richard always spoke so fondly of you that I feel he would have wanted us to be friends," Sophia said. "I would love for you to call me Sophia."

"And you will call me Daphne, I dislike being Lady Daphne because everyone makes it sound as if I am ten years old," Lady Daphne said. "I have so many questions—oh, but I'm not annoying you, am I? It's not as if I'm bothering you for a prophecy, because my friend Viola is a Seer, not an Extraordinary Seer, but a Seer, and people are always asking her to Dream for them, and she hates it, and I imagine you probably feel the same way. And I know all these people are hovering around wondering how I dared to speak to you—"

"Daphne, please don't trouble Mrs. Westlake," Lady Claresby said.

"But I'm not—oh, I am, aren't I?"

Daphne looked so downhearted that Sophia laughed again and clasped her hand.

"You are not in the slightest," she said, "but I believe Almack's is not the place for such conversation. May I call on you both tomorrow?"

"We would be delighted to welcome you," Lady Claresby said with a smile.

"Please do!" Daphne said, squeezing Sophia's hand in return. "I promise to keep my excitement in check."

"I look forward to it," Sophia said, and watched Lady Claresby and her irrepressible daughter move off into the crowd.

She had forgotten Richard had family beyond his immediate one; his mother was the Marquess of Claresby's sister, Lady Penelope St. Clair, and her marriage to the wealthy and highly-rated Mover Archibald Westlake had been the talk of London thirty years before. Probably the St. Clairs were not truly family, having been related by a marriage that had ended so tragically, but Richard's parents lived in Bath, and Sophia's family all lived in Derbyshire, and she found herself pleased at the thought of finding relations closer to her adopted home.

She turned to resume her seat and discovered, to her amusement, that one of Cecy's many friends from her Speaker reticulum had taken it, and the two women were deep in conversation about something Sophia had no knowledge of. Well, she did want Cecy to enjoy herself.

She surveyed the room. From the way several men quickly averted their gaze, she knew they had been staring at her. How foolish, that they had to wait on an introduction to approach her, when it was clear they were interested in making her acquaintance. How terrible, that she had to rely on Lady Daveril to provide her with those introductions. Too late, she realized she might have asked Lady Claresby for assistance. Who knew what the Countess might come up with?

"Mrs. Westlake!" The Countess's booming voice cut across the noise, startling Sophia. It was as if her thoughts had summoned the woman. "There you are! I almost believe you have been hiding from me."

"No, Lady Daveril," Sophia said as the tall woman approached.

"There is someone you should meet," the Countess said. "Lord Endicott, do not be so shy. Mrs. Westlake, let me introduce Lord Endicott. Mrs. Westlake is newly returned from Portugal and is eager to make new friends."

Lord Endicott. The world tilted, and Sophia's vision went grey at the edges. *How is he here? Is there some other Lord Endicott?*

But no: there was the tall, well-Shaped form, the splendidly turned calves and broad shoulders, the golden hair and bright green eyes that Nature and not talent had gifted him with, since neither could be Shaped, the strong mouth that at the moment was smiling at her in what probably looked to everyone else like a friendly, even admiring, expression. She could not bring herself to smile back at him. His was the face of her nightmares.

CHAPTER 2
IN WHICH SOPHIA DREAMS, AND FORMS A RESOLUTION

"I did not know it was Mrs. Westlake to whom you wished to introduce me," Lord Endicott said in that beautiful baritone that had always been able to captivate his listeners. "We were acquainted in Portugal. Mrs. Westlake, your servant."

"Lord Endicott," Sophia said, hoping it came out sounding normal and not filled with the fury and humiliation raging through her. "I did not know you were in London."

"My business in Portugal is finished," he said, "and London is where society is, this time of year. Do you not agree?"

He looked so friendly, sounded so charming, and she had to stop her hands from closing into fists and smashing that beautiful face. "I suppose," she said. Why could she not think of some way to cut him? To extricate herself from this conversation? But Cecy was preoccupied with her friend, and Daphne and Lady Claresby were gone, and Sophia had just enough self-control not to begin screaming accusations at Lord Endicott.

Lady Daveril laughed, a sound as booming as her voice, and said, "Ask her to dance, Endicott, or I'll have to do it for you, and you know I will."

"I would enjoy dancing with you, Mrs. Westlake," Lord Endicott said, offering her his hand. Sophia felt numb. She could not. She absolutely could not spend one more moment in his presence. She should turn and walk away—

—and commit social suicide, declare herself haughty and stiff-necked, be even more the subject of gossip than she already was. She took his hand and bobbed a curtsey to him. "Thank you, my lord," she said, and was proud that none of her turmoil showed in her voice.

Their first dance was fast, with much hopping and weaving, certainly too exuberant for conversation, but after a minute of silence, Lord Endicott said, "I am glad to see you participating in society, Mrs. Westlake."

"And why should I not?" Sophia replied, trying for a light tone.

Lord Endicott shrugged. "I was afraid you would allow what happened to make you bitter. You are far too young and lovely to let one mistake sour your life."

His face was so innocently friendly. *Does he practice that look of concern in his mirror every morning? Or is he Shaping his face as he speaks?* "Your concern is touching," she said.

"I see no reason why we should not be friends. I bear you no ill will."

"How generous of you."

"Then you are bitter, after all."

Sophia's temper began to rise. *Just two dances. Half an hour.* "Again, I thank you for your concern, but *I* see no reason why we *should* be friends, simply because Lady Daveril has taken an interest in my social life."

Lord Endicott's look of concern turned to one of injured sorrow so perfect it could not be real. How, *how* could he so readily put up such a false façade? "I have forgiven you for your mistake in accusing me of a terrible crime," he said. "I believe you should be able to forgive yourself. I wish there were something I could do to aid you in that."

"Forgive my bluntness, Lord Endicott, but I have not asked for your help, nor do I believe I need it. I would prefer this conversation be at an end."

"I don't believe I deserve that. I could have had you arrested, you know. The law is not gentle with Seers convicted of lying about their

Dreams. I choose to believe you were mistaken rather than untruthful."

"So I am to show you gratitude, that you only had me humiliated and not imprisoned as well?"

"The humiliation was all yours, Mrs. Westlake. There is no shame in a Seer being wrong about a Dream or a Vision. I understand they can be very difficult to interpret correctly. You were the one who chose to continue claiming not only that I was engaged in business like some common tradesman, but that I was an embezzler and a thief, when all the evidence said otherwise."

"Evidence *you* manufactured."

"And then made yourself appear unhinged by *that* accusation." Lord Endicott continued to sound sorrowful, not angry, and it infuriated Sophia. Why was he playing this game with her? Was he not satisfied that her reputation within the government was shattered? "I truly do not wish to be your enemy, Mrs. Westlake, but if your pride—"

"Say nothing more," Sophia said in a low, intense voice. Surely everyone dancing within ten feet of her could feel the anger radiating off her like heat off a summer pavement. "You were guilty. You and I both know it. You found a way to hide your guilt. We both know this as well. I lost my position thanks to you, and now the government considers me unreliable and irrational. There is nothing I can do to change their minds about me. All I can do is put it behind me—and resolve never to be in contact with you again. So do not, I pray you, continue this farce."

"Forgive me for upsetting you," Lord Endicott said. "I meant only to extend an olive branch—but I see your hatred of me has disordered your good sense." He smiled at her again, still perfectly sorrowful, but his eyes were alight with pleasure at her anger. If only she dared slap him across that beautiful face! Fury filled her, made it impossible for her to speak, and for that Sophia was grateful, because anything she said now would no doubt come out as a shriek.

She moved through the figures of the dance automatically, without looking at her partner more than was necessary. He spoke to her once or twice more; she ignored him each time, and finally he fell silent. If she had any doubt about his character before, his deliberate torment of her confirmed that he was an amoral, soulless villain who, not being satisfied with defeating her, was compelled to torture her as well.

This was how he'd accomplished it; this was how he had convinced everyone he was an innocent victim. He was handsome as only a Shaper could be, he spoke smoothly and with great feeling, he knew how to conceal his wrongdoing from everyone except her, and her knowledge of his crime was irrelevant. That he was also politically powerful only gave more weight to his words, at least as far as the War Office was concerned. Had she not known the truth, had she not been certain of his guilt, she might have thought him truly interested in making peace between them.

She endured the rest of their dances, and his escort back to where Cecy sat, alone now, with a stoic demeanor. Lord Endicott bowed, then walked away without a word. Cecy watched him go, imperfectly concealing her horror. "Sophia, do not tell me you accepted his invitation to dance!" she said in a low voice.

"Lady Daveril was standing right there. I had no choice. Oh, Cecy, may we not leave?" Sophia was furious that her enemy might drive her away so readily, but she was so overwhelmed she could not bear another moment in this hot, overcrowded, noisy room that was too bright and filled with too many awful people.

"Of course, dearest. Let me arrange for my carriage to be brought around."

Cecy stood and walked away, and Sophia sat and waited, feeling too exhausted to move. The stares continued, but no one else stopped to speak to her; no one asked her to dance. She felt as isolated as if Lord Endicott truly had spread the word of her "mistake" and his own status as wronged innocent.

But there was nothing she could do, except avoid him. He could still choose to reveal all—she had never understood why he had chosen not to do so, since there was no pressure the War Office could bring to bear that would have any influence on him, and she could admit to herself that she *was* grateful not to have to suffer through public humiliation and ostracism. But she would sooner die than admit that to *him*.

Their ride home was silent; Sophia's inner turmoil kept her too preoccupied to speak, and she suspected Cecy's pain had increased. They parted company in the hall outside their bedrooms, and Sophia undressed as quickly as her lady's maid could help her, then climbed into bed and pulled the blankets around her ears. Her time in beautiful, temperate Lisbon had made her sensitive to cold winters, and now she shivered as her body too-slowly adjusted to the sheets imperfectly heated by the warming pan.

Is this what I am destined for? Tormented by Lord Endicott, unable to defend myself, knowing myself to be right when all the world believes me wrong? She rolled over to lie on her stomach and burrowed her head beneath her pillow. *Sometimes I even doubt myself. I have a perfect accuracy rating; was I simply too proud to accept that the great Sophia Westlake could be wrong?*

She reviewed, as she did every night, the Dream that had revealed Lord Endicott's crime. Dwelling on it was pointless, but she could not stop herself, and every time, every recalled detail confirmed the truth of what she had seen. *He knew I had found him out, somehow, and concealed his crime. Was it coincidence, that that clerk died before his testimony would have proven me right? He is a thief and a liar and I should be content with knowing I was right.* But it was not enough.

She fell into Dream as a diver drops into a deep pool, blue waters parting to let her body slip between them. In all directions, above and below and to the sides, stood the doors of Dream, insubstantial and cold, though the last was her imagination, as in Dream she could not feel any such thing. Some stood ajar, inviting her; others were fast closed and would need an effort to pass through. Sophia wandered among them, having no particular intent in Dreaming tonight.

As she approached each door, it grew opaque, and on its surface shifting figures danced, hinting at what knowledge might lie beyond. Had she meditated on a subject before sleeping, she would have found doors specific to the information she sought; as it was, her Dreams simply grew from things she knew or had experienced recently. Until six weeks ago, all her Dreams had been focused on the Peninsula. Now they were random glimpses into lives she barely remembered encountering.

She passed a door whose images were little better than masses of inchoate color, then went back a few steps to look at it again. A face formed from the colors, faded, came into focus again. Sophia's Dream-self gasped, and the Dream shook briefly as her living body reacted. She calmed herself, afraid of waking; no Dream could be returned to once a Seer woke. The face re-emerged. *Lord Endicott.*

Of course, it was logical she might Dream of him, even obvious, given the emotional effect he'd had on her. She put her hand palm-first on the door, and it dissolved as if absorbed by her skin. As it disappeared, she was drawn forward until the Dream surrounded her, as if she stood inside the room that was the locus for the Dream image.

The room itself was nebulous; it could have been the grand entry at Carlton House or a shack near the banks of the Thames. It contained waist-high wooden crates, none of them labeled even when she imposed her will on the Dream to bring that part of it into focus.

For an ordinary Seer, part of interpreting Dreams was learning to identify meaningful images by how they appeared in relation to the rest of the Dream. Some Dreams were colorless except for certain parts that were bright red or pale yellow, while other Dreams persisted in staying out of focus but for one important object. Sophia, an Extraordinary, was capable of manipulating the stuff of Dreams to extract their meaning more directly.

The room held nothing more than the crates. Sophia stepped back and pictured one of the lids flying off. It did so, vanishing as it went, which told Sophia its contents and not the crate itself were the core meaning of the Dream. She looked into the crate and saw silver. Loose coin filled the crate, an impossibility because no one but a Mover could lift a crate thus filled. Her perspective shifted, and the silver turned into rifle balls, then back again.

Confusion dragged her out of sleep. She already knew that Lord Endicott, concealing his involvement with a company producing war materiel, had embezzled from the government, billed for twice as much as he delivered, then blackmailed the clerk to alter the records. Why would she see this again? She sat in her bed in the darkness and rested her chin on her bent knees. She had no interest in Seeing anything to do with that vicious liar, so why did her Seer's brain drag up his image?

Of course. Though the War Office had not believed her accusation of Lord Endicott, they knew of the embezzlement and were investigating the crime. Lord Endicott would have been forced to abandon that plan; no wonder he said his business in Portugal was finished, because he could not afford to be identified as the perpetrator. But he was an amoral villain, and it was impossible that this was his only criminal enterprise. She had exposed him once, or tried to, and there was no reason she should not do so again. She would prove him a liar and a criminal, and she would have her revenge.

She lay down on her back, her left hand flat over her navel and her right over her heart, just below her left breast, preparatory to meditation. It was unlikely she would learn anything tonight; she would need to do more reading to give her mind images on which to base her Dreams. But she *would* succeed. She had never failed before, and it was impossible she should do so now.

CHAPTER 3
IN WHICH SOPHIA IS OFFERED EMPLOYMENT

"There are more than a dozen London newspapers, dearest; must you subscribe to all of them?" Cecy said. She picked up *The Times* and riffled its pages. "Not that I object to your exercising your talent, but this seems rather excessive. I mean, you have both the *Morning Chronicle* and the *Morning Post*."

"Both of which offer the same information from different viewpoints," Sophia said, wielding her scissors to remove yet another clipping. "I need to know as much as possible if I am to accomplish my goal."

Cecy laid down *The Times*, sat down next to Sophia, and sighed. Sophia was certain the sigh had nothing to do with how she had spread her various newspapers over the end of the breakfast room table opposite to where she and Cecy and Lewis took their meal.

Gauzy curtains diffused the light enough to keep it from glaring off the shining brown surface of the table—the part not obscured by newspaper, that is, which was not very much of it. The detritus of the morning meal still waited to be cleared away, and Sophia briefly wondered if she had actually eaten everything on her plate, or if her excitement to begin had distracted her from her stomach's demands. No, she felt no pangs of hunger, just a rising need to absorb everything these papers had to offer about Lord Endicott and his activities, criminal or otherwise.

"Sophy, are you certain this is a good idea?" Cecy said. "It is too late to convince the War Office that you were correct. Should you not leave it in the past?"

"Lord Endicott had the clerk, Mr. Tate, killed to prevent his speaking out," Sophia said, laying down her scissors. There was newsprint on her left index finger and thumb, which she rubbed at with her other hand. "He has shown himself without conscience and ready to commit any foul action to protect himself. I seem to be the only person who knows his true nature. How can I sit by and permit him to continue in his crimes? Especially if it might mean saving a life?"

"That is an excellent justification," Cecy said drily, "but I am certain you have other reasons for pursuing Lord Endicott." A servant entered the room and, with a hesitant glance at them, began clearing dishes away. Cecy lowered her voice. "You and I both know you have a tendency to become obsessed when you are faced with a problem. Tell me, what was it that happened when we were at school and your pet bird went missing?"

Sophia flushed. "That was different."

"You spent so much time in Dream that you collapsed and had to be sent home for a week of bed rest," Cecy said. "When it was clear to everyone that the obnoxious creature had escaped to the forest to live a carefree existence where its shrill and horribly intermittent cries could not disturb innocent girls who only wanted to sleep during the dark hours as God intended."

"All right," Sophia said, torn between irritation and amusement. "I will concede your point that I sometimes become..."

"Obsessive."

"*Overly focused* on a problem," Sophia said. "But it is that quality that has brought me my greatest successes, as I'm sure you'll recall."

"I believe the Fleet of the Americas is grateful to your *obsessiveness*, with all those weeks of analyzing Visions that led you to understand the fundamentals of how they work," Cecy said. "And then more weeks of training your fellow Extraordinaries to use the technique against the remaining pirates. But you came close to collapse again, and you cannot expect me to be happy about that, no matter how much success you had."

"Cecy, I swear to be careful. I cannot achieve Lord Endicott's destruction if I collapse; you don't believe I drive myself to the breaking point because I enjoy it?"

"I believe you do not always know where the breaking point is."

"Then *you* will have to remind me," Sophia said. She picked up her scissors and waved them in Cecy's direction, snipping the air with a couple of metallic tearing sounds. "I will stop you overexerting yourself, and you will stop me forgetting to eat and bathe."

Cecy wrinkled her nose. "I daresay I have the less pleasant task."

"But *you* are the more recalcitrant of us. Will you see Dr. Garland today?"

"Tomorrow," Cecy said, "though I feel horribly guilty, dragging her here three times a week only to wait on me and repeat the same temporary treatment every time."

"You forget she sees your condition as a challenge. Do not deny her the pleasure of treating you like an experiment."

Cecy laughed. "How strange that the idea does not make me feel angry or dehumanized." She pushed a few papers aside. "Is there anything I can help you with?"

"You can examine the *Morning Chronicle* for references to Lord Endicott," Sophia said, handing over that newspaper and a second pair of scissors. Having Cecy's cooperation, even if it was not completely whole-hearted, lifted her spirits. She would not admit it to Cecy, but the piles of newspapers daunted her a little. So much to read, and she knew from experience that little of it would have bearing on the Dreams she sought—but she could not know which of them might contain what she was looking for, and she could not risk missing a key piece of information by ignoring one simply because it seemed an unlikely source.

She had a moment's irritation at Lord Endicott that had nothing to do with how he'd humiliated her or her current pursuit of his criminal activity. What she *wanted* to do, now that she was free of her government service, was pursue a greater understanding of the mechanism of

Dream, as she had Vision. Aside from Bounding, Dream was the least understood of all the talents.

Seers knew that immersing themselves in the facts surrounding a person or event led to more detailed and accurate Dreams, but not why this was so, and no one understood how knowing facts, which necessarily existed in the past, could produce knowledge of the future. Sophia was convinced there was an answer, but she had no *time*, thanks to Lord Endicott. Proving him guilty was crucial. Proving him guilty in a way that caused him maximum public humiliation...it was not necessary, but it would satisfy her in a way she felt vaguely guilty about.

She snipped another story out of *The Times*. Lord Endicott was speaking to Parliament yet again in favor of the war. Possibly he was involved in some other crime connected with the military, if he were yet so passionate about Britain's continuing support of the fight against Napoleon.

Sophia, though she was in favor of her country defending itself against a merciless aggressor, nevertheless was uncertain about the morality of taking action against civilians who were in the thrall of an Extraordinary Coercer such as Napoleon. He had the gall to brag about his talent, as if it were not something foul that corrupted everything it touched; how could the ability to sway the emotions of multitudes, to make them believe they loved him, be anything but a curse?

No Coercer, Extraordinary or otherwise, had emerged in England for more than one hundred years, but the unexpected manifestation of an Extraordinary Scorcher talent had made some question whether Coercers might not simply be concealing themselves. Two of Sophia's newspapers had sections devoted to speculation as to which prominent member of Parliament might owe his power to a secret talent, though Sophia thought they were simply fond of looking for conspiracies where there were none to be found. She hoped. The idea of having her emotions manipulated frightened her.

"You intend to call on Lady Claresby this morning, yes? Would you mind stopping in at Floris? They know which scent is mine, you need only ask after my name," Cecy said.

"I would enjoy running your errand, as the day seems so pleasant, though I am certain you simply want me away from my obsession for a few hours."

"You know me so well," Cecy said with a wink.

※

IT WAS, IN FACT, A BEAUTIFUL DAY. THE SKY WAS CLEAR, brightening the winter sun and warming the chill air so that Sophia asked Peter to lower the hood of the barouche. She even considered leaving her pelisse behind. But she settled for respectability, and relaxed into the leather seat that warmed with her body's heat and that of the sun until it was perfectly comfortable.

All of London appeared to be out today, enjoying the respite from the oppressive frozen fug that had gripped the city for the previous three days. The pedestrians Sophia passed seemed more animated than before, as if they too had been gripped with immobility by a winter that already seemed as if it might never end.

She resolved to run Cecy's errand first, so it would not weigh on her during her visit with Lady Claresby and Daphne. The route took them near King Street, which brought Almack's to mind again, and Sophia found, to her surprise, that rather than being infuriated by the memory, she felt pleasure—pleasure at knowing she could bring Lord Endicott down if only she applied herself. She turned around in her seat after the carriage passed the turn that led to Almack's, watching until it was hidden by the shops of Jermyn Street. *Yes*, she thought, *I will have justice*, and stifled the fleeting thought that perhaps justice would not be enough.

She found that Floris, at least, was one of the shops that had not changed during her absence—that likely had remained the same for more than eighty years. She always enjoyed her visits there, with delicate scents in the air that were discreet and never overwhelming. She chose a comb for herself while waiting for Cecy's purchase to be wrapped. The shop seemed designed to lure one into making a purchase, if only for the pleasure of holding one of the little boxes, beautiful in itself as well as for the jewel-like treasure it contained.

Sophia held her parcel and went to the multi-paned window, nearly filling the front wall of the shop, to watch Jermyn Street's constantly moving traffic. The edges of the glass where they met the leading were slightly curved and made the passing men and women flicker as they passed. Sophia amused herself by considering how they would look if the window had the power to magically transform them to match those brief flickers. Tall and skinny, like the pair of chattering women with arms linked who strode rapidly down Jermyn Street? Or spherical, like the large man who stood outside near the door as if waiting for someone? Why he would choose to wait in the cold instead of the comfortably warm shop was a mystery.

She accepted her parcels with a smile and exited the shop only to nearly run into the spherical man, who still stood near the door. He was several years older than she, and not really spherical, of course, but well over six feet tall, and powerfully built. His dark eyes came to rest on her with such swiftness that Sophia was unsettled. "I beg your pardon, sir," she said, taking a few steps away.

"No, I should beg your pardon, Mrs. Westlake," he said. His voice was deep and smooth, and in tone unnervingly like Lord Endicott's, though in a much lower register. His well-bred accent was completely at odds with the pantaloons and undistinguished greatcoat he was wearing. "I was not paying attention to where I was standing."

"You know my name," Sophia said, trying to conceal her irritation. Once again her red gloves left her open to impertinences. It was not uncommon for admirers, or supplicants, to follow her in the hope of convincing her to perform some service for them, regardless of propriety; had she been any ordinary gentlewoman, it would have been the height of bad manners for this man to accost her on the street. Many Seers enjoyed their notoriety, and most accepted commissions—at a hefty fee, of course—as a way of making a living. Sophia, having no need of money, found the whole thing annoying. "I do not accept commissions, sir."

"I'm not interested in a commission, not the way you mean it," the man said. "My name is Rutledge, and you used to work for me."

"I beg your pardon again, sir," Sophia said, "but I know the men and women of the War Office for whom I used to work, and you are not among them."

Mr. Rutledge took Sophia's arm and drew her a few steps away from the shop door before releasing her. Sophia was too startled to resist. "My...employer...has no Extraordinary Seers—no Seers of any kind—of its own," he said. "General Omberlis occasionally loaned me your services. You must remember that some of your Visions seemed unrelated to the war?"

"I am not at liberty to discuss my military service," Sophia said. His size, and the deepness of his voice, and the way he stood so near to her, were beginning to make her nervous. Granted, he was unlikely to assault an Extraordinary nearly on the doorstep of Carlton House, but if he did, the fact that he would face a long prison sentence would be no comfort. She began assessing the distance from where she stood to her waiting carriage. Why did the stupid driver not see her predicament?

"Then I will tell you about it," Mr. Rutledge said. "You entered the service in aught-nine, when you came of age, as is expected of an Extraordinary Seer. You had an exemplary record for over three years. Perfect accuracy. And then you had a Dream that was disproven and you refused to admit you were wrong. The War Office expelled you, though it concealed the details of that expulsion to protect you and it both. Am I correct?"

"How do you know that?" Sophia said.

"I told you. You used to work for me. And now I would like to employ you on a somewhat more regular basis. I have need of an Extraordinary Seer. I know and respect your abilities. And I believe I can offer you something beyond money."

"And what would that be?" Sophia said.

"An opportunity to reclaim your reputation. To prove you are still as reliable as you ever were."

Sophia caught her breath. Vindication. *Someone*, finally, realized she had been telling the truth. "Then you are employed by the government," she said. "Who is your employer?"

He shook his head. "I can't tell you that until you've agreed to work for me. I can assure you it would not be immoral or degrading work, but I am not at liberty to reveal my connection to it to anyone who is not similarly committed."

"I am not comfortable with that."

"Are you comfortable with how things stand now? With the War Office considering you unstable and irrational?"

It was like a blow to the chest. "I say you are impertinent, sir," Sophia said.

"I apologize if my words were inappropriate, but I believe they are no less true for all that," Mr. Rutledge said.

Sophia considered briefly. "And how is my work for you to redeem my reputation? How does it involve Lord Endicott?"

"It has nothing to do with Lord Endicott," Mr. Rutledge said, frowning. "I thought you had put that behind you."

The ache in her chest tightened. "Then you believe my Dream was false," she said.

"I don't believe you deserved to be expulsed simply for one incorrect Dream," Mr. Rutledge said. "The War Office acted out of fear of what political pressure Lord Endicott might have brought to bear, and that was wrong."

Sophia focused on his face. He was surprisingly attractive for a faithless deceiver who was stupid enough to be taken in by Lord Endicott. How attractive would he be if she balled up her fist and struck him in the eye? "My Dream was not incorrect," she said, winding her fist into the fabric of her gown so it would not attack him independent of her control. "Lord Endicott is an embezzler and he arranged the death of Clive Tate. And I refuse to work for someone who believes I am a liar."

"I do not believe you are a liar," Mr. Rutledge said. His tone of voice, so patronizing, was that of someone soothing an injured animal. "You made a mistake—"

"The mistake was in speaking to you at all," Sophia snapped. "Do not approach me again."

The pleasant expression fell away from the big man's face. "I expended a great deal of political capital to get the—my employer to agree to my proposal at all," he said. "Some of those in positions of power have learned of your expulsion and believe you to be a liability. I am the only one who still has faith in your abilities. You cannot be so foolish as to reject that."

"Perhaps you should have spoken to me before you wasted all of that effort," Sophia said. "I am not so desperate that I will go crawling back to a government that thinks so poorly of me. I have no need of your offer, sir, and if repudiating what I know to be true is what it will take to reclaim my reputation, then I would rather the War Office continue to consider me unreliable."

"You are making a mistake."

"I believe, in your eyes, I am making *another* mistake. I wonder you can have any need of my services at all, if you believe me to be so entirely in the wrong."

"I—" Mr. Rutledge stopped. He appeared to be controlling his impulse to shout. "Mrs. Westlake," he continued in a calmer voice, "I wish I could tell you the details of how you have assisted me in the past. I believe it would convince you of my sincerity in offering you this position. We need never speak of your service with the War Office again, if that would satisfy you. I know you. You have a passion for justice that I believe would be put to good use in working for my employer. Please reconsider."

Now it was Sophia who had to struggle to control her desire to shout at him. "Mr. Rutledge," she said, after a moment's tense silence, "you and I have never met before this day. You do *not* know me, and I am at a loss to understand why you believe you do. I will do you the courtesy of accepting that you mean me no insult in choosing to disbelieve my story. After all, everyone else feels the same; why should you be different? But this means that you can only think of me in one of two ways: either I am a liar, or I am deluded, and I cannot accept a close association with anyone who believes me to be one of those. So I must decline your offer and ask you not to approach me again, because my mind will not change however you renew your request."

Mr. Rutledge's lips thinned as he pressed them hard together, probably trying to contain the words that wanted to escape his tongue. "As you wish. It seems the War Office was right. Forgive my importunacies." He took a few steps away from Sophia and bowed, raising his hat to reveal dark hair swept back from his brow, then turned and walked away up Jermyn Street.

Sophia watched him until he was a few yards away, then came to her senses and went to Cecy's carriage. "Don't leave yet," she said to Peter, and kept her eyes on the tall retreating figure until he reached the end of the street and turned left out of her sight. "All right," Sophia said. She scooted down in her seat in case they passed him, but the barouche turned right instead of left and Sophia could breathe more easily.

The encounter had left her as angry as her dance with Lord Endicott had, though in a completely different way. How Mr. Rutledge could expect her to work for someone who believed her either a liar or unstable was a complete mystery. No, she had been inaccurate in making that claim; he simply believed her to be wrong, and she probably should not hate him for that, since it was true there was no shame in being mistaken. But she knew she was not wrong, knew it the way she knew what her Dreams meant, and that was what ate at her, because she could have endured making a genuine mistake.

He thought I should be beholden to him, that I should be grateful for his intervention on my behalf, she thought, and that infuriated her all over again. She didn't need the War Office's approval or good will. She needed to see Lord Endicott brought low. She needed the world to see what evil hid behind that beautiful face. And she needed him to know she was the architect of his destruction.

CHAPTER 4
IN WHICH SOPHIA DISCOVERS A
NEW ALLY

S ophia emerged from Dream into her dark bedchamber and fumbled about for the lamp, momentarily disoriented at not being able to simply think the light into existence. Her groping fingers knocked the pencil lying on her bedside table to the floor just as they found the lamp's round base. She should have left it burning no matter how long this Dream might take.

Grumbling, she lit the lamp, then leaned out of her warm nest to reach, upside-down, for the pencil where it had rolled beneath her bed. Such a fuss over what was surely her most disappointing Dream to date, but she dutifully noted it down in the diary she kept by her bed:

Everything shifts. People whose faces change—possibly members of E.'s organization, disposable? More money, all bills of low denomination, this time fading from bills to roast chicken of all things!

She closed the book and set it down with more than necessary force, then turned off the light and lay back on her pillows. She would Dream no more tonight; three in a night was exceptional, even for her, and she could feel her mind clouding over with exhaustion. She was almost certain, after nearly a week of studying and meditating, that she was closing in on a detail, *the* detail, that would show her what crime Lord Endicott was engaged in now. And then—well, she had no plans for "then," but there was no point in making plans until she knew what she faced.

She had gone out in society almost every night since the disastrous evening at Almack's—to private parties, the theater, more dances—and had not seen Lord Endicott at all. The mysterious Mr. Rutledge had not made an appearance, either. She chose not to relax her guard, reasoning that preparedness was an excellent policy when unpleasant men were in the habit of appearing where they were least welcome. No, that was probably unfair to Mr. Rutledge, who had been very pleasant despite being impertinent and entirely wrong. Even so, she had no interest in seeing either of them again.

She closed her eyes and tried to relax into a normal sleep, in which the doors of Dream would not appear. It was far easier to fall into a Dreaming sleep, since she had been trained to do it since she was twelve, but Dream provided no rest, and even if she refused to enter any of the doors, a Dream would eventually find her. She flexed her toes, contracting and relaxing the muscles, then her calves, then her fingers and hands, and gradually the exercise sent her off into sleep.

Unfortunately, it was a restless sleep, and Sophia was plagued with ordinary dreams in which she was expected to box up piles of unwanted things, but the piles kept multiplying, and the boxes were hard to find, and when she woke it was to a sense that she had failed terribly at some important task.

She carried the feeling with her through breakfast and dressing to ride with Daphne in Hyde Park. She half-regretted agreeing to the outing, but the idea of staying indoors with nothing but her unpleasant thoughts to keep her company was repellent. And Daphne was an excellent companion—talkative, yes, but Sophia had been surprised to discover that her conversation was clever and interesting, if one could keep her from being distracted by some tangential thought.

She almost regretted her decision again when they joined the few other riders in Hyde Park that morning. It was far colder than she had expected from the brightness of the sunlight and the clearness of the pale blue sky, and traffic through the park was consequently thin. Sophia smiled at those they passed, but without feeling, and was just as happy that they met no one she would be forced to acknowledge less perfunctorily.

"Your head does not ache, does it, Sophia?" Daphne said. Bare branches cast strange shadows across her face. Sophia shook her head, but did not elaborate. Her horse Fidelius—such a perfect name for the placid chestnut gelding, so responsive to her hand on the reins, always so happy to see her—seemed not to mind the cold, but then he enjoyed their rides, no matter the weather. She patted his neck, and he tossed his head in response.

"It's only that you are so quiet, and I thought you would have things to say about the performance last night—I cannot abide clowns, they are so eerie when they don't speak, though I suppose—but then I know you prefer the ballet, and they don't speak either, I wonder what the difference is, because I am not unsettled at all by dancing—"

"I had an uncomfortable night, that is all," Sophia said. She had learned early on that Daphne's conversation was often like a flood that would not stop unless stemmed by the dam of someone else's interruption. "Unpleasant dreams."

"Not prophetic Dreams, though? Because I know Seers dream like everyone else, but I thought Dreams, the prophetic kind, did not disturb your sleep. Viola says they are like watching a play, if you were allowed to watch from onstage and wander amongst the players."

"That is true, and yes, they were ordinary dreams." She chose not to mention the Dreams she'd had before trying to sleep; Daphne was not privy to the details of her expulsion, nor her desire to prove Lord Endicott's crimes.

"*I* dreamed of flying, but then I often do—I wonder if Movers dream of flying, the ones who are not Extraordinaries I mean—I don't suppose Extraordinary Movers need dream of Flying, since they do it anyway—I've never met an Extraordinary Mover, have you?"

"One or two, during my time with the War Office."

"Did you meet the Earl of Enderleigh, then? But I suppose you wouldn't have, as he is serving in the Caribbean, and you were in Lisbon, and—I would imagine he might like to meet *you*, since you were of such help to him—are you ever tired of being famous? I wonder—"

"I find that few people understand what it is I did to help defeat the pirates. Most know only that I did something remarkable that makes me slightly more notable than my peers, but people are in general too polite to plague me for details."

"Oh," Daphne said, and went uncharacteristically silent.

"What is the matter?"

"It's only—" Daphne shrugged. "I was about to ask you what exactly it was you did."

Sophia laughed. "Therefore being impolite enough to plague me? I don't mind telling *you*, Daphne, because I know you are genuinely interested and do not simply want a thrilling story you can relate to your friends later."

"Is that why you never talk about what you did during the war?"

"For the most part, yes." It never occurred to anyone what kind of horrors a Seer might witness in war, what brutality and violence Sophia had Seen in the course of her service. Her stories could only sicken even the most bloodthirsty soul. Cecy knew a little of what Sophia had witnessed, and often helped deflect the curious, but even she knew none of the details. "But I also do not talk about defeating the pirates because the explanation simply confuses most listeners, who lack the vocabulary Seers use when we talk about Sight. But if you are truly interested, I will try to explain."

"Oh, yes, please do!"

Sophia brought Fidelius up closer to Daphne. The two horses crunched their way across the drifts of dead leaves that spilled into the path. "You know how Visions work, yes?"

"You touch an object, and See... is it memories? Pictures of places it has been?"

"More or less. The past, present, and sometimes the future are visible in an object that has a strong emotional resonance. Your eardrops, for example."

Daphne touched her ear, from which hung a tear-shaped topaz dependent from a round diamond. They were far too ornate for everyday wear, but Sophia had never seen her without them. "My mother gave them to me for my eighteenth birthday," she said. "They were a gift to her from my father on the day of my birth. I was so small, you see, and they were like a promise that I would live. And I did. Well, of course I did—but that makes them doubly mine."

"And if I were to handle one bare-handed, I would see that day, and the day you received them, and places where they have been worn, and I might even be able to see through your eyes. But if you had only just commissioned them at the jeweler's, and worn them but twice, I would see nothing, feel nothing except—it is a kind of hum through the skin, as if saying 'nothing to be Seen here.'"

"I understand that. So why could you not track the pirates that way? With a piece of their ships, or something like that? They must be saturated with emotions—or must they be happy thoughts?"

"No, any strong emotion is enough—hatred, fear, love, passion, anything like that. And a piece of something does allow an Extraordinary Seer to track the object to which it belonged. But acquiring such objects was impractical. We needed some other way to find them."

"And you discovered that!"

Sophia smiled. "Emotionally rich objects throw off... I call them 'echoes' now, but until recently we thought of them as false Visions, because it was clear they were unconnected to the objects we handled. It is something I cannot explain to you, the way in which Extraordinary Seers put together past and present by way of Visions, but if you can imagine...you can tell the difference between leather and silk by touching them, and Seers feel a difference between true Visions and the ones that are 'wrong.' Though it's nothing like touch or any other sense."

"I will imagine it. Please go on!"

"What I discovered was that those echoes—no, that is the wrong way to say it. I found that the false Visions Extraordinary Seers were perceiving were actually Visions associated with objects identical to the ones they were handling. The echoes were true Visions; they simply belonged to other items. And then I discovered that emotionally inert objects could be compelled to produce Visions of their counterparts, and from there it was a simple step to using a generalized—and now I have lost you. I did say it was complicated."

33

"I understand, a little, I was just amazed that you could speak so casually of what seems to me very difficult."

"It was." All those days and nights spent in Vision, hundreds of objects, comparing results with her fellow Extraordinaries, pages upon pages of notes, and then the breakthrough—holding a model of one of the Navy's fourth-rate ships and seeing *Breton* itself in Vision, cruising through those blue Caribbean waters, and that intense joy at feeling her talent spread and expand to encompass possibilities no one had ever imagined. It was a victory the War Office could not take from her.

"You must be so proud," Daphne said. "*That* is something I understand. I am still so much smaller—the people at Whitehall, when I was trying to convince the War Office to take me on early, some of them called me the Littlest Bounder where they thought I couldn't hear—it is so *infuriating*, but I can already do things no other Bounder has ever thought of, and I know I will be the first to Bound to an outdoor location—not Skipping, but true Bounding, and everyone thinks that is impossible. But I am certain people probably believed what you did was impossible too."

"No one even knew about it to call it impossible," Sophia said, "but it comes to the same thing. I cannot believe anyone would be so dismissive of you."

Daphne shrugged. "They thought they were being funny. I resolved to make them eat those words by becoming the most famous Bounder ever."

"A goal I hope will give you great satisfaction, though I cannot say fame is as wonderful as everyone thinks. Did you know people follow me, wanting Visions?"

Daphne gasped. "Doesn't that frighten you?"

"No, not at all," Sophia said with a laugh, "as none of them would dare harm me and lose their chance at the Vision they crave. It is simply annoying, to turn around and see five people behind me suddenly become very interested in the shop windows."

Now Daphne laughed so hard she was forced to rein her horse in and stop, or risk falling off. Sophia came to a halt a few steps on and regarded her cousin with amusement. "I did not consider it that funny," she said.

"Oh, but Sophia, I can just picture it, all those people standing with their hands behind their backs and their brows furrowed, as if they had only been walking about and were surprised to find themselves in that street!" Daphne covered her mouth as if to hold in her mirth, then turned about in her saddle to look behind them. "I see no one of that description now."

Sophia looked as well. "No, we have no followers. Such a pity, that you have no opportunity to witness fame first-hand. It might change your mind about your future."

"Oh, bah, if fame follows my achieving my goals, I will have to endure it." Daphne turned to face forward, then said in a low voice, "But I believe *this* is one of your followers; he's certainly intent on us."

Sophia turned to look where Daphne was discreetly pointing, and felt suddenly paralyzed. Approaching them was Lord Endicott, as beautiful as only a Shaper could be, on a black mare equally beautiful and groomed until she shone. Had he arranged this encounter? It was entirely possible. And he was certainly making directly for them.

"He is not my follower," she said quietly to Daphne, prodding Fidelius into movement. Could she pretend not to notice him? Likely he would simply raise his hat to them and continue past. Except—his eyes were fixed on her, he was smiling in greeting, that friendly smile that concealed any number of sins.

"Mrs. Westlake, what a pleasure to see you again," he said. "May I be introduced to your charming friend?"

There was no getting out of this encounter. That had probably been his plan, as it had been at Almack's, to force her into conversing with him in a public place where ranting at him or insulting him would harm only herself. *It is almost enough to wish myself in prison, away from him,* she thought, then was stunned by a realization. He enjoyed tormenting her, was going out of his way to do so, and suddenly it made perfect sense why he would not have accused her publicly of misusing her talent—that would have put her beyond his reach.

She glanced at Daphne and saw the same expression everyone always wore when looking at Lord Endicott, that captivated, almost worshipful look, and it made her furious that society's obsession with beauty made so many unable to look beyond it to a person's true nature. Why she had thought Daphne would be any different...

"Of course," she said, hating herself for letting her anger seep into her voice. "Lady Daphne, this is Lord Endicott. Lord Endicott, Lady Daphne St. Clair."

"Quite a pleasure, Lady Daphne," Lord Endicott said, raising his hat an inch or two off his head, as gracefully as he did everything. "I am surprised to see you here, Mrs. Westlake. I had believed you to have left London."

"Why would you believe that, my lord?"

"I have not seen you at all these last two weeks. You seemed dissatisfied with Almack's, when we met there, and I thought perhaps you had tired of the city."

Hah. He thought he had driven me out entirely. She had already begun to thwart him. "Why, no, my lord," Sophia said, "the company here is excellent, and I find I meet so many interesting people. I have *no intention* of leaving. I hope that is not a disappointment to you."

Lord Endicott displayed his charming smile, but his eyes were empty of any emotion, and she felt a moment's fear that she dismissed immediately. "On the contrary, I am glad to hear it. You know I enjoy your company. You always have the most... interesting... conversation."

"I wonder that you say so, my lord, since I believed our last conversation displeased you."

"Not at all. I wish only to make you think well of me."

Sophia glanced at Daphne again. It infuriated her that Lord Endicott was making himself appear so pleasing to her innocent young friend. "I appreciate your concern, my lord." *I will see you brought low, and then we shall see if you still enjoy my company.* She knew her inner turmoil was evident on her face because the brilliant smile widened.

"And you, Lady Daphne," he said, turning his attention to her. "Do you dance?"

"I do, Lord Endicott," Daphne said, casting her eyes down demurely. Sophia's anger grew. How *dare* he captivate Daphne that way? How *dare* Daphne be so easily captivated?

"Perhaps you will do me the honor of standing up with me one evening?" Lord Endicott said.

"I should like that, my lord," Daphne said. "Soon, I hope."

"Indeed," Lord Endicott said. "I am glad to have met you, Mrs. Westlake, and happy to have made your acquaintance, Lady Daphne. Until later, ladies." He clicked his tongue at his horse, which had stood as placidly as Fidelius during this exchange, and moved on down the path.

Sophia took a deep breath to calm herself. "We should return soon," she said. She urged Fidelius into a brisk walk without waiting for Daphne, who had to scramble to catch up.

"I don't believe I've ever seen a handsomer man," Daphne said. "Though of course one is always conscious of a Shaper's beauty—he *is* a Shaper, yes?—still, he was *very* handsome."

"Yes," Sophia said. "That is what everyone believes."

"He certainly doesn't like you very much, does he?" Daphne said with an air of consideration. "He was almost spiteful—did you do something to annoy him, or is he simply bad-natured? Because he likely thinks too well of himself, being so beautiful, and such people often take offense at the smallest things—"

Sophia gaped. "Daphne," she said, "do not tell me you saw past his demeanor?"

Daphne glanced at Sophia with a wry expression. "Extraordinary Bounders must be observant, to learn essences," she said, "and it would take a much better liar to deceive *me*. I am nearly as good as a Discerner, though I realize that sounds like bragging—but is it, really, when it's true? He thought he had done something to make you leave London, and when he said he enjoyed your company, the tone of his voice told me what he enjoyed was saying things to needle you. And there is something not quite right in the way he looks at one, as if he is working out what to say by rote instead of with feeling. Come, Sophia, I would suspect him of being your enemy, if I didn't believe you incapable of doing anything that would inspire enmity in anyone, you are so kind and generous."

Her words made Sophia blush. "You do not know me well enough yet, Daphne; I can be spiteful and mean-spirited, particularly where Lord Endicott is concerned."

"Then he *is* your enemy. Oh, tell me, Sophia!"

Sophia hesitated. "Daphne, it is a very great secret—"

"If you're about to suggest I cannot keep a secret, I will never speak to you again."

"No, my dear, but I feel—it is uncomfortable for me to share it." But Sophia, looking at Daphne's eager face, felt that secret clamoring to free itself from her heart. "And you must swear to tell no one."

Daphne rolled her eyes. "I swear it. And it's mean of you to suggest I might tell someone, because I am *excellent* at keeping secrets."

"Very well," Sophia said, "but let us return to your home first. Hyde Park might be thin of traffic today, but it is still rather public."

Safely settled in the drawing room of Lord Claresby's town house, with a proper tea spread and the servants dismissed, Sophia settled into her chair and recounted the whole terrible story for her cousin, who listened intently, her expressive face passing from astonishment to consternation and then to anger. When Sophia finished, Daphne said, "But that is *completely* unfair! How dare they expel you simply because Lord Endicott has a beautiful face and is a viscount and has a strong voice in Parliament? Of course your Dream was correct!"

"I am glad to have your support," Sophia said, "but the evidence was all to the contrary. And it is not unknown for a Seer to misinterpret a Dream."

"Don't try to defend them, Sophia. They were entirely in the wrong to turn you away, as if your record and your talent counted for nothing. Are you often forced to meet Lord Endicott? How awful!"

"That was only the second time I have seen him since returning to London. I hope he was not implying he had been looking for me, these past weeks. I *believe* he is merely opportunistic in tormenting me when our paths happen to cross."

"Well," Daphne said, taking up a tiny sandwich and biting into it with some ferocity, "I will refuse his invitation to dance if we ever are at the same ball together, and I hope to do it as publicly as possible."

"Don't, please. He believes no one outside the War Office knows the truth, and—" Sophia took a sandwich of her own to cover her confusion. It should not matter if her friends shunned Lord Endicott, but the idea disturbed her, and she needed a few moments to work out why. "I do not know how Lord Endicott was prevailed upon not to reveal my accusations, and I am afraid he might change his mind if he knew the story had spread beyond the War Office. I never realized what a coward I am, Daphne, but the idea of being exposed as a liar, or sent to prison... knowing myself to be in the right would not be enough of a defense."

"You would not go to prison."

"I would, if Lord Endicott chose to sue me for slander." She remembered the moment in which Lord Endicott's eyes had been empty of anything human and shuddered to think of herself in his power.

Daphne flung herself out of her chair and began to pace the room, snatching up another sandwich as she went. "It is *incredibly* unfair," she said. "Is there nothing you can do?"

Sophia took a long drink of her tea, which had gone cold in the telling of her story. It was one thing to tell Daphne the truth of what had passed between herself and Lord Endicott. Involving her in the quest to bring about Lord Endicott's downfall... she knew enough of Daphne's character to guess that the young woman would not be content to simply observe Sophia's actions. "Nothing," she said, "except avoid him, and hope this all fades with time."

Daphne made a face, sipped her tea, and made a different face, this one of distaste. "This tea is cold," she said, "and I believe I will ring for a fresh pot. Then we will talk about other things, pleasanter things— did I tell you I Skipped from St. James's Square to Bath yesterday?"

"You say it as if I am to be astonished, when I know you made that same journey three days ago."

Daphne brandished a shining silver pocket watch at Sophia. "But now I have one of Gutermuth's new watches, the kind that tells seconds as well as minutes. I wanted to set a record, but I was seven minutes and twenty-three seconds too slow. And Standiford's doesn't want me to try again, now that I know three locations in Bath to Bound to and need not Skip there. It is so hard to remember that they employ me, and are entitled to make that sort of demand."

"Shouldn't you respect their wishes, if they are paying you?"

"It's not as if I don't appreciate their generosity in hiring—though I don't know that it's generosity, when papa approached them on my behalf, after the War Office rejected me and I wanted *something* to do that was not paying calls and doing needlework, and I certainly don't need the money, but papa—he is very clever with money—he says even if I need no money, and *they* reap the benefits of having it known that an Extraordinary is one of their couriers, it's unprofessional not to have a fiduciary relationship."

Daphne set her cup down as a young woman entered the room with a fresh pot of tea and another plate of tiny cakes, from which Daphne helped herself to three. "I have the most atrocious manners when I'm at home," she said, "though I manage not to speak with my mouth full, and mama is in despair at ever making me into a lady—I don't know that I care about that, since *I* want a life of adventure—don't you ever grow tired of being so *constricted*, annoyed at all these rules about what a proper woman is allowed to say or do?"

"I have never felt constrained by society's rules," Sophia said, eating her cake with more delicacy than her cousin, "but I believe that is because society's rules so often bend for an Extraordinary. Do you imagine a non-talented young woman of gentle breeding would be allowed to work for a public courier service? And you are not only employed, no one dares criticize you for it."

"That is because papa is so powerful—oh, I see, you mean the rules are already laxer for us than for other women." Daphne helped herself to three more cakes. "And it's true that papa and mama indulge me—they were entirely supportive of my attempts to enter the War Office three years early. I suppose I should be grateful for what I have."

She sounded so *ungrateful*, with her face scrunched up into a scowl, that Sophia had to laugh and say, "There are still many restrictions on us that seem foolish. I see no reason why you should not continue pushing the limits of what you are allowed to do. Perhaps it will make a difference to the next Bounder who comes along."

"At least no one dares tell a female Extraordinary she is less valuable than a man," Daphne said. "Not in England, at any rate. They cannot afford such stupidity, especially during wartime."

"Indeed," Sophia said, and sipped her tea. Its hot astringency soothed the last remnants of her irritability after encountering Lord Endicott. He believed her to be cowed by him, the helpless victim of his torment, because she was a woman and had no political power or noble rank to meet him on his own ground, and because she was a Seer whose Visions were disregarded by everyone who did have those things and might be convinced to act against him on her behalf.

These thoughts made her anger rise again, and she took another drink, but its soothing power was weaker now. *Justice*, she thought, only half paying attention to whatever Daphne was saying, *justice will not satisfy me. He tried to destroy my life—succeeded, as far as he is concerned. I will be content only with vengeance.*

CHAPTER 5

IN WHICH SOPHIA
CONTEMPLATES MONEY

S ophia woke from Dream, but continued to lie still, flat on her back in her bed, her eyes still seeing the last images of Dream superimposed on the high, shadowed ceiling. *Money, again, bank-notes fading to piles of red muslin—why red?—and then to money again—always such prosaic things!* It had now been two weeks since she began her quest to bring about Lord Endicott's downfall, and nothing she Saw gave her any hint as to how she could succeed. *No, that is untrue,* she thought. *All these images are meaningful, but I cannot understand them.*

Money turning into things—well, that was probably a literal inter-pretation of how money was used to buy food and clothing and any number of other items. Did it mean Lord Endicott was going from government contracting into private trade? But there was nothing illegal about being a merchant, or a trader; it would merely be embar-rassing if it came out that he, a viscount and a Shaper, were engaged in something so beneath his social status.

Or did it mean he was buying something the ordinary things in her Dreams might represent? Could he be involved in the slave trade? *That* would be an excellent way to capture him; selling and buying slaves had been illegal for more than five years now.

The bedroom door opened. "Sophia, I don't—*Sophy!*"

Guilt propelled Sophia off her bed. "Cecy," she began.

"You have been Dreaming almost in the middle of the day? Oh, Sophy, you *promised* you would not become obsessed!" Cecy closed the door behind her. She was gowned elegantly in pomona green silk with short, puffed sleeves, and wore pearls twined through her blond hair. "You are not even ready for this evening!"

"It will take me no time at all to dress. You look lovely tonight!"

"Do not change the subject, Sophy. Why are you Dreaming now? Isn't night-time enough?"

Sophia sat on her bed and picked up her pencil, twirled it in her fingers, then set it down. "It was only one Dream. It took barely any time at all. Now, I should call Beeton to dress me—"

"And how many Dreams in the last twenty-four hours? Don't think I did not realize what you were doing when it took you nearly an hour to join me after breakfast this morning." Cecy sat heavily next to Sophia and took her hand. "I will not tell you that your... your *project* is not important. But you must know, dearest, that it is not so important that you should drive yourself to breaking."

"I am not near breaking, Cecy."

"If our situations were reversed, and I were the one overexerting myself, you would insist I go to bed and stay there. I don't like that you believe my concerns for you can be easily dismissed, when you insist on overriding *my* judgment about myself so often." Her voice was shaking, and Sophia's guilt turned into a burning ache inside her chest.

"Please forgive me, Cecy," she said, putting her arm gently around her friend. "I should not disregard your concern. And you are right—I am spending too much time in Dream. Even if it does not exhaust me, I am neglecting my other interests. And you."

"You must remember Lord Endicott believes himself secure from the law," Cecy said. "He certainly does not suspect you of still trying to prove him guilty of wrongdoing. You are simply impatient."

Sophia sighed. "I know." She stood and stretched, aware that her hair had become disordered from the pillow and her gown was no doubt horribly wrinkled behind. "Now I will dress, and I will be ready to leave for Lady Montclair's dinner party, and I swear not to think of Dream at all this evening!"

"Oh, I don't expect you to do the *impossible*, and not think of it at all," Cecy said with a smile. "But you will have many opportunities to discuss politics with Lord Montclair and his guests, and I imagine that will keep you distracted."

"You know me so well! Now, take yourself off, and tell Lewis that I am, in fact, attending the dinner party. He never says it, but every time we go somewhere I can see that he is wondering 'How is it that Sophia always takes so much time to ready herself, when Cecilia is always done in half the time and is twice as beautiful to boot?' "

"He does not," Cecy said, laughing, "but of course if he did not believe me more beautiful than you, he would be a very poor husband. Though I have always envied you your auburn hair."

"And I have always wished to be blonde like you. Such a pity hair color cannot be altered by an Extraordinary Shaper! Imagine how much business she would have!"

With Cecy gone, and Beeton summoned, Sophia hurried through her toilette as quickly as she dared. Carelessness in her dress was unthinkable, even for a private gathering such as Lady Montclair's dinner; she was always conscious of being on display, like an elegant bolt of satin brocade laid out in a shop window. The image was a little too apropos tonight, since she had spent so much time in Dream the last several days; it made her feel as if Dream were all there was to her, as if it made her some commodity to be admired, or sold, irrespective of the woman she was.

She picked up a pearl ear-drop, let it twirl and glow in the lamp-light, then set it down with a sigh. Remembering Cecy's dress, she passed over her favorite green gown in favor of a golden muslin that brought out the red highlights in her hair, donned a coral necklace and earrings, and submitted to having her hair coiled high on the back of her head and secured with golden pins tipped with tiny beads, so she appeared to be wearing a nearly invisible crown of gold. Cecy clapped with delight when she saw her, and Lewis bowed to her with exaggerated courtesy.

"I take it you've achieved new heights of sartorial splendor," he said as they all settled themselves in the four-seated landau, which was securely hooded against the November night. "I'm afraid I know nothing of these things."

"I would suppose a Shaper would have to at least be aware of the common ideas of beauty, in order to Shape his form most elegantly," Sophia teased.

"You know I settled on this form when I was eighteen," Lewis said, smoothing back his black hair, "and I've been satisfied with it ever since. And as Cecilia seems to find it appealing, I have no need to look to other models for change." He was tall, and lean, with an aquiline nose that suited the smooth masculine contours of his face and well-modeled lips that were always quirked as if he expected any moment to see or hear something to make him smile.

"You are certainly the handsomest man I know," Cecy said.

"I agree," Sophia said, "and it is such a pity you are already spoken for. Whatever are the rest of us to do?"

Now Lewis did smile. "I thought you had resolved not to remarry," he said.

"True, but I might agree to be swept off my feet."

Cecy made an O of pretended astonishment. "And what characteristics ought a man possess in order to do this sweeping?"

Sophia pretended to think. "He should be of no more than average height," she declared, "fair-haired and fair-skinned, quick to laugh and to make me laugh. Intelligent, but not too sober-minded; fond of the theatre; a good dresser; and just poor enough to appreciate my fortune. And I believe I would like to marry a Mover. I loved Richard, but he was not a comfortable husband, always Bounding off even before we both entered the service."

"Oh, Sophy, you spoke too quickly," Cecy said, laughing, "I wish to write down your list so I will know to whom I should introduce you, and whom to help you avoid!"

"I ought to provide Lady Daveril with my list, and let her do all the work!"

They were still laughing as the landau pulled up to the Earl of

Montclair's town house near Oxford Street, and were barely able to contain themselves when the footman took their cloaks. They were among the first to arrive. Lady Montclair, a young woman only a year or two older than Cecy and Sophia, tall and thin with brown hair elegantly styled in a manner that did not show her to advantage, greeted them warmly and ushered them into the drawing room.

The Earl of Montclair possessed no talent, and his fortune was not large; the dimly-lit drawing room was of no more than average size, large enough for perhaps ten people to gather comfortably and fifteen to stand cheek by jowl. The furnishings crowded the room like a second set of guests, Grecian-inspired sofas and cabinetry that were ten years out of date, suggesting to Sophia that Lady Montclair could not easily afford to replace anything. But the furniture was well-tended and showed no signs of wear. Rosewood pedestals carved with oak leaves flanked the fireplace, bearing large arrangements of hothouse flowers that gave off a strong, sweet scent and were already beginning to wilt from the heat.

Cecy immediately made for the low-backed sofa upholstered in soft fabric with narrow green stripes, a very un-Grecian design, to begin an animated conversation with a woman already sitting there. For someone who was frequently homebound, Cecy had a surprising number of friends drawn from all levels of their social class; being a Speaker kept her from the kind of isolation that might otherwise be her lot. Sophia left her to her conversation and wandered the room alone.

The wide entry hall connected the room to another, slightly larger room opposite, decorated in the same classical style, where card tables had been set up for the guests' entertainment after dinner. It was only in Sophia's imagination that they seemed huddled together, plotting her downfall. Not everyone would choose to play cards, and with any luck those who did not would be people Sophia wished to speak to. She was a terrible card player, unable to remember the rules of loo and vingt-et-un, even worse at reading the faces of her partner or her opponents.

Cecy teased her about it, saying that surely a Seer ought to be able to know what cards everyone else held, though she knew Sight did not work that way. Sophia tried not to let her distaste for the pastime show, as it was not uncommon for her to arrive at some event only to discover that the hostess had arranged the entire thing with an eye to what would please her. It made her uncomfortable, feeling that the entire success of some evening was dependent on her enjoyment of it, and she sometimes had to struggle not to let her true thoughts about some tepid gathering show, for fear of hurting her hostess's feelings.

"Mrs. Westlake," her current hostess was saying, "I am so pleased you chose to join us. And—" her voice dropped to a whisper, though there was no one nearby "—I cannot thank you enough for the Vision you gave me last week. To know my poor brother is still alive—though of course he cannot return to England, not after what came of his duel, but I am so relieved. Thank you."

"It was my pleasure, Lady Montclair," Sophia said, wanting to wince at the woman's tight grasp. "And... the other matter?"

Lady Montclair lowered her gaze. "It is true I am increasing," she said, even more quietly. "My husband is so pleased. We had thought—" She looked across the room to where Lord Montclair stood near the fireplace, talking rather animatedly to Lewis and a young man with tousled blond locks so perfectly disordered they could only have been arranged that way intentionally. The Earl was a short, round man, ten years older and two inches shorter than his wife, with prematurely greying brown hair parted in the middle and breath that smelled of tobacco, but Lady Montclair gave him such a fond look that Sophia was a little embarrassed at having witnessed such a private thing. Love certainly appeared in the most unlikely places.

"Again, it was my pleasure," Sophia said. Lady Montclair gave her a last grateful look before turning away to greet her new guests. Sophia smoothed her dress, realized her palms were sweating inside the silk gloves from Lady Montclair's firm grip, and went to a quiet corner to remove them briefly. Only a few more guests, and the fire would be unnecessary. She was already more relaxed after speaking with Lady Montclair. Cecy was right: she had been spending too much time in Dream and needed to socialize. Besides, Lord Endicott was socially and politically prominent; it was not beyond reason that someone here might know something of him that would give her Dreaming the detail she needed.

The door opened again, admitting more guests, and Sophia donned her gloves and turned in time to hear Lord Montclair say, "Rutledge! Come, man, tell us what you think about this news out of the north."

CHAPTER 6
IN WHICH MR. RUTLEDGE MAKES
AN APOLOGY

The room, which had formerly seemed warm, now stifled her. A familiar large figure came into the drawing room, straightening his coat, which was disordered from removing his greatcoat. When she had spoken with him before, his clothes had had a shabby look to them; now he wore knee breeches and waistcoat and a well-starched shirt and cravat, but his tailcoat was undistinguished, his breeches a muddy brown, and his overall appearance was that of someone who had only a nodding acquaintance with fashion.

He saw her in her corner, but gave no sign that he recognized her other than the briefest widening of his eyes, and passed through the room to join Lewis, Lord Montclair, and the fashionable blond man in their group at the fireplace. The heat of the room made Sophia dizzy. How should she react to him? He clearly wanted to pretend they had never met before this evening, but did she owe it to him to play along? *Don't be ridiculous,* she told herself, *what would be the point of claiming acquaintance with him?*

She strolled around the room to give herself time to reclaim her composure. It still infuriated her that he had assumed so casually that she would leap at his offer, that she would be willing to retract her accusations against Lord Endicott, and remembering that made it difficult for her to maintain her calm, though maintain it she did. Lady Montclair deserved better than to have her valued guest begin shouting accusations at someone her husband was clearly friends with.

Sophia made her fists relax. Mr. Rutledge had been impertinent, had accused her of lying—no, he had said he thought her mistaken in her Dream, but that was only a slight difference—and he had offended her. He knew how she felt about him. He would likely not approach her, and the two of them could both pretend they had not met before.

"We should ask Mrs. Westlake," Lewis said, and Sophia realized her perambulations had brought her close to the fireplace. "Sophia, how is the Army payroll distributed?"

The question was not at all what she had expected, and she felt a moment's anger at Lewis for asking her anything to do with the war, knowing her history with the War Office. But the four men were looking at her with patient expectancy, so she said, "There is a Bounder corps attached to the quartermaster's office, tasked with bringing the money each month for distribution to the units. It is a relatively new system—Field Marshal Wellesley is a great innovator, but his superiors are slow to accept change."

"Sounds damned uncertain to me," the blond man said, "trusting all that money to a single person. Should've continued sending it by ship."

"It only took one capture of a ship carrying the Army's payroll to convince the government of the greater security of Wellesley's plan," Mr. Rutledge said. Sophia avoided looking at him; his deep voice was pitched to carry no farther than their little group, which made his conversation feel uncomfortably intimate.

"Security from France, maybe, but not from theft by some light-fingered Bounder." The blond man jerked his head, making his curls gleam in the firelight. "They're always flitting away without so much as a by-your-leave, be hardly any trouble for them to make off with the money."

Sophia, infuriated on Richard's behalf, sucked in a breath to blast the stranger with an angry retort, and Lewis overrode her, saying, "I imagine the Army has already considered that, *isn't that so*, Mrs. West-lake?" He accompanied this with a warning look that said as clearly as speech that her host would be offended if she started a fight in his drawing room. She glared back at him. Her host had said nothing in counter to his obnoxious guest's comments—but then, Lord Montclair likely knew nothing of Bounders and would certainly not remember Sophia's husband had been one.

"Yes, Mr. Barham, the Army has many safeguards in place," she said. "The coin is counted three times before it leaves Whitehall, and again when it reaches Lisbon, and the Bounder signs for it—she is accountable for any missing money, and I assure you the punishments for a shortfall are severe. But our greatest security is of course that our Bounders are as patriotic, and as committed to winning the war, as anyone."

"You see, Skeffington?" Lord Montclair said. "The government isn't as cavalier with our money as you'd like to suggest."

"And yet they insist on paying in coin, when there is such a shortage of it," Skeffington said. He jerked his neck again as if he had some kind of nervous spasm, but likely he was simply drawing attention to how beautiful his hair was. Since he was standing next to Lewis, he merely looked ridiculous, like an overbred pony trying to draw attention away from an elegant stallion.

"What alternative would you suggest?" Mr. Rutledge said. Now he sounded amused, as if he already knew what Skeffington would say, and that it would be something idiotic.

"Well, banknotes, of course," Skeffington declared, and Sophia had to choke back a laugh.

"I believe our soldiers would have some difficulty finding anyone in Spain or Portugal willing to accept a piece of paper in exchange for goods," she contented herself with saying.

"Are you implying English money isn't good enough for the *guerrillas*?" Skeffington exclaimed.

"The Spanish are in the middle of a revolutionary war as well as fighting the dominance of France," Sophia said. "Those bills might have been scrawled out by a soldier instead of printed by a reputable bank in England or Scotland, for all the good they will do them. Paper money is only as good as the gold or silver it is backed by, and everyone instinctively knows that."

"And with so many smaller banks failing thanks to the gold shortage, there are many people in England who feel the same as our hypothetical Spaniard," Mr. Rutledge said. "With banks prohibited from paying out in hard money, people have no choice but to accept banknotes, but there is still a feeling, as Mrs. Westlake says, that they are not truly money. You yourself pointed out the greater value of specie, Lord Skeffington, when you alluded to our shortage of coin. We would not have a shortage were people not convinced of the superiority of gold and silver, due to the precarious situation many banks find themselves in these days."

"That, and the need for bullion to fund the war, given that our Continental allies are also reluctant to take paper," Lewis said. "Another reason for using Bounders to transport money, rather than shipping it—those French privateers armed with Scorchers have no fear of attacking our ships of the line."

"That we need that bullion is even more reason not to dump it all on the Spaniards," Skeffington said. "They're hardly the most useful of allies. Hiding in the bushes instead of attacking directly the way an Englishman would."

Hiding in the bushes. The *guerrillas* had so often been her eyes—the Spanish were reluctant to allow the English to attach Speakers to their bands, but their reverence for Seers meant they were agreeable to Sophia and the other Extraordinaries following them in Vision, relaying what the *guerrillas* saw. They were better at reconnaissance than Bounders, more familiar with the territory and more committed to defending it, and she had watched them strike at French troops despite being poorly armed and small in number, watched them fight and watched them fall. Her natural vision had sometimes been blinded with tears as she relayed the last moments of Sight before the Vision went black forever, clinging to some doomed man or woman as if that distant connection could be enough to keep the person alive.

Her heart beat faster with fury at the stupid, vain man, and she had to turn away from him briefly to maintain her composure. In looking away, she met Mr. Rutledge's eyes, and his expression mirrored what she knew hers to be so exactly that she had a moment of perfect accord with him. It made her forget, for the space of a moment, that she was angry with him. *If he were not so intent on believing me wrong, we might actually be friends*, she thought, and that ended her feeling of camaraderie and reminded her again of why she disliked him. At that moment, Mr. Rutledge's expression of good humor and shared resignation at being forced to endure that fool's company vanished, and he looked away from her, and she felt unexpectedly guilty, as if she'd slapped him in public.

"...expect them to simply steal what they need?" Lord Montclair was saying. "They *are* Englishmen, after all, and men of honor, even if they do come from the lower classes."

Memories of what she had Seen some of their English soldiers doing rose up uncontrollably before Sophia's eyes. "I—" she began, then realized there was no graceful way to end that sentence. How to explain that few men, even good men, were able to withstand the brutalities of war? "They are expected to behave honorably," she said.

"Which includes paying for things in hard coin," Lewis said.

"And that brings us back to the currency shortage," Lord Montclair said. "You're in favor of paper money, Skeffington, aren't you worried about counterfeit banknotes?"

"Too much effort to be worth it," Lord Skeffington said. "Forging receipts, possibly, on an individual basis, but banknotes are designed to be hard to counterfeit, what with all the engraving and scrollwork they put on them."

"On the contrary, forgery of banknotes has been a problem for years," Lewis said. "People often don't know the difference between a legitimate note and a false one, especially if it's issued by some small bank no one's ever heard of, which gives those counterfeiters an advantage."

"I thought the Bank of England had resolved all of that—or possibly you're too young to remember this, Barham, Mrs. Westlake," Lord Montclair said. "They made a big push about fifteen years ago to wipe out forgery. It drew in all the Bow Street officers and most of the provincial police as well. Covered the whole country."

"Fifteen years is a long time for criminals," Mr. Rutledge said. "I understand forgery is on the rise again. The lure of the easy profit is too great for some men to withstand, even with the threat of execution should they be caught."

"Well... that's what the Royal Mint is for, isn't it?" Skeffington sputtered. "Keeping our money safe from damned criminals."

"Would the Warden of the Mint have jurisdiction, though?" Sophia asked. "I mean, one thinks of minting as something relating to coin, not printed money."

"The Mint does not," Mr. Rutledge said. "It is the banks that have to deal with it, individually. Which is why the Bank of England has, in the past, taken a prominent role in opposing forgery. It has the resources to offer the kind of rewards that entice the Bow Street officers to actively hunt down forgers. They would not promise to pay out so much money were forgery not a serious problem."

"How much success have they had?" Sophia asked. Something was niggling at the edge of her awareness, like a memory she could not quite grasp.

"Not as much as they have in the past," Lewis said. "Most forgers are caught when they try to pass their false receipts, but forged banknotes are more difficult to spot. Better if they could find those counterfeiters before they can distribute the forged money, but this generation of criminals is clever—more clever than the average thief. I've even heard it suggested that this is not several forgers working independently, but an organization run by only a few, and that is how they manage to stay ahead of the police. The Chief Magistrate at Bow Street must be tearing out what little hair he has left in frustration."

Coin turns to food and back again. Banknotes turn to clothing to coin and then to notes. Every Dream Sophia had had in the last two weeks slotted itself together, joined by this one piece of information. *Could my Dreams mean counterfeiting? Money that is not as it seems? I must not jump to conclusions, I need to Dream again, but—if Lord Endicott is behind this, no wonder the criminals are so clever!* She wanted to rush into the street and run all the way back to the Barhams' house. Or—would it be too much a breach of good manners to ask Lady Montclair for the use of a bedchamber? An absurd thought, but one with some appeal. The evening now seemed interminably long—dinner, and then cards, and then the drive home...

She suppressed her need to Dream and made herself pay close attention to the conversation. "I had no idea this was such a problem," she said, overriding Lord Skeffington, whose mouth was open to say something inane or ignorant or offensive or, more likely, all three at once. "No wonder the government is so concerned about it, since I understand they run almost entirely on banknotes these days."

"It should have little effect on you, Mrs. Westlake," Lord Montclair said. "The chances of you being passed a false banknote are very small." He nodded to her. "Lady Montclair indicates that dinner is served; will you join her?"

Of course. With no titled Extraordinaries present, and Lady Durston merely a viscountess, Sophia took precedence over every other woman there. Sophia went with Lady Montclair into the dining room, which was more brightly lit than the drawing room and chilly. The walls were an icy shade of white that made the room seem colder than it was, as if they were walls of snow that might begin to melt at any moment. Fat tapers lit the room and the snowy cloth covering the table, which bore a vast number of dishes Sophia was certain the Montclairs could ill afford to share, and it made her feel guilty all over again, guilty and obligated to return their hospitality by eating more than she wanted to.

She took her seat to Lady Montclair's right hand, smiling to cover her discomfort, and they waited while the others found their places. Cecy was nearly at the other end of the table from her, which Sophia might have expected. What she did not expect was the man who settled into the chair on her right side. "I hope my company is not unwelcome," Mr. Rutledge said in a low voice, almost too deep to hear, "but this is where custom demands I sit."

Sophia's guilt redoubled. "I would not be so ungracious, I hope," she said, "and I apologize if I appeared so, before."

Mr. Rutledge nodded, but said nothing more, instead applying himself to the soup before him. Sophia did so as well, but was keenly aware of his large presence at her side, to the point that she responded to Lady Montclair's conversational gambits distractedly. She was grateful when the Countess turned her attention to Lady Durston, seated on her left, and Sophia could eat her fish and asparagus, no doubt a product of the cousins of the hothouses whence the flowers had come, with at least the appearance of placidity.

"Mrs. Westlake," Mr. Rutledge said in the same low voice, and she dropped her fork with a clatter that fortunately drew no one's attention. Her face reddened, and she did not dare to look at her companion. "I didn't mean to startle you," he said.

"I was simply... lost in my thoughts," she said.

"I wish to apologize to you," Mr. Rutledge said, "for the manner in which I approached you the other day. I should never have suggested that you owed me gratitude for my offer, nor that you were required to accept it."

"Thank you," Sophia said. She still could not bring herself to look at him. "I accept your apology."

"Please believe I came to you in a spirit of genuine admiration," he continued. "General Omberlis would not at first tell me your identity when he offered me your services. I believed you to be a man." He chuckled. "As time passed, and your predictions continued valuable, I became more effulgent in my praises, and I believe the General took pleasure in revealing the truth and enjoying my surprise. He is very proud of your talent."

The room's frozen white walls threatened to fall on her. "He *was* proud," she said, trying to sound as if she were stating a simple fact that was not central to everything she had lost.

"Don't——" Mr. Rutledge said. His voice grew quiet. "Believe me when I say I do not wish to cause you pain. Mrs. Westlake, your Dream reports came to me written in such a lively, intelligent voice that I wished to know you better. Can we not find a way to be friends without this... this event interfering?"

Now she looked at him, this time wondering why he was making such an effort. His dark brown eyes, so dark they were nearly black, were fixed on her with that same intensity that had left her so unsettled at their first meeting. He had a strong chin, a very straight nose, and his mouth showed no signs of the humor she had heard from him only moments before. He looked as if he might wait forever for whatever response she might give him, and she wondered again why it mattered to him that he have her good will. Likely he believed this new approach would carry his point as the first had not.

It is not as if we will see one another again, she thought, and said, "I feel you have me at a disadvantage, Mr. Rutledge, since I know almost nothing of you."

He smiled, his eyes again twinkling with good humor, and he said, "Very well. My name is Alexander Rutledge, I am seven-and-thirty years old, I have no talent, I own property here in London and in Derbyshire, and I am extremely wealthy."

"I believe that last item is not something you should declare," Sophia said, suppressing a laugh. He had looked so very somber, saying it, and but for the twinkle in his eye she might have thought him hopelessly arrogant.

"Well, it's something people seem to find important, and I dislike the idea of prodding poor Montclair into taking you aside and whispering, 'That Mr. Rutledge is rich as Croesus, upon my word.'"

"I see," Sophia said with a smile that surprised her. "Well, now I can converse with you on at least a *slightly* more equal footing. Did you know my family resides in Derbyshire, Mr. Rutledge?"

"I did not know that. Would you like to play the game of discovering our mutual acquaintances, or is that a subject for the drawing room rather than the dinner table?"

"I know almost no one there. My family took up residence while I was abroad."

"Then we will avoid that topic. Besides, I am only there on business, or for the hunting."

"Should you not be there now?"

Mr. Rutledge's amusement faded. "I have other concerns keeping me in London," he said.

"Oh," said Sophia. "More things we dare not speak of." The idea made her unexpectedly downcast.

"Not entirely," Mr. Rutledge said. "I have business interests to manage here as well, and I enjoy the varied company of London." His face went comically somber again. "And what brings *you* to London, Mrs. Westlake, if your family is in Derbyshire?"

The twinkle in his eye dispelled her low spirits, challenging her to respond in kind. "That is an impertinent question, Mr. Rutledge," she said, pretending to be offended. "Suppose my relations with my family are not cordial, and my reasons for avoiding them a great secret?"

"Then I would be embarrassed, and we would have to fall back on conversation about the weather and the flavor of the duck I am about to serve you," Mr. Rutledge said. "And since I have no reason to imagine the duck anything but ordinary, I hope that is not the case."

"It is not. I am here because Cecy—Mrs. Barham needs a companion, and she is my dearest and oldest friend."

"That is a much happier response than I had hoped for. She is often ill, is she not?"

"Yes, and I enjoy spending time with her no matter her condition."

"I would call that laudable, but I imagine you take so much pleasure in your friend's company that it is no hardship."

Sophia blinked at him. "You are correct," she said, "but I must admit you are the first to understand that truth."

"I understand friendship, I hope," Mr. Rutledge said. His eyes were once again fixed on her with that intensity that made her wonder what he truly wanted from her. She wished, now, that she could remember any Dreams or Visions from her time with the War Office that might have been in his employer's service. It was uncomfortable, him knowing so much about her when she knew practically nothing about him. True, they seemed to have some things in common, and true, he had a sense of humor she found appealing, but was that really enough to base a friendship on, when there were so many other things that stood between them? It surprised her to discover she wished their circumstances were otherwise.

"Mrs. Westlake," Lady Montclair said, "would you care to join us in the drawing room?"

Sophia rose, still looking at Mr. Rutledge. "It was a pleasure, Mr. Rutledge," she said, and meant it.

"Likewise," Mr. Rutledge said, standing politely. She brushed past him—he really was very large, as if he were built to a scale bigger than that of other men—and went to take Cecy's arm. *He did not believe me,* she told herself, but it was a weak, petty voice, and she chose to ignore it. If he wished to be friends, well, why should she be ungracious? *What matters,* she thought more firmly, *is that I finally have the clue I need to tell me what Lord Endicott is doing, and I will prove his crimes. I will be vindicated, and everyone, including Mr. Rutledge, will know it.*

CHAPTER 7

IN WHICH SOPHIA HAS A MEASURE OF SUCCESS

Sophia placed her palm flat against the door of Dream, absorbing it into her skin as it dissolved with a quaver. Her sleeping mind told her it tingled, though she could not actually feel any sensations while in Dream; if she did, it would mean she was too close to the surface of sleep to make any sense of the Dreams she entered. As the door dissolved, she was drawn into the Dream as if pulled forward—or possibly it was the Dream that came to meet her. The result was the same.

The room's walls were nebulous, telling her she lacked the information to know where this place was located in the waking world. That was unimportant; none of her Dreams about Lord Endicott's counterfeiting plan in the last four days had been specific as to *where* he was committing his crimes, but much as she would have liked a street address or, failing that, an image of the outside of one of these places, that was not essential to her current plan. Time enough to track him down physically. All she needed at the moment was a face.

The indeterminate room was small, perhaps fifteen feet on a side, and contained only a square wooden table that looked as if it had been put together by someone who had never actually seen a table before. Its top was splintery and gray; it looked like driftwood, but not planed and polished the way Sophia had seen such wood sculpted in Lisbon. Rather, it seemed as if the unknown craftsman had simply walked along the shore and gathered what planks he could find, then hammered them together.

Because it was such a clear, detailed image, Sophia concluded its irregular form could not mean lack of knowledge on her part. More likely it meant something slapdash, something for which rapidity of assembly was more important than long-term stability. She had seen images like this one frequently enough that she concluded Lord Endicott's operation relied on an ability to move quickly between locations, leaving no traces behind. Not that this would be enough to thwart her, once she had enough information.

The ramshackle table had a single drawer, which, in contrast to the table, was of shining, polished mahogany with brass fittings. Sophia imagined it sliding open, pretended she could hear the scrape of wood on wood, and looked inside. A single banknote lay within. It was a two-pound note, beautifully printed and inscribed with the name HAMMOND BANK, which Sophia had never heard of. There was a chance it was a fictitious bank, dreamed up by Lord Endicott for the purpose of passing false notes, but thus far every banknote she had seen in Dream was drawn on a real institution. She had no idea why this was so, and reminded her sleeping self that this was one more item of knowledge to pursue.

The banknote was dated and signed; the date was two days from now. Sophia's Dreaming self breathed out in relief. She had directed her meditations at predicting the near-future, but until tonight she had only seen Dreams of events that were too late to be useful to her. Banknote, bank, and now she needed a face.

A part of the unfocused wall moved as if it were a door swinging open, and a man entered the Dream. He wore trousers, like a working man, a rough linen shirt open at the neck with no cravat, and his coat looked like a sailor's—but he had no face. The Dream shook with Sophia's annoyance and disappointment. Seventeen Dreams, and not a single face to put to Lord Endicott's men. She calmed herself, focused on the man's image, and carefully pulled at it as if she were trying to remove a shroud from his skin. This time, it would work; she had to believe it was so.

Slowly his features began to coalesce, trembling into focus the way the Dream door had dissolved into her skin. It was a thin-featured face, freckled across his cheekbones, his chin pointed so sharply it looked as if it had been carved that way, and his light brown hair fell forward over his forehead and into his eyes until he pushed it away. She memorized the face for reproduction when she woke. Drawing was a skill all Seers were expected to master, and while Sophia's skills were not as refined as those of some of her peers, she was still more than capable of producing a recognizable sketch.

The man approached the table and removed the banknote from the drawer. It came away in a series of jerks, and when Sophia looked, there was another, identical banknote in the drawer. So this did not represent an isolated forgery; that was yet more evidence of a criminal organization rather than one man acting alone. Instead of folding the first note and putting it away in his coat, the man held it out at arm's length and turned, making it seem as if the note were pulling him, or guiding him, like a compass.

Sophia held her breath. This part, discovering what he would do with the note, was even more difficult than revealing his face had been. She turned her attention to his hands where they gripped the banknote; that was the key, maintaining the connection between both images. The man began to walk forward, away from the table and away from Sophia, and she carefully followed him. Her Dream self could not move too quickly, for fear of waking her physical body, but go too slowly and she would lose the man entirely. She told herself that they were both walking in place, that it was the undefined room that was sliding past them, then with an effort of will swept the walls away to reveal—

—a street scene, with light coming from everywhere instead of the sun in the sky, so the Dream location had an unreal appearance, like the set of a ballet. It was in a poorer part of London, with plaster-walled shops crammed close together. They, too, looked like set decorations rather than real buildings, with their windows painted on and their doors empty holes. Even so, if she looked at the setting as if it were a painting, looked at more distant landmarks and the way the streets fit together, she was confident it was located in Whitechapel. The banknote in the man's hand now swung back and forth like a magnet seeking iron, until it dragged him along to a door above which hung three exaggeratedly large blue balls, each more than a foot in diameter. The banknote pulled the man through the doorway, and the Dream shivered and vanished.

Sophia sat up and lit the lamp, then took up her diary and pencil. With swift strokes she sketched the face of Lord Endicott's man, tore the page from the book and crumpled it in dissatisfaction, then drew again until she was confident anyone could identify the criminal from her portrait. She again tore the page out, but carefully this time, then wrote rapidly:

Pawnbroker in Whitechapel. There is an abandoned building on one side and a used clothing shop on the other.

Hammond Bank. Find it. Warn them.

This is only the first step.

She laid the portrait on her page of notes and closed the book on it, then extinguished the light and lay back on her pillow, blinking away the afterimages of the glow. This was a slender thread indeed. Everything relied on this man being able to reveal the identity of the person who had given him the forged note, and even then that second person might not provide a link to Lord Endicott. But the point of meditation before Dreaming was to prompt a Dream that would give you what you wanted, and Sophia had no reason to believe her Dream would fail her. It had shown her this man because he was the link she needed to Lord Endicott's operation.

She considered Dreaming again, with the intent of Seeing the result of the man's apprehension, but that was too far in the future, and anyway she had promised Cecy. Even though her friend was not there to witness, Sophia felt again the rebuke Cecy had given her the night of the Earl of Montclair's dinner party and resolved not to overwork herself.

She pinched the bridge of her nose, trying to stave off the headache gathering behind her eyes despite her caution. So Lord Endicott had gone from embezzlement to counterfeiting. If he were desperate for money, she had heard nothing of it, but that was the only reason she could think of that he might be engaged secretly in business, let alone two such criminal operations. *I wonder why he does not marry*, she thought, *since so many women would love to be Lady Endicott, and he might have his pick of heiresses.* How unfortunate for him that her fortune was not at his disposal. She closed her eyes, made her muscles relax, and eventually, despite her excitement at finally having made a break-through, fell into a natural sleep.

She woke early the next morning and rushed through her morning chocolate and toasted bread and her toilette. She gathered the newspapers and set them aside without reading them, then sat down to her writing desk as if preparing for battle. She trimmed her pen nib, opened her inkwell, and wrote in her most elegant script:

Sir,

The somewhat unattractive man whose portrait is enclosed will enter your store on the fifth of December. He will attempt to pay you with a £2 note drawn on Hammond Bank. The banknote is a forgery, and I am sure you will agree with me that it is a poor one. Give this letter to the Bow Street officer you summon to take the man into custody. Officer: your captive is a member of a criminal organization engaged in forging banknotes. If your superiors are sensible enough to offer him transportation rather than death, he will reveal the identities of the man or men responsible for giving him the fraudulent note. This is the extent of my Sight.

Sincerely,

Sophia Westlake, Extr. Seer

She waited a moment for the ink to dry. It had been tempting not to act until she found a link that would directly prove Lord Endicott's involvement and guilt, but nearly a week's worth of Dreaming had shown she would not have enough information about the counterfeiting operation unless she struck it a blow. Lord Endicott's response to this action of hers would cause ripples that would make themselves felt in her information sources, inspiring more accurate and useful Dreams.

Unfortunately, her involvement in the man's apprehension would be made public, and Lord Endicott's reaction to that was something she could not yet predict; would he believe her discovery was anything but chance? It was possible he would break his agreement with the War Office, whatever it was, and reveal her "false" accusations against him to neutralize her, but she was certain he would not risk exposure by doing so just as she accurately predicted a crime. The War Office, at least, might find that too much of a coincidence. She hoped. The entire thing was risky, but it was a risk worth taking.

She folded the paper into an envelope, wrote the direction after a moment's walk through Whitechapel in memory—refreshing her familiarity with the city had been her first action upon returning to London, and one she did not tell Cecy about, since it took her through places decidedly not fit for a well-bred woman to roam—and sealed it with her personal emblem, surmounted by the stylized curlicues of an Extraordinary Seer. Then she rang for a footman and handed it over for delivery. Simon looked at the direction, gave her a dubious glance, opened his mouth as if to say something, but then simply left the room. He had no right to look dubious; her instructions for finding the pawnshop were perfectly clear, and she was a little insulted that he had apparently been about to challenge her.

Sophia leaned back in her chair, feeling as spent as if she had briskly walked from Cecy's front door all the way to the pawnshop and back. Now there was nothing for it but to wait. The two days she had been so glad to see now seemed interminable. She pushed back her chair and went to gather her newspapers. It was unlikely she would learn anything new until Lord Endicott's man was apprehended, but there was no point in not staying informed, and it was something to do. In two days, she would strike her first blow against Lord Endicott. *In three days*, she reflected, holding her scissors in the air and working the blades idly, *I will be cutting out stories bearing my name*.

❧

THREE DAYS LATER, SOPHIA TOOK HER SEAT AT THE TABLE AND folded her napkin neatly in her lap. "The story is not very prominent," she said, "but I am not so vain as to believe my every action is worthy of front page notice."

"This is quite unexpected, Sophia," Lewis said. "Did you know your

64

Dream would have such a dramatic effect?" He folded the newspaper and set it beside his plate, then picked up his fork and knife to attack his sausage as if it were likely to turn on him at any moment.

"I did not," Sophia said. It was mostly true. She had only known that the man in her Dream would lead the Bow Street magistrates to his confederates. "But it is extremely satisfying to know that two other men were also apprehended, and at least a hundred forged banknotes discovered. I wish only that I knew whether those men revealed the location of the printing press that produced those notes."

"You received more than usual notice at church this morning," Cecy said, "which tells me some of these people saw the newspaper early this morning. I wonder if that is entirely in keeping with the spirit of Sunday worship."

"I am accustomed to being stared at," Sophia said, but "accustomed" was the wrong word for the fizzing, lighthearted feeling that came over her when she made a Dream public. Was it a sin to be so... *exhilarated* by her fame? No, not her fame, but that of her talent. Interpreting Dreams left her feeling stretched out, but in a good way, as if her mind were expanding to encompass ideas and images beyond her waking self. Seeing those Dreams come true, particularly in the public eye—it felt as she imagined it would feel to have a child who played the pianoforte with such skill that everyone admired and praised her. Having others admire and praise her Dream filled her with joy on its behalf.

"Will Bow Street enlist your help in finding more counterfeiters?" Cecy said. "Since you have proven your accuracy."

"Possibly, though forgery is not the only crime they are concerned with," Lewis said, "but I would be surprised if the Bank of England did not contact you."

"I... that had not occurred to me," Sophia said. The idea left her feeling angry and guilty at the same time. Of course the Bank of England would want every advantage in pursuing the counterfeiters, though no doubt they had their own Seers working on the problem. And as generous as their rewards were, they likely could not afford her services—or, rather, the going rate for the services of an Extraordinary Seer, given that Sophia herself never took money for her Sight. But forgery was a serious problem, an attack on the foundations of the government and society, punishable by death; was it her duty to help stop it, regardless of Lord Endicott's involvement?

That thought made her anger override her guilt. She had no interest in any forgers except Lord Endicott, and the idea of possibly allowing him to escape justice for the sake of capturing some other criminal was unthinkable. She would uncover Lord Endicott's crimes, and send evidence to Bow Street, and they would capture him and see him tried and hanged, and *that* would be justice, both for herself and for England. But she would not hand over control of her talent to a committee of fiduciary-minded men who would direct her to use it as *they* saw fit.

"Wouldn't that be exciting, having such important work?" Cecy said. Sophia knew she was thinking of her pursuit of Lord Endicott, and now her anger was supplanted by unhappiness, because she could guess by Cecy's tone of voice that she thought Sophia would do better to turn her efforts in a direction that would not leave her so isolated. Cecy didn't understand. It seemed no one did.

"I believe it is unlikely I will be asked," she said, "but of course I would be happy to help." She took a bite of her egg; it tasted bland, like sulfurous water. She no longer felt hungry; she felt filled with right-eous anger, ready to attack the newspapers and extract the information she needed for another Dream. Now that a hoard of false notes had been discovered, she was confident she could reach for Dreams that revealed the location of others, and with enough of those, she could guess at the location of the press. Then it would become complicated. She had to find a way not only to locate the press, but to tie it to Lord Endicott.

She salted her egg and took another bite; still bland. One step at a time. First, the notes, and with luck, more of Lord Endicott's men. She felt certain in a way she hadn't since her expulsion from the War Office. Strange, how that event had weakened her belief in herself in ways she hadn't realized. Well, she no longer felt weak. She was ready to take on whatever challenges might lie between herself and the accomplishment of her goal.

CHAPTER 8
IN WHICH HUNTING IS
DISCUSSED

"You are in pain, Cecy," Sophia murmured. The noise of the crowd surrounding them made it unlikely that anyone would hear, but Sophia kept her voice low regardless. Almack's was far too public a place to have such a conversation.

"I feel very well," Cecy said, looking everywhere but at Sophia's face. "Do you suppose Lady Hartwell is here? I have not Spoken to her in weeks and she must feel sadly neglected."

"Your lips are pinched and there are creases at the corners of your eyes. You are unwell. Let me take you home."

"It's strange, but somehow discussing literature is not the same when one does it over the reticulum," Cecy said. "I would like her opinion on this new collection of essays by Bakewell. I believe he over-states his case for the Stuart kings' reliance on Speakers to maintain their power. Though it is true Queen Anne had quite the reticulum of her own despite not being a Speaker."

"Cecy—"

"Sophy, do not tease me, I am perfectly well."

"You are not—"

"And if I am not?" Cecy finally brought her eyes to meet Sophia's.

"I refuse to be an invalid, Sophy, and if I choose to endure a little pain, that is my business."

"A little pain will become a great pain—"

"Excuse me, Mrs. Westlake, but might I have the pleasure of the next dance?" The man addressing her was short and fair, and she recognized his face but could not for the life of her remember his name. She suppressed her annoyance at his interruption and smiled at him.

"Of course," she said. "Cecy, I—" She turned back to her friend only to find Cecy had moved off into the crowd and was speaking with a woman whose bright red hair made a dramatic contrast to the brunettes and blondes surrounding her.

Sophia ground her teeth. Cecy had been confined to the house for eight days, and long confinement made her restless and angry at her weakness, and consequently led her to self-destructive behaviors—such as exerting herself to go out in public, despite her knowledge that it would leave her in much greater pain than if she had stayed home. Sophy was always torn between sympathy for Cecy's situation—she knew she would likely be as resentful about her lot as her friend was—and frustration that Cecy often refused to be sensible about her limitations.

She turned back to address her partner, desperately trying to remember his name—and found herself face to face with Lord Endicott.

She was unable to stifle a gasp, and he smiled more broadly, and bowed. "I believe this is our dance," he said.

"I—no, my lord, I am engaged to another," she said, but he was shaking his head with amusement.

"I informed the gentleman that you had agreed to dance with *me*, and you would be happy to oblige him later," he said, his smile broadening until it threatened to split his face in two. "He was very understanding."

"You are presumptuous, my lord," Sophia said. Her heart was beating too rapidly, furiously, and she wished she dared slap him. "I have not agreed to any such thing."

"I apologize for my presumption, but I felt I could not wait for another dance to have your so-pleasant company," he said, extending his arm to her. His smile was one of innocent pleasure, as if he truly cared for her. "Though of course you are free to repulse me. It's not as if anyone is looking at us, here at the center of the room."

Her temples throbbed. She risked a quick glance around. Of course everyone was watching them. Him, because he was beautiful; her, because of the detestable gloves that now might as well be a beacon the way the red-headed woman's hair was. She accepted his arm. *He is your prey. You will destroy him. Two dances are nothing.*

The thought was enough that, when she faced him as the music began, she was able to bestow a genuine smile on him. She took further pleasure in seeing his friendly expression waver, just a little, nothing anyone but she could see. "Are you still enjoying your stay in London, Mrs. Westlake?" he said.

"I am," she replied. "I wonder you are still here, as I am told this is the best hunting season. Or perhaps you do not hunt."

"Not this year. I prefer the pleasures of London. And your delightful company."

"I imagine hunting would be very exciting. Learning where your prey will be, knowing its movements, then running it to ground... is the chase more exciting than the kill, do you suppose?"

They separated in the figures of the dance, though neither looked away; it was as if they were physically linked by the music, which pushed them apart and then drew them back together, beat after measured beat. "I believe it depends on the prey," Lord Endicott said when they were once again close enough for conversation. "Some of them are more wily than others. And the kill is not always inevitable. Sometimes the creature eludes one's gun."

"But I imagine it would be *very* hard for the prey to evade a hunter who knows its every move before it does."

"That would be a rare hunter indeed." Lord Endicott had stopped smiling, though his expression was still pleasant.

"How fortunate for the poor animals that it is so," Sophia said.

"Then you have sympathy for the prey?"

"Sometimes," Sophia said. "But some animals are dangerous, and deserve their fate at the hunter's hand."

"Do you feel confident you can determine what fate the prey deserves?"

Sophia shrugged. "I judge them by their actions. The ones who themselves prey on the innocent—I believe their fate should be self-evident."

Lord Endicott nodded. "Though a hunter should be careful," he said, "because those are the very animals most likely to turn and savage their pursuer. Many a hunter has come to a bad end at the teeth of a predator."

"Does that mean the hunt is pointless, my lord?"

It was Lord Endicott's turn to shrug. "That should only serve as a warning to those who hunt... dangerous game. Such animals have no pity, no fear of reprisal. Were you to engage in such a hunt, Mrs. Westlake, the animals would not treat you with gentleness simply because you are a woman."

"I understand that, my lord," Sophia said. "Were I a hunter, I would of course take steps to protect myself. But I would not allow fear to prevent me participating in such an exhilarating and personally satisfying exercise."

"I understand you as well," Lord Endicott said, and this time his smile was a baring of teeth that did not touch his eyes, though again Sophia was certain no one but herself could tell the difference. Again, an unbidden shiver went through her. It was as if he were two men, one affable and well-mannered, the other devoid of compassion and human feeling. How he managed to conceal the one behind the charming smiles of the other was a mystery beyond her understanding.

They finished their dance in silence, and when the next began, Lord Endicott spoke of trivialities as if their earlier conversation had never happened. Sophia was barely aware of answering him. He knew she was pursuing him; he was not afraid of any threat she might pose. Yet.

When their dances were over, he escorted her to a spot near the far wall, chosen seemingly at random, and Sophia only had time to register that it was a relatively quiet corner when Lord Endicott said, "I hope you will remember what I said about hunting dangerous game, Mrs. Westlake. I would hate to see any harm come to you."

"Why, my lord, you cannot imagine I will take up hunting!" Sophia said with a laugh. "No one would credit me with the strength and agility for such a sport. But I find the whole thing compelling. I assure you, if I *were* to engage in such an activity, *you would be the first to know it.*"

Lord Endicott's smile shifted, the corners of his mouth flexing downward as if he could not control his Shaping. He bowed to her and walked away; Sophia watched him go, admiring his form, which *was* beautiful even though the rest of him was repulsive. Now they were at war.

She had a moment's concern as to how he might strike at her; she was still convinced he could not afford to reveal her "mistake" without drawing attention to himself, which left him with... what? She knew so little of him personally she could not begin to guess. That might be a true mistake on her part, to strike at him without knowing in what way she should defend herself. But the first blow had been delivered, and it was too late for her to turn back now.

She glanced across the room, looking for Cecy, and instead saw the familiar figure of Mr. Rutledge approaching. He was dressed formally and properly in tailcoat and knee breeches, neither of them stylish, and his dark hair was again swept back from his face in defiance of fashion, though she had to admit the unconventional style suited him. An unexpected frisson of anticipation bubbled through her, and she suppressed it. Attractive he might be, pleasant his company might be, but he did not believe her, and how then could they be friends?

"Mr. Rutledge," she said, "how are you this evening?"

"Very well, now that I have you to converse with," he said amiably. "I hoped to persuade you to dance with me."

"*You* dance?" she exclaimed, and immediately knew her mistake. Her face went hot with embarrassment.

"You mean, because I am rather large?" Mr. Rutledge said, but he sounded amused. "I believe I can avoid stepping on your feet, if you will give me the opportunity to prove myself."

She took the arm he extended. "I meant—well, I must admit I did mean... what you said... but you also seem so sober-minded, I did not imagine you would engage in a somewhat frivolous activity."

"You consider dancing frivolous?" he asked as they took their places and bowed to one another. "I believe it a serious business, myself."

"How so?"

"It is a metaphor for life, I believe. For the ways in which men and women relate to one another. Knowing where to step in order to keep harmony, partnering with one yet encountering others—and then, of course, there is the way in which dancing allows unattached men and women to explore their interest in one another. I believe it is no coincidence that dancing so often leads to matrimony, in our society."

"I daresay you are right."

To her surprise, and shame, Mr. Rutledge was an excellent dancer. He was even better than Lord Endicott, whose dancing was perfectly correct but always had an element of showiness, as if he were more conscious of being admired than of his partner's pleasure. Mr. Rutledge, on the other hand, was simply graceful, and Sophia was embarrassed all over again.

To cover her confusion, she added, "It is certainly true that agreeing to dance with someone for the space of half an hour is like a temporary engagement. You are committed to your partner for that time, and should not give your attention to anyone else."

"I hadn't thought of it in that way. I will have to add that to my collection of sober thoughts, so I will not disappoint you as to my character."

Sophia flushed again. "I apologize. That was rude of me."

"You know little more of me than my appearance and fifteen minutes' conversation. I'm not surprised at the conclusions you drew."

She lifted one hand and turned it so his attention was drawn to the red glove. "I am always the subject of people drawing conclusions about me simply from the sight of this. I should have known better."

Mr. Rutledge nodded. "And now that we have each mortally offended the other, we cannot help but be friends, don't you think?"

His smile was so wry Sophia's mouth fell open, then she laughed. "I fail to see why that matters so much to you," she said.

"I told you," Mr. Rutledge said, "your reports were written in a voice that I found interesting. I wanted to meet the person behind them. And you are the only Seer I have ever met, Extraordinary or otherwise, and I admit I'm as fascinated as the next man by what Seers do. Is it too impertinent to ask how you discovered the existence of that forged banknote?"

"That is likely a conversation too long for the space of two dances," Sophia said, "but the short answer is that I Dreamed of the note, then meditated on its owner until I found a Dream of him as well, and put the two together." She chose not to tell him how much research she had had to do to have enough information to Dream any of that. He didn't need to know the details of her hunt for Lord Endicott.

"Did our conversation at the Earl of Montclair's home spark that Dream?" he said.

"...Yes, it did, to an extent," she said. "It certainly must have started me contemplating the subject."

"It was generous of you to share that Dream with its intended victim."

"I find I cannot sit by and allow a crime to be committed, if I can stop it."

"But not all Seers feel that way, is that true? They use their Dreams for personal gain?"

"Some of them do. I have no need to use my Dreams to support myself, but many Seers depend on that income to live. So I can hardly fault them, except that I have complete disdain for anyone who allows others to be hurt so she can profit by it."

"I believe I agree. I suppose the committee of the Bank of England has approached you, asking for your help," Mr. Rutledge said.

"They have not," said Sophia, "though I do not feel insulted. I am certain they feel satisfied with the efforts of their own Seers."

"A pity, given that you've proven your worth," Mr. Rutledge said. "And I understand there is evidence that the banknotes they found were part of a larger supply. The Hammond Bank is teetering as the news spreads that they may not have the reserves to back up their supply of notes."

"I believed Parliament had prohibited banks from paying out in gold."

"Yes, but public expectation is still that banks should *have* that money, against the day when the war is over and the restrictions will be lifted. I have heard that the Hammond Bank received a number of forged banknotes in the last two weeks, likely more than they actually detected, but they kept the incidents concealed—foolishly, to my mind —to prevent this sort of panic. So the rest of the banknotes, the ones not discovered by your Dream, still pose a threat to the bank."

"I wonder why the Hammond Bank was targeted," Sophia said. "Is there something special about it?"

"Not to my knowledge, except that it is small and easily toppled by someone who has the means and desire," said Mr. Rutledge. "If the notes were found... it makes sense that they might be near the printing press the forgers are using, and *that* would be quite a blow to them."

"It would," Sophia said. Finding the press... that would hurt Lord Endicott quite a lot, if she could tie him to it. "Do you suppose this is more than one person, then?"

"There were three men captured thanks to your evidence, though none of them knew anything more than that they had received the money and were to pay it out in small amounts. That speaks to a larger group, an organized group with a plan behind their actions. Who knows what that plan might be?"

"Indeed," Sophia said. In her heart, she was already at home, preparing to Dream. "They might choose to target a different bank next."

"Or go after the Bank of England directly, if they have enough success with the smaller banks. Though I shudder to imagine the implications, were they to become so bold."

"Then I hope the Bank is well defended," Sophia said. So many possibilities for Dream—could she convince Cecy to leave early?

"But this is hardly conversation for dancing," Mr. Rutledge said with a smile. "I should instead ask you how you find London, after so many years spent abroad."

Sophia's heart froze. Surely he did not mean a back-handed taunt, a reminder that had Lord Endicott not ruined her, she would be in Lisbon still? "Very cold," she said.

"I understand the Barhams have a lovely country home. London must have some appeal, to bring you here instead."

"Mr. Barham has his interests in the East India Company and the theater, and Mrs. Barham loves visiting her many friends."

"That seems a mismatch, to me."

"Ah, but Mr. and Mrs. Barham are very happy, I assure you."

"How so, where their interests do not align?"

"I beg your pardon if I am impertinent, Mr. Rutledge, but that question tells me you know little of marriage."

"You are correct. I am a lifelong bachelor. I fear I would make some woman a terrible husband."

"And why is that?"

Mr. Rutledge laughed. His gloved hand, touching hers in the steps of the dance, gripped it firmly for half a breath. "Mrs. Westlake, you are dogged in your pursuit of the truth."

Again her heart felt icy, as if he meant her pursuit of Lord Endicott, which he could not possibly know of. "Have you some dire secret you keep hidden from the world?"

"No, I simply know so little of what makes an excellent marriage, I feel I am doing the world a favor in not entering into that felicitous state myself."

"Mr. Rutledge, I am surprised at you. I took you for a man who does not allow fear to govern him."

"Then teach me, and perhaps I will change my mind."

Sophia clasped his hand briefly and stepped away. "I was married only a few short years, but they were joyful years. Richard—my husband—enjoyed traveling with me, though I never did become accustomed to Bounding. But it was being united with him that gave me joy, not the places we went, or the breathless wonder of Bounding. That is what marriage is, being one in heart if not in mind as well."

"So shared interests are not essential?"

"Pleasant, yes, but I have found that dissimilarity gives you things to speak of together. I enjoyed sharing my passion for politics with Richard, even though he cared little for Whig or Tory or Parliament."

"Then I am even more convinced unmarried life is for me. I would have difficulty shackling myself to anyone who could not share my interests."

"If you consider it 'shackling,' " Sophia said with a smile, "you are probably correct."

The music came to an end, and Mr. Rutledge offered Sophia his arm, which surprised her; she had been so caught up in the conversation she had not realized two dances had passed. "I should escort you back to your friends, but you seem rather unaccompanied tonight," Mr. Rutledge said.

"Mrs. Barham is here somewhere, and you need not wait on me to find her."

"I'm glad to hear she is well enough to enjoy company."

"I am happy about it, too. I am also grateful that she has so many Speaker friends to entertain her when she is confined to the house."

Mr. Rutledge nodded. "Then I will leave you now, but... thank you, Mrs. Westlake, for your company, and your conversation."

"Thank *you*, Mr. Rutledge, for forgiving me my *faux pas*," Sophia said, curtseying to him, then watching as he walked away. Now that she was paying attention, she realized he walked with as much grace as he danced, and she blushed again at her foolishness. He was interesting, and clever, and handsome, and he danced well, and he... well, did it matter whether he thought her wrong, when all the world did as well? Perhaps they might be able to be friends, after all.

She began circling the room, barely noticing the people who stepped out of her way, and found Cecy sitting alone on a bench upholstered in pale gold. "Cecy," she began, and Cecy lifted her face to Sophia's and said, "I need to return home." Her face was set and white, and tears threatened to spill over her cheeks. Sophia forgot the chastisement that was on her lips and helped her friend stand.

They rode home in silence, Sophia unable to think of anything to say that would not come out as *I told you so*. Cecy held herself so still, as if she were trying not to touch anything that would make her pain worse, that Sophia could not bear to reprimand her. "You should send word to Dr. Garland," she finally said.

"I Spoke to her assistant and asked if she would come to us at the house, but the doctor was away and Mr. Rally did not know when she would return. Sophia, you were right."

"That doesn't matter now. Dr. Garland will help you, and you will sleep and feel better in the morning." Sophia reached out to take Cecy's hand, but changed her mind when she remembered how painful even the gentlest touch could be when Cecy was in this condition.

Outside the carriage, snow was falling in fat white clumps of flakes clinging together against their eventual landing. In the morning, the world would be white, and Cecy would be well, and Sophia could once again plan her attack against Lord Endicott. *More banknotes, somewhere,* she thought, *more notes, and the plates that produced them. That is more than enough.*

CHAPTER 9

IN WHICH SOPHIA GOES ON THE ATTACK, WITH UNEXPECTED RESULTS

In the morning, the snow was still falling, and Cecy was not well. Sophia brought her tea, and bathed her forehead, and prayed for Dr. Garland to come soon. Dark shadows under Cecy's eyes told Sophia she had not slept at all that night. "It hurts," she whispered to Sophia when she brought her another cup of tea and helped her sit up to drink it, then fell silent.

Lewis had vanished—Cecy had told them both, long ago, that she could not bear to see the look on his face when he watched her suffer —and Sophia sat alone with her friend, even after she finally fell asleep, unwilling to escape into Dream and be absent if Cecy woke and needed something.

Dr. Garland came just after noon and expelled Sophia from the bedroom. "She'll be well enough soon," she said. Sophia stood in front of the closed bedroom door feeling bereft. She had been so preoccupied with Cecy that she had forgotten to eat, and she did not feel hungry now, but she went downstairs and rang for a light meal: cold meat and cheeses and hot tea. She ate, and returned to her room and sat on her bed. Dreaming might take her mind off Cecy; she refused to consider she might have more selfish motives instead. She lay back on her bed, fully clothed, with her palms pressed to heart and navel, and closed her eyes to meditate. Mr. Rutledge's comment about finding a press near the banknotes resonated with her. *The banknotes, then.*

Meditation, for a Seer, was a matter of becoming aware of her body, of how the blood flowed through it like an unending river, how air rushed in and out of her lungs like a warm summer wind, then bringing a single idea to mind and letting it sink into that movement until it flowed through her as her blood did. It took Sophia only a few minutes to attune the idea of the banknotes she had Seen to her body, then she dropped easily into Dream and waited for the right door to appear.

She was surrounded by doors crowding close together around her now, an event not uncommon when she was focused on a particular goal. Her Dreaming mind offered her a host of options, all of which would have something to do with Lord Endicott, but she wanted a particular Dream, so she ignored them. Some of them might recur, though with slight differences; no Dream ever repeated itself. She was experienced enough not to fear that she might miss something important, and simply leap through the first door she encountered.

Above, she saw the door she wanted; the gauzy, faded image of a banknote rippled in and out of view. She laid her palm against it and was drawn into the Dream, into a room somewhat more solid than was usual. It looked like a shed, or a room in some run-down lodging house somewhere in the city, windowless and dark even in the regions of Dream where no light was needed to see clearly. It was unfurnished and lacked the marks on the floor or walls that would indicate where furnishings had once stood. Sophia turned around in a tight circle. There was a door, but it was little more than a rough outline against one of the walls and lacked a knob or latch or even hinges. Time enough to deal with it later.

She returned to her original position and saw that a splintery pallet had appeared on the floor. Its light, unfinished wood looked strange against the dark floorboards, out of place, and it wavered in the Dream, reminding Sophia of the transitory nature of Lord Endicott's plans. Banknotes began appearing on it in tidy stacks until the pile reached the ceiling and became compressed by it. Stacks of notes slid down its sides and onto the floor, disappearing as they landed. Then the banknotes began to disappear as if time had been reversed, until the pallet was empty. After a few moments, the process began again. Sophia watched it cycle twice more before turning her attention to the empty room. The press had to be here somewhere.

She tugged at the shadows, trying to force them into definition, but they resisted her. Impatiently she turned the pallet and its load translucent and whisked it away, like sweeping up cobwebs, to give herself a better view of the room. It seemed empty. She walked slowly in the direction of the walls, which receded from her approach until she felt she was walking down a dark, circular tunnel. She looked behind her, and the room drew her back as if she were entering one of the doors of Dream. Once again, she stood near its center. The tunnel vanished. She made a circle of the room, careful not to walk toward the walls, but saw nothing. The pallet had reappeared and was beginning its cycle once again. It seemed there really was nothing left to find.

She turned her back on the pallet and looked at the wall where the door hung. Granted, this was Dream, and nothing existed the way it did in the waking world, but doors and windows within Dream were complicated even by the standards of that strange other-world. They represented the concept of two places being linked, rather than an actual door one could open and step through, and using one took great concentration, even for a Seer as experienced as Sophia was. She let her eyes go unfocused and concentrated on the thin lines defining the door, pictured them deepening and broadening to let even more of the non-light of Dream through. It was smooth, she told herself, smooth and lacking the splintery grain of the wall surrounding it, and as she thought this the door shrank further, rotated as if it were on an axis that ran vertically through its center, and disappeared. Sophia took a step toward the open space that shimmered with pale emptiness, and with her second step had left the unfinished, empty room behind and emerged into a place that appeared to be on the banks of the Thames.

The world was once again lit with the non-light emitted by everything around her. The river looked like a child's drawing, with passing ships sitting on top of the water instead of resting within it. The part of the city across the river was outlined in a few strokes, with no detail to identify the buildings, though London Bridge was a swoop of black ink across the sky about a mile upriver from where she stood. She turned and saw that the building she had exited was an old, grey warehouse that came nearly to the shore of the river, with a roof half caved in and boards missing from its walls. No one with legitimate business would consider using it.

There were other warehouses lying nearby, all of them in better condition. Sophia walked away from the warehouse and stepped onto the solid "water" of the Thames, which to her Dreaming mind felt like soapy old stone. She continued to walk backward across the water until she had a better view of the shoreline and could commit it to memory, counting off buildings and looking for landmarks. Then she stood and looked out at distant London Bridge, which in Dream was strong and sturdy, completely unlike the decrepit monstrosity that blocked river traffic and always looked as if it were a breath away from complete collapse. Plans to rebuild it had never come to anything, and it was likely nothing would be done until it fell apart completely. How easy it was, in Dream, to fix problems that seemed insurmountable in the waking world.

She woke herself and lay still for a moment, staring at her ceiling. It was flat and boring and made her think of a coffin lid, though it was far too high for her to become claustrophobic from that thought. Then she sat up and began sketching a picture of the outside of the warehouse, then on another page drew a diagram of where it sat in relation to the river, the bridge, and the other buildings. She went to the drawing room and scribbled out a note, addressed it to Sir Arthur Rowley, Chief Magistrate at Bow Street, then called for Simon to run the papers there. "Quickly," she added, though she knew the footman would not need encouragement. Then she put away her writing desk and went to see Cecy.

"She's asleep," Dr. Garland said when Sophia knocked and opened the bedroom door. The doctor looked as tired as Cecy had, with the black hood of a female Extraordinary Shaper covering greying hair that made her look older than her forty-six years. "Outside now, Mrs. Westlake." She took Sophia's arm in her grasp, her bony hand firm and smoother than her face, and pulled her along, though Sophia had no intent to resist her.

"Thank you so much, doctor," Sophia said. "Will she be better, when she wakes?"

Dr. Garland looked grim. "I hope so. I have no idea what causes her pain. Her body is reacting as if she's being stabbed everywhere at once, but there's no physical cause I can see. The best I can do is soothe her nerves, give them a conflicting message, so to speak, but..."

"Is there anything we can do for her?"

"Make her rest. I've left you something that will help her sleep, if the pain returns. *When* it returns, I should say, and it gripes me that I have to say it. But there's no way to tell what makes her pain flare up like that, so aside from keeping her from exerting herself when it starts to be severe, there's nothing I can tell you."

Sophia nodded, hesitated, then said, "What of... of children? She won't talk about it, so I thought—"

"I can tell you what I told Mr. Barham. There's nothing wrong with her female organs, nothing that ought to prevent her having children, and I imagine the reason she hasn't conceived is that she's too caught up in worry about it. Sometimes our minds can hamper our bodies like that. Does she desire children?"

Sophia nodded.

"Then I'll talk to her about it when she's suffering less. There might be something I can do."

"Thank you again, doctor."

"Don't thank me until she's cured." Dr. Garland shouldered her satchel, which she always carried even though she had never used its contents on Cecy, and went off down the stairs.

Sophia went quietly into Cecy's room and took her seat near the bed. Cecy already looked better; her face had lost its pinched, painful look, and there was color in her cheeks again. Sophia leaned back and let her thoughts drift until she fell asleep, where she dreamed of dancing with men she knew and men whose faces she barely remembered seeing before, and she was the hunter and they the prey. Lord Endicott had the face of a tiger and clawed at her when she tried to escape dancing with him, and Mr. Rutledge was a giant bear that stepped between them so she could not see Lord Endicott at all.

"Sophy," Cecy said, and Sophia startled out of sleep and sat up, wiping away a tiny bit of saliva leaking from the corner of her mouth. She leaned forward and put her hand on Cecy's narrow shoulder, pressing her gently back into the pillows to keep her from rising.

"You need to rest," she said. "Please lie still."

"I will rest, I am simply hungry and I want to sit up," Cecy said. "Sophy, please forgive me for not listening to you—it's just that I get so impatient—" She wiped a tear from her eyes, then scrubbed her damp hand on the counterpane.

"I understand, dearest, and no one's blaming you for being ill." Sophia stood and went to the door. "I will tell Lewis to come to you, and I will order food; do you have a preference?"

"Something simple and warm, like soup, if that is not too much trouble. It is late enough they should be serving dinner soon."

Sophia looked at the clock. How long had she slept? The men from Bow Street might be taking Lord Endicott's men into custody right now. "I am certain soup will be no hardship. I will return soon."

She went down the stairs and into Lewis's study, which was like stepping into the disorderly back room of some museum dedicated to preserving remnants of every culture in the world. Sophia pinched her nose to keep from sneezing at the fragrant dust that filled the air as if it too had been carried here from India or the mysterious islands beyond China. Lewis had traveled far in his youth, gone entirely around the world twice, and his study bore the evidence of those travels: carved masks from deep within Africa, colorful rugs from marketplaces in Morocco and Cairo, painted and jeweled statues of Hindu gods, silks purchased from merchants off dhows in the China Sea and not from warehouses in London.

Even now, he continued to collect artifacts from around the world until he had a collection any actual museum would envy, if it were not a disorganized mess. Lewis simply "arranged" it by putting things on shelves and walls wherever there was an empty spot. Had he wanted to continue his travels, to show Cecy the wonders of the world? But he had known Cecy's condition when they married, knew it was likely she would be an invalid all her life, and Sophia had no doubt he did not regret giving up that dream.

Right now he looked as haggard as a Shaper ever could, which meant he was unshaven and his eyes were bleary. A decanter of brandy sat in a clear spot on his desk, with a small glass next to it, but the decanter appeared full, and she suspected Lewis had simply put it there to keep himself company. He stirred a pile of ivory discs that had angular runic shapes burned into them, some kind of fortune-telling apparatus, he had once said. Unfortunate that they were unlikely to reveal the secret of Cecy's malady. "I am not drunk," he said without looking at Sophia.

"I know," she said. "Cecy wishes to see you."

He pushed back from his desk heavily. "If there were something I could do for her…"

"I know."

Someone knocked once on the door, and Simon entered. "Mrs. Westlake, you have a caller from Bow Street," he said.

Sophia's whole body began to hum with anticipation. "Go to her, Lewis, and you, Simon, tell the cook Mrs. Barham wants soup, that hearty stuff she makes with plenty of chicken. Tell her I don't care that it's not sophisticated and neither does Mrs. Barham. I must—Lewis, both of you, just go!"

She exited the room so quickly she bumped up against the footman, who could not step out of her way quickly enough. That brief contact was enough to bring her to her senses, and she walked at a more sedate pace down the stairs and to the front door. That was as far as Simon, whose sense of propriety was greater than hers, would have allowed a Bow Street officer to enter the house.

The entry to the Barhams' town house was a narrow chimney of a room, though white instead of sooty black, and smelled of floor wax and the dusty dry artificial flowers Cecy insisted on during the winter. The man stood only a few steps from the door; his rigid posture, and the way he ran his fingers along his trouser seam, suggested that in his mind he was already finished with this errand and off on his next. He was dressed informally, in nondescript brown trousers and coat, and his shoulders were a bit damp from where the still-falling snow had melted. He removed his hat when she appeared and bowed to her, revealing brown hair streaked with blond that was somewhat flattened from his hat, which appeared to be a size too small for his head. "Mrs. West-lake?" he said.

"I am she," Sophia said.

"Sir Arthur sends his thanks, and you're to know, ma'am, we recovered nothing from the site your Dream sent us to," the man said.

The hum of excitement vanished. "How is that?" she exclaimed. "I assure you my Dream was a true one." *No,* she thought, *no, I refuse to be wrong, I will not be called wrong again.*

"There was evidence showed something were there once, but they was gone afore we came," the man said. "Likely we was too slow." He eyed her cautiously, and Sophia interpreted his look to say, *Or you were too slow in sending to us.* She nodded, acknowledging both his spoken and silent words. It was possible she had been too slow. Or the footman—whom had she given the message to? She would have to speak to him—had taken too long about his errand. Anything might have gone wrong.

"I take it Sir Arthur will not reject any future warnings I might send, simply because this one arrived too late?" she said.

The man scratched his nose with a dirty fingernail, and shrugged. "We never ignore a Seer's messages when they've the reputation you do, ma'am. But we'd like not to be called out for nothing."

The oblique rebuke startled her. No ordinary constable, none of Bow Street's foot soldiers in their ongoing battle against London's rising crime rate, would have dared to speak so to her. Despite his somewhat slovenly appearance, this must be a principal officer, popularly referred to as a Runner, one of only eight men tasked with investigating crime throughout England. "What is your name, sir?" she asked.

He nodded to her again. "Benjamin Vane, ma'am."

"Mr. Vane, I assure you I will not send word unless I am certain you will be able to act on it. Frivolous warnings can only harm my reputation—and I do not wish to waste your time any more than you wish to have it wasted. I apologize if my warning was too late."

"Didn't mean to insult you, ma'am," Vane said, and she could see he meant it. "Your drawings led us straight there, no question which warehouse it was. We could see something heavy were stored there once, and found one banknote they'd left by accident, trodden into the mud. So you were right, and we'll all have to act more quickly next time."

"Thank you, Mr. Vane." She would have to put more of an effort into finding Lord Endicott's hiding places quickly, give him no time to relocate. "If I have any more Dreams involving crime, I will be more prompt in bringing them to your attention."

Vane put his hat back on, bowed to her, and left without waiting for the footman to show him out. Sophia looked at the puddle of dirty water his feet had left. The snow would hamper Lord Endicott's movements, surely, prevent him from emptying other warehouses or shifting his press. She would need—

—no, she would need to stay with Cecy again. Or... *She is with Lewis, she has no need of me.* Sophia turned away from the dirty splotch on the glossy floorboards and went up the stairs. *It will be just one or two Dreams, and then I will return to her.* She went to her room and lay on her bed. *She will not want me hovering over her. Half an hour's Dreaming, and she will hardly miss me.* She slipped into Dream as easily as oil slides through water and left all other concerns behind.

CHAPTER 10
IN WHICH SOPHIA WRITES MANY LETTERS

December 1812

9 Sir Arthur,

Enclosed is a map of an area in Spitalfields where you will find a supply of forged banknotes. I have indicated the house in question with an X. The notes are guarded by two men, one of whom will be drunk when you approach on the northwest side. He will probably be grateful to be apprehended by you, as I am sure his criminal superiors will be displeased with him in a fatal way. This is the extent of my Sight.

Sincerely,

Sophia Westlake, Extr. Seer

10 DECEMBER 1812

Mrs. Westlake,

My thanks for your warning. Unfortunately, the house was empty when we arrived. The neighbors informed us there had been some comings and goings last night, but no one could provide us with more information.

Rowley

"Sophia!"

Sophia came out of Dream with the sensation of walls of silk flowing over and past her Dreaming face. She struggled upright and patted her head to make sure her hair was not disordered. Footsteps neared her door; she leaped up and hurried to sit at her dressing table, which Beeton had tidied despite knowing Sophia would simply disorder everything within moments of sitting. Sophia opened her jewelry box and picked through its contents. Would Cecy believe—

"Sophy, have you anything that will match this new gown of mine?" Cecy said, opening the door and entering unasked. "I believed my shoes to be... but no, they are entirely the wrong shade, and it's too late to do anything about it now."

"You may help yourself to any of my shoes you like, except the ones I am wearing now," Sophia said, not turning to look at her friend. "Do you imagine these pearl ear-drops will do?"

"They are lovely, Sophy." Cecy compared two pairs of dancing-slippers side by side. "I don't know that the Armentrouts will have dancing, but it's better to be prepared, don't you agree?" She came to stand next to Sophia and put her hand on her shoulder. "I am *so* glad you aren't Dreaming as much, dearest," she said to Sophia's reflection. "You were becoming so worn-out."

"I know, and I feel much better," Sophia lied. "Are you going to wear those? I don't believe they will fit you."

Cecy poked Sophia in the small of her back. "*I* believe you are worried they will fit *too* well, and I will look better in them than you do."

"That's true of nearly everything," Sophia said.

14 December 1812

Sir Arthur,

If you will send your men to 8, Crescent Road, in Limehouse, you will discover a merchant sailor who has been staying at the lodging house at that address for ten days, making himself extremely unpleasant to his landlady. He has used forged banknotes drawn on Hussey's Bank during that time to purchase food and drink and to pay for his lodging. He is short and fat and wears a knit cap of dull olive green, has brown eyes and grey hair, and walks with a slight limp in his left leg. He received the false notes directly from another man to whom he will be able to lead you. I have Seen the second man only as shadow, but he is taller than the first and, I believe, younger, and wears a silver ring on the third finger of his right hand. This is the extent of my Sight.

Sincerely,

Sophia Westlake, Extr. Seer

14 December 1812

Mrs. Westlake,

Thank you again for your information. The woman at the lodging house confirmed that a man of your description had been staying with her for several days, but left two days ago after settling his bill. Only two of the notes he gave her were forged. We also asked the nearby establishments about the man; they said he had paid in coin and not in notes recently, though we did retrieve some forged banknotes. None of them were witting accomplices to the forgery.

Rowley

❦

"AND I SAY," EXCLAIMED THE TALL, JOWLY MAN WHOSE NAME SOPHIA had not heard, "if these little banks fail, it's no real loss! People ought to put their faith in the Bank of England, is what I say."

"And you believe the Bank of England is immune to failure?" said Lewis.

"Not immune, but they can protect themselves better," the jowly man said.

"I presume you refer to their anti-counterfeiting measures," Mr. Rutledge said.

The jowly man shook his head. "I meant," he said, "they've the manpower to protect their printing presses from these dastardly criminals."

"They cannot prevent anyone from using a banknote as a model to engrave their own plates," Sophia said. "Though—but I see dinner is announced, gentlemen, and we must continue our conversation later." *Later, if we return to it. If you have all not forgotten. I cannot simply leap back into it and drag you all with me.*

She found herself once again at the lower end of the table, next to her hostess, and she was about to lay her napkin in her lap when the chair on her other side was drawn out, and Mr. Rutledge said, "As I knew I would be seated next to you again, I have been trying to think of horrible insults to deliver, but the best I can do is to compliment you on your appearance."

"Thank you, Mr. Rutledge, and I am afraid my supply of insults has run dry," Sophia said with a smile. They had met several times since that night at Almack's, and she had discovered she enjoyed his company and looked forward to seeing him again. He had a good sense of humor, and interesting conversation, and it had become not at all difficult to forget the circumstances of their first meeting.

Now she watched him take his seat next to her, feeling warm pleasure at his presence. His hands, pulling out his chair, fascinated her, with their square-cut nails and well-shaped fingers—she cast her glance at her soup plate, conscious of staring.

He settled into his chair with a small grunt. "You are keeping well, I presume?"

"I am, and you, sir?"

"I believe I was happier with insults, if the alternative is this insipid small talk," Mr. Rutledge said. "I know we are capable of better than this."

Sophia laughed. "Very well," she said, "tell me what you meant by anti-counterfeiting measures, a moment ago."

Mr. Rutledge's eyes widened in mock surprise. "Weighty stuff for a dinner conversation, don't you agree?"

"But certainly not insipid, you must admit."

"Very true." Mr. Rutledge put down his soup spoon and turned to face Sophia more directly. "The Bank of England has used special paper to print their bills upon for more than a decade. It has a watermark that is difficult to duplicate. Forgers would not only have to have the right plates, they would have to steal the right paper as well. I wouldn't agree with our vocal friend that the Bank of England is the only secure bank in the British Empire, but he's not wrong that they would make a difficult target for forgers."

"So who produces this paper?" Sophia asked.

"I don't know," said Mr. Rutledge, "but I believe it would be a difficult secret to keep. No doubt those suppliers keep a close watch on their paper, just in case."

"No doubt," Sophia said.

18 December 1812

Sir Arthur,

The paper mill owned by Terence Chastain will be robbed in two days' time, at approximately one o'clock in the morning on December 20. Their target is paper manufactured for the use of printing banknotes, this order being designated for the Bank of England. There are six thieves and they will approach from the west, having bribed the night watchman to leave the shipping doors unlocked. They have been hired by the man whose face I still cannot see, who wears a silver ring on the third finger of his right hand. One of the thieves will remain with the wagon they bring to carry the paper away, one will stand lookout, and the rest will remove the paper from the mill. Two of the thieves have a distinctive pattern to the nails in their soles. One of them wears a scarf wrapped around his face, into which he coughs, trying to muffle the sound. They do not work well together and it should be no trouble at all for your excellent men to apprehend them. This is the extent of my Sight.

Sincerely,

Sophia Westlake, Extr. Seer

· · ·

21 DECEMBER 1812

Mrs. Westlake,

We observed the Chastain mill for three hours last night as you directed and saw no thieves. The night watchman insisted he knew nothing of any bribes, and he was vouched for by Mr. Chastain as a hard worker of seven years. I wonder if you were perhaps mistaken about the night or about the name of the mill?

Rowley

SOPHIA THREW THE LETTER AT THE FIRE; IT CAUGHT THE DRAFT from the chimney, which lifted it a foot into the air, then sent it fluttering to lie on the hearth rug. Daphne went to pick it up. She read it silently, though Sophia had already read it aloud, then crumpled it into a jagged-edged ball and tossed it somewhat more accurately into the heart of the flames, which rose up higher in acknowledgement of her offering. "He makes you sound unreliable," she said.

"Because I *am* unreliable, as far as these prophecies go," Sophia said. She hunched into her chair, which was an uncomfortable seat with hard cushions and rough upholstery that looked as if it were embroidery done on burlap. "I have not been correct once since my success with Hammond Bank. Sir Arthur is being polite in not saying what he is actually thinking, which is likely 'why are you wasting my time?' And I begin to agree with him."

"No, Sophia, you aren't unreliable!" Daphne dropped to her knees next to Sophia's chair and leaned against it, then reared back with an exclamation of disgust. "How can you bear to sit in this thing? It's scratchy and hard, and I have no idea why anyone would choose to have it in her home. Mrs. Barham can't possibly know about it."

"Oh, I don't mind it, Daphne," Sophia said, though now she was developing an urge to scratch. She took another letter from the salver and read the direction, then wrinkled her nose in distaste. "The Duchess of Lenshire again, asking for a Vision. The woman is relentless."

"What Vision does she want?"

"The subject is irrelevant, with her. She simply wants the social cachet of having an Extraordinary Seer perform for her friends." Sophia scanned the lines quickly and sighed. "Very well. I shall have no peace until I do as she asks."

"You could reject her outright. It's not fair that you be treated like a performing animal!"

"Fairness has little to do with it. If she were evil, or cruel... but no, she is only foolish and self-centered, and much as I dislike being on display like a cake in a shop window, I dislike more gaining a reputation for arrogance in rejecting what most would see as a reasonable request."

"But should you not be concerned that others will take her example, and plague you with requests?"

"I am more concerned about how many failures I am accumulating, even if my Dreams are only too late to be useful rather than actually wrong."

"You should Dream about something other than forged banknotes," Daphne said, rising and moving to a different seat that looked more comfortable than Sophia's. "It's almost as if you're obsessed with them."

"It's only coincidence," Sophia said, and felt guilty about lying to Daphne—but what good would it do for Daphne to know the truth about why the banknotes were so important? "A Dream about one thing usually leads me to consider it more frequently, which leads to more Dreams on the same topic. What would *you* have me Dream of?"

Daphne grinned. "You could Dream of my great successes in the War Office. I'd like to know where I will be sent. Do you imagine I will meet the Prince Regent? I saw him once at Carlton House, at least I saw part of him, he was rather surrounded by admirers—why do you suppose it is they crush about him so, but give you space to move? Since you're almost as famous as he is, and—"

"I wonder that myself, but mostly I am happy not to be crowded," Sophia said. "And I do not believe my Dreams would be very useful to you; they are only good for short-term prophecies, and you still have five months to go before your service."

Daphne wrinkled her nose. "Four months, twenty-seven days," she said. "I am so *impatient* all the time. Though Standiford's is busier than ever, this time of year, and I am grateful I can Bound instead of having to drive through the cold and the snow, grateful when I remember to be, that is. Well, then, you can Dream of...of the man you will fall in love with!"

"That might be rather long-term as well, since I have no intent to remarry."

"No?" Daphne leaned back in her seat and pulled her knees up to curl into a corner of the sofa. "Why not?"

Sophia opened her mouth and found she had no ready answer, which surprised her. "I already have social status, and I have no desire for a title," she began.

"Which is fortunate, because the Prince Regent won't give titles to women," Daphne said.

"*Rarely* gives titles to women," Sophia said, "and I would not marry to gain a title no matter how much status I lacked. I have sufficient fortune to keep myself comfortably for the rest of my life, and a talent that would allow me to increase that fortune if I chose, so I need not marry money."

"You might fall in love," Daphne pointed out.

"I might, but I consider that unlikely. Every man I meet is more interested in my notoriety than in my person." She felt a brief discomfort at her own words that she could not identify, and pushed it aside. "It was so much easier, with Richard. We met, we fell in love, and five months later we were wed. But I was only nineteen—everything is different when you are young."

"I know," said twenty-year-old Daphne, "because men are always pretending to be interested in me, when what they want is to be married to the Marquess of Claresby's only child, or to an Extraordinary, and—but it is so *discouraging* to be so observant, and to know the truth of their intentions! On the other hand, suppose I *did* meet someone I could love, and then I might want to give up on all the adventures I mean to have! So I'm just as happy none of them are sincere."

"What a declaration!" Sophia said with a laugh.

☙❧

22 DECEMBER 1812

Sir Arthur,

The man who has been issuing orders to the counterfeiters of whom I have warned you resides at Wharf End Lane, north of Billingsgate, in a lodging house marked with a picture of a sheep's head and the word Witters. He is tall, with black hair and black eyes, wears fisherman's boots and a long scarf of undyed wool, as well as the silver ring I have mentioned before. He will be in possession of a few forged notes drawn on several banks throughout London. I include his portrait here. This is the extent of my Sight.

Sincerely,

Sophia Westlake, Extr. Seer

22 DECEMBER 1812

Mrs. Westlake,

No one of that description is reported as living at that address, which is not a lodging house, but a mercantile office. I believe it might be better that you direct your reports to the Bank of England's committee, which will be able to use your Dreams better than we can.

Rowley

☙❧

SOPHIA LAY WAKEFUL IN HER BED, TOO TIRED TO DREAM AND NOT tired enough to sleep. No, it was not exhaustion that kept her from Dreaming, but fury. How *dare* that wizened little man imply that her Dreams were unreliable? *Except that they are,* she reminded herself, *and this last one was simply false. I cannot believe I failed so utterly to interpret it!*

She had been so exhilarated to finally put a face to the shadowy figure that had hovered at the edge of Dream so many times, she had drawn a copy of his portrait for herself and hidden it in her wardrobe where she could look at it when she needed a reminder of what her goal was. And now, to be told not only that the man was not to be found, but that the place to which she had directed the Bow Street Runners was not a residence... she put her hands over her mouth to muffle her scream of frustration. She had failed at her goal, and worse, she looked like a fool.

She went through her relaxation routine, flexing and relaxing each set of muscles in turn, but found herself still too restless to sleep. She could ring for a glass of hot milk, which was disgusting but might help her fall asleep, but that would require leaving the warm comfort of her bed for the chill air of her bedchamber. She could light her lamp and read for a while, but her current book bored her, and getting another would again mean leaving her cocoon. So she closed her eyes and slipped into Dream once more, fighting her tiredness and her feelings of humiliation when she remembered what had come of her latest Dream.

The idea of entering a Dream about Lord Endicott's counterfeiting wearied her, but she had done her work too well, and all she saw on every side, above and below, were doors leading to Dreams of counterfeit banknotes used for purchases or paying bills or redeeming debts, sheets of paper and gallons of ink, the shadowy silhouettes of presses (shadowy because she had never yet seen one and had only the vaguest idea of what they looked like) and the shapes of faces she never recognized. She wandered among the doors, feeling another weariness, this of the spirit, descend over her. What was the point of Dreaming if her Dreams could not enact change in the waking world? She chose a door at random and laid her palm flat against it, and was drawn into the Dream as smoothly as silk sliding through a brass ring.

She entered a large shop of some kind, more elegant than most of those she had seen in Dream lately, in which faceless figures moved, handled the merchandise, and spoke to one another in chirps like a flock of canaries—it was rare to hear sounds in Dream, and most of them were symbolic rather than literal, a bell standing for laughter or a dog's bark representing a fight.

It seemed to be a clothing warehouse, with yards of fabric stretched out like webbing across the wide space which grew wider whenever Sophia's attention went to the walls instead of the people. Watching them was something to do, so Sophia made her way through the shop, amusing herself by bringing items into focus and altering them, changing muslin into satin and then into netting. Of course her changes went unremarked by the patrons; it was all a construct of Sophia's Dreaming mind. But it was an emotional release, a feeling that she was at last in control of *something*.

She approached a woman who was paying for a dress and saw the flickering movement that meant the banknote was fraudulent. On a whim, Sophia made an effort to draw the woman's face into focus. She had no idea where this warehouse was, but it seemed ungenerous to the Dream not to at least try to make use of what it gave her. The woman had a narrow face, and a narrow nose, and narrow eyes...

...and the Dream was fading all around her. In the space of two breaths, Sophia found herself surrounded by the doors of Dream again. She turned around in a slow circle. The door she had entered had vanished. The Dream was gone.

This was an impossibility. One entered a Dream, then rose from it into the waking world. One did not return to the doors of Dream. One certainly did not exit a Dream without choosing to or being startled out of it.

Sophia reached out to a nearby door, but stopped herself before she could touch it. A stray thought flashed through her mind—*am I losing my talent?*—but it was a ridiculous, impossible thought, not even worth entertaining. Something else had happened. Something... something improbable, something suggested by the limits of Dream and the boundaries of a Seer's talent and the place where they intersected. She stopped herself speculating and reached out, instead, for more information, and for the nearest door.

She did not bother examining the details of this Dream closely, but instead cast about for the image at its heart. A man sat counting banknotes on a stool, laying them out in stacks on an invisible table. As she moved around to see the face of the man, the Dream shuddered, faded to mist, and she was once again surrounded by doors.

So. Let us apply reason. Dreams show what may be, if circumstances remain as they are. A Dream may be countered if the right action is taken. So a Dream that vanishes before it can be acted upon is a Dream whose possibilities have been eliminated, even as I become aware of them. No. Because I become aware of them. Eliminated by someone who is in a position to change those events, who knows what I See. Someone—

She gasped, and her Dreaming self did the same, shaking her concentration enough that her last thought before rising out of Dream was: *Oh, no. He has his own Seer.*

CHAPTER 11

IN WHICH SOPHIA DISCOVERS SHE HAS A COUNTERPART

Sophia sat up in her bed and lit the lamp with unsteady hands. Another Seer. Of course. What a fool she'd been not to realize it sooner—but then, in her time with the War Office, she had always been the one disrupting the Dreams of Napoleon's Seers. She had never been on the other side of that contest, never known how it felt to the Seer whose Dream she intercepted and changed. Uncertainty, and fear, welled up in her, and it took some effort to convince herself these were irrational feelings. She knew what the unknown Seer was doing, because she had done it many times before. She simply had to work out how to prevent that Seer from interfering in her Dream.

She lay down again and prepared to meditate. The first step in disrupting a Dream was knowing what your enemy might reasonably Dream about. Lord Endicott knew she had set her sights on his counterfeiting operation and would have instructed his Seer to meditate on the Dreams Sophia would have related to this topic. That would create doors revealing what Sophia Saw, and from there it was a matter of telling Lord Endicott to, for example, move a batch of forged notes from one warehouse to another, or to warn one of his men not to pass a fraudulent banknote to a particular person. It was difficult, because there was no way to know which of the many doors of Dream Sophia might enter, and therefore Lord Endicott would be forced to make many alterations to his plans, but if his organization was large enough, as she believed it was, he would have the resources to do such a thing.

But for Dreams to disappear before she could act on them... the enemy Seer seemed to have discovered a way to predict which door Sophia would choose before she entered it, and was able to take action to erase the possibility that the event would happen at all, preventing her Seeing it. She had never heard of such a thing before.

Fear made her lose her concentration briefly, and she focused on her breathing, in through her nostrils, out through her mouth, until her whole body resonated with the sound of her lungs working and her heart beating. This enemy Seer was powerful. She was clearly experienced. But Sophia was a master of her craft too, and the idea of pitting herself against someone who was her peer in ways no one else had ever been was... exhilarating, actually, and exciting. She would take a different approach and let it lead her back to this other Seer. *Show me my enemy*, she told herself, and dropped into Dream.

She had hoped one door of Dream, at least, would bear the visage of her enemy, but of course she knew too little of the woman for luck to be on her side. The doors of Dream, as usual, displayed images related to counterfeiting. Sophia stood and watched them for a few moments. If the enemy Seer were powerful enough to make those Dreams vanish before Sophia entered them... that was a possibility that didn't bear lingering on.

But nothing happened. The doors simply surrounded her in all directions, still and unmoving except for the shapes on their surfaces. So either the Seer's perceptions did not extend this far, or she was toying with Sophia. Sophia chose to believe the former. *Let us experiment, then.* She chose a door with the hazy image of a press on it—as long as she was experimenting, she might as well try for the high-hanging fruit—and passed through it with ease.

In this Dream, the press was an angular, spidery creature crouched in a nest of wires that connected it to the unseen walls on all sides. Sophia folded her arms across her chest and waited. Nothing happened. She took a step—

—and she was once again surrounded by doors. She took a few steps, trying to keep her balance. That had been far more abrupt than the last time, too abrupt for her to grasp some other aspect of the Dream that would lead to the Seer rather than the press. Quickly she turned and passed through another door at random, found herself in a tavern, saw the flickering motion as a banknote changed hands—

—and the Dream was gone. Her sleeping self responded to her Dreaming body's increased heart rate, her growing fear. If she could not find something to hang onto, something to follow back to the enemy's own Dreams... She calmed herself and began entering door after door, trying everything she could think of: paying close attention to the Dream's central object, paying *no* attention to the Dream's central object, focusing on the surroundings, walking toward the walls and letting them tunnel out before her. Nothing worked. Time after time, the Dreams vanished, one after another until she was sick and dizzy. Then there were no more doors.

Sophia crouched and put her head between her knees, breathing deeply, then remembered she had an actual body that was not nearly so exhausted and dizzy as this one, and let herself wake. Her heart was still beating too rapidly, and the lamp's flame had rings around it that went away only after Sophia blinked rapidly several times.

She lay back and stared up at the ceiling. The enemy Seer was far more experienced than Sophia had expected. She knew how to conceal her presence so Sophia could not follow the Dream back to her. Sophia squeezed her eyes shut. Very well. She would simply have to go at this from an unexpected direction. She might not be able to pursue her prey through Dream, but her Dreams were anchored in the waking world, and there was no reason one of them might not give her more information. Particularly the only one that had been false.

She rose from her bed and dressed. She would have to forgo her stays; it was nearly eleven o'clock, and calling on Beeton to help her dress would raise the kind of questions she wanted to avoid. So she fumbled into a dark, plain gown and sturdy shoes, found a heavy grey cloak with a voluminous hood, and tiptoed downstairs. The narrow door to the ground-floor stairs squeaked as she pushed it open, but there was no one around to hear it, and she descended quietly into the dimly lit hall that led to the offices and the kitchen.

Here, someone would be awake, anticipating Lewis and Cecy's return from spending the evening with friends. The hall smelled of supper and hot candle wax, the latter of which came from a dozen candles burning behind glass shields in the servants' dining hall. At the center of the room stood a battered oak slab of a table that at the moment was bare of cloth or table settings. Three men sat at its far end, playing cards, each of them with small stacks of coin in front of him.

Simon glanced up at her entry, then threw his cards down and leaped to his feet. The other two were slower to respond; the butler, Traviss, wiped his hands on his knee breeches, while Peter the coachman gave his pile of coin a little shove, as if hoping to hide it from her notice.

"Mrs. Westlake, ma'am," Traviss said. "You... is there something I can do for you?" He wiped his hands down his breeches seam again, and Sophia saw beads of sweat spring up along his receding hairline. She had of course never come below stairs before, and had no idea whether gambling was permitted or not, but the three men certainly were behaving as if they were children caught stealing pies from under the cook's eye. Good.

"I need the carriage, Traviss, and a lantern," she said. "I have an errand to run."

"At eleven o'clock, ma'am?" Traviss blurted, then went pale when Sophia raised her eyebrows at him.

"I don't recall inviting you to question me about my actions," she said, "and in fact I believe it would be better if you—" she encompassed all three men in her gaze—"did not discuss this evening with anyone. I know *I* will not." She left that sentence hanging in the air, and waited.

Traviss cleared his throat. "Yes, ma'am," he said. "Peter, bring the coach around. Simon, a lantern for Mrs. Westlake."

Peter nodded, scraped his coin off the table furtively, and exited the room without looking once at Sophia. Simon, glancing quickly from Traviss to Sophia, left his coin on the table and followed Peter. That left Traviss and Sophia eyeing each other. She had never seen the tall, stoop-shouldered man so discomfited.

"Are you enjoying your evening?" Sophia asked. She couldn't help herself. He simply looked so *guilty* it was hard not to needle him. Why Lewis might forbid gambling was beyond her, since he enjoyed a good wager himself, but as long as the three men were afraid she might give them away, she could feel confident of her excursion remaining a secret.

"Indeed, ma'am," Traviss said. He seemed to be regaining his composure. They fell back into silence until Simon returned holding a lantern and handed it to Sophia.

"I beg your pardon for intruding," she said. "No, please do not trouble yourselves, I do not need an escort." She went back up to wait in the entry hall. If Lewis and Cecy returned home early... but no, they would not be back for a few hours, and it was not very far to Billings-gate. Well, it was a few miles, but that was nothing. She could investi-gate the supposed mercantile office, learn why her Dream had failed, and return before anyone but those three men knew she was gone.

After five minutes, nervous of being discovered, she opened the door and looked for Peter. There were no gas lamps yet in Hanover Square, just ordinary ones that flickered as if they, too, were shivering in the cold. The smell of a coming snowstorm overrode the distinctive smell of London, crisp and wet, promising a white Christmas. It had been a mild winter to date: just enough snow to be pretty without being an inconvenience. She closed the door and resumed her wait.

Finally, the door opened, and Peter peered inside. He too was bundled up against the cold, the striped woolen scarf wound several times around his neck and his heavy coat making him look bulky. "Ma'am, the carriage," he said.

Sophia accepted his help into the carriage and settled her cloak around her. "Wharf End Lane, north of Billingsgate," she told Peter, who frowned at her.

"That's not a place a lady ought be going, this time of night special-ly," he said. "You sure about it?"

"Of course I am," Sophia said, "and as I have you to protect me, I need fear nothing, yes?"

Peter put his hand on his coat pocket, which was deep with a wide mouth, easily large enough to hold a horse pistol. "Let's hope it don't come to that, ma'am." He shut the door and climbed into his seat, and with a jerk, the carriage moved forward. Sophia settled back into her seat and watched the street slide past, the lanterns casting stripes of light across her hands in their red gloves. She needed a plan.

Well, it was unlikely anyone would be at a mercantile office this late in the evening, and there might be little foot traffic there because so many of the neighboring buildings were businesses—she ought to have known better when she Saw the address so clearly, and it made her furious how easily that enemy Seer had made a fool of her. No matter. She would find a way into the building and discover why her Sight had failed her. Then she would... well, she would determine what her next step would be after investigating the office.

The Barhams' carriage was well-sprung, and jostled her only a little over the irregular stones of the road. Sophia readied herself for meditation, which was made only slightly more difficult by the movement of the carriage. *Show me the future in which I find a way into the office*, she told herself, then fell into Dream and looked about her for the right door.

She had worried, for a moment, that there would still be no doors there, but her Dreaming brain had summoned more to replace those the enemy Seer had destroyed. Most of them still dealt with counterfeiting, but a handful bore images that were harder to distinguish, indicating that her meditation had generated a new set of possibilities. She went to look at these, using her instincts to draw her where they would, and found herself in front of a door which bore a single knob in its center, silvery in the non-light of Dream. The doors of Dream never had any fittings to them; this represented the contents of the Dream. Sophia laid her palm on the door and was drawn into it.

She stood in a narrow alley between two buildings—no, they were like a child's drawing of buildings, outlined with strong black strokes of ink, windows sketched roughly into their faces. They extended high above her head until they disappeared into clouds far too low to be real. She looked to either side; the alley became immaterial only a few feet from her in both directions, and when she turned around to face the drawing behind her, it went immaterial too. So, only one of these constructions mattered.

She turned to face the first edifice again and took a step back to see it better. The whole thing wavered as if she were seeing it through water and had just flung a stone at the pool. She held still, afraid it might dissolve entirely, but it settled back into immobility, and she had the feeling that the shimmering motion was part of what she needed from this Dream. So she took another step back, and then another, and with each step the wavering grew more intense, but also shrank until it was centered on a fat barrel beside the door.

Sophia steadied herself and drew on that barrel, bringing it into focus, and as she did so her view tilted and swayed dizzyingly until she was looking at one of the upper windows. It wavered, then went from being a child's drawing to a real window, framed in wood that had once been painted white and was now scratched and peeled. One pane was missing, and Sophia looked inside and saw it would be easy to reach the latch through that missing pane. She examined it more closely; she would fit through the window opening without much trouble. So— alley, barrel, window. Very likely it would be more difficult than the Dream suggested, but she was confident she could overcome any difficulties she encountered.

She let the Dream go and rubbed her eyes. *One more, as a precaution,* she thought, and found a Dream thronged with faces. She entered it and found herself at the end of an alley, looking at the carriage pulled up to the edge of the street nearby. Faceless people walked past in both directions, none of them looking her way, far more than she imagined ever came down this street in the waking world.

She watched, and waited, and presently the crowd thinned until there was only one person, whose face shivered into clarity as she watched. His footsteps slowed, then he turned toward her and raised his arm, and a heavy stick appeared at the end of it. Sophia made him freeze and walked around him, examining him, then rose out of Dream and breathed slowly and deeply until the dizziness passed.

She had probably spent too much time in Dream tonight, and she would pay for it in the morning, but no one said she had to rise early, and she had nothing planned for the day until attending the Duke of

Lenshire's party tomorrow evening. She could certainly be excused a little extra sleep to fortify her for an evening of dancing and conversation—oh, and she was committed to having a Vision for the Duchess. Why she had agreed to do it so publicly... but she had, and there was no sense regretting what she had no way of changing.

That was something Mr. Rutledge had said—what had they been discussing? She couldn't remember, but he had said it in response to some comment she had made, and it had made her feel guilty, as if he had been talking about her expulsion from the War Office and somehow knew her secret campaign to expose Lord Endicott and reclaim her reputation. He had an uncanny knack for seeing to the heart of whatever she was saying and responding in a way that increased her understanding of her own opinions. He was—

—actually, she thought about him quite often, didn't she? And she looked forward to seeing him, and she felt that rush of pleasure when he was near... *Sophia, you are falling in love with him, aren't you?*

The idea made her face flush. True, he was quite a bit older than she, but that was not so remarkable; Lord and Lady Montclair, for example, were quite happy despite the difference in their ages. And Mr. Rutledge was clever, and shared her interests, and was handsome despite his unfashionable attire... why should she not feel an attraction to him? Perhaps the way he always sought her out meant that he, too, felt something more for her than friendship.

She blushed again. How embarrassing, after having declared frequently and decidedly that she did not intend to marry again, to consider—well, she could bear Cecy's teasing, and there was no one in society save perhaps Lady Daveril who would criticize her for falling in love with him. Just the thought was enough to send her heart racing.

She pressed her gloved hands to her hot cheeks. *Be sensible.* It probably did not matter. Despite how often he sought out her company, he had never given her any indication that he felt anything but friendship for her, and no doubt he would be embarrassed if he knew the ridiculous turn her thoughts were taking. No, he was a friend, and he would stay a friend, and both of them would be happier that way. One of them would be, anyway.

She leaned against the fabric of the hood to cool her cheeks and saw they were approaching the intersections she had seen in Dream and nearing Wharf End Lane. She leaned forward and said, "Keep going to the end of the street, and turn." Cold air brushed her face, raising a chill along her arms and cheeks, and she clenched her hands in their red silk gloves together in her lap. Now nothing would stop her from learning the truth.

CHAPTER 12
IN WHICH SOPHIA TAKES UP A
CAREER AS A BURGLAR

W harf End Lane was narrow, wide enough only for one
carriage to pass at a time. Sophia hoped it was a through
street and not a dead end, hoped even more fervently
that they would not meet anyone coming the other way. With no
householders to maintain lights along the street, it was dark and fore-
boding, as if it knew Sophia's purpose in coming here and was drawing
in on itself for protection against her incursion.

The wooden structures lining both sides of the street sagged as if
depressed, and though they did not seem as run-down as they would if
they were abandoned, the weathered grey doors made it impossible to
imagine they had ever been new. Few signs indicated the shops'
purposes; presumably if you knew enough to find the way there, you
knew which building you wanted.

The street was as empty as she'd hoped. She had only been in this
part of London once, familiarizing herself with landmarks, and that
had been at two o'clock in the afternoon, not nearly midnight, and she
had only been able to guess at what it might look like now. The
carriage passed a few men, hunched up against the cold, who walked
on without showing any interest in them. Another man, walking alone,

glanced up at her, and she reflexively shrank back where she could not be seen, uncertain what she was afraid of.

A bundle of rags tucked into an alley between two of the closely-packed structures moved, revealing a man curled in on himself so he would fit into the small space. Sophia realized she was still clenching her fists and forced herself to relax. She had Seen far worse things happen to men in the war, and yet the sight of that man wedged between the buildings made her feel sick and horrified in a completely different way.

She sat up and watched carefully until she saw the sheep's head sign, the name illegible in the dim moonlight. Aside from that, it looked no different from its brothers, except that its doorknob was brass instead of iron. Sophia had no idea if that was significant or not. Then they were past, and Peter was turning at the end of the street and coming to a halt. "Ma'am, what you want to do now?" he said.

"Wait a moment." The front of Witters had not resembled the "building" she had seen in Dream, which suggested there was a back way in. Sophia got out of the carriage and walked a short distance up the new street. It was colder here, so close to the Thames, and a breeze had come up that blew the smell of the river away. There were no lamps along this street, nothing but the light of the full moon soon to be covered by storm clouds, but not too soon—it would not interfere with Sophia's plans. She had plenty of time.

She paced down the street until she could see past the buildings of Wharf End Lane—what a grand-sounding name for such an ordinary, tired-looking street—and into a narrow alley that seemed to run parallel to it, behind the buildings, for most, if not all, of its length.

"Wait here," she told Peter. "A man will try to attack you in a little while, but if you are alert, and show him your pistol, I believe he will run. He is the sort of person who will attack weakness and flee from strength."

She retrieved her lantern from the carriage and held it out for him to light. By its flickering glow, Peter looked extremely nervous, but said nothing as she entered the alley with her lantern held as close to her chest as she dared. It cast odd shadows on the walls she passed and made the windows in the upper stories, those with glass panes, flicker like ghosts keeping her company as she walked. There were no windows at ground level, and no sign that there ever had been. The blank walls were like a narrow canyon that made her feel suffocated. She hugged herself briefly, rubbing her arms against the cold, and continued on.

The alley was full of rubbish: battered crates and broken bottles and the half-frozen waste of dogs or cats. She stepped around a heap of cloth she fervently hoped did not conceal a person and reminded herself of why she was here, trying to maintain the calm she always felt in Dream. From this perspective, here at the bottom of the alley, the buildings really did seem to extend all the way to the sky, and Sophia kept her gaze firmly ahead.

It was unnerving to be in a place so like, and so very unlike, what she had seen in Dream, and that was when she realized she had no idea whether she would recognize the rear of Witters. She had not bothered to count how many doors lay between the end of the street and her goal, and she would have to retrace her steps all the way back to the street and face those dour, sinister men whose disinterest might not persist when they saw she was a lone, defenseless woman.

She stopped for a moment, lowering her lantern, and nearly gave in to despair. This was the most ridiculous idea she had ever had, and she should be home now, safe in her bed, not wandering through a filthy alley on a futile errand that no doubt would teach her nothing.

Something moved behind her, and she whirled, holding out her lantern like a talisman. A dog so painfully thin she could see its ribs even at ten feet's distance skulked out from between two of the buildings and whined at her. Sophia brandished the lantern. "Shoo!" she said, waving the light a little, praying it would move on. She had read of wild dogs attacking people, and although this one looked peaceful enough, its appearance could be a ruse.

The dog whined at her again, then limped away down the alley toward where Peter waited with the carriage and his reassuring pistol. Sophia relaxed and lowered the lamp, turned around, then looked more closely at the battered wooden wall next to her. It reminded her of what she had seen in Dream, though the weathered gray boards bore little resemblance to the stark black and white construction her

Dreaming mind had conjured. She looked up and saw, well above her head, a window that reflected the scant light in a strange pattern, as if some of the glass were missing. This had to be the right building; she refused to consider the alternative.

She looked around at the refuse clogging the alley and saw an empty barrel canted atop a pile of bricks. Strange, to find bricks in this place built mainly of lumber, but she didn't care enough to speculate on their presence. She took hold of the barrel and, with some rocking, managed to pull it off the heap and onto its side, then roll it to a spot directly under the window. It was not difficult to upend it, and it seemed sturdy enough to support her weight, so she set her lantern on the ground and climbed atop the barrel.

She stretched out her fingers and was able to grip the window ledge, curling her fingers through the space where the pane was missing—and that was all. She reached up with her other hand and fitted it through the same space, but even with both hands together she could barely find purchase on the sill, never mind pull herself up. She let go and stood balanced on the barrel for a moment. Just a few more inches...

She climbed off the barrel and went back to the refuse heap. There were the bricks, of course, and a few lengths of rope too small to be of use to anyone, and two or three boards perhaps three feet long and the width of her two hands. She pulled at one of them and it slid easily from the pile. The board alone would not give her enough height, but it might still be of use.

She dragged one of the boards to her barrel and laid it on top, then began hauling bricks to it, stacking them neatly on the board until she had a pillar six bricks square and four high. She laid another of the boards across the pillar for stability, then carefully climbed atop her makeshift stool. It teetered beneath her, but did not fall apart, and now she was chest-high to the window and able to reach inside and open the latch easily. She climbed back down for the lantern, which she carefully set on the floor inside the room, then awkwardly hauled herself through the opening. With a final scramble to keep from falling on her face, she was inside.

Sophia straightened her clothes, tugged at her gloves, and looked around. The room looked smaller than it probably was by the lantern's flickering light, containing only a few small crates and an empty bookshelf. She took a deep breath and smelled only old wood and dust. If this office sold anything, her nose detected none of it. She adjusted her gloves again, then exited the room through a flimsy door that stuck in its frame.

She found herself at one end of a short hallway that terminated at the far end in a staircase that ascended and descended out of Sophia's sight. Two more doors lay between her and the staircase. Faint blue moonlight shone from beneath them, giving them a sinister look, as if something evil were going on behind them. Sophia sternly told her imagination to be silent and went forward through the open doorway directly opposite her, into a room lit more brightly by the glow of the full moon.

Most of the front wall was taken up by a window with dozens of thick, palm-sized square glass panes that made it impossible to see anything outside clearly. It looked as if the window itself were the source of the blue light, and Sophia had the momentary impression that she was back in Dream, where impossible things like glowing glass happened as a matter of course.

She shook her head to dispel the illusion and turned around to examine the room. It appeared to be where most of Witters' business was transacted. There was a clerk's desk in one corner, and a counter filled most of one side of the room, with the detritus of business covering it—an inkstand or two, a discarded pen, a pair of ledgers. Behind the counter were some cubbyholes, some of them containing folded or rolled papers. Whatever trade Witters engaged in, it was not the sort that invited thievery, and no doubt everyone in the neighborhood knew it.

She went down the hall toward the stairs and tried the doors. Both were locked. She considered falling into a Dream to see if they were important, but chose not to worry about it until she had exhausted the possibilities of the staircase. It was dark in both directions, and silent, and extended beyond her lantern's light, giving no indication which way her Dream might intend her to go. After a moment's consideration, she determined to go up first.

The stairs creaked under her weight like a symphony scored for rusty nails and dry wood, making her nervous. She told herself they were not going to collapse, and there was no one to hear her in any case, and moved on.

The stairs ended at another hallway, this one lined with doors on both sides. Five of the six doors matched the rest of the building, grey and depressed-looking, with tarnished doorknobs. The sixth, however, was sanded and painted and bore a shining brass knob. Sophia stood and regarded it for a while, because it looked completely out of place in this decrepit building where nothing had been painted for at least ten years. Then she opened the door and went inside.

It was a bedroom. No, not just a bedroom: a room in a lodging house. The bed frame was shabby, but its brass was polished. The blanket on the bed was worn soft, but not threadbare, from much washing. The porcelain bowl and pitcher on the cupboard with its three drawers had a few chips, but were otherwise intact. A lamp stood on the cupboard, waiting to illuminate the room for its occupant. Even the chintz curtains were free of dust and would no doubt give the room a cheery, homey look when they were drawn back to allow sunlight to enter.

Sophia realized her mouth was agape and shut it. Someone had gone to a great deal of trouble to make this room look like lodgings for someone. Then her brain caught up with the rest of her senses, and she became furious. They had *tricked* her. Lord Endicott had done this on purpose to make her look unreliable. That... that *bastard*.

She had been too confident, and she had underestimated him, and he had made her look the fool. And now Bow Street would not take her seriously, leaving her to fight him with only her own resources. He had a Seer, he had all the power, and she had... what? Determination? That was all very well, but in wartime determination needed to be backed up by military strength to be useful, and this was most certainly a war.

Wood creaked, somewhere nearby, and Sophia went very still, listening. Nothing. Then, again, a creak from the symphonic stair as someone took a step, then another.

Sophia extinguished her lantern and looked around for a place to hide. Under the bed was something that only worked in books, since it depended on your pursuer being an idiot. She rushed to the window and began prying at it with her fingers, but it was not made to open, or had been painted closed, and she gave up. She could not scale the side of the building in any case, so exiting by that route was pointless.

She snatched up her lantern and went to stand behind the door, where she would be concealed oh-so-briefly when whoever it was entered. She would smash the lantern on his head, then run, and hope not to trip and fall to the bottom of the stairs in the darkness. She gripped the lantern in both hands and swallowed to rid herself of the dry, panicked feeling in her mouth.

The person drew nearer, making the creaky music crescendo. She raised her makeshift weapon above her head, and waited.

A man much bigger than she entered the room, moving quietly. He took a few steps further into the room, and Sophia stepped forward and brought the lantern down toward his head. The man turned with incredible speed for someone so large and caught the lantern with one hand as it descended. With the other he grabbed Sophia's arm and twisted it behind her back. She gasped in pain and struggled to escape, but the man's grip was like a raptor's claw. "Let me go," she said, panting with fear.

The man released her. "What are you doing here, Mrs. Westlake?" Mr. Rutledge said.

CHAPTER 13

IN WHICH THERE IS AN UNHAPPY REVELATION

S ophia gasped. "What am *I* doing here? What are *you* doing here?" she exclaimed, forgetting to speak quietly.

"At the moment, wishing I had sent Stewart on this errand," he said in his low rumble. "You are the last person I would have expected to find in this place, though I realize as I say those words that it makes perfect sense for you to be here."

Sophia rubbed her arm where he had grasped it. "I am here because I wanted to know why my Vision failed," she said. "You have no such excuse."

"No, I don't," he said. "Why don't we leave before someone notices the activity going on behind these windows?"

Sophia didn't budge. "You were surprised to find me here, which means you were not following me," she said, "and you certainly do not live in this part of London, so you were not investigating a potential burglary near your home. So why *are* you here?"

Mr. Rutledge rubbed the bridge of his nose. "My men were watching this building because of your Dream," he said. "Because it proved so—my apologies—so dramatically wrong, I became suspicious, and determined to watch for anyone approaching this office who might know the truth. I did not consider that you might also be interested in knowing why your Dream had failed, nor that you might pursue that interest directly."

"Your men? Watching the building? How do you know of my Dream? Mr. Rutledge, are you with the Bow Street Runners?"

Mr. Rutledge walked toward the window and leaned heavily on the ledge. "No," he said, "I work for the Bank of England."

Sophia gaped. "But you..." Too many words crowded into her head. "You said you worked for the government!"

"No, Mrs. Westlake, that was a conclusion you drew. I apologize for allowing that misapprehension to stand, but correcting it would have meant revealing the truth, which, as I said, I was not at liberty to do."

"But the Bank—then you are pursuing the forgers!" Sophia put a hand on the bedframe to steady herself against the startling revelation. "Is this what you wanted me to do? To work for the Bank of England?"

"Ultimately, yes. It was clear to me that one of the counterfeiters is a Seer because they are always two or three steps ahead of me. I wanted to enlist you to counter that person."

"Then why all the mystery? It is surely no secret that the Bank has a committee supervising those who pursue forgers on their behalf. Your identity need not be concealed."

"The Bank hired me," Mr. Rutledge said, "because I have previous experience, in a somewhat different capacity, exposing criminal organizations. I do not, however, have any experience in banking, and for me to be publicly associated with the Bank would raise questions I cannot afford to answer. As I said, I wish you had not discovered me. Though I believe I know you well enough to trust you will tell no one of our encounter."

I know you. He had said that before, when they had first met. All their interactions, every one of their conversations, presented themselves to Sophia for reevaluation, and she wanted to weep. "You used me," she whispered.

"What was that, Mrs. Westlake?"

"You used me!" she shouted. "You—all those conversations where we spoke of money and forgery and the consequences—you gave me information knowing I would Dream about it and would have to act on it! I told you I would not work for you, and you found a way to trick me into doing so!"

Mr. Rutledge turned to look at her. "I gave you that information because it was obvious it mattered to you," he said. "Sir Arthur Rowley sends copies of all reports relating to my task on to me, and that includes your Dreams. I was certainly not going to throw that away simply because you refused my offer."

"And am I to believe you were simply a disinterested party, altruistically helping poor deluded Mrs. Westlake with whatever mad obsession has her in its clutches?" Sophia said. "I am certain that makes a comforting lie you can tell yourself when your conscience bothers you, not that I believe you have one."

"That is *not* what I think of you," Mr. Rutledge said, swiftly crossing the room to take her arm again, roughly. "I have the greatest respect for your abilities. I—" He looked down at where he held her and released her arm. "I knew, if this last Dream of yours seemed false, something was wrong. The counterfeiters made it seem this was a lodging house, didn't they? They wanted to steer you wrong, or make you seem unreliable, or both. They failed to do so.

"Mrs. Westlake, don't you see what we could accomplish if we work together? I have no idea why you chose to pursue these counterfeiters, but I can give you every resource at my command to continue that pursuit. And it would give me great pleasure to share my work with you. Please reconsider."

It was hard to see his expression in the moonlight, but he sounded sincere. She had thought him genuinely sincere, all those times he had sought her out. What was the truth, now? She recalled what she had considered in the carriage, how she had thought so fondly of him, and humiliation surged through her. How could he possibly care anything for her, if he could trick her so?

"You took advantage of me," she said, barely keeping a quaver out of her voice, "and used my Dreams for your own purposes. You befriended me so you could more easily give me information that would create more of those Dreams you needed so much."

Mr. Rutledge took her arm again, this time gently. "No," he said, "I assure you, my friendship for you is genuine. And I..."

He took a step closer, apparently searching for more words. She wrenched away from him. "Save your assurances," she said bitterly. "You cannot possibly expect me to believe you now."

"Would it have made a difference had I told you from the beginning who my employer was?"

"I would..." She looked up at him, at the shadowed pools his eyes were in the dimness, and felt a great weariness descend upon her. "No," she said. "It would have been more honorable, but I still would have refused your offer. As I refuse it again now."

"Why? Tell me the truth, Mrs. Westlake. Why are you pursuing these counterfeiters? Why not work with me to do so?"

Half an hour earlier, ten minutes earlier, she would have told him the truth about Lord Endicott. Now she could not bear the thought of him looking at her again with disdain or pity. "You did not trust me," she said. "And I cannot trust you."

She turned away from him and walked down the stairs, their creaks now sounding like the wails of the damned, high and long. He didn't follow her.

Exiting through the window, trying to find her footing on that unstable pile of brick and board she had created, struck her as ludicrous. She left by the front door and went down the street toward where Peter waited with the carriage, not caring that she was walking alone. The men she passed either could sense her pain and humiliation or could not be bothered to molest her, because no one tried to stop her. She only remembered about halfway to the carriage that she had left the lantern behind in the "lodging house." Mr. Rutledge could have it for all she cared.

Peter was still sitting on the driver's seat, huddled into his coat and scarf as if he were trying to hibernate. "Take me home, please," she said, remembering the "please" almost as an afterthought. She had good manners. She could be polite. She would never use her friendship with someone to gain the use of that person's talent.

The ill feeling had turned into a rocky lump in her stomach. She swiped at her eyes, inwardly cursing how her tears spotted the silk. She had thought him her friend, and he had turned that friendship against her. No, he was not a friend, but someone much dearer to her than that. *Forget about love,* she told herself, *you do not love him,* but she knew she was lying. In love with a man who believed her obsessive and unstable; how much greater a fool could she be?

She leaned her head against the yielding fabric of the carriage top and closed her eyes. She had no idea what time it was. The way this evening was going, it was possible she would return home to find Lewis and Cecy already there, Cecy worried or angry or disappointed at her absence, and she would have to explain where she'd gone, and then Cecy really would be furious. Yes, that would be the perfect ending to this day.

The house was still and dark when she returned, and when she reached her bedchamber, Cecy was not waiting within, demanding an explanation for Sophia's absence. Relief made her weary, and she undressed in the darkness, feeling too tired to light the lamp.

Safely in her bed, she stared up at the distant ceiling and pondered what she had learned. Lord Endicott's Seer had created a false Dream for her; that should be impossible. And yet... the mystery man, the black-haired man who was almost certainly one of Lord Endicott's associates, and an important one, he had not been false; she had been seeking him out since his existence was first hinted at in Dream. So at least the Seer could not generate entire Dreams; she could only manipulate the circumstances of true ones to trick Sophia. And that would not happen again.

Because she can make my Dreams evaporate before I See them, she thought, and rolled over to put the pillow over her head again. This Seer, whoever she was, had a tremendous advantage over Sophia, and now that she was alone and heartsick and exhausted in her bed, Sophia had difficulty not falling into despair. *In the morning,* she told herself, and forced herself to fall asleep.

⊗⊗⊗

"You were much missed at the dinner party last night," Cecy said. "The Peabodys—" She stopped abruptly and took an overly-large bite of egg.

"Yes?" Sophia said, though in truth she did not care about the

Peabodys, who were shallow and not very bright and no doubt only missed Sophia because of the social cachet she would have brought to their gathering. She took a bite of her own egg, which had grown cold, and willed her incipient headache to vanish.

"It was nothing," Cecy said.

Sophia laid down her spoon and stared Cecy down. "It did not sound like nothing."

Cecy shrugged. "They made such fools of themselves, asking after your health every other minute, and Mrs. Peabody talking of 'dear Sophia' as if you were bosom friends. I found it amusing, but you seem not to be in the mood for humorous stories."

"Very humorous indeed. How glad I am I did not attend. Though, naturally, if I had been there, Mrs. Peabody would have insinuated herself into every conversation I attempted to have, laughing that horrible whining laugh like having icicles driven into one's skull. I wonder that we put up with them at all."

"They are foolish, but not evil, Sophy," Cecy said, "and I believe they are more to be pitied than hated."

Sophia scowled. "You are far too sweet, Cecy."

"And you are far too out of sorts this morning. Did you not sleep well?" Cecy paused with her fork halfway to her mouth, then laid it down, precisely bisecting her plate. "You did not spend the night in Dream, did you?"

"I did not, and you may stop looking at me that way." Sophia retrieved her spoon and took another bite of lukewarm egg.

"I fail to see how you can know how I am looking at you, since you refuse to meet my eyes. Sophy, you *promised*."

"I had but one Dream last night," Sophia lied, "and then I slept poorly, and now my head aches, and I wish you would leave off accusing me of things I promised you I would not do!"

Cecy was silent. Sophia risked a glance at her and saw her lips were set and white with anger. "Do not lash out at me simply because I am concerned for you," she said. "You are not being honest with me. Sophia, seeing Lord Endicott punished is not worth it if you must destroy yourself to accomplish it!"

"I am not destroying myself. I am being careful. He is simply a difficult quarry to run to ground, that is all."

"You have a history of not knowing when you are close to destruction. You make promises, and you intend to keep them, I know you do, but your passion drives you beyond what you can bear. Sophy, perhaps this quest of yours is a bad idea."

"How, bad, when it will bring an evil man to justice? Can you truly say that outcome is a bad idea?"

Cecy leaned forward as if she wished to take Sophia by the shoulders and shake her. "If it ruins your health, how is it worth that price? And is it not a little prideful to insist you are the only one who can reveal Lord Endicott's crimes? Someone will find him out. It need not be you."

"Cecy—" Sophia felt as if her friend had struck her. "I, prideful?"

"You have a powerful talent. It makes sense you would take pride in it. But you are not omnipotent, Sophy. Let this go. Please. Even if only for a few days, perhaps a week."

Sophia shoved her chair back and stood, feeling her hands shake. "I thought you understood," she said. "The world believes the façade he displays. No one even thinks to look for evildoing beneath that beautiful face. If not I... there is no one else, Cecy! How can you not see this?"

Cecy regarded her calmly, the clenched muscles of her jaw the only sign that this was not a normal conversation. "I see my dearest friend in danger of tearing herself apart," she said. "How can *you* not see I cannot bear to watch that happen?"

Sophia turned and strode out of the breakfast room, pushing the door open with so much force that it struck the wall and rebounded in her face. She stormed up the stairs and to her room, where she again flung the door open with a satisfying thump. She paced, trying to control her anger. Cecy understood *nothing*. She was in no danger from Dream; she had pushed herself a little too far last night, but that was in pursuit of important knowledge, and it would not happen again. She would find a way to counter that Seer, and then she would find the black-haired man, and he would lead her to Endicott, and she would have vengeance.

She eyed her bed, but her head still pounded, and it was unlikely she would be able to enter Dream at all, let alone find a productive one. She did not want to face Cecy right now; she did not want to go riding, or to the shops, or to visit people. Her head hurt enough that reading or sewing seemed like too much work. And—she groaned—the Duchess of Lenshire was expecting a Vision tonight, and if Sophia sent her regrets, the woman might very well come to Cecy's house and demand the reason for it. She sat on the edge of her bed and massaged her temples. Why could not the world simply run the way she wanted for once?

Someone knocked on her door. Beeton entered, and said, "Lady Daphne is here; shall I have Simon show her to the drawing room, or are you indisposed, ma'am?"

Sophia began to shake her head, then changed her mind. "Tell her I will join her directly," she said, then squeezed her eyes shut and willed her headache away. Daphne's chatter might make it worse, but she could not bear being alone with her thoughts for one more instant.

"Oh, Sophia, you look unwell—you should have said something, I could return another time," Daphne said, rising from the sofa when Sophia entered the drawing room. Her cheeks were pink from the cold, and her blond hair was, as usual, in some disarray.

Sophia said, "Did you Bound here, or ride?"

"Oh, I took the carriage, I still cannot Bound to a room as crowded —though it's not the kind of crowded you probably imagine, it's different for Extraordinary Bounders, it's just that its essence is complicated, but in any case I would not Bound into the hallway downstairs, which—yes, I could Bound there, but it's so impolite, bursting into someone's home without an invitation—"

"Sit down, Daphne, and we will have tea," Sophia said. The fire was a little low, so she poked at it and stretched out her hand as if to caress the flames that leaped up. Daphne sat down in a chair near the fireplace and warmed her own hands.

"I came to invite you to our Christmas dinner, as you are family— the house is rather full now of relatives of all sorts," Daphne said. "Papa always likes to have the table crowded round with people, so there are relations we only see once a year—it's exciting, actually, except for Uncle Ernest, who likes to pinch my bottom—I can Skip away from him though, so it's not as if I really mind, except he—really, how dare he take such liberties! But I told Mama you would probably want to dine with the Barhams, so you needn't feel obligated."

"I thank you for the invitation, but yes, I intend to dine here," Sophia said, feeling a spark of anger at Cecy that for the briefest moment made her consider Daphne's invitation seriously. "Please do thank Lady Claresby for me."

"I will," Daphne said, turning away from the fireplace as a maid came in with the tea tray. "Oh, I do love a cup of tea on a snowy day like this! Though I hear it will not last—not that it matters to me in my work, but I am sure all those poor horses pulling hackneys would prefer not to drive through the snow. Sophia, are you certain you're well? Because you—or is it rude to say you look as if you haven't slept in days? That's how you look, anyway."

"I am quite well, Daphne," Sophia said irritably. This was a bad idea. Daphne was so unrelentingly cheerful, it made Sophia wish her anywhere but the Barhams' drawing room. "I wish people would stop commenting on my appearance."

"Who—has Mrs. Barham said something, too? I'm sure she's only concerned for you. Have you been Dreaming much lately? That would explain it, you don't get any rest in Dream, at least that's what Viola says—"

"I have *not* been Dreaming too much, and will you leave off chattering at me!" Sophia said.

Daphne set her teacup down and regarded Sophia closely. "Yes, you have," she said, sounding distant, as if her thoughts were coming to her from a great distance and she had to work at reaching them. "You have been Dreaming several times a night. It's interfering with your sleep, I can tell. You have this tense look to your eyes, and you keep tapping your fingers on the arm of the sofa as if you're only waiting for me to leave so you can get back to something more interesting. But what—" She leaned forward. "You are pursuing Lord Endicott, aren't you? You want to bring him to justice!"

"And if I do? I don't see that it is anyone's business but mine." Her headache was increasing. Was it so obvious? Or was it only that Daphne was far too insightful for Sophia's comfort?

"It matters to everyone who cares about you. Sophia, aren't you worried you're pushing yourself too hard?"

Sophia flung her teacup at the fireplace, making Daphne jump as it shattered and sprayed its fragments in all directions. "No, I am not," she said, grinding out each word, "and I believe I know better than *you* how much Dreaming is too much. I do not recall inviting you to comment on my appearance or my actions, but then what else could I expect of a scatterbrained *child* like you?"

Daphne stared at her, her eyes wide and her mouth slightly open in astonishment. Then she vanished with a faint *pop*. Sophia realized she was on her feet, her breath coming fast and hard as if she'd been running. She held the saucer to her shattered teacup in her left hand and lifted it to examine it, feeling as if she'd never seen anything like it before. Then she threw it, hard, after the teacup, and was satisfied by the chiming sound it made as it smashed against the back of the fireplace.

She picked up Daphne's abandoned cup, thought about throwing it too, but settled for pouring the remaining liquid over the flames and listening to them hiss like an injured animal. She felt like one herself, struggling and suffering in the course of vindicating herself, with no support from the people who supposedly cared about her. Everyone was obsessed with the amount of Dreaming she was doing, when *she* was the Extraordinary Seer and knew better than they did what her capabilities and limits were. And she had not even begun to reach those limits.

She left the drawing room and went back to her bedchamber. Her headache had diminished somewhat; shouting at Daphne had helped relax her. Perhaps she had been a little harsh, but if Sophia did not challenge Daphne on her occasionally dangerous Bounding experiments, Daphne had no right to criticize Sophia's use of her own talent.

She lay down fully clothed on her bed and settled in to meditate. Her enemy seemed focused on destroying the Dreams Sophia had of Lord Endicott's criminal activities, so Sophia would turn her attention to the black-haired man. Dreaming of him would lead her to her quarry from a different direction, and then it would not matter what the enemy Seer tried. She would not let that unknown woman defeat her.

CHAPTER 14
IN WHICH SOPHIA REACHES HER LOWEST POINT

"You look lovely tonight," Sophia said to Cecy, who sat opposite her in the carriage, her red pelisse trimmed with ermine pulled close around her. Cecy glanced at her, then went back to looking out the window. Given Cecy's naturally cheery temperament, it was the equivalent of punching Sophia in the face.

If she will not accept my offering of peace, so be it, Sophia thought, sitting back and looking out the other window. Her head would not stop aching, her fingers were frozen inside her gloves, her left shoe pinched her toes, and she was certain her new gown, with the demi-train and the puffed sleeves, made her look awkward. Not that anyone would care, once she produced the Duchess's Vision.

A pity she was forced to attend this dinner party with Cecy, or she would deliver her Vision and then return home immediately. She could not even remember what the Duchess wanted her to See, nor why she had agreed to it, but it had no doubt been because the Duchess was a relentless woman who never failed to gain whatever she wanted. That included the Duke, who had been a confirmed bachelor before Clarissa Taylor, as she had been, set her sights on him and his title.

The Duchess had simply worn Sophia down until it was easier to give in than to endure her teasing any longer. She was like a terrier, yapping away until she got what she wanted or was hauled away by force. Since no one dared lay hands on the Duchess... Sophia tried to remember what she had promised, but came up with nothing. If her head would only stop throbbing for five minutes!

The carriage pulled up in front of the Duke's townhome, and Peter assisted Cecy and Sophia out. He refused to meet Sophia's eye, which satisfied her; the fewer reminders she had of the previous evening's debacle, the better. It had been—

Sophia nearly stopped in the middle of the pavement. *No.* Mr. Rutledge was to be in attendance tonight. Of all the people in the world she least wanted to see! Her headache intensified until she imagined its throbbing was visible. She took a deep breath and calmed herself. He would not be so crass as to approach her, or attempt to speak to her, as if nothing had changed between them. The Duke's fondness for entertaining guaranteed the party would be large, and no one would think it strange that Mrs. Westlake and Mr. Rutledge, who were such good friends, found no opportunities to speak to one another all evening.

Cecy did not wait for Sophia, but climbed rapidly up the steps, where she was announced by the footman. Sophia walked more slowly, wishing with all her heart that she could be elsewhere, then put on a smile she thought looked genuine and passed through the tall, white entryway. It was larger than the Barhams' drawing room, with grey-streaked marble underfoot, a high white ceiling above, and white walls unadorned save by sparkling lights. It gave Sophia the impression that she had entered some fairy prince's icy palace. Even the railing of the curved stair that circled the room and the ironwork of the chandelier had been painted white, as if someone had made an effort to eradicate every trace of color that might ruin the palace's frozen perfection.

Sophia handed off her pelisse to the footman and quickly made her way into the drawing room, which was not much more inviting than the entryway but at least did not make her feel as if she were about to be bleached to suit the décor. It was well-lit, with pale blue walls that somehow managed not to look frozen, and was empty of furniture except for a pianoforte in one corner and a couple of chairs and a sofa grouped in the middle of the room, all of them unoccupied despite the crowd milling about on the Duchess's extravagant Oriental carpets. Paintings on the walls depicted country scenes, most of them of men riding to the hunt, and to Sophia they looked washed out, dull, with little of the animation one might expect to see in such lively subjects, as if they too were frozen in place.

She and Cecy had been a little late to arrive, due to their mutual unwillingness to seek one another out, and nearly thirty people turned to look at her when she entered the drawing room. It was unnerving, having so much attention focused on her, and she responded the way she always did, which was to half-smile and nod. Richard had always said it made her look mysterious, like a sibyl out of Greek myth. She would rather be thought mysterious than awkward and tense, which was how she actually felt.

The crowd parted for her as she moved forward, which forced her to continue, as she had only stepped into the room because it was expected and now she had no destination in mind. She settled for circling the perimeter of the room, nodding and half-smiling at everyone, exchanging meaningless greetings with people she knew. Mr. Rutledge was either not present, or not visible; *probably not present*, she thought, *because he is so fat he would be obvious*, and then she felt guilty at having had such an ignoble thought. Mocking and exaggerating his physical attributes just because she was angry with him should be beneath her. Her headache had gone from throbbing to a steady pain that felt as if her head were swollen to twice its size.

"Mrs. Westlake. How good to see you," the Duchess said. Sophia made her curtsey. The Duchess was a fair-haired woman of middle age, with protruding front teeth and too-thick eyebrows, and her smile was lopsided, giving others the impression that she was smirking at them. Tonight she was gowned spectacularly in coquelicot satin with strings of rubies around her neck and in her hair; it was far too ornate, far too gaudy, for—actually, Sophia could not imagine an occasion for which the Duchess's garb would be appropriate, but her Grace had never been one to care about other people's ideas of what was appropriate. "And what an unusual gown. So daring of you."

"Thank you, your Grace," Sophia said, conscious now of how

terrible she must look to elicit such a comment from the Duchess. She would burn the awful gown when she returned home.

"But then I imagine you need not worry about your appearance now that you are—but I forget myself," the Duchess continued, leaving Sophia confused as to her meaning. The Duchess delighted in keeping others off-balance. "I hope you are prepared for my Vision. You will See for me before we go in to dinner, as I believe anticipation is hard on the digestion. Everyone here is naturally agog to see you perform."

Like a trained animal, barking on command, Sophia thought, but said, "That seems wise, your Grace."

"Please enjoy yourself," her Grace said with a little wave of her hand. "I know political conversation is a pleasure of yours. I cannot see the appeal myself, but a good hostess knows to provide for the entertainment of *all* her guests." Her emphasis on "all" made Sophia imagine the Duchess rounding up her politically-minded guests and penning them somewhere away from the fireplace, where their conversation would not disturb more sensible people, and she had to hold back a smile. She would have to tell—

Sophia's good humor disappeared as she realized the person with whom she was accustomed to sharing such ridiculous thoughts had betrayed their friendship, and as she surveyed the room she realized further that, aside from Cecy, she knew no one here well enough to call "friend." The realization sent a spike of pain through her head that made her eyes water.

She continued to wander the room, saying a few words to acquaintances but not letting herself be drawn into conversation. The noise, and the warmth of the room, and the pain in her head left her disoriented, barely able to remember why she was there in that overcrowded room. Her words began to sound meaningless, and it surprised her when she spoke a stream of nonsense syllables and people responded as if they understood her speech. She bounced between knots of guests without knowing how she had passed from one to another, until she fetched up against someone who took hold of her elbow with a large hand and tethered her to the ground.

"You look unwell," Mr. Rutledge said, in a voice lower than usual.

The familiar sound woke Sophia out of whatever fugue state she had been in, and she pulled away from his grasp.

"I am perfectly well, thank you," she said. It came out breathy and weak, and she cleared her throat and continued, more firmly, "Please do not trouble yourself."

"Your eyes are glassy, and you were weaving. I am astonished no one else noticed," Mr. Rutledge said. "I believe you should sit down."

"I did not ask for your opinion," Sophia said, but the idea of sitting down had some appeal. On the other hand, she did not want him to believe she could be guided by his opinion, so she continued to stand, staring him down despite how uncomfortably acute his dark eyes were. How could he show concern for her, as if nothing had passed between them? "I believe I know whether I am unwell or not."

His eyes narrowed. "Very well," he said, and walked away, brushing past her as he went and making her wobble—not enough that he noticed, Sophia reflected thankfully.

As soon as he was well away, she found a chair upholstered with gaudy tapestry work—it still seemed odd that there were only two chairs in the entire room—and fell into it, doing her best to conceal the fact that that was what she was doing. The room wavered, then settled back into place. Perhaps she needed to see Dr. Garland—not, of course, because she was ill, but surely a headache this severe should not last this long?

She put her fingers up to massage her temples again, then dropped her hands to her lap. If Mr. Rutledge were still watching, she did not want to give him the satisfaction of being right about her condition. Which he was not.

"Ah, Mrs. Westlake. Are you ready to begin? A trifle early, but that will give you plenty of time to examine the possibilities of Vision," the Duchess said. She stood next to Sophia's chair and clapped her hands three times, loudly enough to cut across the noise of conversation. "Mrs. Westlake has agreed to have a Vision for me," she called out. "You are all welcome to watch, but do not crowd, and do not speak, as that interferes with her Sight."

This was untrue. Sophia had had Visions in the middle of a battle-field with no difficulties. On the other hand, the lessening noise accompanied a lessening of the pain beating on Sophia's skull, so she welcomed the Duchess's error.

"What object have you for me, your Grace?" she said.

The Duchess sat on the overstuffed chair matching Sophia's, opposite her and near the arm of the unoccupied sofa. "A ring," she said, pulling a man's signet off her thumb.

"And is there something you would like me to See?" Sophia asked. "Something you wish to learn?"

"Whatever you can tell me about its most recent owner," the Duchess said. She handed the ring to Sophia, who laid it in her lap so she could remove the red silk gloves. "Particularly if you can tell me where he is now."

"I will do my best, but you must understand Visions of that nature may take many hours to identify," Sophia said.

The Duchess frowned. "I was led to believe you are the best England has to offer," she said. "Are you telling me this is not true?"

Sophia smiled at her, wishing she could use whatever hammer was pummeling her head to pound some understanding into the Duchess's skull. "Many hours' *is* the best, your Grace," she said. "Anyone but I might take days to discover such knowledge. I simply do not want to give you false hope."

"Very well," the Duchess said. "Begin."

Sophia nodded, closed her eyes against her headache, and picked up the ring.

Whirling images buffeted her, making her sway with their ferocity and speed. It had been several weeks since she had had a Vision, and she was unaccustomed to how strong they were, how many possibilities of past and present and future flowed through them.

Vision was entirely different from Dream. Instead of walking through the images her Seer's brain created, she looked out through a hundred windows on a hundred different times and places. Some of them were static pictures, powerful moments frozen in place by Vision to show how important they were; others flowed as events unfolded, played out to the end, then started over. Some were hazy, as if seen through gauze; those were Visions of possible futures that might be depending on how the present fell out.

With care, a Seer might trace those Visions to the presents on which they depended, and from there discover what actions might guarantee those futures occurring. And in all these shifting images was one window that showed the present as the person most closely connected to the object saw it.

She opened her eyes to look at the crowd surrounding her, most of them strangers; Cecy and Mr. Rutledge were not in sight. She closed her eyes again—Visions did not depend on ordinary sight—and thought, *Echoes. Let us be rid of those.* With an effort of will greater than usual, she whisked away the Visions attached to other signet rings in other places and other times. The spinning whirl of images lessened dramatically, to the point that Sophia could begin to make sense of what remained despite her dizziness.

Unfortunately, this was an old ring that had seen much since its creation, and working out which of the Visions pertained to its most recent owner was difficult and slow. "Many hands have held this ring," she said, thinking to keep her audience, and her overbearing patroness, entertained. "Four hands. A family." She let herself be drawn into one of the moving Visions to examine it the way she did Dream, but the excruciating pain in her head redoubled, and she blinked away tears and could not bear to do it again.

She sorted and discarded Visions, casting irrelevant ones away, deciding to focus on finding the Vision that would show what its owner saw, wherever in the world he might be, which would take less time than describing all of the images related to him; the Duchess would have no idea that Sophia was, in a sense, cheating her. This was much easier, as that Vision would be a moving one, and most of the Visions associated with this ring were static images she could eliminate.

Her quest was going much more rapidly than she had believed it would, given her headache. Perhaps she could give the Duchess what she wanted, then excuse herself. Would Cecy respond if she thought Sophia was ill, or was she still too angry?

The Visions had taken on a reddish tinge, like tiny windows rimmed with ruddy copper, and it hurt to look at them directly. "The owner of this ring has a stable of horses of which he is proud," she said, glancing into one window and then casting it away before it could overwhelm her. "He has... he is a landholder, possibly noble—no, not— I believe he is an Earl—" She was nauseated from the motion of the Visions that simply would not sit still for her. "His property is in Hertfordshire," she added, and the reddish tinge turned ruby, and *then* the Visions went still, and her head stopped pounding, and she closed her eyes in blessed relief at freedom from the pain, and everything was black and perfectly still behind her eyelids.

She became aware, after what seemed no time at all, that she was lying down face-first on something soft but prickly, and the beautiful blackness had given way to a reddish brown, and her head had begun to hurt again. Someone rolled her onto her back and straightened out her legs—she had not realized they were bent awkwardly under her until that moment—and then he lifted her and laid her gently on a cushioned surface. "Back away, and give her air," Mr. Rutledge said. She opened her eyes and blinked up at him. He was looking up and away from her, then Cecy was there, holding her tight and sobbing her name. Sophia reached out with an arm made of stone and laid it on Cecy's shoulder. "Don't cry," she tried to say, but her mouth was too heavy to move.

"Is that how a Vision is supposed to end?" said the Duchess. "I didn't expect that."

"Mrs. Westlake has not been well," Mr. Rutledge said, "and I imagine she simply overexerted herself. I am sure she will oblige you with another Vision some other time."

"Oh, that will not be necessary. I was simply curious. This ring has no special meaning," the Duchess said. "Will she be recovered in time for dinner, do you suppose?"

Cecy sat up abruptly, releasing Sophia with some vehemence, and opened her mouth to say something that, even from her awkward angle, Sophia could tell would be fierce and angry. Mr. Rutledge put his hand on Cecy's shoulder. "I believe Mrs. Westlake will need to return home," he told the Duchess. "Mrs. Barham would like her carriage brought around, if you don't mind."

"It will cause the most awful imbalance at my table," the Duchess said, but turned away to call a footman.

Mr. Rutledge dropped to one knee beside Cecy. "Please allow me to accompany you home, Mrs. Barham," he said quietly. "Mrs. Westlake appears incapable of walking, and I believe you would find it difficult to maneuver her in and out of your carriage."

"What she said—" Cecy began, and Sophia had never heard her so furious.

"Is unimportant," Mr. Rutledge said. "Let us get Mrs. Westlake home so she can recover. Mrs. Westlake, can you hear me?"

With great effort, Sophia nodded, setting her head throbbing again. Why was everything suddenly so difficult? And how dare Mr. Rutledge insinuate himself into Cecy's confidence? They did not need his help. She tried to stand, and found herself utterly incapable of doing so no matter how she strained; the effort left her feeling even more exhausted. They needed his help. She closed her eyes against the tears she refused to shed. How humiliating, to be so completely help-less. To depend on someone she could not bear to see again.

"We are waiting for Mrs. Barham's carriage to take you home," Mr. Rutledge said. "Don't be afraid. You will be well with a little rest."

Sophia closed her eyes again rather than acknowledge him. A little rest. Her humiliation deepened. She had driven herself past breaking, just as Cecy and Daphne had said, had let her need for vengeance over-ride her good sense, and now she had collapsed in front of a room full of people who would no doubt be dining out on this tale for a month. She had been so wrong—she had said such awful things to Daphne!—and it had been for nothing, because exhausting herself had not got her any closer to her goal.

She opened her eyes and stared at the ceiling, refusing to cry. She would not humiliate herself any more than she already had.

CHAPTER 15

IN WHICH DAPHNE HAS A CUNNING PLAN

A small commotion turned out to be the Duchess's footman, come to tell Cecy the carriage was waiting. Sophia once again tried to stand, but none of her muscles responded, and she had to endure being lifted by Mr. Rutledge, as easily as if she had been an infant, and carried through the icy palace of the entryway and into Cecy's barouche. Her cheek pressed against the smooth fabric of his tailcoat, which smelled, unexpectedly, of cinnamon and cloves, as if Mr. Rutledge had come to the Duke's home from some distant, exotic market in Marrakech or Shanghai. It was a pleasant smell, and it made her feel more humiliated that she took enjoyment in any part of this farce.

She hoped to be allowed to lie still on the rear-facing seat, her face hidden in the darkness, but Mr. Rutledge supported her in a half-sitting position, his arm securely around her shoulders to keep her from sliding off the seat and her cloak draped over her body. She closed her eyes again and pretended to be asleep. If only this night-mare were over!

"Thank you so much for your help, Mr. Rutledge," Cecy was saying as the carriage bumped its way toward home. "I am sure Sophia is grateful to have such a friend as you."

"She has a better friend in you, I warrant," he said. "Mrs. Westlake, are you comfortable?"

Sophia kept her eyes closed. She had nothing she wanted to say to him. Not that she could speak.

"I believe she is sleeping," Cecy said. "I wish she had listened to me! I knew she was spending too much time in Dream."

"So she did overexert herself," Mr. Rutledge said. "Is she normally so... determined?"

Cecy laughed. "Such a polite way of saying 'stubborn', sir. She is always... *determined*... when she is pursuing a passion."

"What passion could possibly be worth hurting herself?"

It was fortunate Sophia's muscles were too exhausted to respond, because she would have tensed all over at this question if she could. If Cecy told him she was pursuing Lord Endicott, Mr. Rutledge would believe her still obsessed, and treat her with pity or condescension. She hated herself that his opinion still mattered so much to her.

"She is... searching for someone," Cecy said. Sophia would have relaxed if her body were at all under her control. "Someone difficult to find."

"I see," said Mr. Rutledge. The carriage jolted, nearly knocking Sophia off her seat, and Mr. Rutledge's arm tightened around her, holding her steady. "Then for her sake I hope she finds him soon."

"Because even this will not persuade her to be cautious, you mean? So do I."

Cecy sounded so bitter that Sophia could not keep a few tears from welling up. Her selfishness had hurt more than just herself. It was her responsibility to help Cecy in her times of pain; Cecy should not have to worry about *her*.

She shifted her position and was relieved to find herself capable of moving, though she was beginning to ache as if someone had given her a shovel and ordered her to dig from Cecy's house to Whitehall. Her proximity to Mr. Rutledge was becoming uncomfortable, far too intimate even though he was only touching her to keep her from falling to the floor of the carriage. She moved again, trying to sit, and Mr. Rutledge restrained her with ease.

"I do not believe you can sit unsupported yet," he said.

"Sophy, *please* do not exert yourself," Cecy said. She sounded as if she were crying again, so Sophia gritted her teeth and tried not to think about how awkward and embarrassed she felt. He gave off warmth more steady and consistent than a fire, which chagrined her further that she was so grateful for it. She was cold, and as she registered that feeling, she began to shiver and could not stop herself even when he put his other arm around her and drew her closer to provide more warmth.

It had been years since she had been this close to any man. The smell of cinnamon and cloves was stronger now, and his embrace was gentle but firm, holding her securely so she would not fall. She rested her head on his shoulder and wished with all her heart it meant something more than the simple need to keep her on the seat.

She was having trouble remembering why she was angry with him —oh, yes, he had manipulated her and betrayed their friendship... though that did not explain why he was being so solicitous of her needs now... Could he, too, regret what had passed between them? Could he, too, wish things were otherwise? Her head was beginning to hurt again, and she pushed all of those thoughts aside.

"I have asked Dr. Garland to come in the morning," Cecy was saying, "though it is just a precaution. I know from the past that Sophy simply needs to rest, and to give over Dreaming for a few days."

"I..." Sophia's mouth was too dry to articulate words. "Forgive," she managed.

"Never mind that," Cecy said, and the carriage bounced to a halt.

Sophia watched her friend exit the carriage, then Mr. Rutledge lifted her again and backed down the steps to the pavement without her head so much as grazing the side of the door. He turned, and she slipped. Without thinking of how hard it was to move, she put her arms around his neck to stop herself falling. He paused, just for a moment, before hitching her up to a more secure position. The smell of spices filled her again. "Forgive," she repeated, and withdrew her arms in favor of clasping his coat front.

"I won't drop you," he said. He took her through the front door and up the stairs to Cecy's sitting room, where Cecy was directing one of the footmen to drag the chaise longue around closer to the fire. Mr.

Rutledge set Sophia down on it and stepped back to make way for Cecy, who moved pillows to support her head and feet and spread blankets over her. She was still unaccountably cold, though the fire had been built up until it seemed almost large enough to spill out over the hearth and consume her.

She looked to where Mr. Rutledge stood at the foot of the sofa, his dark eyes fixed on her, his expression unreadable. "Thank you," she said. At that moment she felt no bitterness toward him, nothing but gratitude and regret that they could not return to what they had been before.

He inclined his head to her. "It was my pleasure to be of service to you, Mrs. Westlake," he said, sounding as if she were no more than a stranger he had helped to cross the street.

Regret stabbed at her heart again, and she cast about for something else to say, something that would keep him by her side, but he had turned away and was having a low-voiced conversation with Cecy she could not make out. Then he left the room without looking back.

"Do you suppose you can sleep? Or do you want something hot to drink? You were shivering so badly, there in the carriage," Cecy said, coming to lower herself to the floor near Sophia's head.

More tears began forming. "You...too good," Sophia said. Cecy's face crumpled into tears.

"You scared me!" she exclaimed. "You told me you would not push yourself, and you did—you were so white, and for a few moments you stopped breathing, and then you fell, and I thought you might die in that stupid woman's drawing room with all those horrible people watching and hoping that you *would* die because then they would have something horrible to tell their horrible friends! If Mr. Rutledge—"

She shuddered, and tried to control herself, even as tears continued to spill down her cheeks. "You are fortunate to have had *one* friend among those ghastly people, and I do not know how I would have got you home without him. Sophia, *why* do you do this to yourself? Lord Endicott means *nothing*, do you hear me? I know he hurt you, and I know you want justice, but you will kill yourself over it and nothing will change!"

Sophia reached out from beneath the blankets and groped for

Cecy's hand. Her friend clung to her, crushing her hand, but she welcomed that little pain; it was something real, something more powerful than the aching immobility that gripped her. "Yes," she said. "I... was foolish. Forgive me."

"You know I do," Cecy said, wiping away her tears with her free hand. "Sophy, *please* let this go. I need you. And I don't want to see you suffer."

Sophia nodded. It took less effort this time. "Yes," she repeated. "You're right. I don't need to do this. Forgive me."

Cecy's grip relaxed. "Just... just sleep, please? You will feel better in the morning, and Dr. Garland will make sure of your recovery." She stood, too slowly, and grimaced.

"You are ill," Sophia said.

"I should not have knelt on the floor, that is all," Cecy said, but her eyes said she was lying. "I will sit with you until you fall asleep, and then I will go to my own bed." She smiled. "You see, *one* of us is capable of sensible behavior."

"I wonder about that," Sophia said, returning her smile.

☙❧

"EXTREME PHYSICAL EXHAUSTION," DR. GARLAND SAID, RELEASING Sophia's hand. "Nothing a little rest won't cure, though I've done what I can to accelerate the process. Seers and Shapers are prone to it if they aren't careful. Seers shape Dreams out of the same physical reserves Shapers draw on to alter flesh. Do it too often, and your body runs out of those resources faster than you can replenish them. No more than two Dreams in twenty-four hours, Mrs. Westlake, unless you want to collapse again and give Mrs. Barham cause for alarm."

"I understand, doctor," Sophia said. She pushed herself up on the chaise longue and felt no more than a small ache. "Thank you."

"Well, don't make it necessary again," Dr. Garland said, straightening with a spine-popping yawn. "And I suggest you spend the rest of the day lying down, just as a precaution."

"I will."

Dr. Garland shouldered her satchel and nodded at her, then nearly bumped into Cecy as she exited the room. Cecy apologized to the doctor, then came forward to sit near Sophia. "Are you well?" she asked.

"Very. But I intend to rest here for today, if only to keep you from fretting."

"If my possible fretting keeps you from exerting yourself, then I will gladly hover over you like an anxious hen. Though I doubt any chick in the history of the world was as recalcitrant a patient as you."

Sophia scooted further up to sit against the arm of the chaise longue. "You are not to wait on me, Cecy," she said. "I brought this on myself. I should not be rewarded by being brought food, or tea, or books, or the papers. Beeton will see to my needs."

"Don't be ridiculous. How many times have you waited on me when *my* unwise exertions caused me to collapse?" Cecy drew a chair closer to the sofa. "Besides, it makes me feel virtuous that I have not once said 'I told you so.' "

"I believe you said as much several times last night."

"Only in spirit. Those exact words have never escaped my lips. Now, what would you like? Not food, because breakfast was only an hour ago. A book?"

Happily settled with her book, Sophia assured Cecy that she would call for her if she needed her, but when she opened it, she discovered she could not focus on the words. After reading the same sentence three times, she laid it down on its face in her lap and stretched. She was more at peace than she had been in days. Weeks, even. Deciding not to pursue Lord Endicott further had lifted a weight from her heart she hadn't realized was there. There were so many other things she could do with her talent, though having Visions for the Duchess of Lenshire was not one of them.

Had the woman actually implied that Sophia's collapse had ruined her dinner party? And asked her for a Vision out of a frivolous desire to see Sophia perform? That she had collapsed in the service of someone so arrogant and thoughtless... well, that did not matter now, because she would refuse to acknowledge the Duchess again, and the woman would find that offending an Extraordinary Seer carried with it social consequences that were not inconsiderable. The thought cheered Sophia even more.

The door banged open. "The rumor is you died at the Duke of Lenshire's home last night," Daphne said, "which I knew could not be true, but I thought I should see for myself what really *did* happen. It was all the Dreaming, wasn't it? I like being right, but not under these circumstances."

Sophia sat up straighter, and said, "Daphne, I do beg your pardon—"

"Oh, I didn't take offense, your mind was clearly disturbed, and I knew you did not mean a word of it. I only left so you would not give yourself more reasons to feel guilty later," Daphne said. She pulled a chair around so she could face Sophia directly. "You really are angry at Lord Endicott, aren't you, to push yourself to such extremes. I apologize for not understanding that before."

"I will not pursue him any longer," Sophia said. "Cecy is right—he is not worth my health, or my life. He can do nothing to me save anger me when we meet in public, and I believe I can control myself enough that he will eventually lose interest in that. There are so many other things I can do with my talent."

"But Sophia, you cannot simply give up now!" Daphne exclaimed.

"No, Daphne, it is not worth the risk. Cecy was so distraught—I can't make her endure that again, and I am so bad at knowing my limits. Really, it's better I give up this mad quest."

"I see," Daphne said, leaning back in her chair and extending her legs as if she were wearing her Bounder uniform, with its trousers and sturdy boots, instead of an attractive muslin dress that at the moment was rucked up under her arms. "So you're quite decided on leaving Lord Endicott alone."

"I am. Why? Daphne, you look positively wicked."

Daphne grinned more widely. "Because I can get you into his house."

CHAPTER 16

IN WHICH SOPHIA EMBARKS, AGAIN, ON A LIFE OF CRIME

"Hiis... house?" Sophia said

"His town house! It will be a challenge, but that is exactly the sort of thing I like. And you can take something of his so you can have Visions, and follow where he goes, and see to whom he speaks—you see? It's the perfect plan!"

"Daphne," Sophia said, "it is not a perfect plan, it is insanity. Breaking into someone's home is illegal, and if we are caught... being Extraordinaries would not protect us, never mind the scandal. I appreciate how you wish to help me, but I truly do not want to pursue Lord Endicott any longer."

But it was too late. She could not stop herself thinking of what she might do with some possession of Lord Endicott's, how much that would help—*I promised Cecy! How can I even consider this?* She closed her eyes as if that would ward off temptation. *You did not actually promise her anything,* a tiny, wicked voice told her. *And Vision is different from Dream. The right Vision might actually make your Dreams more effective.* The wicked voice was *very* good at justifications.

"I believe you *do* want to pursue him, and you are simply trying to be virtuous," Daphne said, "but isn't it more virtuous to expose a criminal who might bring down the government?"

"It is not that dire, Daphne."

"I've been reading about it, forgery that is, and it *is* serious, because it undermines our economic foundation, and—you know people have been sentenced to death for forging so much as a one-pound note? That seems very serious to me. You would be serving your country, and so would I, because I won't let you do this alone, you've already shown what poor judgment you can have."

"Daphne—"

It would be easy to find something small, something he would assume he had misplaced. How useful would it be to be able to see through his eyes. And she would be very, very careful not to hurt herself. She could tell the whole truth to Cecy when it was all over, and Cecy would be angry, but she would have to admit Sophia had done something important and valuable. "I do not understand how you can possibly enter his house," she said.

Daphne sat up and clapped her hands in delight. "It is the easiest thing in the world," she said, "though that's an exaggeration, just a little, and I would—it's actually quite complicated, but not hard, if you understand me. The hard part is knowing when he will be gone—why could he not have gone into the country for the hunting, that would— oh, but then he would take his important things with him, so it would do us no good—"

"I can discover where he will be," Sophia said, "and when, though I do not believe I can accomplish that without revealing my interest in him. He will probably assume I am trying to avoid him. I suppose—" She put her hands over her face. "Daphne, this is madness!"

"No, it is sensible, since I don't believe you will be able to stick to this new resolution of yours. At least my plan has the virtue of providing you something concrete to focus your attention on, instead of fumbling around with Dreams."

"I don't fumble!"

"You know what I mean."

"Well, we can do nothing for the next several days. Today I must rest, and tomorrow is Christmas Day, and it may take me some time to learn when Lord Endicott will be away from his house."

"That's all right. I'll call on you every day starting day after tomorrow, and then we will make further plans. Oh, this is so exciting! Is this how it feels to work in the War Office?"

Sophia closed her book and ran her fingers across its buckram cover. It was as if her blood were fizzing in her veins, as if she could leap from the couch and run through the streets of London. "No," she said, "it is so much better."

⁂

LEARNING THE DETAILS OF LORD ENDICOTT'S MOVEMENTS WAS AS simple as asking Cecy and Lewis, before accepting an invitation, whether he would not be there. Cecy gave her the most sympathetic look when she asked the question that Sophia felt horribly guilty at lying to her—but Cecy would be happier not knowing her dearest friend contemplated embarking upon a life of crime. Not that Sophia intended her criminal activities to extend beyond illegally entering Lord Endicott's house once. The idea still excited her, and not just because of the possibility of thwarting him; it disturbed her that stepping outside the law, even to this small degree, could make her feel so exhilarated.

She had prepared herself for a long, patient wait, imagining herself as a lioness waiting, crouched in tall sunburnt grasses, waiting for the zebra to come calling at the waterhole, so she was surprised when, in the drawing room on the third day after Christmas, Cecy said, "You need not fear, dearest, Lord Endicott will not be at Almack's tonight. Lord Chumleigh is hosting a gala, and Lord Endicott is certain to attend." She made a face. "The Viscount and his friends play very high, and I sometimes suppose Lord Chumleigh might as well turn his home into a gambling house, and save himself the trouble of sending out invitations. But I am grateful, this once, that Lord Endicott is so fond of gambling, if it means you do not have to deny yourself the pleasure of going out in public."

"I am so relieved to hear it," Sophia said, rubbing her temple in a way she hoped looked offhand. "It would be so difficult to have to endure his company. I am afraid that makes me a coward."

"No, not at all! You have no way to defend yourself against him—

that means it is simply common sense. And if you feel you would like to leave the city, we could always go back to Reedings for the rest of the winter, or to Bath—"

"I will *not* have him believing I have run away from him! No, I will simply avoid him when I can, and endure him when I cannot." This time she rubbed her temple and gave a little wince of pain.

"Do you have a headache, Sophy?" Cecy asked.

"Just the tiniest twinge," Sophia said. "Nothing of consequence. Would you like me to read while you sew? Or are we expecting company?"

She kept up the pretense of being in pain all morning, though she protested she felt well enough to sit and write letters when Cecy insisted she rest. Having posted a message to Daphne as well as to her parents, she finally gave in to Cecy's demands and went to lie on her bed after a light meal just after noon. With the prospect of Vision within her reach, she felt no temptation to Dream—had, in fact, done no Dreaming since the Duchess's disastrous party. The memory of lying collapsed on the Duchess's Oriental rug made her cheeks burn.

She tried not to consider the aftermath at all. Mr. Rutledge had been so solicitous of her comfort, had tricked her into using her Dreams on his behalf, had rescued her from the Duchess and the prurience of her guests, had pretended to be her friend so he would have an excuse to converse with her... Those things were all so at odds with each other that she could not tell what was true anymore. It didn't matter. If she could avoid Lord Endicott, she could avoid Mr. Rutledge, and not be put in a position where she would have to express her gratitude, for she *was* grateful; she simply could not bear to be indebted to him.

By suppertime, Sophia really did feel ill, having spent the time in her room fretting over the upcoming burglary when she was not trying to bolster her resentment of Mr. Rutledge, which had, to her frustration, begun to fade. She ate, but listlessly, and in the end did not have to complain of a headache, because Cecy said, "You look terrible, Sophy, and I believe you should not come to Almack's tonight. Stay home and try to sleep, please."

"I will," Sophia said, and went back to her room. She waited half an hour before summoning Beeton to help her dress in a dark, plain gown. "I feel well enough to sit and read, but this gown is too wrinkled now," she said. Eventually she was settled in the drawing room with a book she pretended to read. After fifteen minutes, she stole downstairs, retrieved her cloak, and slipped out the front door and down the street.

Daphne was waiting in a gaudy landau around the corner. Its top was down, and a man in a heavy black coat and hat sat on the high seat with his hands on the reins and an air of complete indifference to whatever his passenger might do. Daphne wore her Bounder uniform and a dark cloak much like Sophia's own, her hair was pinned tightly about her head, and she was flexing her fingers in their tawny kid gloves when Sophia approached. "I have been waiting *forever*," she said, "and I'm sure poor Brutus wishes we were moving, he hates standing still in the traces. We had to drive around the street once because people—though there are not many people about at this hour, but this is a rather striking vehicle—I know, but it was the only one Clevis could justify—"

"I apologize for the delay," Sophia said, climbing up awkwardly to sit next to Daphne, "but I suppose it will be better if we do this in darkness, though it will be harder for us to see well."

"I agree. Clevis, please take us to Windermere Street."

Clevis snapped the reins next to the horse's ear, and the landau moved off at a brisk pace. "Clevis is devoted to me," Daphne said, "and he won't tell anyone where we went tonight. Though," her voice dropped to a whisper, "I didn't tell him anything of what we planned to do, as I'm sure he would consider it his duty to tell mama and papa. So he will let us off some short distance from where we want to go, and then return home. I hope we are not pursued, because we would have no transportation, and then we might be caught."

She did not sound upset by this possibility. Sophia's stomach clenched in anticipation. Being caught was unthinkable.

"You are certain you can get us both inside?" she said.

"Very certain! But there is a degree of luck involved. There must be an open window—not open exactly, just not curtained—so I can see the room I will Bound to. And you will have to come with me, because

I won't be able to Bound back for you, not to the outdoors that is. You see, every indoor space has a different essence—that is its shape and what it contains and where everything is, not like the signatures ordinary Bounders use—so if I can see the room, I can memorize its essence and Bound to it. Though it will take a little time, because it is dark—but at any rate this becomes much simpler, and I daresay the simpler we can make it, the better."

"I see." Sophia relaxed a little. Daphne's enthusiasm had worried her with the possibility that her cousin was not taking this seriously. "So you will Bound us inside, and we will locate the right object, and then... how do we escape? Why do we not have Clevis wait for us?"

"Because, as I said, I can't Bound to an outdoor location. It's far too complex, even for me," Daphne said without a trace of modesty. "So we will Bound back to papa's house, and then Clevis will take you home! See how simple it is?"

"I believe there are still a dozen things that might go wrong, starting with being caught by Lord Endicott's servants, but it is a very clever plan, Daphne."

"Of course it is. And as I said, simple is best. The real danger is it might take you a while to find the right object, because the longer we are inside, the more likely it is that someone will find us." Daphne groped around by her feet and came up with a small lantern. "This should provide enough light without giving us away, if the house is dark, which I hope it is. Oh," she said, suddenly crestfallen, "you are right, there are so many things that might go wrong!"

"Yes, but we are prepared," Sophia said, forgetting her objections for the moment. "We will stay close together, and remain hooded, and if a servant sees us, you will Bound us away before he can raise an alarm or recognize us. And... well, that would probably mean the end of this plan, as they will be more alert if they believe someone tried to burgle the house, but we will simply have to find some other way."

"That's very sensible. All right, we are prepared, and everything will go well," Daphne said. "We should be at Windermere Street in a few minutes."

They fell silent, each thinking her private thoughts. Sophia watched the other carriages and wondered what they thought of the brightly painted landau, with its two passengers who had not bothered to raise the sides against the chill in the air. It was warm by comparison to Christmas Day, where frost had rimed every window in the Barhams' house and Sophia had been more than usually grateful for the warmth of the fire. The Christmas service had been lovely, and they had had an excellent dinner, and Sophia was able to put her troubles aside for the space of twelve hours. She felt a little guilty now, guilty at having deceived Cecy, even if it was for her own good. She would be happier not knowing what Sophia was about at that moment.

She realized they had reached their destination just as they passed Lord Endicott's townhouse and Clevis took them down the street and around a corner. "Thank you," Daphne said as he helped them both down. "I will see you at home soon." She grinned. "We might even beat you there!"

"That sounds like a challenge, Lady Daphne," Clevis said with a grin that matched hers, and set the horse to trotting away. Daphne turned to look at Sophia and clasped her hands, which for once were gloved sensibly in white kid; if they were seen, she did not want to be identified by the red gloves.

"Walk slowly, and let us hope anyone who sees us believes you are a very short young man," Sophia said. They linked arms and proceeded around the corner. Lord Endicott's town house was located in the center of a row of red brick buildings with foundations of white stone blocks, accented with more white stone around the windows and at the corners of the row, like the gap teeth of some monster that intended to consume them all. Miniature versions of Greek temple façades complete with tiny pediments surmounted each door, sheltering them from the weather, though the more modern fanlights surmounting each dark oaken door seemed out of place next to them.

Lord Endicott's town house was half again as wide as its neighbors, with two windows on each side of the door at ground level, and a row of five windows indicating the story above. Each window had its curtains drawn except those of the very top level, which were small and square compared to the larger rectangles of the lower floors, and light shone out from two of those smaller windows. There was no way to see inside those rooms, which were probably servants' quarters and occupied, making them unsuitable in any case.

"Keep walking," Daphne whispered, and she moved faster, drawing Sophia with her around the corner. "Did you see it?"

"See what?"

"One of those curtains wasn't fully closed. There is a small—well, smallish—slit between them. I can go up to the window and look inside, but you will need to watch to make sure no one approaches us. Though if they do, I will simply Bound away. But I believe it will not take much time for me to memorize the essence of the room."

"Daphne—"

"Do you have faith in my talent or not?"

Sophia sighed. "I do."

"Then after I memorize the essence, we will walk away around the corner again, and then I will Bound us into the room. You simply have to watch for anyone who might be too interested in what we are doing. Strangers peering into someone's house might draw attention, but I imagine anyone passing at night will not want to become involved in someone else's problem."

"I hope you are right."

They strolled around the corner again. Sophia was now acutely aware of every carriage that passed, and grateful that there seemed to be no pedestrians other than themselves. She kept her gaze forward, thinking if she met the eyes of a driver or his passengers, they would instantly know what she intended, and leap to the ground to apprehend her and Daphne.

As they drew nearer Lord Endicott's townhouse, Daphne's gait slowed until it was barely more than a saunter. "All right," she said, "you start watching the street, and I will—oh, no."

"What?" Sophia said, alarmed and ready to flee.

"It is... rather taller than I am," Daphne said in a remote voice that told Sophia she was thinking up another plan.

"What should we do? If I lift you... that will surely draw attention."

"I can do it, but it will be more obvious. We will simply have to take the chance."

"Daphne, if it is too dangerous, we should simply go home."

"Not dangerous. I'm going to Skip to where I can stand on the sill. You can see how that would look very obvious."

Sophia closed her eyes. Something had gone wrong already. "We are not giving up yet," she said. "Wait for my signal. I will look far down the street and tell you when there will be a long gap between carriages. How long will it take you to memorize its essence?"

"Half a minute. Possibly less."

"Then we will simply have to pray no one comes along for half a minute."

Sophia walked away from the buildings, tugging at her gloves the way she always did when she was nervous. It was not nearly so soothing when the gloves were not her familiar, comfortable red silk ones. A landau with its hood fully raised passed her; the driver and passengers ignored her. She might look like a beggar, although a prosperous one, standing by the side of the road waiting for someone generous to stop and give her a coin or two.

Another landau, and a barouche, then a high-flyer phaeton raced past with its occupants cheering and shouting. That was dangerous, driving like that in the darkness, but then young men always seemed to believe they were immortal. Even Richard had taken unnecessary risks, and in the end they had got him killed. Small wonder she was uninterested in marrying again, if the pool of hypothetical applicants for her hand were all young and foolish.

Lord Chumleigh, for example, Lord Endicott's gambling friend—he seemed to believe he was doing her a favor by bestowing his attentions on her. Mr. Hawley had that tittering laugh that always accompanied some frivolous statement; the Earl of Mulcester cared more for fashion than politics; Mr. Spencer always eyed her as if he were imagining what she looked like without her gown. They were all the sort of men one could imagine racing down Windermere Street at ten-thirty in the evening in a high-flyer phaeton, possibly while drinking. No intelligent woman would consider marrying anyone so foolish. Older, sensible men were by far more attractive— She flushed, remembering Mr. Rutledge's arm around her shoulders, and regretfully dismissed those thoughts.

Two more carriages passed, these at a more sedate speed, and then the road was clear in both directions for as far as Sophia could see. "Now, Daphne!" she said. Her cousin Skipped from the pavement to the window casement and gripped hard with her hands so she wouldn't fall, pressing her knees in their thick woolen trousers hard against the sides of the frame.

Sophia turned her attention back to the road, which was still empty. Her hands were sweating inside the too-thick gloves, her heart was pounding, and every sound was a carriage turning onto Windermere Street from a side road, where she would not see it until it was too late. Nothing moved except a stray cat strolling along on the far side of the street, as unconcerned about their presence as any of the carriages had been.

Movement, to the left. A large carriage turned onto the street and lumbered toward her. Not a landau, but a post-chaise, bigger and heavier and almost certainly full of more people, including the driver and a postilion. Sophia dared not distract Daphne, could not move, could not do anything except watch doom come rumbling toward them. It neared the corner of the row of townhouses, and Sophia finally said, "Daphne!"

"What?" Daphne said from close behind her, and pulled Sophia away down the street, away from the post-chaise and around the corner. "Let's keep walking, shall we, in case they were paying attention and might want to know why we're not still walking along this side-street," she added.

"Did you—"

"Yes. I almost Bounded us in right then, but I thought they might see us go, and even though there must be many Bounders in this city, no sense drawing attention to ourselves, yes?"

Sophia's heart was still pounding far too rapidly, and she breathed in and out, as if preparing for meditation, until it slowed. "Very sensible," she said. "What room are we Bounding to?"

"I believe it's a dining room," Daphne said. "At least, it seemed to— oh, I will show you," and she put her arms around Sophia's waist and lifted her, and—

emptiness, like gauze, floating though there is no air

—and Sophia stumbled as Daphne set her down in darkness, the only light coming from narrow slits that defined a door some distance away. "Wait for your eyes to adjust," Daphne whispered, but Sophia had already closed her eyes tight shut, and when she opened them, faint outlines were visible all around: a long table lined with chairs, some sort of centerpiece rising high above the table, and the suggestion of more furnishings farther away.

"The next room is lit," Daphne said, unnecessarily, "so we will have to move carefully."

"There are two windows in this room," Sophia said, looking around more carefully and seeing the faintest vertical line that must be where the curtains were slightly open, "so the next room is likely the entry, and the lights are burning so Lord Endicott need not stumble about waiting for his footmen to light the room. We need to reach his bedroom; that is where we are most likely to find success."

"Follow me," Daphne said, and went silently to the door. She pushed it open a little, looked out, then turned to Sophia and nodded. Sophia took a deep breath, tugged at her gloves, and followed Daphne out the door.

CHAPTER 17
IN WHICH SOPHIA ADDS EAVESDROPPING TO HER LIST OF CRIMES

They crept out of the dining room and into a warm and inviting space Sophia could not believe had anything to do with hard, cruel Lord Endicott. If it were true that houses reflected the character of their owners, it ought to be angular and cold, lit by iron lanterns and filled with portraits of handsome, nastily-smiling men and women. Instead, a dozen lamps shed a golden light on the warmly polished wooden floor and the staircase that curved along one wall until it reached a landing, where it turned sharply and continued up. Daphne was already halfway to the stairs; Sophia came out of her reverie and followed her.

There were portraits on the walls of the stairwell, but they were of ordinary-looking people, some of them with a Shaper's beauty, but most no doubt possessing talents that did not show themselves on the skin. Their gilt frames reflected the lamplight that continued up the stairs, lighting them far too well for Sophia's comfort. Carpeting made their steps nearly silent, though the *swish* of her skirts sounded too loud and too distinctive to be anything but a woman creeping about where she should not be.

Daphne stopped, and Sophia nearly ran into her; she turned to Sophia with her finger pressed to her lips, and Sophia realized someone was passing down the hall they were about to enter. Daphne's hearing must be incredibly acute, Sophia reflected, but then they were moving on and she had no time to think about anything but moving quietly.

At the first floor landing, a doorway opened on a dark room that bore the suggestion of sofas and low tables, and Sophia concluded it was a drawing room. Another door, this one closed, stood next to it, and a short hallway extended the width of the house to another set of stairs, this one uncarpeted, at the far end, ascending to the top of the house. The hall was lined with doors, four of them, and Daphne turned to Sophia again, this time with her eyes asking the question *where next?* Sophia stepped past her and looked down the hall. Two of the doors had light shining from beneath them. She put her lips to Daphne's ear and said, "Did the person you heard go up the other stairs?"

Daphne considered for a moment, then shook her head. That meant one of those two lit rooms, at least, was occupied. They had no way of knowing which was Lord Endicott's bedchamber... although...

Sophia took in the scene as a whole. There were two doors on either side of the hall. On the side facing Windermere Street, the doors were equally spaced; on the side facing the rear, they were off-center, with much more wall space between the far door and the end of the hallway. Enough space for a bedchamber and a dressing room? She had no doubt a man like Lord Endicott, for whom appearance was paramount, would require plenty of room for his wardrobe. He would likely not want his chambers looking out over Windermere Street, with all its traffic. And the door was unlit. She slipped past Daphne and beckoned her to follow, went to the far left door and opened it.

It was a bedchamber ornate enough that the Prince Regent himself would not complain about sleeping in it. A brocade canopy, its color indistinct in the dimness, draped the upper half of the bed, which was neatly made up with a heavy counterpane, and the walnut footboard looked as if it had been set to guard the sleep of whoever lay down on it.

Sophia flinched as Daphne lit the lantern, shielding it with her body so it would not shed any light beneath the door. Its light revealed the canopy to be dark gold, worked with brighter gold threads that sparkled as if they were actual metal. The rich green travertine of the fireplace was flanked by columns that were the smaller twins of the ones warding the portal of the house's doorway, and the fire was banked but not extinguished.

Sophia put out a hand to balance herself on a round table, also walnut, that stood at the foot of the bed. Between the two windows lay a dressing table with an oval mirror that was cluttered with knick-knacks, most of which seemed out of character for Lord Endicott: thimbles and pincushions, tiny snuffboxes with enameled lids (Lord Endicott did not, to her knowledge, use the stuff), tangled bits of ribbon.

"Look in here," Daphne said, holding open a narrow door. By the light of Daphne's lantern, Sophia saw Lord Endicott's dressing room was extremely untidy. What his valet was thinking, Sophia couldn't begin to imagine, but the man was definitely failing in his responsibilities if he allowed his master's possessions to remain so disordered.

Sophia went inside and pulled off her right glove, running her hand over Lord Endicott's clothes and cravats and shoes. She did not expect to find any resonance with such everyday things, but it was surprising what people became attached to. Little drawers in an ebony chest with curved legs turned out to hold nothing more exciting than handkerchiefs and a loose collection of buttons, none of which held any significance to Lord Endicott.

She returned to the room to find Daphne picking through the detritus on the dressing table. "What about this?" she whispered, and held up a man's ring. Sophia took it and was immediately struck by dozens of whirling images, and had to set it down quickly.

"It would work," she whispered, "but I believe he would notice its absence."

Daphne nodded and continued her search. Sophia joined her. She thought for a moment that they should not disturb anything, but realized in the next moment it was unlikely, with how untidy it was, that Lord Endicott or his valet would notice anything was out of order, and if they did, they would probably blame it on one another.

Object after object yielded nothing, and soon Sophia was handling things automatically, not paying much attention to what she touched. It had been a nice idea, but impractical, though perhaps... *could* she get away with taking the ring? No, Lord Endicott would blame a servant. She could not bring herself to allow some innocent person to be punished for her actions, however important the ring might be to her cause.

Her hand landed on something hard and cold, and once again Visions sprang up around her, whizzing past so quickly she could barely see the real world. She let it go, waited for the afterimages to subside, then picked it up with her gloved hand. It was a watch fob, a simple bell-shaped fob with a ring at one end to attach it to a watch chain, engraved with a flower of some sort, a lily or a rose. "Wait," she told Daphne, and passed the fob from her left hand to her right, steadying herself against the rush of images. It was such a common item that about half the images turned out to be echoes, but even then it was difficult to begin sorting through the rest, there were so many of them. Unlike the Duchess's ring, only one man had ever held this object; Lord Endicott had no doubt had it commissioned specifically for himself. This was the key to tracking her prey.

"Sophia," Daphne said, going to the door. "I believe someone is coming."

Sophia took the fob with her left hand and turned to say something to Daphne, and saw the doorknob begin to turn. Daphne looked at her in horror. She was too far away. Without another thought Sophia flung herself to the floor and wiggled beneath the bed, and heard the *pop* of Daphne Bounding away. *This is the stupidest place I could hide,* she thought, and then the door opened, the lights came on, and someone rushed into the room and flung open the door to the dressing room.

The man was muttering to himself, low words Sophia could not make out, and then there were thuds, perhaps of shoes landing on hard surfaces, and the deep rustling sound of fabric rubbing across fabric. The bedroom door opened again, and the noises cut off. Then Lord Endicott said, "You will pack your things and leave in the morning, Thomas. And you need not expect a reference."

"My lord, I apologize, I didn't realize you'd be home early," Thomas said. His voice was muffled, as if he were still inside the drawing room. "I was—there were other—your boots—"

"I have been gone for two hours," Lord Endicott said. "I believe it is not unreasonable for me to expect you could black my boots and bring order to my dressing room in that time."

"You know you like them to be perfect," Thomas said. "I was out of the things I use—the secret concoction others would like the receipt for—it took time—"

"Stop whining, Thomas." Lord Endicott sounded bored rather than angry. "Very well. But this is your last chance."

"Thank you, my lord, I promise I won't disappoint you, my lord."

"Take my coat, and no more protestations of fidelity tonight. I'm not in the mood."

"You are home early, if you don't mind my saying, my lord."

"The company was bland and I won too readily. I prefer a challenge. And there's still time for me to attend Almack's, if it's not too much trouble for you."

"No, my lord! I beg your pardon, I have your breeches ready right here, and that new coat—"

"And my shoes? At least you've buffed them up nicely. I would *hate* to have to wait for you to take basic care of my wardrobe."

"Yes, my lord, thank you, my lord."

"Pity they don't serve better refreshments there, but one can always return home for a drink before bed, yes?"

"Yes, my lord."

Silence, broken only by the sound of cloth sliding over limbs. "I hope the women aren't all such frights as the last time I was there," Lord Endicott said. "Miss Ravencroft, possibly, or young Lady Daphne St. Clair. A pity she's fat; she'd be quite pretty if she would reduce."

"I thought my lord fancied Mrs. Westlake, if it's not too bold of me to say."

Lord Endicott chuckled, and Sophia shuddered at the sound. "Ah, yes," he said. "Mrs. Westlake. I do enjoy her company. How unfortunate for me the feeling isn't mutual."

"I don't understand."

"No, you wouldn't, would you? Sufficient to say she wishes me at the devil, when I have never done anything but give her the most devoted attention."

"But the rumor is—I beg your pardon, my lord, but it's common knowledge you intend to marry her."

The chuckle turned into a full-bodied laugh. "Oh, that would be something indeed! My home life would be the envy of all London. No, she'd never have me even if I *did* ask her to marry me, to my great sorrow."

"I see, my lord." Thomas did not sound as if he did see what Lord Endicott was talking about. Sophia understood very well, and wished she had the power to rise up from this narrow, dusty space and shoot Lord Endicott dead where he stood. So *that* was how Lord Endicott's attentions to her were viewed by society! When they had spoken only a handful of times—what had he said about her when she was not present?

All those whispered comments and sidelong looks she always received... of course no one she knew would be so crass as to speak of an undeclared engagement to her directly, so she could not have guessed some of them were speculations about her attachment to Lord Endicott! Sophia had no doubt he himself had spread that rumor to further torture her, expose her to the prying attentions of every gossip in London, link her name to his in a way she could not repudiate except by showing herself to be shrewish and possibly faithless as well, since she would never respond to him with any sign of affection.

"Oh, my lord, I almost forgot," Thomas said, "but Mr. Baines was here today, while you were out."

There was silence for several breaths. "Baines came here?" Lord Endicott said. "What did he want? No, I already know he would not have said anything to you or anyone else in this house. When was this?"

"Nearly two o'clock, my lord. He said, exactly, 'two days, the warehouse.'"

Lord Endicott swore, a blistering word that made Sophia blush even though she had heard it many times from soldiers in the field. "He'll have to be taught a lesson," he said. "I forbade him to come here. Anyone might see him. Did he speak to anyone but you?"

"No, my lord."

"Fortunate for him." Sophia heard the sound of more fabric moving across fabric. "I expect these rooms to be spotless when I return tonight," he said, "or you'll face worse than dismissal."

"Yes, my lord, I know, my lord."

"Good." Feet encased in very fine shoes passed across Sophia's narrow field of vision. She heard nothing for a moment, then Thomas let loose a torrent of profanity even more blistering than Lord Endicott's. "Damn him and his damned wardrobe," he said finally, and Sophia heard him moving around, saw his feet in much less fine shoes cross and re-cross the bedroom.

She drew in too deep a breath, her nose tickled, and she pinched it tight to avoid sneezing. Where was Daphne? She must know Sophia had not been caught, or there would be a great uproar, but other than that Sophia could not guess what Daphne was thinking. Sophia's back and neck ached from the awkward way in which she was pressed into the floor by the sag of the mattress above, and her eyes were watering from the dust. She prayed Thomas would continue to be slovenly and not choose to impress his master by sweeping under the bed.

The sounds of cleaning continued until Sophia thought she might go mad with frustration and impatience. Surely even the vain Lord Endicott could not have *that* many clothes? But eventually she heard the ticking and clinking of small things being moved, the louder *ting* of porcelain ringing on porcelain, and finally, *finally* Thomas turned out the light and shut the door behind him.

Sophia counted to one thousand before emerging from her hiding place. She had been luckier than she deserved, which meant, she hoped, that God looked with favor on her little crime. Even so, getting out of this house was now urgent. She brushed at the front of her dress, which was now grey and fluffy with dust, to no effect, pulled on her right glove, and wrapped her cloak close around her before going to the door and opening it a crack.

The hall was empty and dark. Golden light rose from the entryway via the stairwell, and a paler glow came from the stairs near her that led to the servants' floor, but the two doors that had previously had light spilling from beneath them were as dark as the others. Sophia crept along the hall to the stairs and made her slow, patient way down their elegant curve. She heard nothing, saw no one. The silence was so perfect that when she reached the ground floor and began crossing the polished wood of the entryway, the noise her shoes made seemed as loud as if she were some giant out of myth, trying and failing to draw no attention to herself.

By the time she reached the dining room door, she was breathing as heavily as if she'd been running, and she almost flung herself inside, then leaned against the door, trying to stay calm. "Oh, I am so glad!" Daphne whispered, and Sophia had to choke back a shriek as the girl detached herself from a shadow on the far side of the room. "You were gone so long, but I couldn't think what else to do but wait, and I was so—I thought, either you would return here, or I would hear the entire house up in arms because you had been caught! Was it Lord Endicott?"

"Yes," Sophia said, "and I will tell you the entire story tomorrow, but I believe I should return home as quickly as possible, because it is getting late and I have no idea whether Cecy will believe she should return early to tend to me."

She did not feel entirely safe until, having Bounded to Daphne's home and then been conveyed back to the Barhams' by the taciturn Clevis, she was in her own bedchamber, undressing with Beeton's assistance, having reassured herself Cecy was still not home. Beeton eyed her filthy gown with suspicion, but Sophia gave her a cool stare that dared her to make an issue of it, and Beeton just shook her head in resignation and took the gown away for cleaning.

Sophia settled into her bed, having traded her kid gloves for the red silk ones, and turned the watch fob so light gathered along the curve of its side and turned it bright silver. She would not attempt Visions tonight; her nerves were too frayed for her to focus properly. But tomorrow... tomorrow she would attempt a new approach toward proving Lord Endicott's crimes.

He had sounded so smug, so sure of himself, that her desire to see him fall had intensified one hundredfold. Except that he had not sounded so smug when Thomas had mentioned that man, Baines. A man whom Lord Endicott had forbidden to come to his house. It did not seem too much of a stretch to guess Baines had something to do with the counterfeiting operation. A warehouse, two nights from now...

Sophia again turned the watch fob in her hands, then put it away in a drawer and removed her gloves. If she could locate the Vision that let her see through Lord Endicott's eyes before then, she would be able to watch whatever happened at that warehouse, and that might give her more information on which to base her Dreams. But first, she had to track and eliminate her new prey. She would need to find that enemy Seer.

CHAPTER 18

IN WHICH SOPHIA FINALLY ASKS
FOR HELP

S ophia sat on the uncomfortable chair in the drawing room, half-listening to Cecy tell her about something one of her many friends had said. She had no chair in her bedchamber, and would have endured even this lumpy one with its rough upholstery if only she could transport it to her room without anyone realizing. But there were no chairs in the entire house whose absence Cecy would not notice, and she would want to know why Sophia wanted one in her room, and Sophia could not tell her she wanted it for Visions without having to lie about which Visions she was trying to See.

She had never been good at inducing Visions while reclining, as their motion nauseated her, and although she had tried it with Lord Endicott's fob anyway the day before, she had succeeded only in glimpsing a few meaningless images from his past and one clear Vision of the black-haired man she had seen many times in Dream. Whoever he was, he had the natural gift, possessed by a random few, for holding mutually contradictory intentions in his head at once, which defeated Dream for a time, but she was certain she would eventually be able to predict his actions, if that became necessary.

It was a relief knowing Lord Endicott had in fact impressed something pertinent of himself on the lump of silver, but it brought her no nearer knowing which Vision would let her see through his eyes, and Sophia was beginning to despair of discovering that before his appointment at the warehouse sometime today. Tonight. She hoped.

"Sophy, I beg your pardon, but am I boring you?" Cecy said. "Whatever are you thinking about?"

"I was listening," Sophia said. Cecy gave her a skeptical look, and Sophia laughed. "All right, so I was not *entirely* listening, and I beg your pardon. I was thinking of the Gates's gala on Twelfth Night and wondering what new spectacle Eleanora Gates has in mind."

"I hope it is not the same as last year, when we all drew names out of a hat and had to pretend to be that person for the evening," Cecy said. "I realize it is traditional, but Eleanora should have given more thought to which names she put into the hat, or at least had separate hats for men and women. I had to be Iago and was terrible at it."

"I can only imagine," Sophia said. "I think it would be quite entertaining, all those men simpering around as if that were the only distinguishing characteristic any woman has."

"Well, I am sure she's learned from the experience. Perhaps it will only be charades. She is very good at charades—planning them, I mean."

"She always invites good company. I am looking forward to it, after so many years away."

"I am so glad to hear that, dearest." Cecy leaned forward and clasped Sophia's hand briefly. "You have seemed so melancholy since the Duchess of Lenshire's fiasco. I wish you would not hide yourself away so. I've told you, no one who matters is talking of your collapse. Your friends are all very concerned, in fact."

Sophia's awareness of the watch fob hidden in her drawer burned. "I am simply not feeling entirely well yet," she lied. "And the chance of meeting Lord Endicott—you said he appeared at Almack's that night when he was not expected, and I do not feel ready to encounter him again."

"Yes, and I hate to say it, but I consider it fortunate your headache kept you home that night. Even so, you cannot avoid him forever, and the sooner you face him and show yourself indifferent to him, the sooner he will leave off tormenting you."

"You are probably right. But... not tonight."

"All right," Cecy said with a sort of amused exasperation, "not tonight, but soon. Really, aren't you bored with staying home all the time? Even you must grow weary of novels, and newspapers can only occupy you for so long."

"I do Dream occasionally," Sophia said, "mostly on your condition, though I am afraid I do not know enough about the human body to make sense of what I See."

"You are not to exhaust yourself on my behalf, much as I love you for trying to learn how to cure me."

"I am being very careful. No more than one Dream in a night." She still had not Dreamed since the night at the Duchess's house, and guilt at lying to Cecy stabbed at her again, though doing so was unavoidable. Cecy should not have to worry about her when her own condition was still so painful, much as she might claim otherwise. She would only upset herself to know Sophia was still pursuing Lord Endicott, and Sophia wanted nothing more than to protect her.

"Good," said Cecy, and rose from her chair. "I am going to see Miss Travers, and you need not accompany me, I feel perfectly well and I know you dislike her."

"You make me feel guilty," Sophia said. "There is nothing more wrong with her than her penchant for laughing at her own jokes, which are rarely funny, and I feel ridiculous laughing with her. You are so much nicer a person than I."

"I am not so nice a person as that. She is always helping the poor and it makes me feel virtuous to accompany her on her expeditions. So my motives are more selfish than not."

"I am sure the poor appreciate your generosity, whatever the motives. That is in scripture somewhere."

"Well, I intend to be back late this afternoon, and we will dine in, but *tomorrow* you will attend the theater with Lewis and me and we will all have a splendid time, even if it is *Othello*, speaking of playing the part of Iago. It is vaguely unsettling, watching something so serious during a time devoted to revelry, but Lewis is so eager for it I have not the heart to deny him."

"I am looking forward to it as well. Enjoy yourself, dearest, and I will see you later."

Sophia sat looking into the fire for several minutes after Cecy left, then rose to go to her bedchamber. She could sit on the bed, at least, because time was short and she would need to have success not only before Lord Endicott's meeting, but before Cecy returned. But when she was seated on the edge of her bed, fob in hand, she rolled it over and over in her gloved palm until it was warm. This was the only sensible course of action. She might butt heads with that enemy Seer in Dream for days, or weeks, while Lord Endicott pursued his criminal activities, and if she wanted to have any effect at all on his plans, she needed a different approach. That Seer might be able to thwart her Dreams, but could do nothing to interfere with her Visions. Cecy would understand, when it was all over. She drew off her right glove and took the watch fob between her fingers.

She once again swept away the echoes that crowded her Visions and the pressure she always experienced in Vision lessened, an unpleasant but not painful sensation, as if a weight were bearing down on her shoulders. Spending a great deal of time in Vision was not as exhausting and not as dangerous as too much Dreaming, and during her service with the War Office she had sometimes spent as many as sixteen hours in Vision without feeling more strain than an ache in her shoulders and lower back. Much longer than that was impossible, as tiredness eventually drove the Visions away, popping them like blue-tinged soap bubbles, so her current activity would not lead to a collapse so long as she did not also Dream excessively. She had no intention of worrying Cecy again.

Though if you collapse here, at least Mr. Rutledge will not be present to humiliate you further, she thought, then banished that memory and sat up straighter on her bed. Mr. Rutledge had not humiliated her; the humiliation was hers alone. She had not seen him since the night of the Duchess's gathering, and could not determine if that pleased or grieved her. And now she was wasting time. She would have to concentrate in order to See clearly. She had no doubt that, given time, she would be able to see the world through Lord Endicott's eyes. Whether that would be in time to achieve her purposes was the real question.

She could, for the moment, ignore the static images that appeared like the most detailed paintings one could imagine, crisp-edged and focused with the background fading to pastel. They might be of interest later, but now she needed a moving Vision. She picked one at random and let it draw her in the way Dream did, though this was more like flying than the gentle flowing pull of Dream. Dancing—a ballroom—a woman—nothing of importance there. She released the Vision and went back to scanning the images. Here, a moonlit night— there, horses running free—here, a boxing match, and a great deal of blood—she let that one go with a shiver of distaste. She reached for a different, less disturbing Vision, then stopped herself. She might be at this for hours, and be no closer to her goal. She would need to try a different strategy.

She closed her eyes to shut out any possible distractions and relaxed, breathing from her abdomen until her shoulders drooped and she felt as if she might slide off the bed. Her left hand, resting on the smooth counterpane, began tingling as if she had been sitting on it for an hour; she brought it up, slowly, to close over her right hand, which still gripped the fob hard enough it would leave dents in her palm. She had done this once or twice before, applying Dream meditation to her Visions, with no success, but it was worth the attempt, if it meant the possibility of bringing her more quickly to her goal.

Breathing slowly, she watched the Visions begin spinning with greater force and speed than before, dizzying her until she thought she might fall over. She let them spin, let her eyes of Vision go out of focus, and—it was as if she had an invisible hand that reached out and plucked a Vision from the whirlwind. The Vision pulled her into it so rapidly it dizzied her further, taking her a moment to make sense of what it showed.

It was not Lord Endicott's current perspective. She slouched a little more in disappointment and tried to regain her balance by looking at the Vision more closely. It was an image of a short, slight, grey-haired man sitting at a desk, writing something—and then the Vision began again, little man at a desk, hand on paper, pen with ink glimmering at the tip of the nib, dipping down to scrawl words across the paper she could not make out. Sophia blinked the Vision away and swallowed against the nausea the swiftly flowing images had induced. It was not the Vision she wanted, but suppose her meditation had brought her something else of importance?

She went looking for the little grey man in other Visions, and found him. Lord Endicott saw him frequently, though the Visions, both moving and static, in which he appeared were all extremely boring: talking, writing, sketching, more writing. All passive things; no Visions of him with any of the accoutrements of the forgery business. And yet she had a feeling his dealings with Lord Endicott were shady; the places where they met were rundown warehouses or litter-strewn alleys or offices—if one could call them that—in parts of London no respectable gentleman went.

She watched the man fold a sheet of paper and seal the envelope; the address was Lord Endicott's townhouse. Sketches, clandestine meetings in dark alleys, letters to Lord Endicott; this must be the enemy Seer. She had no basis for this belief other than circumstantial evidence and her own instincts, but it felt right, all the way down to her bones.

She dismissed her Visions and checked her pocket watch, the gift of a grateful Swiss banker and one of her most prized possessions. Almost two o'clock, and Cecy would be returning soon. It was a small success, but she still needed to be able to See through Lord Endicott's eyes, and she was fast running out of time.

⚜

SHE HAD TROUBLE CONCENTRATING ON THE CONVERSATION AT dinner that night, and it took her nearly the entire meal to realize Cecy was also unusually quiet. When she brought it up, Cecy said, "I am merely tired, Sophy, nothing dire," and Sophia left it at that. At the end of the nearly silent meal, Lewis went to his study and Sophia and Cecy retired to the drawing room, where Cecy took up her sewing and Sophia settled in with a book.

"Miss Travers asked to be remembered to you, and to thank you for your generous donation to the foundling home," Cecy said.

"Now I feel guilty at disliking her, when she is so kind and unselfish," Sophia said.

"She is tedious. I wish I had not visited her," Cecy said, but her last words came out choked with tears.

Sophia dropped her book and went to put her arms around Cecy. "Oh, my dear, what is it? You are in pain, aren't you? Oh, you should have stayed home, you have exerted—"

"I am not in pain," Cecy said, shaking her head violently from side to side. "It is nothing."

"Cecy, do you imagine me stupid, to believe those words when your tears tell a different story?"

Cecy shook her head again. "No, but I—it is nothing, I can bear it, I do not wish to burden you!"

"You are not a burden, you *know* that! Now, tell me what is wrong."

"I don't," Cecy began, then drew a great, shuddering breath as if it were all that stood between her and death. "We visited the home," she said.

"Yes? Everything is well?"

"It is," Cecy said, nodding, "but I...." She wiped her eyes. "So many children," she said, "so many unwanted babies, and I have nothing, Sophy, I want my own baby and I will never have children, and it is so *unfair*! I wanted—Sophy, I wanted to snatch one of them up and carry it home with me, *tell me why*, Sophy!"

"Cecy," Sophia said, "of course you will have children. Dr. Garland said there was no reason you should not."

"And yet five years of marriage is not enough. Dr. Garland is telling me what I want to hear because she knows the truth will devastate me."

"Dr. Garland never tells anyone a comforting lie, Cecy, you know that." Sophia hugged her more tightly. "She says you worry about it too much, and it keeps you from conceiving. It will come, I promise you. Why didn't you tell me how this was troubling you?"

"Because you were already so burdened with your worries about Lord Endicott, and you already bear me up when I am ill, I did not want to complain." Cecy began to cry again, and Sophia held her close and rocked her like the child Cecy so desperately wanted. This happened so often, Cecy concealing things from Sophia in order to spare her pain—

I am a hypocrite. And I have been treating Cecy like a child.

All her justifications for not telling Cecy the truth seemed shameful now. She remembered how she had told herself she was doing the right thing and cringed inwardly. How could she be in the right if that required her to lie to her dearest friend?

Cecy's weeping had faded to a few shaking sobs now and then, and she wiped away tears and then put her own arms around Sophia. "I should not have kept this from you," she said. "I feel better not to be carrying it alone."

"See, that is the sensible way to look at it," Sophia said, detaching herself from her friend and pushing her a little to make room for her to sit on the couch. "And you will remember I forgave you for doing something so wrong as to try to spare my feelings, yes?"

"That sounds more like a chastisement, Sophy."

"No, I simply have something to tell you that will likely make you angry." Sophia clasped Cecy's hands and said, "I am still pursuing Lord Endicott."

For half a moment, Cecy looked confused. Then anger creased her brow and she tried to pull away from Sophia's grasp. "Sophy, you *promised*! How could you lie to me like that? Let me go!"

"Because I wanted to protect you, and I was going to tell you when it was all over, but we both agreed it was wrong to do something like that and I am very, *very* repentant, and I am telling you now!"

Sophia let go Cecy's hands and Cecy jerked them away, hard. "What were you going to do if you collapsed again and died? Sophia, you cannot do this!"

"I am not Dreaming. I... acquired... something of Lord Endicott's, and I am following Visions looking for something I can use against him. You know that is not dangerous. Cecy, I don't want to hurt myself, but I cannot allow him to go unpunished. I *cannot*. It hurts me to know the world thinks so well of him—did you know he has been spreading the rumor that we are close to an engagement? He continues to use me, and he will not be satisfied until he has destroyed my spirit the way he has my reputation. Please understand, Cecy. *Help* me."

Cecy looked away. "I will not help you kill yourself."

"No, but I believe—Cecy, I should have asked for your help weeks ago. I believe you can keep me from being absorbed in Dream. Is that your only objection, that I will be overwhelmed by Dream?"

"I don't know." Cecy was still looking in the direction of the fire. "How did you get something of Lord Endicott's?"

A lie sprang to Sophia's lips and nearly escaped before she remembered she was done deceiving her best friend. "Daphne and I went to his house... secretly... and we stole it."

"*What?*" Cecy said, turning to face Sophia so rapidly that her hair sagged out of its pins. "Sophia, that is *illegal*! Whatever possessed you —no, of course I know what possessed you. You are desperate." It was her turn to put her hand on Sophia's. "You are that desperate, dearest, and I had no idea. You should have come to me sooner."

"We have both been trying too hard to protect one another. You are not fragile, and I am not weak. Will you help me, Cecy? And let me help you?"

Cecy nodded, and then they were clinging to each other, Sophia shedding a few tears of her own. Then Cecy began laughing, and when Sophia drew back in surprise, she said, "You went to his house and stole it. That was no doubt Lady Daphne's idea. What did you take?"

"A watch fob," Sophia said, and related the whole experience, making Cecy laugh and gasp by turns. "I cannot believe I successfully hid under Lord Endicott's bed," Sophia concluded. "It seems so ridiculous now—well, it seemed ridiculous at the time, too."

"And he has been telling people he is deeply attached to you!" Cecy said. "Making you seem fickle, or a tease, when you treat him with coldness. I *insist* you destroy him, Sophy."

"That is the kind of encouragement I need," Sophia laughed, "but I still do not know how to see through his eyes, and I will not be able to see where he goes tonight."

"True, but even if he does go somewhere significant, he is no doubt accustomed to moving his operations often to avoid your Sight," Cecy said, "and you already know the name and face of one of his important co-conspirators, so that knowledge would not be new even if you could See what he sees. So I believe you should turn your attention elsewhere. I believe you should pursue this enemy Seer."

"I have thought as much myself, but he is already blocking me at every turn, and I cannot See his intentions without them dissolving around me."

"Then Dream of something else. Dream of him. If he is employed by Lord Endicott, it is impossible that forgery is the only thing with which he is involved, yes? And he will not know to block that Sight. Who knows what you might be able to do, with the right Dream?"

"You are positively glowing, Cecy."

"Because this is exciting! Oh, Sophy, you should have told me all of this sooner, because I am now entirely distracted from my own problems." Cecy curled up at the far end of the sofa and wrapped her arms around her knees. "You should make a list."

"A list?"

"Yes, of questions to pursue in Dream. So much better than to allow random possibility to dictate your Dreaming. I will begin. Ah... what about 'where does he live?' Or is that too direct?"

Sophia could not contain herself any longer. "Cecy!" she said, her laughter spilling out of her. "I believe you should call in at Bow Street and ask to be made a Runner! I doubt any of them is more tenacious and logical than you."

"Yes, but none of them dress very well, and I understand the pay is often poor," Cecy said. "I am quite serious about the list. Let us go to your room and use one of the numerous Dream notebooks you imagine I don't know about."

"Very well," Sophia said, "but I wish to Dream tonight, and I believe you should watch over me when I do. I would prefer not to fall back into bad habits."

"I will provide myself with a book, then. Sleeping people are boring, even if they are thwarting evildoers as they Dream."

They had sat like this before, Sophia remembered, when they were girls at school, their legs folded under them as they whispered secrets after the lights were out. Sophia had sought specific Dreams then, too, other girls' requests for secrets about the mistresses and the young men in the town near the school, but she had never before plotted the destruction of a man.

And it will have to be destruction, she thought as she chewed the end of her pencil. *Lord Endicott must not be allowed to benefit from the Seer's knowledge anymore.* It was impossible the Seer was an innocent in all of this; she had seen him so viciously happy at revealing others' secrets. Even so, she hesitated with the pencil's tip hovering just above the paper long enough that Cecy said, "Sophy, he tried to ruin you."

"He did," Sophia said. "He took pleasure in it." He thought he'd won, thought he had made her a laughingstock in the eyes of the law, and anger swept away her uncertainty. "What was it you said? 'Where does he live?' Let us start with that."

"And 'whom does he live with?' Or is 'how does he block your Dreams?' more important?"

"Both, I suppose." Sophia wrote them down, then added, *What has Lord Endicott ordered you to Dream about?*

Why do you work for him?

What do you love?

CHAPTER 19

IN WHICH SOPHIA GOES ON THE HUNT ONCE MORE

Sophia came out of Dream with a gasp. Cecy lowered her book. "That did not sound good," she said.

"It is nothing—no, truly, I am not pretending for your benefit, I was simply horrified by what I Saw. King is a detestable man. Dream after Dream of his threatening to expose people's secrets if they do not pay him to remain quiet... I cannot even find it in myself to be appalled at the kind of secrets some people will pay to keep hidden, because he takes such pleasure in tormenting them."

"That seems to be an excellent way to attack him, if it is such a common Dream," Daphne said, returning from where she had been pacing near the windows.

"Possibly." Sophia sat up and stretched. "At least I feel I am making progress. Five days ago I was not nearly so confident."

"We eliminated so many possibilities, though," Daphne said, "even though it did feel as if we were going nowhere. But I'm growing impatient. Aren't you tired of looking only at the past?"

"Dreaming of his past has given me a sense of who he is that I believe will refine my prediction when I am ready to seek it out. Are we agreed King's blackmail is not only in the past?"

"Yes. And I believe Lord Endicott is the kind of man who would not like his underlings to exercise their own initiative in carrying out crime," Cecy said. "So if King *is* still blackmailing people, he is either doing it with Lord Endicott's blessing, or he is risking his wrath by doing it secretly."

"I would guess the latter," Daphne said, "because he looks like the sort of petty, greedy little man who enjoys others' pain, and—you know I believe he might do it because of that, and not because of the money?" She flicked the sheet of notepaper where Sophia had drawn the Seer's likeness. "So when *will* you be ready to Dream about the future, Sophia?"

"Is impatience a Bounder trait?" Cecy teased.

"It is not, Cecy, and I hardly think it's impatience when you simply cannot wait for things."

"I believe that *is* the definition of 'impatience,' Daphne."

"Well, maybe it is. But can you both just sit there and tell me you're not anxious to be *doing* something about this vile person?"

"Soon," Sophia said, retrieving the notebook from Daphne. "Let us review what we know, so I may narrow my Dreaming yet again." They crowded around as Sophia turned the pages. "His name is King—I feel confident about that now that I have seen him sign his name three or four times. He lives somewhere in Spitalfields, in surprisingly nice lodgings—"

"Far nicer than he deserves," said Daphne.

"Yes. He is a creature of habit—dines in ordinary at the same place every day, buys the *Morning Post*, which I find strange, from the same urchin, and either he never washes his clothing, or his suits of clothes are identical. He rarely meets with Lord Endicott in person, or at least has not done so as far as I can See, preferring to put his Dreams to paper. I say 'prefer' but I suspect this is Lord Endicott's demand, as I doubt someone of King's character would be comfortable giving anyone the means to blackmail *him*, which is how those Dreams could be used against him."

"Wouldn't Lord Endicott be implicating himself if he used those letters in court?" Cecy said.

"Not if he could conceal the fact that he had acted on them. He could prove King tried to entice him into crime, and it is illegal to use

Dream to coerce someone else. But that is not how we're going to attack him."

"Then you have a plan," Cecy said.

"The beginnings of one. I intend one more Dream today, this time to predict whom his next victim will be, and then we can use that information to destroy him."

Daphne returned to pacing in front of the window. "We can reveal it to Lord Endicott... no, that wouldn't make sense."

"It would be satisfying to let Lord Endicott punish King for us," Sophia said, "but you are correct that we have no practical way of giving the information to Lord Endicott without him knowing from whom it has come."

"And we can't guarantee he will believe it worth eliminating King from his organization," Cecy added. "Since it's unlikely he has another Seer available."

"Right. So we will have to arrange for King to be apprehended in a more traditional way," Sophia said.

"The Bow Street Runners will not listen to you."

"I know, and that is a weakness of my plan. But I depend on the two of you to find a solution where I can't."

"Since your task is the most difficult, I believe it only fair Daphne and I should shoulder part of the burden."

"Then I believe I should Dream again. I may need to Dream once more after this, Cecy, but I promise that one will be the last today."

"You do not seem fatigued by your efforts, so I imagine it will be safe."

"Thank you, Cecy." Sophia lay back and laid her gloved palms on heart and navel. "This might take a while," she said, closing her eyes. She heard the other two women shuffling about, then the calm sound of her breathing filled her ears, the *thump-thump* of her heartbeat made every part of her body resonate with it, and she thought, *Show me his present crimes*, and slipped into Dream.

Her Dreams in pursuit of King had grown darker the closer she came to understanding him, the doors of Dream turning black and twisted. There was no light in Dream because it was not needed, but Sophia felt as if she were wandering deeper into a forest where the branches tangled overhead and blocked out the comforting lights of sun and moon and even stars. She was accustomed now to find few doors related to her prey; he was isolated, self-contained, in a way that implied he did not even want the friends he had, and he was unlikely to call them friends at all.

The better she came to know King through Dream, the fewer yet more reliable the doors became. This time, searching for his present crimes, she found only four. Two of them bore the marks of the counterfeiting operation, and she ignored those. The other two were marked with faces; on one, a teeming horde of people, on the other, a lone man's face. Difficult to choose. Did the mass of people represent his attitude toward all of humanity, that anyone he met was a potential victim? Or was the lone face the man he was currently blackmailing?

It was irrelevant, Sophia realized, and after the slightest hesitation she laid her palm along the center of the lone man's face, and let the Dream draw her in.

The shifting walls told her this was a Dream of something that might happen in the near future. King was speaking to the man whose face had been on the door; King displayed a large sheet of paper, and the man disintegrated into piles of banknotes and loose coin. Interesting. She let herself be drawn to the narrow, black-limned door in the nebulous wall and stepped through it to a street sketched out, as usual, with thick, generic lines and little detail. She looked around and was astonished. *Pall Mall. You are reaching beyond your grasp, I believe.*

A white painted circle in the sky told her it was mid-morning, so what she wanted would be... there. She quickly crossed the street to pick up a sheet of newspaper that was trying to disintegrate into Dream. Those sorts of objects left only transitory impressions on reality, and despite her considerable skill, this one vanished after only a few moments. It was more than enough time for her to read *5 January 1813* at the top. Tomorrow's date.

She woke from Dream and lay still for a moment, savoring the feeling of settling back into her physical body, as if her spirit had flown from it, untethered, into a different world. "He is still engaging in blackmail," she said, startling Daphne and Cecy, "and tomorrow, ladies, he is ours."

ॐ

IT WAS STRANGE, CONCEALING HER RED GLOVES UNDER A HEAVY FUR muff, but Daphne had said, "Suppose word of this comes back to Lord Endicott? We don't want him to know anything of your involvement yet," and Sophia had had to agree with her. If they could make it appear King had been apprehended due to his own carelessness, Lord Endicott might not be as quick to defend himself against Sophia's renewed attack.

They had also had a discussion over whether all three of them should go, or just Sophia, Cecy pointing out that three women shopping together would not be an unusual sight and Daphne complaining that she did not want to be left out of the fun, but in the end they determined Sophia should go alone. "Much as I wish to see King's face when he realizes he has lost," Cecy had said, "I believe men like our Mr. Parris are rather timid, and if we all come surging at him like a regiment over a hill, he might fail us."

"Oh, bah, you don't have to be so reasonable," Daphne had said.

At the moment, with Cecy's carriage jouncing her all over the seat and a cold draft seeping through a crack where the hood was imperfectly joined, she almost wished for their company. She did not believe it breaking the spirit of her agreement with Cecy not to tell her how anxious she was over the upcoming meeting. Sophia *knew* her Dreams to be true, *knew* herself to be accurate, and yet the memory of that last letter from Bow Street made her cringe.

This man, this Gerald Parris, would not dare to question her veracity; her reputation was unsullied, at least as far as the public was concerned; she need not fear bringing her Dream to him. What she ought to worry about was how he would react to her revelation that she knew his secret. Convincing him that she was not the blackmailer he should worry about might be difficult.

The carriage proceeded down Pall Mall and came to a stop at her destination, and Peter opened the door and assisted Sophia out, something made more difficult by her refusal to remove her hands from her muff. More carriages passed by, going in the other direction, and the normally placid horses stamped their feet. Sophia thought her nervousness might be catching. "I will return shortly," she told Peter, and swept through the front door of 89, Pall Mall and into Harding, Howell and Company.

That King would dare blackmail *anyone* in this bastion of female fashion, packed full of silks, laces, furs, muslins, and anything else a woman with plenty of money and a desire to be at the forefront of society might want, astounded Sophia with his sheer effrontery. It even smelled of wealth, though the scent was more likely that of the rich furs being stroked and appreciated by customers on either side of the door. Sophia kept moving, slowly, waiting for the shop assistants to notice her in her expensive muslin gown and the cerulean blue bonnet she almost never wore because it shouted *Money!* at anyone who looked at her. The furs really were beautiful. She would need to return someday on a genuine shopping expedition.

From the corner of her eye, she observed a man wearing an imperfectly fitted black coat—surely the store would want its employees dressed well?—and a cravat starched so thoroughly it could probably stand on its own approaching her, just ahead of one of his fellows whose appearance was a little more spruce. Their resemblance to a pair of hunting dogs both trying to corner the same fox forced her to conceal a smile. "Can I help you, miss?" the lucky shop assistant said.

"Mrs.," Sophia corrected him, "and I would like to speak to Mr. Parris."

The shop assistant looked a little taken aback. Sophia guessed he thought respectable, wealthy women were not supposed to know the names of lowly tradesmen. "I am certain I can help madam with whatever her needs are," he rallied.

"My needs are to speak with Mr. Parris," Sophia said, "though I believe you are quite capable at your job." If she had to reveal the red gloves to compel his obedience, she would, but that could ruin her plan. She stared down the overly helpful shop assistant and pretended she was Lady Daveril, who would certainly not put up with such behavior.

The shop assistant reddened, and said, "This way, madam." Sophia followed him through two more wide openings, each topped with a row of fanlights, and toward a counter in front of a wall of drawers and shelves full of pasteboard boxes and, high above, giant bolts of fabric from which slivers of color were visible. Larger swaths of silk and satin hung from rings set into columns at intervals throughout the room. The shop assistant pointed toward the counter, bowed, and walked away as if in reproof that she did not appreciate his service. Sophia took a deep breath to calm herself and approached the counter. Everything depended on what happened next.

CHAPTER 20
IN WHICH THE LIONESS FINDS
THE RIGHT WATERHOLE

The man behind the counter was the older, slightly fatter twin of Sophia's guide, though his coat was of a richer fabric and a much better cut, and his cravat was tied in a complicated pattern that probably had a name like the Algebraical or the Montmorency. He was showing a length of puce silk to an elderly woman who huddled into the folds of her pelisse like a badger going to ground.

"I am sure madam will look splendid in this color, it is so rich and mature," Mr. Parris said. He glanced at Sophia once, smiled pleasantly at his customer, then glanced at Sophia again as if wondering why she did not move on. Sophia stood with her hands gripped tightly inside her muff and returned his glance with a placid expression that said she was prepared to wait forever for his full attention. "It... it is worth every shilling," he continued.

"Do not patronize me, young man," the elderly woman said. "I know very well your job is to sell me the most expensive thing you have and pass it off as a bargain. Well, I've no interest in your game. Show me the lavender again."

Mr. Parris nodded, and Sophia realized to her dismay this was the sort of woman who would take all day deciding on a gown, and in the end purchase nothing. She was old and wealthy and very likely bored, and Sophia had no time to waste. So she said, "Lavender is entirely the wrong color for you."

The woman turned, slowly, to face Sophia. "I don't believe I heard that," she said. Wrinkles dragged down the corners of her mouth and eyes, but Sophia guessed she had got in the habit of frowning at things long before Time had had a hand in souring her disposition. Sophia quickly took in the rest of her: hat designed for a much younger woman, neckline too low for day wear, hair styled in an attempt to mimic...

"I apologize for speaking out of turn," she said, "it is only that you bear a striking resemblance to Lady Cowper, and she, naturally, would never wear lavender."

The woman touched her hair. "I do? That is... yes, I have been told so."

"I assumed that was why you were looking at the puce silk. I saw Lady Cowper at Almack's just the other night, and she was wearing a gown of almost this color. The fabric was not nearly so fine as this, however." Sophia sent up a silent prayer that this woman was ignorant as well as vain; the lovely Lady Cowper, patroness of Almack's, preferred pale colors.

The woman put her hand out to touch the puce silk. "Not as nice as this?"

"No, much more faded. This is so vibrant, I am sure it will draw everyone's attention."

"I believe you are right. Ten yards, young man, and be quick about it."

It took Mr. Parris several lifetimes to arrange for the silk to be sent to the elderly woman's modiste, and several more lifetimes for Sophia to extricate herself from conversation with her new friend, during which time she agonized that someone else would approach her prey and she would have to do the whole thing over again. But presently the old woman was gone, and Mr. Parris said, "I ought to share the commission on that sale with you, miss."

"Mrs.," Sophia said again, "and you will not thank me when you learn why I am here. Is there somewhere more private we might go?"

His face went wary. "This isn't that kind of store, miss. Madam."

"Nor am I that kind of customer," Sophia said, withdrawing one hand from her muff long enough for him to recognize the glove. His wary expression disappeared, replaced by fear and anticipation in equal measure. He glanced around—it was before noon, and the shop was not busy—and beckoned her to a corner partly sheltered by draping lengths of richly brocaded satin, where he stood so his body blocked hers from view.

"Do you have a Vision for me, ma'am?" he said, his voice breathy, as if he'd been running.

"You are Gerald Parris, residing at 15, Larkspur Street. You are supporting your younger brother, who is enrolled in a school you can barely afford, and your infirm mother." Sophia took a deep breath. "That is why you began embezzling from your employer, to supplement your income."

Mr. Parris took a step forward and raised his hand as if to strike her. His eyes were wide and his breath was coming even more rapidly now. "It's a lie," he said. "You're telling damned lies."

Sophia laid her palm flat on his chest and could feel his heart pounding. "This glove says otherwise," she said. "But I am not here to accuse you. I'm here to save you."

"I—what?"

She was losing him, she could tell. He could not afford to lose this job under any condition, let alone one that could ensure he never worked again. "Listen to me, Gerald Parris," she said, grabbing his chin and forcing him to look at her. "I am not a threat to you. In about an hour, a man, another Seer, will come into this store and ask to speak to you. He is short and slight, with grey hair and a bit of a limp. He will reveal that he knows you have committed a crime, and he will promise not to share this knowledge with your employer if you pay him, and go on paying him. Do you understand what I am saying, Mr. Parris?"

Mr. Parris nodded. "But... what do *you* want? Are you threatening me?"

"No, I am not threatening you. I want your blackmailer, Mr. Parris. I want to see him imprisoned, and what you have done isn't important to me. I don't condone theft, but I have Seen your family and I know what it is to be desperate. If you will do as I ask, and if you will swear to stop embezzling from your employers, I will pay for your brother's education and I will see your mother gets the medical treatment she needs. Do you swear?"

Mr. Parris shook his head, then nodded, then looked confused. "I don't understand why you're helping me."

"No, Mr. Parris, *you* are helping *me*. But you must do exactly as I say. And *no one* must know I am involved. You will be the one who apprehends him, and your employers will look favorably on you because of it. I need no publicity. Now—do you swear to help me?"

"I do. I mean, I will help you."

"Good. Then this is what you must do."

※

Forty-seven minutes later, according to Sophia's highly accurate Swiss pocket watch, a drab, grey little man came strolling into Harding, Howell and Company. From her position behind a fall of silken fabrics, she watched him stop, look around, then make straight for Mr. Parris's counter. The hardest part of these last few minutes had been keeping customers away from Mr. Parris, so he would not be occupied when King arrived. Mr. Parris looked nervous, something Sophia was afraid King might notice and draw the wrong (or right) conclusions from, but there was no help for it.

She shifted her position and wished she were close enough to over-hear them, but of course it was not the kind of conversation they would have if anyone were close enough to listen in. So she contented herself from observing their interaction and making up words to fit their expressions:

Mr. Parris looks very nervous. He has almost forgotten he is simply to greet King. There, King is drawing him in, because Mr. Parris now looks uncertain—oh, now he looks terrified. King must have told him "I am your blackmailer, ahahaha." Mr. Parris is playing his part well. Oh, how I wish Daphne and Cecy were here! No, Mr. Parris, wait until he shows you his affidavit as a Seer—there, now excuse yourself to "get his money." Oh, King, you are mine now.

Mr. Parris left his counter to go into the back of the shop. King waited, as relaxed as if he were not a vicious criminal who was about to

182

meet justice. Sophia had given Mr. Parris everything he needed to make this work, but she could not do anything to stiffen his spine, so she clenched her hands tight and prayed he would have the brazen nerve to carry it off.

There he was again, approaching from a different direction, with another shop assistant—no, this new man had a less subservient walk, he must have more authority, perhaps he was even one of the owners—but they were approaching King now, and Sophia did not care who the man was so long as he reacted properly.

"This is the man, sir," Mr. Parris said loudly, and his voice sounded not at all shaky. "He says he has had a Dream that shows me stealing from the company, and I insist he is lying. I want my reputation restored."

King looked so surprised Sophia wanted to cheer. "I... there must be some mistake..." he began, and Mr. Parris thrust his hand into King's grey, drab coat and pulled out a piece of paper.

"He showed me this and threatened to send it to you, sir, if I didn't pay him," Mr. Parris said. The owner, or whoever he was, took the paper and began reading it. The other customers were looking at the little tableau, whispering, and more people came crowding in at the doorway from the other rooms and were paying the most particular attention to what was happening. King looked as if he wanted to bolt, but didn't know where to run.

The owner folded the paper and put it away inside his own coat. "You're the Elias King named on that Dream affidavit?" he said.

"I—no, it's not me, I was acting on his behalf—" King said.

"That's a lie, sir. He introduced himself as Elias King," Mr. Parris said. "Sir, I have been a faithful employee for two years. He's threatened to smear my good name. I believe you should examine his claims so I can prove I didn't do what he said."

"That won't be necessary, Parris, I know the kind of man you are," the owner said. He took hold of King's arm. "I'm turning you in to the magistrates. Lying about Dreams is a crime, and so is blackmail."

"No," King said, looking wildly around the room for an escape. Too late, Sophia ducked back into her sheltered corner; he saw her, and his fear turned into fury. He roared something unintelligible and smashed his fist into his captor's face, making the man scream in pain and release him. He fled toward the exit, shoving women out of his way and into one another. Sophia tore after him, though her sensible brain was saying things like, *What exactly do you plan to do if you catch him?*

She tripped over a fallen customer, kept herself on her feet through sheer willpower, and emerged onto Pall Mall to see King racing off toward Haymarket Street. She ran after him for a few more steps before her sensible brain brought her to a panting halt. She cursed, loudly, drawing a few stares from passersby. Then she staggered back to Cecy's carriage and ordered a very startled Peter to drive her home. She had failed. Now King would be too wary for her to ever trap him again, and Lord Endicott would know she was still a threat.

She sagged into a corner of the carriage and closed her eyes. She would not give up. She would simply have to think of a new plan.

Nothing suggested itself during her drive to the Barhams' house. She felt drained, as if she had once again been Dreaming too much and it had sapped her will to keep moving. Thinking was too much effort. She dragged herself out of the carriage and up to the drawing room where Cecy and Daphne were pretending to drink tea and enjoy themselves.

Both women leaped up when she entered, Daphne literally Skipping to a spot that put her inches from Sophia's nose. "Well?" she demanded.

"It didn't work," Cecy said. "I can tell from how despondent you look. What happened?"

"It almost worked," Sophia said, and sank down onto the uncomfortable chair to tell her uncomfortable story. She finished by saying, "I believe I want to leave this alone for the rest of the day. I cannot begin to imagine what we could try next."

Daphne sprang up from her seat and knelt at Sophia's feet. "Oh, Sophia, of course it worked!"

"I am afraid I don't see it either," Cecy said.

Daphne hopped up and grinned at both of them. "That is because neither of you has a job delivering messages that sometimes contain sensitive information. When someone tries to steal a courier's bag, or tries to bribe a courier, we try to catch him, of course, but sometimes these people are clever—not cleverer than I, but then no one—well, once someone tried to—but I'm distracted again, aren't I?

"What I was saying was if someone tries to tamper with our messages or packages, and we don't apprehend him, we send the person's description to the magistrates, and then they look out for him so he can't try it again. And *you* made sure they had not only his description, but his name and his Dream affidavit too. I will bet you anything you like the magistrates have already issued a warrant for King's arrest."

Cecy and Sophia looked past Daphne at one another. "Lord Endicott will not want to associate with anyone under such close scrutiny by the law," Cecy said.

"And King knows too much about Lord Endicott's criminal endeavors," Sophia said. "King might have to worry about Lord Endicott finding him before the Bow Street Runners do."

"Hah! I feel as if I could black Lord Endicott's eye for him right now!" Daphne said.

Sophia remembered King's furious, helpless face, and thought of how Lord Endicott might look when he heard the news. "I believe, in a sense, we just did," she said.

CHAPTER 21

IN WHICH A GALA TAKES SOME UNEXPECTED TURNS

Sophia folded the newspaper and set it aside on the table next to the uncomfortable chair. "The *Morning Herald* may have its flaws, but it does the best police reporting, I believe."

"*I* thought they made Mr. Parris sound heroic," Daphne said, "which you said he really wasn't."

"I said he didn't act like a traditional hero, but I believe he was very brave, essentially daring his employer to check the company records, knowing they would show King's Dream to be true."

"But you knew they would not check if he were forthright enough," Cecy said, "because you saw it in Dream."

"Yes, and that is why he was brave, because he could not know until it was over if he had been forthright enough." Sophia stretched. She had not Dreamed for twenty-four hours, but she was still weary from everything she had done to trap King. "I must remember to pay his brother's tuition, and ask Dr. Garland to look in on the mother and find out what is wrong with her so she can be treated. I hope Dr. Garland does not feel we treat her as if she is on permanent retainer with us."

"You can do all of that tomorrow," Cecy said. "This afternoon we will rest, because tonight we will be attending the Gates's Twelfth Night gala. Have you been invited, Daphne?"

"I have, and I am prepared for whatever games Mrs. Gates intends," Daphne said. She scrunched up her face, pressed on her cheeks to make her lips pucker up, and intoned, "I am Montoni, cold and brooding, ahahahaha."

Sophia and Cecy went off into wild laughter. "I imagine Mrs. Radcliff would take exception to your portrayal of her villain," Sophia said, "and besides, Eleanora never does the same thing twice."

"Oh, bah, that means all my preparation is for nothing," Daphne said, grinning, "and I may only approach this evening with dread."

"Last year was anomalous," Cecy said. "It will be very enjoyable, you'll see."

"I hold you to that," Daphne said. "Sophia, what is the time?" Sophia displayed her watch, and Daphne squeaked. "I'm late!" she exclaimed, and vanished with a *pop*.

"I am glad it is not fancy dress," Sophia said, standing and beginning to pace the room to stretch out her legs. She really was more weary than she should be. Possibly a nap was in order. "That is so much work, and one always has to worry that some other woman will come dressed as Athena, or the Five Graces, or something."

"There are only three Graces, dearest."

"So I need worry not only about dressing the same as another person, but of getting that dress wrong."

Cecy laughed. "I am certain Eleanora will come up with something entertaining. And I am assured Lord Endicott will not be there, and Lady Daveril has gone into the country, so it will be enjoyable all around!"

"You relieve my mind, Cecy. Though I am not sure, now, whom I am more loath to face!"

She lay in her bed in her shift and tried not to accidentally slip into Dream. There was one person she had even less desire to face than her two nemeses, but she had been unable to ask Cecy if Mr. Rutledge would be there without starting a conversation she felt powerless to finish.

She had not told Cecy or Daphne about Mr. Rutledge's employer, or that he had wanted her to work for him, or that he had betrayed their friendship by manipulating her talent. The first two were not her secrets to share, and the third... it was connected to the first two, yes, but her reluctance to speak of it came more from her confusion than from a desire to keep those secrets. It had been so much simpler when they were friends. Now, when she thought of him, she felt anger and humiliation and gratitude and even desire, all stirred together like some witch's brew of emotion, waiting on some final ingredient that would determine which of those feelings should come out on top.

Facing him tonight... she seemed to have settled on avoidance as her way of dealing with those relationships that were too uncomfortable or painful or confusing, hadn't she? The thought made her angry enough with herself and her weakness that sleep seemed impossible. Avoiding Mr. Rutledge was not going to do anything but postpone the moment when she had to face him and thank him properly for bringing her home safely, however discomfited it made her feel.

Her longing to see him embarrassed her, mixed up as it was in her humiliation over how he had tricked her. She could not determine the truth. Had he deceived her completely, pretended to be her friend so he could manipulate her? But then why treat her with such solicitude in her moment of need? And was it not in many ways worse if he *were* truly her friend and abused that friendship to gain the use of her talent? In either case, her ridiculous feelings of love for him were... ridiculous, that was all. Foolish to care for someone who cared nothing for her; foolish to care for someone she could not trust.

She lay, sleepless, until Beeton came to dress her in her green silk shift with the ivory gauze gown over it, to arrange her hair and pin her green satin turban over her auburn curls, to help her choose a necklace and a pair of shoes and send her downstairs to join Cecy and Lewis at the door. Cecy looked radiant, as usual; Lewis looked calm and almost painfully handsome. Sophia smiled and contributed a few things to Cecy's chatter on the way to the Gates's town house in Grosvenor Street, but she felt remote, as if this were all happening to someone else—until Cecy said, "And I reassured Mr. Rutledge you would be there. He was concerned there might have been lasting damage from the Vision, which I told him was not the case."

"Thank you," Sophia said, then could not think of anything else to say.

"I really do feel tremendously grateful to him for his help," Cecy went on. "I am surprised he did not call the next day to inquire after your health, but I suppose he is a very busy man."

"He is," Sophia said. "And I'm sure he has faith in Dr. Garland's abilities."

"Certainly that. Perhaps we should have a dinner party, invite him as a way of saying 'thank you.'"

"Do you consider that wise, given your health?"

"I feel well—all right, I know there is no guarantee I will still feel well in the morning. Even so, I want to do something to show our gratitude."

"I am sure he already knows it. He... he is quite generous." Sophia blushed, but did not know why. Praising Mr. Rutledge made her feel as awkward as if he had once again been required to carry her out of some hostess's overheated and unpleasant gathering.

"If you think so," Cecy said. The carriage came to a halt and they emerged to be welcomed into the Gates's town house.

It was one of the largest on Grosvenor Street and the most elegant, thanks to Eleanora Gates's exquisite taste, which made her one of the principal hostesses of London. The mirrored walls of the small entryway threw off reflections of themselves, like Almack's in miniature, and kept the room from feeling cramped. Sophia went through to the spacious drawing room to the left, where the carpets had been removed and the chairs pulled back against the glass-fronted cabinets to leave plenty of room for dancing. Eleanora Gates's cut-glass chandelier, modeled on the famous ones in the Assembly Rooms in Bath, sent warm golden light flickering over the entire room, a warmth echoed by the flames burning low in the fireplace with its creamy mantel.

"Mrs. Westlake!" exclaimed a woman Sophia had met several times before in company, and then the room seemed filled with people calling out greetings and friendly questions until Sophia wanted to hide. They were determined to show her she was valued, and that no one thought less of her from having a moment's weakness, and it made her feel more awkward than if they had said nothing. But she smiled, and told herself firmly she was having a good time. After half an hour passed, and the guests' attention turned to more interesting things, she discovered it was true. How much different from the Duchess of Lenshire's dinner! She did not see Mr. Rutledge, did not see anyone whose presence might interfere with her enjoyment of the evening, and the tension she had felt upon entering began to ease.

"Thank you for coming, everyone, I am so pleased to have you as my guests!" Eleanora Gates called out. Sophia turned away from an interesting conversation about how the Prime Minister might handle the Roman Catholic question to look in Eleanora's direction, and as she did so, she found herself instead looking directly at Mr. Rutledge. His dark eyes were fixed on her, his expression unreadable, and she blushed, but could not look away.

What was he thinking, when he looked at her? Surely not that she was weak and helpless; he was too much the gentleman to hold her collapse against her. But he knew she would never agree to work with him, and he probably believed she hated him... but she didn't hate him, she was angry with him, only she was having trouble hanging on to that anger—

"—so let us begin!" Eleanora said, and Sophia tried to remember the rest of it. Something about a hat—oh, no, she had brought out the old hat with the creased brim no one with any taste would wear, which was why she only used it to hold slips of paper for games. Was it charades? She simply could not remember. Daphne brushed past her, clutching her paper. "Isn't this fun?" she said, but was gone again before Sophia could acknowledge her.

The crowd pushed her forward to where Eleanora stood, and she dipped her hand into the hat and pulled out a folded paper. It was only women doing the selecting, she realized, and unfolded the paper to read LORD CHUMLEIGH written on it in elegant script. It surprised her that Eleanora had invited him, and surprised her further that he had accepted the invitation. He was not a bad man, but he preferred gambling to dancing, drinking to good conversation, and it was unlikely he would find either of those things here.

"Now, find your partners, ladies!" said Eleanora, and a great giggling went up on all sides. Sophia's mouth went dry. Partners for what? All around her, women were approaching men and displaying their papers. Well. It was an unorthodox way to choose dance partners, but Sophia could endure Lord Chumleigh for half an hour, then move on to more pleasant pursuits.

Lord Chumleigh was standing near the fireplace, talking to two other young men Sophia knew to also be fond of gambling. He was short, but well-featured, with blond hair arranged neatly around his face and a sprinkling of freckles across his cheeks that made him look like a boy, though he was a year or two older than she. His coat and knee breeches were of the finest make and his neckwear was a starched and folded dream of a cravat that shoved his chin unnaturally high, making him look disdainful. Sophia concealed a smile when she saw his watch fob was almost identical to Lord Endicott's. He was a bit of a dandy, and completely self-absorbed, but harmless.

She approached him and extended her paper. "I seem to have drawn your name, my lord," she said.

Lord Chumleigh took the paper from her and examined it with a golden quizzing glass. "You have indeed," he said. "But I believe I am the winner, Mrs. Westlake."

"Is *this* Mrs. Westlake?" one of the other young men said. Aside from having black hair, he was the virtual twin of Lord Chumleigh.

"Hah, Florian, you're a damned fool if you can't see the gloves," the third man said. He was fat where the other two were slim, with the look of a former athlete gone to seed.

Florian scowled. "I meant—"

"Never mind what you meant," Lord Chumleigh said. He extended his arm to Sophia. "Will you walk with me, Mrs. Westlake?"

"Certainly, my lord." She expected him to take her to where the couples were lining up for the dance, but there did not seem to be a line forming at all. Lord Chumleigh began strolling around the perimeter of the room, nodding to people but not engaging in conversation. It took Sophia almost half a minute to work out that he was displaying her, as if she were a prize, and then she nearly flung his arm away in her anger. Was *this* what Eleanora had in mind? She was going to have strong words with the woman later.

"Will the dancing begin later?" she said, thinking *It had better be sooner than later, or Eleanora and I will have more than words.*

"After the supper," Lord Chumleigh said. "Gives us more time together, doesn't it?"

"I don't understand."

Lord Chumleigh patted her hand where it lay on his arm. "Partners for the night, you and I! Just as well you drew my name. Anyone else, and a *certain someone*—" he tapped the side of his nose and winked "—well, he wouldn't be so understanding of you standing up with anyone but me. Us being such good friends, of course."

Partners for the night. That explained so much. She was going to pull Eleanora's hair out by the roots when she got her alone. But *certain someone* made a different kind of horrible sense. "I believe I am free to partner with whomever I like, my lord," she said, pretending ignorance.

Lord Chumleigh laughed. "I'll bet that's what you tell everyone, isn't it? Don't worry, I know it's a secret. You can trust me not to talk."

"Can I, my lord?"

"Of course!" He turned her to face him, and she realized he'd had a little, or possibly a lot, to drink before coming here tonight. "Faithful until the end, is what I am. Ivo knows that."

Sophia closed her eyes and turned her head away so she did not have to inhale his stinking breath. Ivo. Ivo, Lord Endicott. Lord Chumleigh was his good friend. Lord Chumleigh believed she and Lord Endicott were not only attached, but secretly engaged. Sophia wanted to scream, and then beat Lord Chumleigh senseless.

She opened her eyes and once again found herself looking directly at Mr. Rutledge. *His waistcoat is so ugly*, she thought irrelevantly, *if he is so wealthy, one would imagine his clothing would reflect that*, then hated herself for the spiteful thought. He was still expressionless, intent on her. She had no idea how she looked: furious, resentful, aggressive?

Then he smiled. It was so unexpected and yet so familiar—how often had he smiled like that at something she had said?—that she smiled back at him in reflex. Her heart beat a little faster, light as a bird. Then he turned his head to face his partner, a tall, slender brunette

Sophia did not know, and she realized his smile had been directed at that stranger instead. She closed her eyes again. Of course he would not smile at her. No matter how much she might wish otherwise.

"—otherwise it's all for nothing," Lord Chumleigh was saying. "Don't you agree?"

"Of course," Sophia said. "Are they forming up for charades over there? I do love charades."

"I don't care for them myself," Lord Chumleigh said, but she dragged him with her to join the others and ignored his protests. She hated charades; she was as terrible at guessing the riddles as she was at cards, but Mr. Rutledge and his lovely companion were conversing with a few other people near the door to the dining room, and this put her as far from them as possible. She laughed, and exaggerated her follies, and pretended she did not feel sick with misery and embarrassment and hatred of her chance-won partner.

The announcement of supper came as a surprise to her, absorbed in the game as she had become. "Shall we go in, Mrs. Westlake?" Lord Chumleigh said into her ear. His breath was hot and still stank of old alcohol, and she closed her eyes for a moment to regain her calm. He might as well have been Lord Endicott himself, hovering over her shoulder to prevent her enjoying herself in his absence. Could she reject his offered arm? Eleanora would be devastated. As angry as she was at her situation, she liked her friend too much to make a scene; everyone else seemed happy with the game. So she smiled, accepted Lord Chumleigh's escort, and they made their way into the dining room with the rest of the throng, customs of precedence ignored for the evening.

They sat near the middle of the table, across from an enormous silver epergne filled with hideously expensive white and gold roses. It blocked much of Sophia's view of the table and made her feel as if she and her companion were sitting in an arbor, sheltered on all sides and suffocated by the cloying fragrance. Lord Chumleigh never asked her which dish she would like, but heaped food onto her plate faster than she could eat it, saying, "Wouldn't want you to feel neglected, Mrs. Westlake, our mutual friend would be disappointed in me," and that oblique mention of her nemesis twisted Sophia's stomach into a knot of anger.

She began plotting an early departure. Perhaps she could persuade Cecy to pretend to illness—no, there she was near the head of the table, laughing at something her partner, Mr. Nevensham, was saying. Ruining her pleasure when she was so rarely in a condition to experience it was unthinkable. She could endure Lord Chumleigh for a few hours more.

The company rose from the table when Eleanora did and returned to the drawing room together. Lord Chumleigh persisted in clinging close to Sophia's side like an unwelcome dog convinced of its irresistible appeal despite its odor and dripping saliva. "Will you dance with me?" he said. "I know I'm not the partner you'd like, but might as well protect the secret, hey?"

"You are entirely right, Lord Chumleigh," Sophia said, and took his hand. *I would prefer any partner but you.*

Lord Chumleigh was a terrible dancer, always missing his step and laughing foolishly at his mistakes. Sophia's face began to feel numb with smiling encouragingly at him. *Surely Eleanora will not expect us to dance only with one man all evening*, she thought, and to her relief someone else solicited her hand for the next dance, and Lord Chumleigh retreated to a seat along the wall, where his friends joined him. He never stopped watching her, though, and now it was Sophia's turn to stumble through the steps, burdened by the weight of his regard. This evening could not have been more miserable if it had been designed with that intent.

She turned down her next potential partner, pleading fatigue, which was partly true; it was fatigue of the spirit, though, and not of the body, that drove her to a seat in a quiet corner where she could watch the dancers and feel grateful to have escaped Lord Chumleigh's supervisory eye for the moment.

Her eye fell once again on Mr. Rutledge—well, it was natural she should watch him, she told herself, because he was half a head taller than any other man in the room, and his graceful dancing made him worth watching. It was not as if she sought him out. He was partnered with the same slender brunette the slips of paper had shackled him to for the evening, though he seemed not to mind it. Sophia made herself look elsewhere. This was the most miserable evening she had endured in months.

"Mrs. Westlake?"

She turned, startled out of her reverie, to find herself addressed by a tall and attractive footman. "A Mr. Vane is here, asking for you."

Vane. The Bow Street Runner. "Did he say what his business is?"

"No, madam. He apologized for intruding on your evening, and asked if you would give him five minutes of your time."

His last three words were spoken into silence as the dance came to an end. Vane's sudden appearance here could mean anything. Had they discovered that Lord Endicott had made her Dreams appear false? "Thank you," Sophia said, rising from her seat. "Will you take me to him?"

The footman led her through the house and down the stairs to the tradesman's entrance off the kitchen. "He said he didn't want to make a fuss, so he's waiting outside," he said.

"Thank you," Sophia repeated, and stepped outside. After the warmth and mugginess of Eleanora's drawing room, the cold air bit into her skin with needle-sharp teeth. No one was there. Apprehension made her take two steps back and put her hand on the knob just as Elias King emerged from the darkness, lunging toward her.

CHAPTER 22

IN WHICH MR. RUTLEDGE MAKES ANOTHER APPEAL

Sophia shrieked and flung herself away, and a cold, sharp pain shot down her arm as his silvery knife slashed her. Her instinctive, terrified movement put King between her and the door, and even in the darkness behind Eleanora's house she could see he knew he had her at a disadvantage. He changed his grip on the knife and grinned at her, a nasty, evil look that set Sophia's heart beating faster.

"You destroy me, I destroy you," he said. "Been butting heads all this time, should've known it would come to this." He slashed at her again, making her jump back. She was trapped back here in this tiny space, unable to outrun him in her thin dancing slippers. Hot blood trickled down her arm, not stanched by her gauzy sleeve.

"Even if you kill me, Lord Endicott will never let you live," she said. It came out as faint and breathy as the puffs of steam that followed her words.

King shrugged. "Still have the satisfaction of knowing you went first." He lowered his head and rushed at her.

She ducked, twisted out of his grasp, felt his blade pass next to her ear, and then they were both on the ground, struggling for control of the knife. She had better leverage, but despite his age and the fact that he was smaller than she, he was still stronger. Tears came to her eyes as she strained desperately against his arm bearing down on her.

Someone grabbed King by the shoulders and wrenched him off her. Mr. Rutledge lifted the man as easily as if he were a kitten and slammed him into the rough brick next to the door, making King cry out in pain. With one hand, he kept the man pinioned there. With the other, he grabbed King's wrist and forced his hand open, the knife clattering to the ground. Sophia staggered to her feet. "Mr. Rutledge," she began.

"Find someone to send to Bow Street to take him into custody," he interrupted her. "But don't go back to the party. It's obvious you were attacked."

Sophia nodded and went inside, looking for a footman. She found the man who had escorted her to the tradesman's entrance; he took in her condition with mounting horror, then ran off without a word when she explained what she wanted. She watched him go, feeling momentarily numb, then remembered Mr. Rutledge. He had not moved since she left except to trap both King's hands behind him with one of his large ones.

"You're bleeding," he said, and pulled a handkerchief out of his coat somewhere. Sophia took it and pressed it over the long slice across her upper arm. It did not seem to be bleeding too badly, but she saw it was on a line with her heart, and then she was shivering harder than the cold could account for and could not stop herself.

"Go inside, Mrs. Westlake," Mr. Rutledge said. "I will wait here for the officer they send and ensure this man does not escape custody."

She shook her head. "No," she said through chattering teeth, "I have to... I will not be able to sleep if I do not..." She looked at King, whose head lolled to one side as if he were unconscious, gasped, and flung herself at him, slapping and kicking him with all her strength.

Mr. Rutledge took hold of her uninjured arm. "Mrs. Westlake, control yourself."

"He is a Seer, he is trying to Dream, don't you see? We cannot let him find a way out of this!" She grabbed his hair and cracked his head against the brick, and he groaned and blinked at her. "You are *not* escaping me again," she snarled at him.

"Try to leave him alive, Mrs. Westlake," Mr. Rutledge said. He shifted his grip and twisted King's arm painfully high above his back. King let out a pained yelp. "Though I admit this is rather satisfying."

Sophia took half a step back, keeping within slapping distance of King. "How did you know I—that he would attack me?" she asked.

"I didn't," Mr. Rutledge said. "I saw you leave, and I followed you. I wanted to speak to you. What did you mean, escape you again?"

"Why did you want to speak to me?"

"Don't change the subject. How do you know this man?"

"You are not my superior. I owe you no explanations."

"Damn it, Sophia!" Mr. Rutledge began, then turned his head away from her. "I would to God I had never taken advantage of you," he said in a calmer voice. "I truly did tell you those things because I wanted to help you in whatever Dreams you were pursuing. It was a complete surprise to me to find, when Rowley sent me your first letter, that you were on the trail of the same people I was. *Yes*, I needed the information you provided, and *yes*, I knew you would object to my using it, but I was desperate, and I told myself you would never find out and that made it all right. That is what I followed you to say. I cannot tell you how much I regret losing your friendship over something so unimportant as all that."

Sophia gaped at him. She tried desperately to hang on to her anger, but it could not stand in the face of such naked honesty. "His name is Elias King," she said, "and I was responsible for exposing his use of Dream to blackmail others. He escaped custody once. I intend to make sure he does not do so again."

"King. At the department store. But your name was not associated with that report."

"I did not want the publicity."

"Why not? It might restore your reputation with Rowley."

He will believe you unstable. Again. "The Dream showed me concealment would bring me success," she lied.

King coughed, then began to laugh, a creaky sound that matched his appearance. "You can't tell him the truth, can you?"

"What truth?" Mr. Rutledge said.

Realization dawned. *She* could not tell the truth, but King could. "Tell him whom you work for," she said.

"No." King laughed again.

She grabbed his hair and slammed his head into the brick wall again. "Tell him!"

"I wouldn't give you the satisfaction," King said. "I'm going to my death anyway, no way around it."

"He can protect you. Tell him!"

"Mrs. Westlake, what are you talking about?"

"Already Seen it," King said. Blood trickled down his face and he licked at it. "No Dream leads anywhere but death. You know why."

Mr. Rutledge shoved him hard against the wall, making him grunt with pain. "Why should I care for whom you work, Mr. King?"

King laughed again. "Beat it out of me."

"As if I could trust anything you said under duress," Mr. Rutledge said, but he twisted King's arm again, cutting off his laugh.

The sound of footsteps put Sophia on edge again, but it was only a couple of roughly-dressed men, followed by the actual Benjamin Vane. "Mrs. Westlake," he said, sounding surprised.

"Mr. Vane," Sophia said. "This is Elias King. I'm sure you have the magistrates' warrant for his apprehension."

"We do," Vane said. "Did he attack you?"

"Yes. I was responsible for exposing his crime."

"That was Gerald Parris."

"My Dream told Mr. Parris what to do. And before you suggest what I know you will suggest, which is that I am making claims to bolster my stained reputation, you might ask yourself what other reason a wanted felon might have for risking capture by attacking someone with whom he has no connection."

Vane looked at her bloody arm, then at her face, and nodded once, slowly. "You should have that tended to, Mrs. Westlake," he said. "We'll have him confined in the Catterwell immediately."

"That may not be enough," Sophia said.

"They're equipped to keep criminals with talent from escaping justice."

"Yes, I know, but I believe someone will attempt to have Mr. King killed to prevent him implicating others in his crimes."

"And what crimes are those?"

A great weariness descended upon her. "Ask him," she said. "I cannot provide evidentiary proof, so my witness counts for nothing at law."

Vane nodded again. "Many thanks," he said. He took King from Mr. Rutledge's hands and handcuffed him, then let his companions lead the man away.

"Come inside," Mr. Rutledge said, leading Sophia back into the passageway and around a corner into the bright warmth of the servants' dining hall, interrupting their supper. "We will need warm water and bandages," he told the room at large when everyone leaped up at their appearance, then steered Sophia to sit at one end of the table, not caring that he was evicting the butler.

Mr. Rutledge ripped the torn sleeve from her gown and examined the wound. "Shallow, but long," he said, "nothing serious." One of the footmen appeared with a bowl of water and a cloth; a maid brought a rolled bandage. "Hold your arm still," Mr. Rutledge said, which made Sophia begin to shake again. In her mind's eye, the knife descended—

A hand gripped hers. "You have survived worse than this," Mr. Rutledge said. She looked at him, at his expressionless dark eyes, and wondered what he saw in her face. He gently washed the blood from her arm, then swabbed the wound, making it bleed a little, and wrapped it up and tied off the bandage. "You might have someone look at Healing that," he said.

"It is not enough to be worth troubling anyone. I will simply wear long sleeves for a while."

"If you wish."

Sophia became aware the servants were hovering around them, and that their meal was still spread on the table. "I beg your pardon," she said, rising, and left the room, but once she was in the passage that led up to the ground floor, she realized she did not know what to do next. She certainly could not return to Eleanora's party in this condition— she touched her hair, realized her turban was hanging down the back of her head and her hair was matted on one side where she had rolled on the ground, and of course her gown was ruined. She removed the turban, which had a smear of dirt along one side, and buried her cold fingers in its folds.

"Let me take you home," Mr. Rutledge said. "I will inform Mrs. Barham that you felt ill and did not wish to disturb her."

"What of your partner?"

He smiled. "She had already arranged to meet someone here, someone younger and more prepossessing than I. A pleasant enough young lady, but her conversation leaves much to be desired."

"I see," said Sophia, feeling pleased. So he cared nothing for the attractive brunette. "And I doubt Lord Chumleigh will note my absence, except as it affects his chaperon duties—" She had forgotten, for the moment, why Lord Chumleigh was so solicitous of her, and she did not want to explain it to Mr. Rutledge, who knew why Lord Chumleigh's belief was completely erroneous. But he did not seem to notice her confusion.

"Wait here," he said, leaving her alone in the passageway. She still felt cold and a little sick. He had come to her rescue, albeit accidentally; he seemed genuinely remorseful about having used her; why could they not be friends again? *Because you are on the trail of Lord Endicott, and you cannot tell him that without looking obsessive and unstable.* That first great obstacle to their friendship, that he did not believe her Dream about Lord Endicott was true, reared up again like a black blot on her memory. Her cold thoughts went round and round her head: *tell him, and there will be no chance of anything between you—don't tell him, and let lies come between you—tell him, and make him see—*

"We'll go out the side way," Mr. Rutledge said, startling her. He held out her heavy pelisse and helped her put it on, letting it rest on her left shoulder rather than trying to ease her bandaged arm into its sleeve. "My carriage is waiting. Mrs. Barham is concerned, but I believe I carried my point that you are not seriously ill. I apologize for deceiving her—I hope she will not be too angry with you when she hears the truth."

"She will not be angry for long," Sophia said. "She never is."

Mr. Rutledge helped her into the carriage and settled himself opposite her after giving the driver his orders. "Are you in much pain?" he said.

"Not much."

"Is there anything else I can do for you?"

"No, thank you." Sophia sat on the edge of her seat, unable to relax. "That is two things I owe you for now."

"I haven't been keeping score. I only want to be of service to you." He looked, if not tense, then not entirely at ease, leaning forward as if he expected she might fall off the seat and he would have to catch her.

They rode in silence for a while, Sophia unable to think of anything to say. How to tell him she forgave him, when a greater secret lay between them, preventing a return to what they had once been?

"Why do you refer to Lord Chumleigh as your 'chaperon'?" Mr. Rutledge said. "Was he not a chance-won partner?"

The knot formed again in Sophia's stomach. "It is apparently common knowledge that I am nearly engaged to Lord Endicott," she said lightly, trying to make it sound like a great joke, "and as Lord Endicott's friend, Lord Chumleigh considers himself bound to protect his interests."

"What a horrible irony," Mr. Rutledge said.

Sophia said nothing. Telling him Lord Endicott had spread the rumor to torment her would do nothing but bring up the forbidden subject they had learned so well to dance around. To her horror, tears formed in her eyes. She *wanted* to tell this man the truth. She wanted him to know how she felt about him. She wanted him to share in her secret misery and give her the same comfort and support Cecy did, and she could not be honest with him.

"Something is wrong," Mr. Rutledge said. She shook her head, afraid tears would spill over with her words if she spoke, grateful for the darkness of the carriage that made him nothing more than a dim, bulky outline across from her. He leaned farther forward, enough that the lights from the street lamps illuminated his face at intervals as they passed. "Mrs. Westlake," he said, "if you can forgive me at all, I wish you would share whatever troubles you with me. I want only to be your friend."

With those last words, a barrier broke free within her. He was telling the truth, she was certain of it, but rather than reassuring her, it made her heart break. "A friend would believe better of me than the world does," she said. She was surprised at how miserable she sounded. His lack of faith in her Dreams—no, in *her*, in her reliability and honesty—wounded her more than she had realized. "A friend would not treat me with such reserve in order to maintain that friendship. I cannot tell you anything without running up against that one truth. Mr. Rutledge, I would like to be your—your friend, but I believe that is impossible."

Mr. Rutledge shifted in the darkness. "Lord Endicott. Mrs. West-lake, you yourself said it to Vane: without evidentiary proof, your Dream can have no power in a court of law."

"And of course that means it is impossible that the subject of my Dream might have had, for example, a Seer to tell him how to conceal his crime? You saw the 'lodging house' that made my Dream seem false. How can you be so intelligent and yet so blind to the clear fact that someone is trying to make me look unreliable to protect himself?"

Mr. Rutledge was silent.

"I have—" The carriage came to a lurching stop. "I have no proof yet," Sophia continued, "but I will have, and I will see Lord Endicott destroyed for what he has done to me. The reason our investigations came together is that he is the man behind the counterfeiters, Mr. Rutledge. I am certain of it, and you may consider me unstable if you like, or a liar, and that will not change the fundamental truth of the matter."

She drew a deep breath to calm herself. "I am truly grateful to you for what you have done for me. I owe you my life. But I cannot be the friend of anyone who believes me wrong when I have asserted, time and again, that I am right."

She wrenched at the carriage door; it stuck, and she wobbled, and his hand came up to steady her. She jerked her arm away and fled, furious with herself, furious at the weakness that brought tears to her eyes again. It mattered little that he had apologized, that he wanted to return to what they had been, because he did not believe her Dream, and even her love for him could not change that.

Safely in her room, she let Beeton exclaim over her injury and said only that there had been an accident, and she simply needed to sleep. But sleep was impossible. Her arm ached, her head was beginning to hurt from unshed tears, and she felt a weariness of the soul no amount of rest could cure.

King was no longer a threat to her. She thought about the possibility that he might be murdered in prison and was a little disturbed that the idea did not horrify her. With him out of the way, Lord Endicott's operation lay open to her Dreaming, and it would take her very little time to discover a way to link him to the counterfeiting. She hoped. Bow Street would not listen to her, which meant any solution would have to be one within her grasp, and that of Daphne and Cecy. She refused to be daunted by this.

She reached into the drawer of her bedside table and removed the watch fob, running her bare fingers over it to trace the faint engraving of the rose, or lily, or whatever flower it was, as the Visions swirled around her head. They made her feel ill, but she was disinclined to sit up, and she could endure a little discomfort. She sorted through Visions, watching Lord Endicott's life unfurl, until she caught a glimpse of one that endured longer than the others. She focused on it, and the nausea rose as it became stationary against a spinning background.

A game of cards—no idea which one, she was so bad at all of them she never could identify them by sight—and familiar hands, wearing the gold pinky ring incised with the Endicott arms in miniature. The hand chose a card and laid it down. Pity she was not an Extraordinary Speaker, able to send thought into the mind of anyone, Speaker or not, to tell one of Endicott's opponents what cards he held—but, of course, if she were a Speaker she could not also be an Extraordinary Seer, and her Speaking would be pointless.

She realized her thoughts were wandering aimlessly and released the Vision, then closed her eyes and willed the nausea away. Now she could watch the world through Lord Endicott's eyes. It was probably too much to hope he would go personally to the site of one of his crimes, but she would find a way to use this Vision regardless. *And I will prove to Mr. Rutledge that I am right*, she told herself, and settled in to Dream.

CHAPTER 23

IN WHICH THE LIONESS STALKS
NEW PREY, AND IS STALKED
IN TURN

Sophia sat next to Cecy and Lewis in their box at the Theatre Royal and listened with half her attention to the actress pacing the stage, lamenting that her hands would never be clean. The lackluster performance of *Macbeth* was responsible only for part of her distraction; in her heart, she was back at home, preparing to Dream yet again of the black-haired man, Lord Endicott's crony Baines. He was a handsome man, which only went to show it was impossible to tell a person's nature by his appearance. He had a face almost as well sculpted as a Shaper's, with finely arched black eyebrows and lips full enough to be attractive without being womanly, and he moved with a graceful confidence, like—*I am not thinking of Mr. Rutledge anymore.*

Sophia's initial Dreams after King's attack, the ones intended to show her in which direction success lay, had all indicated Baines was key to Lord Endicott's downfall. So she had done almost nothing for the last three days but Dream of him. She knew where he lived, or rather, had Seen a number of places where he slept, and knew the parts of London where he was most likely to be found, but every attempt she had made to predict where he might be at a particular time had been foiled by his natural ability to confound Dream. She could not even Dream of the printing press, which Lord Endicott was apparently moving often to confound her Sight, because it was Baines who determined where to move it, and her Dreams attempting to predict its location collapsed as well.

Not that it mattered. Even if she could discover where it would be at a given date and time, there was no one she could tell who might have the power to apprehend Baines or confiscate the press. It was just possible that Benjamin Vane had conveyed her statement to Sir Arthur, and that Sir Arthur might once again trust her word, but that seemed unlikely. And even if he did trust her, he would send her letters to Mr. Rutledge, and the thought of that was unbearable. She would simply have to find a way to deal with Baines, and what he represented, on her own.

It was tempting, here in the relative dimness of the box, with Cecy and Lewis's attention on the stage, to let herself drift off for just a few minutes, but Cecy would be infuriated, and even Sophia realized that behavior bordered on irrational. Besides, she was still unsettled by her most recent Dream, in which, in an attempt to approach the problem from a different direction, she had chosen a door marked with Lord Endicott's face.

She had followed him frequently in Vision these past few days, Seeing what he saw, but even when he went into the rougher parts of the city he was never in proximity to anything criminal. It frustrated her, but she kept watching, feeling vaguely guilty at how intimate her Visions were when used this way. In the past, whenever she had Seen through someone else's eyes, it was with their knowledge and consent; what she was doing now would be wrong if it were not transmuted by some alchemy of necessity into right. But it still made her feel uncomfortable in the rare times she allowed herself to think that way. Even so, Lord Endicott must be destroyed, and a little discomfort was a small price to pay for that destruction.

So when two days ago, a door of Dream appeared to her bearing his face, when she had done no meditating that might create it, she had entered it out of curiosity. It was a long, featureless hall, its walls and floor and ceiling a uniform red like dried blood, with no doors or windows. The ends of the hall in both directions disappeared into a red-streaked grey mist that moved like a curtain in an unseen wind.

Lord Endicott stood next to her, his head tilted in the attitude of someone listening for something very far away. Then he began walking.

Sophia followed him, her Dreaming self easily matching his long stride. The grey mist did not seem to be drawing nearer, and Sophia had begun to wonder if they were walking in place, when something bright came fluttering toward them. It was a butterfly, gold and green, with a wingspan the size of Sophia's two outstretched hands. Lord Endicott stopped walking and held out one hand, and the butterfly alit on his finger, slowly fanning its wings even though it was at rest. He looked at it, and Sophia was surprised at how happy he looked, as if the butterfly were the greatest gift anyone had ever bestowed on him.

Then, with the joyful expression still on his face, he took one of the butterfly's wings in his free hand and tore it off, and the butterfly screamed with Sophia's voice.

Sophia took a step backward, and the Dream shuddered as her real body reacted to her Dreaming self's shock and horror. No Dream had ever made a sound so soul-chilling before. Lord Endicott's smile became even more pleasant. He tore the other wing off, and Sophia had screamed as the butterfly did, making a discordant echo, then had thrown herself out of Dream more quickly than she ever had in her life.

Now she could not stop seeing the look on his face as he tortured that insect. There had been no cruelty, no sadism, only a cheerful, guileless pleasure, and it was far more horrifying than if he had displayed his evil in his expression. She had known he took pleasure in other people's pain, or at least he took pleasure in hers, but she had not realized he was insane, though he was good at pretending otherwise. She had seen it in his eyes more than once, but had not known to attribute that lack of human feeling to madness. Now she wondered that she could ever have believed otherwise.

She shifted as if to lean against the front of the box, remembered she was in public, and sat up straighter. *That he is not sane might explain why he is still pursuing his counterfeiting operation when the sensible thing to do would be to shut it down, now that he does not have King to protect him,* she thought. He wanted to torture her more than he cared about being sensible. The thought made Sophia feel cold, and she rubbed her arms where goose pimples had sprung up despite the warmth of the theatre, crowded with people. Who knew what kind of torment he might devise now that King was no longer available to counter her Dreams?

The sound of the tide washing on the shore translated itself into the applause of the crowd, and Sophia clapped with them, though she had not even noticed Birnam Wood come to Dunsinane, which was supposed to be very dramatic in this new production. She listened idly to Lewis and Cecy discussing the performance, which had been as much a disappointment to them as to her, and followed them through the crush of playgoers and, finally, past the portico, where they waited for the carriage to be brought round.

Revived by the crisp winter air, Sophia began planning another foray into Dream that night. *Only one Dream*, she assured herself, but her frustration at being balked yet again was translating once again into more frequent Dreaming, and she had to remind herself she had promised Cecy not to overextend. Still, she had only Dreamed twice today, and a third would not be excessive. But what Dream? Dreaming of Baines only made her more frustrated, but she knew in her bones there *was* a way to circumvent his infuriating ability, if only she could approach it properly. She was afraid to Dream of Lord Endicott again, and Dreaming of lesser things, like the location of forged banknotes, only made her impatient.

The press of people was increasing rather than decreasing, and Sophia was about to suggest they move to a more sheltered corner when Cecy staggered, then began to turn to look behind her, and Sophia grabbed her and pulled her to one side before her rational mind fully comprehended the danger: the man standing behind Cecy, a perfectly ordinary-looking man except for the large knife in his hand, was lunging at her with his arm outstretched.

Sophia screamed, causing Lewis to look around at them, and the attacker slashed at Cecy's stomach. More screams erupted from the crowd as others saw her assailant. Both Sophia and Cecy took several steps backward, stumbling as they ran into other people who shoved them back toward the knife-wielding man in their own attempts to get away. It was like being caught by a tide that flowed in all directions at once, and Sophia tried to keep hold of Cecy, afraid of what might happen if they were torn apart.

Lewis roared something, and flung himself at his wife's assailant, Shaping himself as he went. Muscles flexed against the fabric of his coat and his knee breeches as his body responded to his need for strength and agility, and he flung people out of his way as if they were dolls whose well-being he had no care for. Sophia saw the attacker's expression go from an eerie dispassion to stunned horror; he threw down the knife and began pushing his way through the crowd, trying to escape an enraged Lewis.

"Sophia, I don't feel well," Cecy said, grabbing at the front of Sophia's fur-lined pelisse and bearing Sophia down with her as she collapsed on the street. Her face in the light of the lamps turning the theatre's façade yellow-white was pale, her pupils dilated, and Sophia's throat felt suddenly tight. She searched Cecy's body for injury and found none, though a long tear in the back of her coat left her breathless and lightheaded with fear. She put her arms around Cecy, who clung to her, breathing heavily. "I feel so dizzy," Cecy added, very quietly, as if words were too difficult to produce.

"You are uninjured, dearest, this is nothing but the shock of being attacked," Sophia said, easing her friend into a more comfortable position and waving away men and women who crowded around. "No, she will be well, it is nothing," she told them, "please do not try to lift her, she only needs air."

The crowd diminished not at all. *So many people, gawking at the spectacle*, Sophia thought, and raised her left hand high, fingers spread wide, and heard the murmuring change tone as the spectators registered the red glove. "*Back away now*," she shouted, and finally they heeded her, and Sophia and Cecy were at the center of a rapidly widening empty circle of pavement.

"These ridiculous things are useful for something," she told Cecy, who nodded. She was breathing slowly in a manner that told Sophia she was using all her concentration to remain conscious. Sophia held her tighter and wished Lewis had not gone after the attacker; they needed to take Cecy home immediately, call Dr. Garland, put her to bed and pray she would not have an episode after all this.

The crowd shifted to reveal Lewis, moving more slowly now and breathing easily. "The fiend must know this area well," he said, "because he certainly could not outrun me, but I lost track of him after only three turns. Cecilia, darling, look at me. Sophia, did he injure her?"

Sophia shook her head. "She is simply overwhelmed. Where is the carriage? It cannot possibly take this long for Peter to return!"

"I'll find him." Lewis stretched and made a pained face. His body was returning to its usual proportions, but he would pay for his too-rapid transformation with exhaustion and severe muscle aches and cramps tomorrow. By the look on his face when he looked at his suffering wife, it was a debt he did not regret incurring. He strode off into the crowd, which made way for him almost as quickly as they had for the red gloves; none of the people he had shoved aside seemed inclined to complain to him about it.

Sophia rubbed the back of Cecy's neck and helped her stay upright, though by the time Lewis returned, she was leaning less heavily on Sophia and her color had started to return.

"I feel so foolish," she said when they were all in the carriage. "It is not as if he hurt me."

"It was terrifying, and your reaction was perfectly normal," Sophia said.

"I wish I'd caught the coward. I cannot believe he was able to attack you in public like that. What could have possessed him?" Lewis said.

Sophia looked across at Cecy where she was tucked under Lewis's arm. "I do not believe it was a random attack," she said.

"Not—" Lewis sat up straighter. "You mean Lord Endicott might have been behind it?"

"Except I cannot imagine why he would attack Cecy," Sophia said. "He cannot possibly know her involvement."

"He knows we are friends," Cecy said.

Sophia thought of the dismembered butterfly, and once again felt colder than the weather warranted. "He meant to torture me," she said. "Killing you, Cecy—he knows what that would do to me, not only your death but your death as retaliation for my attacks on him. He would rather see me suffer than protect his enterprise, or that blade would have been aimed at me."

"He is a monster," Cecy said.

"Yes, and a monster with power," Sophia said. "He knows where to strike at me. Cecy, we cannot continue."

"What? Sophia, after everything we have done, to let him go unpunished?"

"What else am I to do? Your life is far more important."

"We can protect me. I do not go out often, and Lewis is strong and alert to any danger. I will simply never be alone in places where a stranger can approach me."

"My love, you know I would do anything to protect you, but I believe Sophia is right," Lewis said. "Lord Endicott's crimes will not go unnoticed forever. Someone will bring him to justice."

I should be that someone, Sophia thought, but said, "Cecy, we have already struck many blows at him. We can let this rest."

Cecy abruptly turned her head to look out the window. "Then he has made me his tool," she said, her voice furious.

"What? No, Cecy—"

"Then what else would you call it? His hostage? His weapon? I refuse to let him use me like that. I am not a *thing*, to be used to do evil against my will. I am so often helpless because of my condition, and he would make me even more so. No, Sophia, we are not giving up this fight. You will Dream to learn if Lord Endicott intends to make more attempts on my life, and we will act on those Dreams, and Lord Endicott will be brought to justice by us. And if you try to give up out of some ridiculous idea of protecting me, Daphne and I will simply continue without you."

"Daphne would never be so foolish." Even as the words escaped her lips, Sophia knew they were false. Daphne lived for being that kind of foolish. "And if she were," she went on quickly, seeing Cecy shaping a retort, "I am certain I could argue... never mind."

"You see? I am invariably logical when I am right."

"Lewis, talk sense into her," Sophia said.

Lewis was quiet for a while. Then he said, "I believe this endeavor of yours has just become ten times as dangerous as it was. I also believe there is no reason to believe Lord Endicott will leave off tormenting you, and threatening the ones you love, simply because you stop pursuing him. As dangerous as trying to destroy his organization is, it will likely be more dangerous to leave him free to commit whatever crimes he chooses. I can protect Cecilia. You three should continue as you have been."

"Lewis, if he manages to kill Cecy—"

"Don't you believe you will be able to predict when the next attack comes? Sophia, this is the only sensible thing to do."

Sophia leaned back in her seat and sighed. "All right," she said. "But at the moment I feel doubly discouraged. I still do not know how to break past Baines' resistance."

"You have only been trying for three days," Cecy said. "Give it time."

"I am afraid time is something we do not have," Sophia said.

CHAPTER 24

IN WHICH SOPHIA HAS TWO
UNSATISFACTORY ENCOUNTERS

Sophia did not need to enter the door with King's face superimposed upon it to know what it held. She laid her palm against it anyway. She was in some sense responsible for his fate, though she felt no guilt—he was, after all, a criminal, and a despicable man—and it seemed fitting she should witness his end.

Am I so inured to violence, she thought, looking at his body, dangling from a makeshift rope attached to nothing, *that I am neither disgusted nor horrified by this? But it gives me no pleasure, either. I wonder how long it will take his victims to realize they are free?* Had Lord Endicott found a way to silence his now inconvenient Seer, or had King chosen this way out to avoid a more public humiliation and death? In either case, he could no longer indict Lord Endicott, which left Sophia's nemesis free to continue his campaign to torment her.

"King is dead," she told Lewis and Cecy at the breakfast table.

"Was it murder?" Cecy asked.

"I don't know. That seems likely. I wonder if Lord Endicott feels safer now?"

"He is not safe as long as you are on his trail," Lewis said. "It worries me that he has not made another attack in the last three days."

"We have gone nowhere but to church in the last three days," Cecy pointed out, "and I believe he is not yet desperate enough to send marauders into our home."

"You have just given me the most appalling image," Sophia said. "Is that something we should fear?"

Lewis cleared his throat. "That has already occurred to me," he said, "and I have gone over the house with Traviss and the footmen, ensuring the locks are secure and the ground floor windows are firmly barred. I have told the staff only that I have heard rumors of burglaries in nearby neighborhoods and am taking precautions. But I'm afraid they have heard some of our conversations—I don't know what they make of them, but they already know I will not tolerate gossip, so I believe we need not worry that news of our actions will spread. At any rate, we are proof against a casual attempt at forced entry, and if it comes to it, I will hire protection."

"I'm glad you are thinking along those lines, because I certainly was not," Sophia said. It frightened her that she had been so focused on her efforts to predict Baines' movements that she had forgotten about the need for such basic precautions. "Thank you, Lewis."

"It's for my own peace of mind as anything else," Lewis said. "Though I'm vain enough to want this all settled soon. This new form is so unfamiliar I feel I hardly know myself."

"I believe you look wonderful no matter what form you take," Cecy said. Lewis smiled and shook his head. Sophia privately agreed with Cecy; Lewis was taller now by an inch or so, and broader in the chest and shoulders, and his muscles were larger and more well defined, though his new wardrobe mostly concealed the latter. He looked perfectly capable of throwing an intruder through a second-story window without straining himself.

"Then you will escort us to Lord and Lady Ormerod's ball tonight?" Cecy continued.

"I will, and I hope you appreciate the sacrifice, as you know I dislike dancing."

"You danced often with me, when we first met, and I believe you are an excellent dancer."

Lewis winked at Cecy. "But now I have caught you, and need not dance anymore."

"Then we are perfectly matched, for I do not enjoy dancing either. Sophia will have to dance enough for the three of us."

"That is quite a burden to bear," Sophia said, "but I will try not to be overwhelmed by it."

⚜

THREE GLITTERING CHANDELIERS CAST THEIR BRILLIANT LIGHT OVER Lord Ormerod's spacious ballroom, with its high *trompe l'oeil* ceiling rimmed with gold and the windows turned into mirrors by that light. Sophia admired her pale, wavering reflection in one of those windows; the yellow tint to the light turned her hair bronze and her red gown dark orange. She adjusted her hem and turned away, wondering if anyone had seen her moment of vanity, and realized she didn't care if they had.

She felt unaccountably cheerful tonight—yes, Cecy was probably still in danger, and Sophia was still unable to predict Baines's movements or find the printing press, and she would still be the center of uncomfortable attention tonight, but for some reason she was undisturbed by these realities. She had gained many more acquaintances since her arrival in London last September, women she could converse with, men she could dance with. Her worries could take themselves off elsewhere for the night.

"Mrs. Westlake, how do you do this evening?" Lady Ormerod held out a hand for Sophia to take. She was a tall woman garbed elegantly in rust-colored velvet the mirrored windows would no doubt turn orange. "I am so pleased to welcome you here tonight."

"Thank you for the invitation, Lady Ormerod," Sophia said. "Your home is so beautiful."

"Lord Ormerod is very proud of his art collection," Lady Ormerod said. "I must warn you, he intends to ask you to exert your influence on Mr. Barham to induce him to part with that scrimshaw he so admired on our last visit. Please do not be offended."

"I am never offended by Lord Ormerod. He is always so affable," Sophia said. "Though he will be disappointed, as I know Mr. Barham is very fond of that piece."

"Well, Lord Ormerod will simply have to master his disappointment," Lady Ormerod said with a smile that to anyone else would have looked disdainful; Sophia had known the viscountess long enough to be aware that her Ladyship's long nose and narrow eye gave her an appearance that, combined with her tendency toward formality, made her seem haughtier than she was.

"I know you dislike having a fuss made over you," Lady Ormerod continued, hooking her arm through Sophia's and drawing her closer so as to speak into her ear, "but I thought you would not mind if I made *one* arrangement for your benefit."

"That is so kind of you! What arrangement—or is it to be a secret?"

"Not a secret from you, of course. I can see how you might want your privacy protected. No one will know I made a particular effort to invite Lord Endicott here tonight."

Sophia's cheerful buoyancy turned to lead. "Lord Endicott?" she managed.

"And I am *so* pleased for you, my dear. After your husband's death—well, we need not speak of it further. I assure you no one will hear anything of your attachment from me until you are ready to make it public."

"But—Lady Ormerod, where did *you* hear it?"

Lady Ormerod smiled at her again, and this time Sophia could not help but see it as a sneer. "I do have eyes, Mrs. Westlake. Lord Endicott pays you the most particular attention whenever you are together, and he never so much as smiles pleasantly on any of the women who try to catch his eye. Though I should warn you, my dear, you should moderate your appearance of indifference to him. Keeping a secret is one thing, but one might almost believe you dislike him!"

"I... will remember that, Lady Ormerod."

So Lord Endicott would be here. Sophia's first impulse was to find Cecy and flee. Meeting him under these conditions was intolerable. Then Sophia met Lady Ormerod's eyes again. The woman was so innocently pleased for Sophia that she became infuriated. It was one thing for Lord Endicott to torment her, but now he was drawing her friends into his ruse. Lady Ormerod did not deserve to be used so. "Thank you for thinking so kindly of me."

"Oh, it's nothing, really. Lord Endicott is a pleasant guest. I only wish I could feel I had made the match myself. Did you know Lord Ormerod's cousin, the Earl of Enderleigh, met Lady Enderleigh for the first time here in our home? Though I don't know that I had anything to do with that either, but it *is* so exciting to see love blossom, is it not?"

Sophia nodded, and let herself smile—a real smile, though not caused by the simple emotion Lady Ormerod no doubt believed it was. "I look forward to this evening with great pleasure," she said.

And it was a great pleasure. She moved through the ballroom, greeting acquaintances and friends with a restored good cheer, allowing herself to be amused rather than angry at the thought that many of them, like Lady Ormerod, believed her in love with Lord Endicott. What would he do if she avowed the truth of their "engagement"? *He is insane; he would likely do something unexpected and mad.* This cooled her amusement somewhat. He had tried to have Cecy killed; he had ruined Sophia's reputation with the War Office; he might do anything to protect himself. He was dangerous, and she needed to remember that. But she would not let fear prevent her from destroying him.

She danced, and danced again, and while moving through the steps of the third dance saw Lord Endicott in the crowd, watching her. He had Shaped his face to show a subtle blend of emotions—desire, admiration, and a hint of sorrow. It was the perfect expression of unrequited love. The absurdity of their situation struck her for the first time, and as she passed near him, she bestowed a brilliant smile on him that made his expression wobble. He thought to discomfit her tonight. She would turn his ploy against him.

When the dance was over, Sophia returned to Cecy's side, fanning herself with her hand and laughing harder than was warranted over something her partner had said. Cecy gave her a dubious look, and said, "You are far too cheerful tonight—" Then her gaze passed beyond Sophia, and she clutched at her gown, saying in a low voice, " 'Ware the enemy—"

"Mrs. Westlake, good evening," Lord Endicott said. "Mrs. Barham, such a pleasure to see you well."

"Good *evening*, my lord!" Sophia exclaimed. "I had no idea you would be here! Such a pleasant surprise." She took his hand before he could offer it to her. "It seems we never see one another anymore."

"No—that is, I have not had the pleasure recently," Lord Endicott said. He sounded not at all startled by Sophia's aggressive friendliness. "Dare I hope this means you will dance with me?"

"I would like nothing better," Sophia declared, and patted his hand in an affectionate way. A brief scowl distorted his handsome features, so swiftly Sophia doubted anyone but herself had seen it. Then he smiled again and led her to where the dancers were taking their places.

"I cannot tell you how my heart is warmed by your enthusiastic welcome," he said as the music began. "You know my only desire is for you to think well of me."

"Oh, my lord, I believe you know what I think of you," Sophia said. "As I know your feelings toward me."

"Then we should both be happy in that... security."

"Indeed. Though I wonder you can feel happy, given the loss you have so recently endured."

He raised his eyebrows at her. "Loss?"

"Why, Elias King, of course. His death must have been a tremendous blow."

"You are mistaken. I know no Elias King."

"No? I must be thinking of someone else."

"It is no matter. I have always forgiven you your mistakes."

"Yes, you have, and I am so grateful to you for that generosity. You, of course, make no mistakes." She smiled at him, and his calm expression slipped again, this time showing his confusion. What did he believe she knew? How many of his secrets did he believe she held?

"I like to believe I am honest enough to admit to mistakes when I make them," he said.

"Very honorable, my lord. So do you admit to having made a mistake two nights ago? Playing that jack when you should have played the ten? That cost you a not inconsiderable sum."

Lord Endicott went completely expressionless. "I do not understand you," he said, his lips barely moving.

"Not that I know anything of cards," Sophia continued, "but Lord

Chumleigh certainly seemed pleased to benefit from your mistake. I believe that new waistcoat of his is an unfortunate shade of puce, don't you? It makes him look so sallow."

His face looked pale in the bright yellow light. "How odd that you should have heard that trivial story," he said.

"It is not hearing I speak of. As I'm sure you know."

"You Dream of me, then? It gives me joy to know you care for me in that small way."

"You are my great preoccupation these days, my lord. Well, you and one other."

"I am devastated to know I have not your undivided attention. Who is this other?"

Sophia smiled and shook her head. "No one you know, I am certain. He is tall and black-haired, handsome—though not as handsome as you, my lord—and wears a silver ring. I find his movements most interesting."

"I believe you should stop Dreaming of him. You wouldn't want me to become jealous, would you? I might do anything if I thought I were slipping in your estimation."

"That almost sounded like a threat, my lord."

"Of course not. I simply wish to maintain a place in your heart. I cannot bear your teasing, your sometime coldness." The look of Unrequited Love was back.

"Oh, but my... did you say 'coldness'? My coldness conceals a very different feeling. As I'm sure you know."

"I wish I could know what you were thinking. It would certainly influence my actions."

"As my knowledge of you shapes mine. I feel I know you better every day. It's as if we See as one." Sophia smiled again, and Lord Endicott went expressionless again. Did he understand what she was saying? She wanted to take him by the ears and scream *If you hurt my friend, I will stab you through the heart as you sleep*. She would have to settle for oblique hints and warnings. If she had to follow him in Vision every day for the next month to bring him down, she would do it without regret.

They danced in silence for the rest of their dance and half of the next. Lord Endicott had regained his look of forlorn hopelessness, that sad smile that no doubt had every woman in the room wishing she could be the one to make it disappear. Sophia felt utterly satisfied. Now he knew she no longer feared him, and if he were as intelligent as she guessed, he knew she could follow him in Vision. Who knew what he thought she might witness?

"We spoke of hunting, some weeks ago," Lord Endicott said, startling her. "Do you still have an interest?"

"I do, my lord, more than ever," Sophia said.

"Then you recall what I said about the prey turning on the hunter."

"You said other predators are the most likely to savage the hunter, as I recall."

"So you *do* remember. I was under the impression you had forgotten that lesson."

"Not at all, my lord. I have a healthy respect for predators. Or, that is, I would have, if I were a hunter."

"It is fortunate for you that you are not, I daresay."

"Why is that, my lord?"

Lord Endicott's eyes met hers, and Sophia felt a little faint, because his eyes were empty of anything remotely human. "Because I believe you would be the sort of hunter whose pursuit of one foe blinds her to the approach of another, more dangerous one."

"I... believe you are mistaken." She felt like a vixen caught by the hound and backed into a corner; she was afraid to look away from those terrifying eyes.

"If I am, I will be the first to admit it." He smiled, then, and winked at her, his face once again displaying Unrequited Love. Sophia's good cheer evaporated. She had been a fool. *He is mad,* she told herself, *what made you think defying him would provoke a reasonable reaction?* She had wanted only to show him she was not so easily deterred, but now —he might do anything. She cursed herself, and knew her turmoil was visible to him, because he smiled more broadly at her, escorted her back to Cecy when their dances were finished, and kissed her hand, gripping it to keep her from pulling it away from him in a way that told Sophia he knew very well he was making her miserable.

He will not drive me away this time, she told herself, and danced every dance until she was certain her feet were bleeding and her shoes were about to fall apart. She wished she knew what everyone else thought of her interaction with Lord Endicott. Had she made it appear as if their secret engagement were a certainty? She had been a fool all around, tonight, and were it not for her desire not to give Lord Endicott the satisfaction of making her flee, and her reluctance to hurt Lady Ormerod's feelings, she would have left early, gone back to her bed and begun Dreaming again. The need to prove Lord Endicott's guilt had just become more urgent.

She deflected a would-be dance partner and escaped the ballroom, hunting for a place she might be alone for a few minutes, preferably somewhere cooler than the overheated, overcrowded room. How had her life come to this? Was she to spend the rest of her days drifting from ballroom to drawing room to theatre, one tedious round with no variation?

She opened a door and was rewarded with a cold breeze scented with snow. Outside was a small garden, incongruous here in the heart of the city, with little more than a few bare hedges and some empty flowerbeds, waiting for the promise of spring that seemed so far away now. Sophia inhaled the chilly air and felt as if it were blowing away layers of horrible clinging soot, the remnants of her conversation with Lord Endicott. She was close to bringing her quarry down, and however he tried to escape her, whatever the attack he brought, she would be the victor.

She shut the door and went back toward the ballroom, her footsteps dragging. Surely they had stayed long enough to satisfy the demands of good manners? She turned out of the narrow hall that led from the back door and nearly bumped into someone large—

"Mr. Rutledge," she said, so startled that her heart began pounding as if he'd leaped out at her.

"I beg your pardon, Mrs. Westlake," he said. He took a step back, but made no further movement.

"I... did not realize you were here," she said.

"I was a rather late arrival."

Sophia couldn't think of a reply to this. Her heart would not stop pounding. He was looking in her direction, but his eyes were focused on a point just past her head; why would he not look at her directly? "I was about to take my leave of our hosts," she said.

"Then I am glad to have spoken with you before you left," he replied.

"As am I." She had to repress the desire to turn and look behind her, to see what he found so fascinating.

"Are you?" Now his eyes met hers, with that uncomfortable directness she nevertheless could not look away from. "You seemed to wish nothing more to do with me when last we met."

Once again she was left without a reply. It was true, and yet so untrue she felt inclined to laugh, which would no doubt sound hysterical. "It is not I who am the barrier to our friendship," she finally said.

"So you said." It seemed a conclusion, but still he made no move to continue on toward the ballroom. What more did he want from her? She found herself perilously close to tears, and could not understand how he could so often have that effect on her. He didn't believe her; why should she allow his opinion to matter to her at all?

"I should join Cecy," she said. She made as if to pass him, only to be stopped by his hand on her arm. He was not trying to restrain her; she could have pulled away from him easily. Instead she half-turned to look up at him. His touch reminded her of the night he had brought her home from the Duchess of Lenshire's house, and how he had supported her in her weakness, and she blushed hotly until it felt as if her entire body was trying to ignite at the memory of how comforting his embrace was.

He looked as if he were searching for something to say, and she waited, feeling as if whatever it was would be the perfect words to sweep away all the misunderstanding and bad feeling between them and make everything right again. She would settle for friendship if she could have nothing more from him, if friendship were even possible—

He released her arm. "I apologize," he said, "I should not—good evening, Mrs. Westlake."

"Good evening, Mr. Rutledge," she said, turning quickly away so he would not see the ridiculous tears welling up in her eyes. She was a fool. There was nothing he could say that would change what had passed between them. It was stupid of her to believe otherwise. Stupid of her to long for his touch again.

She wandered the hall between the front door and the ballroom, admiring the art, until she was certain her nose and eyes were no longer red. Cecy had always been able to cry without ruining her face, and Sophia envied her as she never had before. Finally she went back into the ballroom and found Cecy and Lewis, talking to Lord Ormerod. The tall, potbellied man brightened when he saw her, and exclaimed, "Mrs. Westlake! I cannot believe we have not spoken tonight. Will you come to see me in three days' time? I am about to purchase some Greek marbles and would like to test their provenance. I'm afraid I don't trust the seller very much."

"Of course, Lord Ormerod, I would be happy to. But I must bid you farewell, if Mr. and Mrs. Barham don't mind," Sophia said.

"We were just saying our goodbyes as well, Sophy," Cecy said. "Thank you again, Lord Ormerod, and good evening."

In the carriage, Sophia said, "I hope that was not a polite fib on my behalf, Cecy."

"It was not," Cecy said. By the light of the passing lamps Sophia could see her face was now pinched with pain. "I am not too badly off, Sophy, you can stop giving me that look. I thought it best to leave before I was."

"Such sensibleness," Lewis teased, drawing Cecy close. Jealousy, hot and sharp like a knife straight from the forge, struck Sophia so hard and so unexpectedly that she flinched, then chastised herself. She had no need to be jealous of what Lewis and Cecy had. *You want that,* she told herself, and once again self-pitying tears began to rise.

What an awful night this had been. Taunting Lord Endicott into who knew what kind of retaliation. Meeting Mr. Rutledge with such unsatisfactory results. And now pining over something she would never have. She would go straight to bed, no Dreaming for her tonight, and in the morning she would be sensible again. She stared out the carriage window, blinking, until her vision was once again clear.

But in the morning, she was groggy and tired, as if she had spent the night in Dream. She lay there, hoping the feeling would go away, but it only pressed down on her more oppressively. Eventually she sat up and rang for Beeton. She would eat something more substantial than her usual morning chocolate, then try to sleep again and perhaps it would clear her mind.

The door flew open. "Sophy, you must see this," Cecy said, rushing at her with a newspaper in her hand. She flung it down across Sophia's lap. "There, just there. Oh, what will we do?"

Sophia smoothed out the paper, which had been slightly crushed in Cecy's hand. At first she saw nothing that might have caused Cecy such distress. Then, in letters much larger than the surrounding print, she read: SEER, OR FRAUD?? *Mrs. Sophia Westlake, Extraordinary Seer, of Hanover Square, is famed for the accuracy and completeness of her Sight—or is she? It is confirmed that Mrs. Westlake was expelled from service with the War Office, having falsely accused an unnamed party of embezzlement and insisting on his punishment, despite there being no evidence to support her claims. Such an accusation can only lead*

Sophia could read no further. Her vision went grey around the edges, and she clutched the paper, crushing it further. Dimly she heard Cecy crying her name, grasping her shoulders and shaking her, hard, but she felt powerless to stop her. "I should have known he would do this," she said. Her voice sounded very faint, so she said, more loudly, "I suppose we should be happy; we must be very close, now." She clutched at Cecy's arms and let Cecy rock her while she stared, unseeing, into the distance.

CHAPTER 25

IN WHICH THERE IS SOME
DISCUSSION OF MADNESS

"It is a very small story; perhaps no one will see it," Sophia said. She unfolded the paper to reveal the heading, and felt sick. "*The Times*. Well, of course no one we know will read *that* rag." She began to laugh, frightening the tiny part of her that was still rational with how mad she sounded.

"Sophia, please don't—" Cecy said, hugging her tightly. Sophia clutched at her friend and tried to control her hysteria. "It is merely allegation. How dare they print 'confirmed' when they do not dare print Lord Endicott's name? No one who knows you will believe it on the strength of this alone."

"You are so optimistic. It is in the paper; of course everyone will believe it. This is my fault. I should never have taunted him. I thought... but apparently whatever the War Office did to induce him to remain silent was not powerful enough. Oh, Cecy." She wanted to weep, but no tears came. Later, perhaps, when the whispering began, and the notes uninviting her to dinner parties arrived, and her supposed friends turned their backs on her.

"This is not the end. You said it yourself. We must be close, to make him panic like this. The War Office will know he released the story, and they will wonder why he did so now, after so much time has passed, and they will—"

"Lord Endicott is not the only person who knows of it. They will believe some other person revealed the truth, possibly in exchange for money."

"But—oh. You are right." Cecy took her by the shoulders and shook her again, gently this time. "We have to prove Lord Endicott's crime!"

"And I have no idea how."

Cecy stood. "Breakfast first," she said. "I don't care how early it is, we need fortification. And then you will learn to track Baines."

"I can't—"

"It is past time for 'can't', Sophy. You found the pirates not because you are an Extraordinary Seer, but because you applied your understanding to the problem. You must stop trying to Dream a way past his defenses and use your intellect instead."

Sophia gaped at her. "Cecy, you are not only an optimist, you are a hopeless one. What makes you believe I can succeed?"

"Because I have faith in you, of course," Cecy said. "Now, dress, and join me at the table. You will tell me what you know of the mechanisms of Dream, and I will ask stupid questions that force you to understand it better." She shut the door behind her with a ferocity that matched her demeanor.

Sophia shut her mouth. Gaping like a startled child would not solve her problem. She rang again for Beeton and began searching her wardrobe for her favorite morning gown. If she were to be excoriated in the court of public opinion, she intended to be comfortable doing so.

She had trouble eating; her stomach insisted it was too anxious for food. She forced down a few bites of toast and some tea that soothed her fears somewhat. "What did you mean by 'stupid questions'?" she said to Cecy, whose appetite was unusually good.

"I meant that, as I know almost nothing of how Dream works, my questions will no doubt have obvious answers—obvious to you," Cecy said with her mouth half-full of sausage. "But I believe you need to look at the problem from the beginning. For example: what makes Dreaming possible?"

"You ask a question with no answer. Extraordinary Shapers surmise that Dream originates in the brain rather than the heart or liver or some other organ, but no Shaper can see inside the brain to determine what about a Seer's brain is different from anyone else's."

"You must at least have some ideas, though."

"We know Dreams are not a prediction of what *will* be, because they can be altered or eliminated if the correct action is taken. But you already know that, since King did it to me."

"I don't understand how he was able to do that."

"He meditated on what Dream I would have, then took action to ensure that Dream could not occur. Cecy—"

"I told you they would be stupid questions. Could you not have meditated to know which Dream he would See, then choose a different Dream?"

"It doesn't work that way." But as she said this, she wondered whether it were true or not. The question resonated with her. "King's meditation would have... or possibly not... I don't know, Cecy. I've never tried it before."

"A pity King is dead, or you could test that theory."

"Yes. I never thought I would regret his death in any way. But it is irrelevant. It is not another Seer I have to thwart; it is someone whose movements are unpredictable." Sophia pushed herself back from the table. "And no one has ever done that before."

"Yet," Cecy said, mirroring her. "No one has done it before *yet.* Just think—you will be responsible for two of the greatest discoveries about Sight ever!"

Sophia laughed, but her heart was growing heavy again. It had taken her weeks to discover the secret of the generalized focus, and might take more than that to learn how to overcome Baines' resistance. If the law determined her actions against her "unnamed party" constituted a misuse of her Seer's talent, she would be doing that discovery in prison.

They went to Cecy's drawing room, Cecy chattering as animatedly as Daphne ever dreamed of being along the way. "Then explain to me how Baines' movements cannot be predicted," she said.

Sophia settled into the uncomfortable chair. She had become fond of it, how it kept her from becoming complacent; it was like an eagle's perch, putting her high above the confounding movement of everyday life where she could See to the ends of the earth, or at least to the outer boroughs of London. "If I knew that—really knew it—then his ability would not interfere with my Sight," she said. "It is as if he never makes a decision about the future until he is in it, or perhaps he is capable of holding several possibilities in his head at once, never settling on any of them until it is too late for Dream to have any meaning. It is a type of thinking often seen in those whose minds are not whole, but I do not believe him mad."

"But you can Dream of Lord Endicott, and he is certainly mad."

"It is not the same. The reality Lord Endicott sees may not be a true one, but it is coherent."

"I understand. Possibly."

There was a *whoosh* of displaced air, and Daphne said, "Did you see —oh, I see you have. I could kill Lord Endicott right now, I swear! Don't you agree?"

"I am not so murderous as you, but yes," Sophia said. "Sit down, Daphne. How on earth were you able to Bound here?"

"I told you, it is all a matter of learning the essence of a place, for an Extraordinary Bounder," Daphne said, throwing herself down onto the chaise longue and stretching her legs out. She was wearing her Bounder uniform and looked as if she had recently been out of doors, with her too-pink cheeks and slightly disordered curls. "And I certainly know this place well enough now, after all the time we have spent in it. I have to work today, but I thought I would come and tell you my plan before I started."

"I feel as if an unstoppable boulder is racing down a hill toward this house," Sophia said. "What plan?"

Daphne grinned. "I told mama I'd heard the unnamed party was Lord Endicott."

"Why did you do that?" Cecy exclaimed.

"Why shouldn't we? You both know Lord Endicott is the one who sent that story to *The Times,* or was behind whoever did send it. So if he wanted his name kept out of it, he must have had a reason, and that means we should make sure everyone who reads the story knows the truth. People will want to know why he has paid such devoted, loving attention to Sophia if she tried to have him arrested as an embezzler. That will throw the whole thing into confusion. Today I will tell everyone to whom I make a delivery the same rumor, claiming that of course it's just a rumor and can't possibly be true. I believe the news will get around London faster than I can Skip from here to Bath. Did I tell you I missed the record by only four minutes and ten seconds this time?"

"Daphne, that's too reckless!" Sophia said, then buried her face in her hands.

"No, I believe she's right," said Cecy. "At the very least it will make people question the veracity of the story."

"I think you have both run mad," Sophia said, raising her head.

"Then we are in good company with Lord Endicott," Daphne said. She leaped off the chaise longue and stretched. "I will return later this afternoon, certainly before five o'clock, to tell you of my progress. And *you,* Sophia, will not fall into despair. Lord Endicott must positively be shaking in his shoes to try something like this."

"That is what I said," Cecy said.

"You see? And we are both very sensible. Find Baines, Sophia." With a *pop,* she was gone.

Sophia massaged her temples. "I cannot now remember what we were talking about."

"You were telling me about the difference between Baines and Lord Endicott."

"Well." Sophia settled herself more firmly. "Lord Endicott is the kind of man who sees the world clearly, but only as he believes it should be. It is not impossible that he genuinely believes he loves me, which is a horrible thought I wish I had not entertained. Baines is—it is as if, in his mind, the world is fractured, and any one reality might be true at any given time. So he keeps switching between them, and Sight does not... I say 'does not know,' but of course Sight has no intelligence to 'know' anything. But it is as good a metaphor as any. Sight does not know which reality he will act on until he has already acted on it. I can clearly Dream Baines' past, just not his future."

"But he must act eventually. Couldn't you try to Dream of those actions?"

Sophia shook her head. "That only—" She stopped, arrested in mid-sentence by an unexpected thought. "Suppose he... suppose we are trying to find the press," she said. "Suppose I attempt to Dream of where he will move it. That Dream will fall apart because Baines makes the decision. But the press must end up somewhere. It can't be in all the possible places at once. If I... no, that wouldn't work."

"What wouldn't?"

"It would still be looking for a Dream of where the press will be. But—Cecy, I need a map of London. A big one that shows even the smaller streets."

"I will ask Lewis if he has one, and if not, I will send him to purchase one immediately," Cecy said. She stood, wincing, and Sophia said, "Cecy, you are not well."

"I am well enough for this. Do not treat me like an invalid, please." She left the room, and Sophia sat back in her chair and thought. She would have to do a good deal of Dreaming, and Cecy would object, but if she insisted on pushing herself despite her pain, she could hardly criticize Sophia for doing the same. Cecy was right; Sophia should have been using her intellect to track Baines, should have gathered more information before resorting to Dream.

She leaped from her seat and ran to her room for one of her note-books and a fresh pencil. Why had she not remembered all the pages and pages of notes that had preceded her discovery of Rhys Evans' secret? If she were lucky, that memory would not be too late to help her now.

"Where did you go?" Cecy said when Sophia returned to the drawing room. Lewis had joined them and was holding a large roll of paper.

"We need to pin this to the wall," Sophia said, casting about for a suitable place.

"I guessed as much," Lewis said, waving a little box at her. "If you will remove those paintings, I will try to control my curiosity long enough to put this up."

Sophia had never realized how many paintings and portraits and miniatures covered the walls of Cecy's drawing room. They piled more than a dozen of them against the wall beneath the map Lewis pinned up. It was an excellent map, rendered in great detail, though as she looked at it she realized they probably only needed the southern half of it. Then she reminded herself she should not make assumptions where Baines was concerned.

"I will have to have several Dreams, Cecy," she said, settling herself on the chaise longue, "and I know you will object to that, but we both know how urgent this is."

Cecy nodded. "What are you looking for?"

"The past," Sophia said. "I realized I have not been thinking clearly. Even Lord Endicott does not control every piece of property, every warehouse in London. Baines only has so many places he can move the press to. It is unlikely he will have developed a pattern, but I believe knowing where the press has been, and when it has been there, may show us something we can use."

"That could mean many Dreams," Lewis said.

"I hope it does not," Sophia said, and settled herself in to meditate, her hands over her heart and navel. *Find me a starting place,* she told her mind, and dropped into Dream.

CHAPTER 26

IN WHICH SOPHIA MAKES USE OF HER INTELLECT

Half a dozen doors circled her, each bearing the hazy, spidery shape of the press she had grown so familiar with. A door thus marked, she knew from long experimentation, revealed one of the press's locations, but none of these bore any indication as to which held the first, original, location of the press. Sophia wanted to scream with frustration, batter down all the doors and force them to show her what she wanted to know. Her sleeping self quivered with her Dreaming self's emotion, and she made herself relax. Anger would not solve her problem.

She walked toward one of the doors and saw the image on its surface sharpen and come into focus. Perhaps she would have more success if she knew what a printing press actually looked like. The idea turned her anger into despondency; she knew of only one person who might be able to provide her access to a press, and he... She made herself relax once more. Thinking of Mr. Rutledge would not solve her problem, either.

She examined the image minutely and discovered a blotch about the size of a penny across its lower left corner. *Strange.* It should either have resolved itself as the rest of the image did, or disappeared entirely. She bent to look more closely at it and saw, as if through a thick layer of gauze, the number 6. She took a step backward and looked at the door, then turned to look at the one next to it. Another blotch, this one resolving into a very faint 12. Further examination showed each door was numbered, though not sequentially; the lowest number was 3, the highest 13, and those numbers were the doors' only distinguishing characteristics. It seemed her Dreaming had produced something useful, after all.

She stood and watched them for a few moments. Once she passed through the door, the others would vanish, and she would learn what she could from her Dream and then have to repeat the process over again. She was already weary from exertion, and the idea of having to do this again and again—at least thirteen times!—sapped her will further. *There is nothing for it,* she thought. She reached out to the door numbered 3 and let herself be drawn through it.

This press had shadowy human figures crawling over it and along its spidery limbs, but she ignored them to exert her will upon the door to the outside. She stepped through, found herself in a street crowded with more shadowy figures, recognized the location, and rose out of Dream in the space of a few breaths. "This will take some time," she said, rising from the chaise longue and crossing to the map, where she wrote the number 3 in the center of a tangle of small streets, "and I cannot make the extra effort to identify the building in which the press has been stored without exhausting myself. But I believe that can wait for another time. The general pattern is what matters now."

"And the numbers will show where the press has been, and when?" Cecy said.

"Yes. I will have to repeat this process several times, because the Dreams are not appearing in convenient numerical order." Her head was already beginning to ache. She chose not to mention this to Cecy. "But at least I now know it is possible."

She Dreamed seven more times before her Sight became red-rimmed and blurry, and by that time her head was pounding as if something were trying to escape from it. She did not need Cecy's urging to take to her bed and sleep for a few hours before continuing her experiment. Sleeping helped a little; the headache still troubled her, but her Sight was once again clear. She returned to the drawing room to find

Daphne had joined Cecy and Lewis. "By the end of my deliveries, people were repeating the rumor to *me*," she said gleefully, and grasped both of Sophia's hands. "Lord Endicott won't be able to extricate himself from it."

"I only hope it will help," Sophia said. "I cannot stop imagining Benjamin Vane appearing on our doorstep to arrest me."

"It will not come to that," Lewis said. "You are still an Extraordinary and they must have evidence you intentionally lied about your Dream."

"It is possible the War Office will intervene at some point. They might appear complicit in concealing the truth. Which they are, in a sense. They would have to say they believed I was simply mistaken, if they want to protect themselves. Unless they think to remain silent, and uninvolved."

"I cannot imagine they would abandon you so completely, Sophy."

"They already have abandoned me once, Cecy. What is another betrayal?" Mr. Rutledge's face came to mind then, and her throat closed up against unexpected tears. "But I will solve this problem before then," she went on, and lay once more upon the chaise longue to continue her task.

"That is all," she said, eight Dreams later, "I have seen nothing higher than 16." She moved her stiff limbs and discovered she could not rise. It was not the horrible semi-paralysis of the Duchess of Lenshire's gathering, but her muscles ached as if she had swum the Thames ten times without stopping.

"You have exerted yourself too much," Cecy exclaimed, and came to help her sit up. "Oh, Sophy, is there no other way?"

"You know there is not," Sophia said. "I would not do this if there were any alternative."

Daphne brought her a cup of tea. "At least you have learned things, so it wasn't a waste," she said.

Sophia sipped the tea and discovered it was lukewarm, but it refreshed her nonetheless. "I believe I can support myself, Cecy, thank you for your help," she said. Cecy gave her a skeptical look, but shifted her position so as not to press so closely against her.

Lewis was drawing lines on the map with the pencil to connect the numbered points, indicating directions with arrows. "This is the path Baines has taken," he said. "He has moved the press sixteen times— seventeen if you count the location he has taken it now that is concealed from us by his ability—but there are only seven locations it has been. I consider it reasonable to say these are the only places to which he has access. And *this*—" he tapped the number 16—"is where it was last."

"But he is not following a pattern," Cecy said. "If he were making a circuit, you could point to the next location on it, but that's not the case here."

"He does have part of a pattern, though," Daphne said, "because he never retreats to the immediately previous location."

"Nor to the one before that," Sophia said. She touched number 16. "So the press is no longer here, and it is not in either of these two places. That means there are only four locations it could be. And all I need do is identify exactly which places those are, which buildings, I mean, and then Dream of them as they are at this moment. And one of them will contain the press. Baines' ability cannot stop such Dreams."

They all sat for a moment in silence. Then Lewis said, "I am sure you know what I'm thinking—"

"—which is that we can't act on that knowledge," Daphne said. "We need someone who can arrest Baines and his men."

"And arresting Baines still does not link Lord Endicott to the crime," Cecy said.

"I believe it does," Sophia said. "The whole point of tracking down Baines was that my Dreams about bringing Lord Endicott to his knees all pointed to Baines as the key to that result. So even if I cannot tell why he is important, I believe Lord Endicott's fate is tied to him."

"Then what are we to do?" Daphne said, jumping up and beginning to pace the room. "We could go to the press ourselves and threaten to turn him in."

"He would not be afraid of that threat, because he must know I have no credibility with the law, and he has all those Movers he would not hesitate to turn against us," Sophia said.

"And even if you find where the press is now, Baines moves it so frequently it's likely it would be gone by the time anyone arrived," Cecy said. "Which means knowing the pattern will not help."

Silence again, broken only by the sound of Daphne's footsteps on the carpet. "I believe we should let it rest for the night," Lewis said. "We may find a solution after a good sleep."

"Well, I don't imagine I'll sleep at all," Daphne said, "but I'll be back in the morning." She vanished with the usual *pop*.

"Neither do I," Cecy said. She tried and failed to stand, grimacing with pain.

"You should have said something, Cecilia," Lewis said. He helped her to her feet. "I will call for Dr. Garland."

"No, I simply need to lie down for a while. But I want to eat dinner first. Do you suppose cook will mind if we eat early?"

"I believe cook is so considerate of your needs she would spoon-feed you if that became necessary," Sophia said, "and I admit to being more than a little hungry myself."

She ate without tasting her food, drifted through the evening barely contributing to the conversation. Lewis and Cecy seemed similarly remote. She hoped they were thinking of a solution to the problem. She herself saw no way out of it, save trying, once again, to enlist Sir Arthur Rowley's help. If he would even listen to her. If he would not simply arrest her on sight. That no one from the Bow Street magistrates had yet appeared on the doorstep did not comfort her as much as it might; for all she knew, the Bow Street Runners were in the process of investigating the truth or falsity of Lord Endicott's allegation, and this was simply fate deferred.

You could send word to Mr. Rutledge, a tiny, idiotic voice in the back of her head told her when she was settled in for the night. She closed her eyes against its suggestion. He would not listen to her any more than Sir Arthur would. *You don't know that*, the same foolish voice said. *He believes in your Dreams.* "All but one," she said aloud, then blushed. How embarrassing, to be talking to the inside of her own head like that. It was only that she wanted him to believe her that she could even consider humiliating herself like that, going to him begging for his good opinion. She was such a fool.

She slept, and dreamed of Dream, doors opening on doors in

endless rows that led nowhere but to other doors. She passed through them, searching for something or someone, but it was as if she had Baines' dubious gift, and her desires changed moment by moment so that no sooner had she focused on one object it disappeared, leaving her to grope about again.

Then she could see Lord Endicott in the distance, covered in butterflies, and she tried to follow him, but he was always two doors ahead of her, laughing and running as if it were a wonderful game. The doors were growing darker and more twisted, as they had when she was tracking King. It was again as if she were running through a dead forest whose branches tangled in her hair and clothes, scratching and stabbing at her so she had to force a path for herself, following Lord Endicott's colorful figure, which always remained clear no matter how many brambles stood between them.

She knew Mr. Rutledge was there before she saw him, could feel his hand on her arm the way he had held her in the carriage, and then he was between her and Lord Endicott, completely blocking the way. In her dream he was a vast giant, much bigger than he was in life, and he held her arm so she could not move around him. He was in the way of her revenge, and she yanked free of his grip, but he looked at her with those dark, intent eyes, and she knew the way one did in dreams that if she could only find a way past him, he would never trouble her again.

She stood looking up at him for a moment, hoping for some sign, something that would tell her what to do, but he said nothing, only reached out to her again. Why would he not help her take her revenge on Lord Endicott? She twisted out of his reach, darted around him, and he vanished, leaving her face to face with her nemesis. There was a pistol in her hand; she raised it, pulled the trigger, and woke to find herself sobbing without knowing what emotion fueled her tears. She wiped her face with her blanket and curled back up in her bed, lacking even the energy to look at her watch to see at what ungodly hour her horrible dream had woken her.

She slept fitfully the rest of the night, waking herself every time she began to dream, and morning found her sitting up in bed, staring at the lightening square of the window, thinking of nothing in particular. She was no closer to a solution than she had been the night before.

She rose wearily and rang for Beeton. Possibly Cecy or Lewis or Daphne had thought of something.

But when she arrived at the breakfast table, Lewis sat alone, his eyes shadowed as if his sleep had been as restless as hers. "Cecy is very unwell this morning," he said. "I have called for Dr. Garland."

"You should have woken me. I would have helped you with her last night."

"I thought it better one of us be alert to watch her this morning, and I wasn't going to be able to sleep anyway. I'm going to bed as soon as I've eaten, if you don't mind."

"Not at all. Will the doctor be here soon?"

"I hope so. Her assistant said she was not very busy this morning. She has already seen to Mr. Parris's mother, so you might convey our gratitude to her when she arrives."

"And I have spoken to my solicitor about his brother's schooling. The young man is a promising student, so I feel I have done a good deed as well as fulfilled a promise."

"Mr. Parris should be grateful you did not reveal his crime." Lewis went back to eating, fiercely, as if his doing so might ease his wife's pain. Sophia found herself again without an appetite, and again forced herself to eat. She would do Cecy no good if she were faint with hunger.

They were both almost finished when they heard the distant sound of a knock on the door. "No, I will go," Sophia said when Lewis began to rise. "You should go to bed. I can help Dr. Garland with whatever she needs."

She hurried out of the room and nearly ran over Simon approaching from the other direction. "Madam, the door—"

"I know, Simon, I'll take her to Cecy," she said, moving more quickly now. "Dr. Garland," she began as she came into the entry hall, then stopped, because it was not the doctor who stood there, but Mr. Rutledge, the shoulders of his greatcoat dusted with snow. He carried a newspaper rolled tightly under one arm and his gloved fingers flexed, once or twice, as if they were cold despite the gloves.

"Mrs. Westlake," he said, "I apologize for disturbing you so early. Is something wrong?"

"Only Cecy's usual illness," Sophia said, echoes of her dream overlapping with reality, leaving her confused. What was he doing here? "Why are you here?" she said, realizing only after the words had left her lips how rude they sounded.

"To make amends, if I can," he said. "Your Dreams were all correct. Lord Endicott embezzled from the Army and he is behind the counterfeiters I have been trying to apprehend."

CHAPTER 27
IN WHICH MR. RUTLEDGE
REDEEMS HIMSELF

"How do you know?" Sophia said. The sense of unreality threatened to sweep her away entirely. Mr. Rutledge could not possibly believe her now, of all times.

"The newspaper," he said, making as if to offer it to her, then withdrawing it before she could accept it. "It's perhaps better you not read today's story. It is somewhat lengthier than the first and has Lord Endicott's protestations that he forgives you your 'mistake' in a manner that makes your guilt seem more certain."

"Then I still do not understand," Sophia said, "why you do not believe that story when it is so convincing."

"Because I know you, Mrs. Westlake," Mr. Rutledge said. His deep voice was practically a rumble. "You are incapable of using your Sight to do deliberate harm to anyone, let alone to someone who was a virtual stranger to you when you made that accusation. I told you I believed you had simply made a mistake." He drew in a deep breath. "I was wrong. There was no mistake. Endicott managed to cover his crime and then, it seems, took great pleasure in tormenting you as revenge for daring to interrupt his scheme. And I should have taken more pains to investigate your claim before simply agreeing with the prevailing opinion."

Sophia realized her mouth was hanging open. "But...why now?"

"I told you. The newspaper. Endicott was the only person who would have revealed that story without including his own name. It made no sense that he should do so now, after months have passed and he has given out he is almost engaged to marry you. I take it you were responsible for attaching his name to this farce?"

"Lady Daphne."

He laughed. "That makes even more sense. I believe the War Office has no idea what they are letting themselves in for." More soberly, he said, "That he should reveal that story in such a manner made me believe I should examine your supposed mistake more closely. To be honest, I was shocked at how haphazardly that investigation was conducted. It seems no one thought to determine whether Mr. Tate's death was suspicious. You have grounds for suing the War Office for defamation of character, if you choose."

"But it has only been one day. You could not possibly have learned all of that in such a short time."

He looked away from her. "In truth, I have been looking into it since you accused me of not truly being your friend. Your words made me feel ashamed. I should have thought better of you, and I apologize."

It was as if she had been carrying around a load of bricks that were one by one lifting away and vanishing into the sky. "Thank you," she said, feeling unaccountably shy. He turned to look at her again, and smiled. It made more of her load fly away.

"Thank *you* for not evicting me summarily," he said. "I would have understood it, but I much prefer having the opportunity to make things right between us."

"So do I," Sophia said, and reached out to clasp his hand. His grip was strong, but gentle, and it comforted her as much as his smile had.

"At any rate," he said, releasing her hand, "I will not insult you by renewing my offer of employment—"

"I need your help, Mr. Rutledge," Sophia said. "I want to find the printing press, and my Dream tells me if we capture the man who has it in charge, he will help us condemn Lord Endicott."

He blinked at her abruptness, then laughed. "Mrs. Westlake," he said, "you continue to amaze me. My resources are at your disposal. Tell me what to do."

Someone knocked again, then opened the door. "I understand my favorite patient is in need," Dr. Garland said, striding off in the direction of the stairs. Sophia began to run after her, then turned back to Mr. Rutledge, who hadn't moved.

"Wait for me," she said, then followed the doctor to Cecy's room, where to her relief she found Cecy asleep and not restless. Dr. Garland settled herself on the edge of the bed and took Cecy's hand in both of hers.

"I'll let you know when I'm finished, Mrs. Westlake," she said. Sophia took that for a dismissal and fled.

Mr. Rutledge was still in the entry hall, looking as if he had taken her request to wait as a literal command to remain motionless. "Come with me to the drawing room, and I will explain everything," she said, leading the way up the stairs again.

Mr. Rutledge examined the map with some interest. "I'm going to guess you are tracking the press," he said, tracing one of the arrowed lines with his finger.

"Now that we are friends again, I can compliment you on your insightfulness," Sophia said. He smiled at her as if nothing had ever come between them, and a few more bricks disappeared until she felt light enough to fly away herself. She explained, briefly, the discoveries they had made the day before, and finished by saying, "I realize it is boring, watching someone sleep, but I must Dream again in order to know where the press will be, and I am not certain how long it will take. But—will you stay?"

"Of course," he said, and pulled a chair close to the chaise longue. "And I assure you I will do my best not to be bored."

"There are books," Sophia said, laughing at his ostentatiously solemn expression. "If you can find any in keeping with your naturally sober thoughts."

"I do read novels, you know. But only sober ones."

"I did not realize there were any of that description. You should be wary. They might make you frivolous, and then I would not recognize you."

"Then I would ask you to dance, and trip over your toes, and then you would know me again."

Sophia blushed, and lay back on the chaise longue to cover the confusion his bantering words sent her into. Were those words of friendship, or did they mean something more? "You must ask me to dance again soon," she said lightly, "when this is all over."

"I promise to do so," he said. His eyes were so uncomfortably direct that she closed hers and went into Dream more rapidly than she had planned, without taking time to meditate. She knew her mistake when she saw the doors thronging about her, none of them what she wanted.

She cleared her mind as best she could. Returning to the waking world so suddenly seemed a waste of Dream, and... yes, she had asked him to stay, but the thought of Mr. Rutledge watching over her as she Dreamed felt intimate, because of her feelings for him, in a way it never was with Cecy or Daphne or even Lewis. She chose to wander until her embarrassment died away, and hoped she might find some door that would give her what she wanted.

Though she had not meditated, it seemed her ordinary dream of the night before had influenced her thoughts, because the doors of Dream were no longer randomly scattered, but lined up in rows so that, if they were doors in the waking world, one might walk through them in a straight line, one after the other. The lines extended into what passed for distance in Dream; they might well loop around and form an infinite circle, if the geometry of Dream allowed it. *I wonder*, she thought, and laid her hand on the door in that infinite loop that was closest to her, and was drawn into it.

She had not paid attention to the image on the door and was surprised to find Cecy standing there, staring into the distance beyond Sophia's left shoulder. She was in her nightgown with her hair braided for sleep, and she was saying something that to Sophia sounded like a high, distant wail. The rest of the space was clouded, meaning that Cecy and her words were all that was important, but what startled Sophia was the door beyond Cecy, standing upright in a nonexistent wall—not an ordinary door, but one of the doors of Dream. It was as if the Dream contained another Dream within it, something Sophia had never seen before.

Curious, she passed Cecy and laid her hand on the door, and was drawn through like silk sliding over skin into another Dream. To her surprise, the new Dream looked identical to the first—Cecy, still in her nightgown, stood there as before, wailing. It was so unexpected she gasped, felt her sleeping self react to her surprise, came close enough to waking to feel Mr. Rutledge touch the back of her hand, and had to calm herself before she was flung free of this new Dream. It was an impossibility for two Dreams to be identical, another impossibility to pass from one Dream to another without waking between them. What had the orientation of the doors done to their Dreams?

She examined the new Dream closely, ignoring Cecy for the moment, though she appeared to be excited about something. Again a door stood upright in the center of the cloudiness that defined the edges of this Dream; she leaned close to it, but did not touch it, afraid to be drawn into yet another Dream before she had exhausted the possibilities of this one. She discovered, upon examination, that there were small differences between the Dreams; Cecy, when she finally looked at her, was wearing a different nightgown, and her hair looked different. She could see nothing that might indicate why this Dream was so similar to the first.

Finally Sophia turned to face the door of Dream. *A Dream located within another Dream,* she thought, *what else might it contain?* She laid her palm against the new door and was drawn through it.

Once again Cecy stood there in her nightgown, and another door of Dream stood opposite her, but now—Sophia gasped, and nearly fell back into the waking world. She had to fight herself to stay in Dream, because what she wanted was to run to her friend and dance and shout with her. She passed her hand over Cecy's hugely protruding belly, which in Dream was insubstantial, then circled her to examine her from all angles. A future, yes, and a much distant future, at least seven months from the present, which was another impossibility, because the future branched so easily and so quickly that Seeing more than a few days into it always failed. So how had this happened?

She looked at Cecy's belly once more, then at the door. *If these*

Dreams arise from other Dreams, then I know what I will find here, she thought, and let herself be pulled into the door to find Cecy cradling an infant, and that was too much for her; she rose out of Dream so fast it left her waking body dizzy and she had to put out a hand to steady herself. Another hand gripped hers, and she blinked up at Mr. Rutledge, then at Daphne, both of whom were staring at her with concern.

"Move," she said, rolling off the chaise longue and pushing them out of the way, running at full speed down the hall and up the stairs and into Cecy's room, startling both Cecy and the doctor. "You're with child," she said, panting, just as Cecy said, "Sophy, I am with child."

Sophia flung herself onto Cecy, laughing and crying, and Cecy clutched at her, saying, "How did you know? Dr. Garland only just told me—"

"I Saw it in Dream, Cecy," Sophia said, "and—" She released Cecy and sat back. "I know how to find Baines," she said. "Remind me to thank Lord Endicott, when this is over. He has driven me to discoveries no Seer ever thought to make before. I can barely think, Cecy, I am so overwhelmed."

"Well, you should try not to overwhelm my patient," Dr. Garland said. "I've done what I can for the moment to ensure you have no discomfort, Mrs. Barham, and I believe you'll find a lessening of your pain in your expectant state, but you should still call on me when you feel an episode coming on. And I'll arrange for a midwife to attend you as well." She stood and shouldered her satchel. "I did tell you it would happen, didn't I? I'm not above gloating a little when I'm right. Good day, Mrs. Barham. Mrs. Westlake."

"Oh, Sophy, I am so happy!" Cecy said when they were alone. "Will you bring Lewis here?"

"I will, and I... oh, I forgot about Daphne and Mr. Rutledge!"

"What do you mean, Mr. Rutledge? And I thought we could not find Baines in time to apprehend him before he moved elsewhere."

Sophia kissed Cecy on the cheek. "It can wait, dearest. I will send Lewis, and when you are able, we will all sit together and I will explain everything."

Cecy began to get out of bed. "I am not going to wait," she said, "because you have a look in your eye that says you are on the hunt again, and I want to be there when you capture your prey."

CHAPTER 28

IN WHICH THERE IS MUCH DISCUSSION OF A TECHNICAL NATURE

"The first thing you should understand," Sophia told her listeners, "is that Dream is, or was, limited to the near future in what it predicts. The future diverges so quickly that asking, for example, the question 'Where will Cecy be on this date one year from now?' can yield no answer, because Cecy might make hundreds of choices between now and then that could put her in any one of a thousand places at that time."

"And that is why you could not simply See where King would be when he was arrested, because it might be days or weeks before that happened, especially since, as a Seer, he could predict you would be trying to have him apprehended," Cecy said.

"Yes, exactly. However, I seem to have stumbled on a way to make Dream reveal those futures. I have yet to understand the technique fully, and I am afraid I may not be able to explain it well to anyone who is not a Seer, but—" She caught Mr. Rutledge's eye, saw his amused expression, and realized she was pacing in a tight circle before her seated audience. She smiled at him in wry acknowledgement of her restless excitement and managed to stop herself and clasp her hands behind her back to still them.

"Dreams arise out of what *is*," she said, "at this moment, and that is

247

as much as anyone understands about how they work. I might Dream, for example, of where Cecy will be tomorrow, and once that has happened—assuming she does not take action to invalidate the Dream —I might Dream tomorrow of where she will be the day after tomorrow. But I cannot Dream today of where she will be in two days; that door of Dream simply would not appear to me. That is, until now."

She started to pace again and stopped herself. "I believe—this is where the explanation becomes confusing. I entered a Dream from which another Dream opened, and another. It was as if, within Dream, I took all those steps I have just described without having to wait, or to exit and re-enter Dream. I saw a reality much further in the future than has ever been possible before."

"How do you know that future will happen? You did say the future branches too much to be reliably Seen," Lewis said.

"It is true that Dream is sometimes difficult to interpret, and a Seer may be wrong about her understanding of it," Sophia said, "but I have always known when I am right about my Dreams, and they have never lied to me." She caught Mr. Rutledge's eye again, and this time his amusement turned into a real smile, which she returned. Having his good opinion made her feel as if she could conquer anything Lord Endicott brought to bear on her.

"And I believe these... far-future Dreams? These new Dreams are no different than the usual kind, in that they may be changed or prevented by someone's intervention. It is even possible that a Seer might have to take an active role in ensuring they are not altered by some other action. But all of that I will have to investigate at another time. What is important now is that I believe this new method of Dreaming will allow me to circumvent Baines' Dream-disrupting ability."

"I understand," Daphne said, "or rather, I don't understand—that is, it's a little like skipping stones across the water, you throw the—or in your case you enter Dream, then go from one to the other until you —well, you don't sink, obviously—what I don't understand is how you can even do that when Baines will disrupt the first Dream—"

"Because you will not be trying to predict Baines' actions," Mr. Rutledge said in his deep rumble.

Sophia laughed. "I suppose it's not that difficult to understand, after all," she said, "since both of you seem to have grasped the principle."

"Well, *I* have not, Sophy," Cecy said, "so please explain it for those of us who are not quite so quick-witted."

"It took me nearly half an hour to understand what they did in two minutes, so I believe I am not so quick-witted either," Sophia said. "As Mr. Rutledge implies, my trying to See what Baines will do always fails because the Dream cannot predict his movements. *But* I am perfectly capable of Dreaming of where he is now, and when he is with the printing press, that appears in my Dream as well. While I cannot predict where Baines will move it, I know he *will* move it, and that it *will* end up in a new location. So I will instead attempt to predict not where it will be moved, but where it will be at some future point after that decision has been made. To be honest, I could have done that before, and I am a little embarrassed that I did not think to focus my Dreaming in that way."

"It would not have mattered, though, would it, because Baines would still have moved on by the time anyone might have reached that location," Lewis said. "And even now that we have Mr. Rutledge's assistance, that will still be true—unless you, sir, have more secrets to reveal," he added with a grin.

Mr. Rutledge shook his head. "My men—or, more accurately, the officers who report to my committee—can still only move so quickly," he said. "But I believe Mrs. Westlake has an idea for how to work successfully within those constraints."

"I do, Mr. Rutledge," Sophia said. "I intend to follow those Dreams within Dreams until I have discovered where Baines will take the press two or possibly three locations from where it is now, and then you and your men may prepare yourselves to capture him at that place."

"Then, if I understand you correctly," Mr. Rutledge said, "you will have to find where it will be just far enough into the future that there is as little time as possible for it to be disrupted, but not so close to the present that my men cannot arrange his apprehension in time."

"You have it exactly," Sophia said. "We know there are seven locations to which Baines has access, but I have not yet identified the exact buildings within those locations, and that means more Dreaming, because I dare not predict where the press will be and then waste time trying to pinpoint where that place is."

"Sophy, that seems like a dangerous amount of Dreaming," Cecy said.

Sophia held out her hand to Mr. Rutledge. "Could I have that newspaper now, please?" she said, and handed it to Cecy. Cecy glanced at the page, then read more closely, her mouth falling open as she did.

"This is absurd!" she said. "How anyone could—he makes you sound dangerously unstable, Sophy!" She flung the newspaper on the floor. "Mr. Rutledge, am I correct in thinking the Bow Street Runners are investigating these allegations?"

"You are, Mrs. Barham," Mr. Rutledge said, "and although being an Extraordinary affords Mrs. Westlake some protection, it is very possible a warrant for her arrest may be issued soon. Endicott has a great deal of political pull, and there is a faction in the government that would like to see Extraordinaries have somewhat fewer legal rights than they currently do. Mrs. Westlake's trial would benefit them enormously."

"I have no time to be concerned about the effects of too much Dreaming," Sophia said. She picked up the newspaper, folded it, and handed it back to Mr. Rutledge. "If it is true Lord Endicott had King murdered in prison, then my confinement there could mean my death. We must find Baines, and quickly."

Cecy stood. "Then let us begin," she said. "Sophy, I will make you as comfortable as possible. The rest of you, take yourselves off. Sophy does not need an audience."

"I should stay," said Mr. Rutledge, "in order to act on whatever information Mrs. Westlake produces as quickly as I can."

"Very well," said Cecy.

"But—" Daphne said.

"I will be fine if everyone stays, Cecy," said Sophia. "But—on the other side of the room, perhaps?"

She settled on the chaise longue with Cecy seated beside her. "When this is over, I intend not to Dream for a month," she said in a low voice, making Cecy laugh.

"If you can manage it, I will be very surprised," she said, then her smile became reflective. "Though not as surprised as I was when Dr. Garland gave me the news. You know she said that is likely why I became so dizzy after I was attacked? Oh, Sophy, it is too wonderful!"

"I am so happy for you, dearest. It is a beautiful baby, too."

"Of course it is! Oh, but you should Dream. We have so many months ahead to talk about this!"

Sophia nodded, closed her eyes, and slipped into Dream. It was so easy, these days, what with all the practice she was getting, that she sometimes had trouble falling into a normal sleep. That frightened her, a little, but the thought of taking her revenge on Lord Endicott kept that fear at bay. She had no time for fear now, either, because she needed all her attention to learn the exact locations where Baines might hide the press.

Time and again she dipped into Dream, wandering the surreal landscape until she Saw something she recognized, then emerging to give the location to one of her helpers. By the time she was finished, she was exhausted and dizzy and nauseated and ready for a true sleep, but there remained one thing to be done.

"I will try to See the place the printing press will be soon, and hope I can also learn when it will be there," she said. It seemed she lacked the energy to rise. Well, Dream did not require one to stand. The others came to gather around her, looking down on her until she felt as if she were surrounded by giant statues, looming over her recumbent body.

"That can wait until tomorrow," Cecy said. "You look as if you are about to fall unconscious."

She searched their faces until she came to that of Mr. Rutledge, who was expressionless. "You know what I have to do," she said to him.

He nodded. "Mrs. Barham, tomorrow might bring anything. I understand your concern, but I believe Mrs. Westlake knows the danger."

Cecy looked terribly torn. "Last one. I promise," Sophia said. Cecy finally nodded. Sophia closed her eyes and thought, *Show me the press*, and once more fell into Dream.

She was so accustomed to seeing Baines in these Dreams that it surprised her when he was not immediately visible. The printing press took up space in one corner of the featureless room, its spidery limbs tossing sheets of banknotes in all directions, where they disappeared before they struck the ground. Lord Endicott's operation was becoming more efficient. Sophia turned in a slow circle and found Baines standing behind her, his handsome face already beginning to blur. How strange, that so many of the villains of this tale looked like the sort of men one would wish to sit next to at the dinner table, but were at heart evil and ugly. Behind him lay the second door of Dream. She hurried past him and laid her palm against that door.

The room beyond was fuzzy and featureless, but there was the press in one corner, and there was Baines, more solid now, and another door of Dream. Sophia looked around for an ordinary door, even one no more than an outline, that would link this room to its exterior, but saw nothing. She rubbed her temples, or tried to; she was as insubstantial as anything else within Dream, and told herself that her Dreaming body could not feel anything, let alone the pain of the headache her living body had been developing all afternoon. She crossed to the door of Dream and passed through it. Press, Baines, door of Dream, but the room was firmer and more well-defined, and there was another, ordinary door in the wall, its carved moldings setting it off so well from the slightly nebulous walls that she opened it with ease, then bolted through it before it could vanish.

The non-light of Dream was too bright and the surrounding landscape too dark, and she had to stand still for a moment to avoid falling down, because it was becoming increasingly difficult for her to ignore her real body's pains and keep herself securely tethered to Dream. Her impossible headache was trying to cleave her skull in half, and everything had pale red rings around it, but she made herself focus on her surroundings. The child's painting effect was more pronounced this time, and everything she looked at wavered, making the red rings surrounding it quiver in a nausea-inducing way. *The day, what day is it,* she thought, and stumbled into the street looking for ephemera.

The first newspaper she snatched at vanished before she could glimpse more than the headline MRS. WESTLAKE ARRESTED!!!

Another sharp pain drove through her head, and her sleeping self twitched, making the landscape bend and twist until she forced it back into place long enough to establish her location in the waking world and match it to one of the locations she had identified.

She found another paper, this one lying in a gutter, half-obliterated, but she snatched it up and read the date just as her sleeping body convulsed and drove her out of the Dream. She jerked again, and then there were hands supporting her, holding her still. "Whitechapel," she gasped, thinking she had gone blind before realizing her eyes were closed and she could not open them. "Late evening, the day after tomorrow. I saw half a sun," she said. Then everything went red, and then black, and the pain was gone, and she slept.

When she next opened her eyes, she was in her own room, lying fully clothed on her bed. Daphne sat beside her, uncharacteristically still, with her hands interlaced on her lap and her eyes fixed on them. She raised her head when Sophia stirred, and said, "You don't have to get up yet."

"I believe I could not rise even if I wanted to," Sophia said. "What time is it?"

"Half past six. Are you hungry?"

Sophia's stomach rumbled. "Apparently I am," she said with good humor, then added, "Is something wrong, Daphne?"

Daphne shook her head. "Everything's fine."

"You certainly seem out of sorts. Are *you* hungry?"

"Not really."

Sophia rose enough to prop herself on her elbows. The pain in her head lessened when she did. "Where is everyone?"

"Cecy and Mr. Barham are in the drawing room. Cecy was in here until about an hour ago. Mr. Rutledge—I still cannot believe he is a spy—well, not exactly a spy, but he certainly isn't what he seems to be, is he? Though now that I say that, I'm not sure what it is he seems to be, just not—at any rate, Mr. Rutledge left to arrange for Baines' capture."

"Oh. That is good. I will have to send him the details of the location." She felt oddly bereft that he had left without saying goodbye, though how he would do that while she was unconscious was a mystery. Then she sat up more fully, ignoring the fleeting pain that went through her head, and said, "No, that is not good. I want to be there when they capture Baines."

"So do I. Mr. Rutledge said, and I quote, 'there is absolutely no way in hell I am taking either of you into Whitechapel at night.' I told him he was being unfair, and that I would tell—anyway, he refused, but he left you this." She picked up a man's ring from the bedside table and handed it to Sophia. "He said he didn't mind if you borrowed his eyes."

It was a heavy gold ring set with a flat onyx stone that bore no design, a ring as plain as the rest of Mr. Rutledge's wardrobe. On a whim, Sophia slid it onto her gloved middle finger, her largest finger, where it hung loosely. *His hands are so large*, she thought, and was reminded of how he had grasped her arm, both in reality and in her dream, and removed the ring, feeling embarrassed at how the memory warmed her. "I will try to find him in Vision later," she said, laying it back on the table, "but now I believe we should eat—are you staying for dinner?"

"No, I am expected at home, but I will return night after tomorrow, and I expect you to tell us all exactly what you See," Daphne said, her old exuberance returning. She hesitated, then threw her arms around Sophia and whispered, "You scared us. Please don't do that again." Daphne released her, and vanished.

Sophia lay back on her pillow and stared up at the ceiling. *I spend so much time flat on my back*, she thought, then nearly choked on her laughter as she thought of how that sentence might be misconstrued. Still, it was true. Was it only the necessity of protecting herself from Lord Endicott that had led her to this? Surely she had not always been so absorbed with Dream. No, it was only after Richard's death that she had begun spending so much time in Dream, or in Vision, and when she had not been exercising her talent she had been thinking about how to exercise her talent.

What would her life have looked like had Richard lived? It was one of those questions that could not be answered, something where the future branched so far from the past there was no knowing where they might have ended up. She might have had a child. She might have been the one killed on the battlefield, not Richard. She might not have been driven to find the pirates' secret, and Lord and Lady Enderleigh might be at the bottom of the Caribbean now.

So many changes that hinged on one man's death. She no longer missed Richard; she could even admit to herself they had both been very young to marry, and that they had begun to grow apart thanks to the pressures of wartime service. Peacetime, when it eventually came, might not have been enough to bind them back together.

She removed her right glove and picked up Mr. Rutledge's ring, steeling herself against the whirling images and the faint nausea that accompanied them. It was a profound mark of trust, him loaning her this ring; he could have no control over what she Saw of his life and history, and she might See some very personal and private things. She resolved not to linger over the images longer than was necessary to find the one that showed his current perspective. He trusted her, and she did not want to betray that trust. She dismissed the echoes, ignored the static images, and went searching through the moving windows in which pieces of Mr. Rutledge's life played out in endless cycles.

She meant only to look at each image briefly, long enough to establish it was not the one she needed, but she soon became fascinated by what she saw. His undistinguished attire and large physique gave the impression that he led a rather boring, sedentary life, or would have if she did not know him so well, but what Sophia saw astonished her: foreign landscapes, exotically dressed men and women, cities in Morocco and Russia and the American colonies and others she could not recognize. A richly dressed rajah, extending a hand for Mr. Rutledge to shake as equals. A woman—she turned away from that one quickly, not wanting to pry, but she was certainly beautiful and they had certainly been *very* well acquainted. He had every right to a relationship like that, did he not? It occurred to her for the first time to wonder why he was not married. Whatever had happened to the woman?

She watched in fascination until Cecy knocked on her door and said, "Are you awake? Oh, I am so glad. Where did Daphne go? She was supposed to watch over you."

"She did, until I woke, and I feel perfectly well except for a bit of a headache."

"Which will no doubt become worse if you persist in playing with Mr. Rutledge's ring while lying down. Come, eat with us, and then you can continue your search. I hope you discover the right Vision before they attempt to capture Baines, or I know from experience you will be unpleasantly out of sorts and likely to inflict it on others."

Sophia set the ring on the table and waited for the whirling images to fade. "I intend to be very pleasant," she said, "because I am close to seeing my enemy brought down, and that makes it impossible for me to be out of sorts."

She continued exploring the ring's Visions after dinner, sitting in her uncomfortable chair and clasping it between her palms. Mr. Rutledge had done so many things in his life. What had brought him to work for the Bank of England? He had said he had experience at capturing criminals, yet he was no Runner; had he worked secretly for the military, or for the government? Now that she had Seen these things, she had so many questions she wanted to ask him. Or—perhaps it would be prying. It *was* prying, wasn't it, spending so much time watching his life flicker past when she ought to be trying to discover the Vision he *had* given her permission to seek out. Embarrassed again, she told herself sternly to focus.

She found the correct Vision almost immediately, though she almost missed it because it looked like a static image, a single sheet of notepaper with the message THIS IS WHAT YOU SEEK MRS WESTLAKE printed on it in large letters. She smiled. Of course he would think of that. If only he had a Speaker Cecy could communicate with, to tell him she had located his Vision. But she knew him well enough to know he would assume she had found him by the night after tomorrow, when that would be crucial.

After a minute or two, the notepaper disappeared, and she was looking at a plate of food, then around a room—it looked like a gentlemen's club. He was dining alone. She set the ring aside and stretched. "I have found Mr. Rutledge," she announced to Cecy, "and in two days we will see Baines captured, and then... oh, Cecy, let us pray I am not arrested before then!"

CHAPTER 29
IN WHICH THE LIONESS CORNERS
HER PREY

S ophia sat in her chair in the drawing room, Mr. Rutledge's ring clenched in her gloved right hand. Cecy, Daphne, and Lewis had drawn chairs and sofas close by and were leaning in as if they, too, might see the Visions if they were close enough to her. "How will we know it is time?" Cecy said.

Sophia glanced behind her, out the drawing room window at where the sun was setting. "Soon," she said, removing her glove. It took mere moments for her to locate the correct Vision this time; nothing could distract her from this.

Mr. Rutledge was somewhere in Whitechapel already. It had been a beautiful, clear, warm day, and now the street vendors lured out by the unexpectedly clement weather were closing up shop for the day. A colorfully dressed woman loitered on a corner, apparently paying attention to no one; Mr. Rutledge's attention lingered on her a moment or two longer than necessary, and Sophia bristled a little before reminding herself that he was not likely to be interested in a common prostitute.

He never stopped moving. Sophia described what she saw as he went, though she left out the part about the prostitute. "He seems to be alone," she added, "and I believe he must be dressed as a workman, because no one is looking at him with the expression that says 'wonder what brings his lordship into the slums.' "

"Is he there yet?" Daphne asked.

"No." He seemed not to be going anywhere in particular, was not walking very fast at all, and Sophia started to become impatient. The sun was going down, and although the lamps hanging well above street level were being lit, they were not well maintained, and the light they emitted did little more than cast shadows into the spaces between them. The narrow streets looked oppressive even at the remove of Vision. How they felt to Mr. Rutledge, she could only guess.

Just then, Mr. Rutledge stopped and removed a notebook from his coat pocket. He wrote, in the same large block letters, STOP BEING IMPATIENT. THERE IS A PLAN. Sophia choked back a laugh. He knew her so well, didn't he? And she knew him.

His eyes stayed focused on the notepaper for nearly a minute, then he put the notebook away and continued walking. Sophia hoped his messages to her would not distract him from, for example, some footpad creeping up on him to rob and murder him. Now he walked more quickly, and his attention flicked in all directions, and Sophia realized he was looking about for her benefit.

The neighborhood, what little she could see of it, was growing rougher, well-kept buildings giving way to tall, narrow houses of crumbling brick that looked as if they might fall down if someone brushed against them the wrong way. People leaned out of unglazed windows two or three stories above the street and, by the movement of their mouths, called out to their neighbors below. Mr. Rutledge turned a corner into a street narrow enough that it looked more like an alley, consulted his watch, then broke into a trot. "I believe he is a little late," Sophia told her listeners, trying to ignore the ache of nervousness that filled her stomach.

"This will work, Sophy," Cecy said.

Sophia nodded, but could spare no more attention to reply. She still saw no one who might be one of Mr. Rutledge's men, only a few roughly-dressed loiterers who did not meet anyone's eyes. The narrow alley came out on a wider street, and Mr. Rutledge's gait slowed back to a walk. This street was still crowded, though it was nearly full dark, with people who leaned against doorways or sat tucked into whatever corners they could find out of the rising wind that made their clothing flutter. Some of those figures were horribly small.

One of the men began sauntering in Mr. Rutledge's direction, only to abruptly turn and walk the other way when Mr. Rutledge shifted his coat. It was a strange encounter, but Sophia had no interest in working out what it meant; she wished only for him to pass through this dismal neighborhood and leave all those tiny shapes behind. She owed Miss Travers an apology, and a large donation. No one should have to live like that.

He was moving so *slowly* now that Sophia's impatience drove her out of her seat to pace, willing Mr. Rutledge to move more quickly, to *finally* reach his destination, and Lewis's hand grabbed her shoulder before she could trip over a low table near her seat. Someone should have moved it where it could not attack her.

"Sit *down*," Lewis said, thrusting her back into her uncomfortable chair. She realized she had lost the Vision, and panic sent the images whirling like leaves in a storm. She squeezed her eyes tight shut and forced herself to calm down. There, the correct Vision was right there. She settled back in to watch.

"He is approaching a warehouse," she said. "It looks deserted, but it is not." It was in terrible shape, bricks missing everywhere, windows smashed in, piles of refuse in the doorways—no, some of those were people, weren't they?—but there were lights burning behind the gaping window holes. They were far too bright for this neighborhood, as if the inhabitants were, contrary to the evidence, wealthy enough not to worry about wasting candles.

Mr. Rutledge did not slow down; he was nearly there, and then he was passing it, and Sophia let out a squeak of indignation. "That must be it, why are they not attacking?" she exclaimed, then squeaked again as the notepaper, almost illegible in the darkness, filled her field of Vision: THE PLAN, it read, underlined twice. "He is infuriating," she said with a laugh, but only shook her head when the others asked what she meant.

Someone was approaching Mr. Rutledge now, someone walking with his head down against what Sophia imagined was now a brisk wind. Those poor children must be freezing. The man turned his head to look at Mr. Rutledge as they passed each other, and Mr. Rutledge nodded at him and received a nod in return.

He was turning, going around to a side of the warehouse where two large double doors stood. They looked newer than the rest of the building, and sturdier, and although they had hasps for a padlock, they were unsecured. Mr. Rutledge approached the doors, and Sophia watched him remove a heavy padlock from one of the deep pockets of his coat and ease it into the hasps, then close it. How much noise had that made? She wished with all her heart that she could hear as well as See.

Mr. Rutledge seemed unconcerned about noise. He took a few steps away from the doors, then continued his path around the warehouse. Two more men passed and received nods. It was dark now, darker than usual because of the high clouds that covered the waxing gibbous moon, and Sophia could see nothing but the lights of the warehouse. If Mr. Rutledge were sending her messages, she could not read them.

He was coming close to one of the smaller doors now, where a bundled figure curled up in its frame, as much out of the cold as it could manage. Mr. Rutledge bent down to shake the person gently; the man looked up at him, terrified rather than angry. Then he looked confused. Mr. Rutledge was no doubt telling him something—"probably that they are about to make an arrest, and he should take himself elsewhere," Daphne said when this was relayed.

Eventually Mr. Rutledge held out a few coins to the man, who snatched them, then half-ran, half-scurried away. Mr. Rutledge surveyed the area, then took out his watch again and brought it close to his eyes—likely more because he could barely read it in the dimness than because he thought Sophia would like to know the time. 8:14. Sophia realized she was clutching the ring so hard it was leaving welts in her palms, but she was afraid to loosen her grip.

Mr. Rutledge put his watch away and reached into his pocket again, and pulled out a long-barreled dueling pistol, which he checked for... Sophia had no idea what one checked a pistol for, possibly whether it was loaded, but her heart was beating fast and her palms were sweating and she could barely remember to tell the others what she Saw, she was so anxious.

Then Mr. Rutledge flung the door open and stepped inside, raising his pistol, and everything was chaos. What lay beyond the door was not a room, it was the entire ground floor of the warehouse, open and without interior walls, and more men were crashing through doors across the way. Sophia could almost hear the shouting and the sound of firearms going off.

She saw what had to be the press sitting near the double doors; it was more squat and less angular than her imagination had shown her in Dream, and Mr. Rutledge looked at it long enough she could see two men ducking behind it and a third running for the double doors. Then Mr. Rutledge advanced into the room at a run, looking everywhere at once, and Sophia realized he was again doing it for her benefit.

She had no idea what the warehouse had once stored, but there were barrels flying toward Mr. Rutledge's men that stopped to hover in midair, quivering as Mover fought Mover for control of the missiles. A few weapons went off, the flash of powder visible even in the bright light, but mostly it was hand to hand fighting, and for a few moments Sophia was disoriented and thought herself back in Portugal, watching a band of *guerrillas* ambush an unsuspecting party of French soldiers. The men at the press were shouting, and the man who had gone to the double doors and found them locked turned around and drew a pistol from his waistband. It was Baines.

"Take him, *take him!*" she shouted, then remembered he could not hear her any more than she could hear him, and sat back down, though she could not remember standing. Mr. Rutledge had put his pistol away somewhere and was in the middle of the fight now, and he was moving so quickly she thought she might become ill from how quickly his perspective shifted.

She clenched her teeth together and made herself keep watching, though the others were all shouting at her to "speak, Sophia, tell us what's happening!" She ducked to avoid a blow aimed at Mr. Rutledge's head, then cried out as another blow connected and made the Vision go dark for half a breath. Then he was out of the melee, and racing toward Baines, and Baines' pistol was raised and aimed at Mr.

Rutledge's heart, *dear God, don't let him die, I cannot bear to lose my love again*—

Mr. Rutledge ducked to one side as the pistol went off practically in his face, grabbed Baines' arm and did something that had Baines folded up over his knee, his face red. Then Sophia saw Mr. Rutledge's pistol pressed to Baines' temple, and Baines lifted his head to look Mr. Rutledge in the eye, seeming not to care how close to death he was. His lips moved. Whatever he was saying was long, and had Mr. Rutledge's attention. Mr. Rutledge's nod dizzied her again.

The pistol withdrew, and Mr. Rutledge brought out handcuffs from somewhere and secured Baines' hands behind his back. He turned to look at the rest of the room. The fighting was over. A number of men lay on the ground, unmoving; others sat with their hands bound, guarded by more men with pistols. The press, untended now, was still and innocent-looking, as if it were not the proximate cause of death and mayhem. Well, that was all to Lord Endicott's blame, wasn't it?

The notebook came out again. Mr. Rutledge wrote BAINES WILL INDICT ENDICOTT IN EXCHANGE FOR FULL PARDON. HE KNOWS MORE THAN ENOUGH.

Sophia released the ring and sat back, breathing as heavily as if she had been in the fight herself. "I cannot believe it is true," she said, and quickly related what she had Seen. "Surely one man's testimony is not enough to convict Lord Endicott."

"It will not be just one man's testimony," Lewis said. "I imagine many of those men will make the same agreement to avoid being hanged. And the printing press is evidence enough that your Dreams are valid. Taken all together, it will mean Endicott will certainly be transported."

Sophia's elation vanished. "But—counterfeiting is a capital offense," she said.

"Endicott still has power in Parliament," Lewis said. "Not enough to escape justice, but his friends will not allow him to hang."

"That is not justice," Sophia said angrily. "He should pay for his crimes."

"Sophy, that *is* payment," Cecy said. "He will lose his fortune, such as it is, possibly lose his title too, have to make a life in the Australian colony—what more will satisfy you?"

Sophia could not bear to look at Cecy's eager, concerned face. "I suppose it is enough," she lied. She picked up the ring again. "Let us see if there is anything else, but I believe it is over."

She was just in time to see Mr. Rutledge close the notebook and put it away. That was a message she'd missed. She would have to ask him if it was something important when she saw him next. He didn't seem to be doing much at the moment, just talking to one of his men, so Sophia put the ring away and pulled her gloves back on. "I am so tired now," she said, though in truth she was too wakeful to sleep.

"Of course you are, dearest. You should go to sleep." Cecy put her arm through Sophia's and drew her close. "Daphne, we will see you tomorrow, yes?"

"Of course. Do you imagine this will be in the morning papers? Or —Mr. Rutledge will still need to conceal his employment, though now Lord Endicott is—oh, I am tired too, I cannot think properly. Good night."

After Daphne had vanished, Sophia let Cecy lead her to her bedroom and help her undress, refusing to allow her to call Beeton. "Remember how we used to have to do this in school because we weren't allowed maids? Oh, Sophy, it has been such a marvelous day. I am so glad you are free from worry about Lord Endicott. Think how much better life will be, now that he can no longer hurt you."

"I know," Sophia said, but she was thinking, *He ought to die for what he did to me, and if he does not, he will mock me, and wait out the term of his transportation—they will not make it permanent, not for someone like him, and fourteen years is nothing—and then he will return, and nothing will have changed.*

Cecy kissed Sophia on the cheek, said, "Sleep well," and shut the door behind her. Sophia stood in her nightdress, staring at the lamp flame until it was burned into her brain, then extinguished it and got into bed. She was still too wakeful to sleep. *I am not free so long as he lives,* she thought, and despite her head, which still ached, she willed herself into Dream, searching for a future in which Lord Endicott was dead and she was truly free of him.

She woke late, feeling as if the house were trembling in its foundations, but it was only Cecy, shaking her awake. "Sophy, you must come quickly," she said. "Mr. Rutledge is here with news."

Sophia dressed more quickly than she had in her entire life and bolted down the stairs to the drawing room. Mr. Rutledge looked rumpled, as if he hadn't slept all night, and one of his cheeks was cut and bruised. "Mrs. Westlake, I apologize for disturbing you this early," he began.

"I seem to recall you telling me that only days ago," Sophia said with a smile. He didn't smile back.

"I'm afraid we were not as thorough as we should have been," he said, his voice a bass rumble the way it always was when he was very serious. "Bow Street sent men to apprehend Endicott early this morning, after receiving my report. He was gone. No one has seen him in any of his usual haunts. We believe someone slipped away from the warehouse and warned him. He's escaped us."

CHAPTER 30

IN WHICH THE PREY ESCAPES
THE TRAP

"That is impossible," Sophia said. "Impossible." If she said it vehemently enough, it might become true. He could not be free.

"It is true," Mr. Rutledge said. "If he had access to the right Bounder, he could be anywhere in the world now. We have no way of finding him."

"Oh, I will find him, you may be assured of that," Sophia said, and left the room at a run. She scrabbled at the drawer of her bedside table, saw faint images crowd her field of Vision, and realized she was not wearing her gloves and had no idea where she had left them. Gingerly, she picked up Lord Endicott's watch fob with her skirt wrapped around her hand, then Mr. Rutledge's ring, and juggling them in the folds of her skirt, she hurried back to the drawing room.

She tossed Mr. Rutledge's ring at him; he caught it deftly out of the air and looked at it as if he'd never seen it before. "Thank you for the loan of your eyes," she said, dropped into her chair, and took the watch fob in her right hand.

She was so angry it took her a moment to find the right Vision, during which time Mr. Rutledge said, "Do I want to know where you got that?"

Cecy replied, "It is better that you don't, Mr. Rutledge."

There, off to the side, a Vision that moved too rapidly by comparison to the rest. She drew it close and watched for a while. "I can only see that he is mounted, and that he is riding in the open, somewhere that might... how strange. I believe he may still be in England."

"You can't be more specific than that?" Mr. Rutledge said.

"Not yet."

"Then he is near London?"

"I cannot tell, Mr. Rutledge, I believe I have already said that."

"Calm down, Sophia," Cecy said. "Why would he not have left the country?"

"He is mad," Sophia said. "Who knows what he might do?"

"Are you speaking metaphorically, Mrs. Westlake?"

"I am not, Mr. Rutledge." She dropped the watch fob into her lap. "I would guess he does not believe he has lost, and has a plan more cunning than the simple solution of going abroad."

"Possibly," Mr. Rutledge said. "If he has no Bounder of his own, there is no reason he could not use a public Bounder service, but few of those have Bounders who know the signatures of any places outside London, let alone England. He may have no choice but to take ship somewhere. Can you tell in which direction he is traveling?"

Sophia once again picked up the fob and looked through Lord Endicott's eyes. "He is heading south," she said. "The sun is on his left hand. South and a little west."

"Portsmouth," Mr. Rutledge said. "Look for signs. Guildford, or Haslemere."

"I have three and a half years of experience scouting for the War Office, Mr. Rutledge. I know how to find my location."

"I beg your pardon," Mr. Rutledge said, but he sounded amused rather than offended. "I forgot myself in my eagerness."

"Thank you." It was such an eerie feeling, Seeing through someone's eyes when he had no idea she was there. She closed her eyes against real-world distractions just as a familiar *whoosh* heralded Daphne's arrival.

"Why have you not taken Lord Endicott to the magistrates?" she exclaimed, and Sophia heard paper rustling. "Look at this headline! Sophia could be arrested at any moment!"

"Lord Endicott has escaped, Sophy is tracking him now, and I suspect Bow Street will not be sending Mr. Vane after Sophy, if you have told them Lord Endicott is the villain, Mr. Rutledge."

"They will not," Mr. Rutledge said. "Though Rowley was preparing to do so when I arrived with my explanation and a line of criminals in tow. I believe he was disappointed he would not be able to make his career by arresting an Extraordinary."

Sophia could not settle whether to be angry or amused by this, but then Lord Endicott turned his head to look at a road sign, and she said, "He is nearing Guildford right now."

"Then he has not gone far," Mr. Rutledge said. "I must hurry back to Bow Street—we will have to round up as many Bounders as we can, if we are to intercept him before he reaches Portsmouth. If we are fortunate, some of them will be able to Bound to one of the towns nearer to Guildford. Please excuse me."

"I can take you to Bow Street," Daphne said.

Sophia dropped the fob into her lap and opened her eyes to stare at Daphne, and saw everyone else was doing the same. "Why are you surprised? It's not as if the magistrates' office is a secret," Daphne said.

"But, Daphne... Mr. Rutledge is... rather large..." Sophia said, unable to look at him for fear she would start laughing, and he would believe she was laughing at him rather than at the absurdity of tiny Daphne lifting anyone larger than she was.

"So what if he is? I want to be more than a courier in the War Office, Sophia, and I have practiced lifting increasingly heavy weights for the last three years, and—you are all so skeptical, but have I ever been unable to do something once I've claimed I could do it?" Daphne walked over to Mr. Rutledge and tilted her head back, looking up at him. "You'll have to balance, but it's only for a moment, and you can do that, can't you, Mr. Rutledge?"

"If you can save me the carriage ride to Bow Street, I can balance for as long as you like," he said. He looked down at the ring in his hand, then extended it to Sophia. "Hold this, for now," he said, "and I will try to communicate with you as we learn more."

"But I will be Seeing through his eyes," Sophia said.

"As a precaution, then," he said. He looked so serious despite the bruise that gave him a rakish look that she took the ring and swiftly dropped it into her lap before the swirling Visions could fill her Sight.

Daphne crouched next to Mr. Rutledge. "It is all about balance, and center of gravity," she said, wrapped her arms around his legs just above his knees, and heaved—and Mr. Rutledge's feet left the ground, and before he could do more than wobble, they were both gone.

Sophia gasped, then began to laugh, and Cecy joined her. "I would not for the world make fun of her," Sophia said when her laughter had subsided, "but that is the funniest thing I have seen in ages."

"I hope she doesn't strain herself," Lewis said. "That was... I don't mind telling you I don't believe *I* could lift him, even in this augmented form."

"Daphne continues to amaze me," Sophia said. She picked up Mr. Rutledge's ring rather than the fob. He was, in fact, inside the magistrates' office, with Daphne beside him—she appeared to be listening closely to something he was saying, and nodding in agreement.

Whoosh. "Mr. Rutledge wants me to help transport the men to Portsmouth," Daphne said, "so I will do that, and then return—no, I will take a few moments to learn the essence of some of the places nearer—I wish I had known I would need to know them, they—it will make my Bounding more—unless you believe—"

"That makes sense, Daphne," Sophia said, half her attention on her cousin and the other half on Mr. Rutledge, who had just written WE WILL FIND HIM in his notebook. That he could take the time to reassure her when he was scrambling to catch up to his prey warmed her heart.

"Then I will return later," Daphne said, and vanished. Mr. Rutledge was talking to Sir Arthur now, and Sophia set the ring down. Right now, she wanted only to See what Lord Endicott saw. The warm feeling she had from Mr. Rutledge's regard turned into a fierce, joyful, angry flame when she thought of how her nemesis was riding to his doom, even if no one but she seemed to understand his death was essential to her peace of mind. She picked up the fob again. He was not stopping in Guildford, but he would need to change horses sometime, and eat—

"Cecy, I am hungry," she said. "Is there anything to eat?"

She found it unexpectedly exhausting to watch the interminable landscape through Lord Endicott's eyes without cease, and eventually settled into a pattern: watch for ten minutes, rest for half an hour, watch again. He did nothing to vary his journey except stop in some town she failed to glimpse the name of, to change horses and eat a nuncheon that was no doubt far coarser than what he was accustomed to. Lewis went off to his study. Cecy sat with her sewing and occasionally asked if Sophia Saw anything interesting. Sophia answered her briefly, and sometimes commented on what she Saw.

She thought about setting the fob aside to See what Mr. Rutledge saw. What would he do, when this was all over? He had told her his working for the Bank of England was something new; based on what little she had seen in Vision, she suspected he had worked clandestinely for the British government for many years, or possibly the East India Company. Some organization that could afford to send him all over the world, at any rate. If Lord Endicott's criminal activities were now permanently at an end, would the Bank of England have need of him anymore? More likely he would return to what he had been doing before this interlude.

She set the fob aside and leaned back in her chair, and closed her eyes. He might need to travel again. The British Indian colonies were always in conflict with the local rulers, and she had Seen him there before; his employers might determine his experience was necessary there. Or they might send him to America, where the Iroquois Confederacy seemed once again to be on the verge of war with the colonies, disrupting trade as well as government. And then it would not matter that they had reclaimed their friendship; he would be gone, and it would be as if she had never met him.

"You seem very somber now," Cecy said. "Is something troubling you?"

Sophia smiled, but did not open her eyes. "You mean, aside from worrying that my enemy will yet escape punishment?"

"Yes, aside from that." Cecy set her sewing down. "Are you content, dearest?"

"With what?"

"Content that Lord Endicott will be punished, even if it is not what you wanted."

"Does it disturb you that I want him dead?"

"It does, a little."

Sophia sat up and looked at Cecy. "He tried to ruin me," she said. "He took joy in seeing me suffer. He would have had me arrested and imprisoned and I have no doubt he would have tried to kill me, given enough time. How am I wrong for wanting him dead?"

"Because it is hurting you," Cecy said. "I know you have been trying to protect yourself, but you are taking as much pleasure in hunting him down as he did in tormenting you. If it was evil of him to do it to you, how is it any less evil when you do it to him?"

"You are not calling me evil, Cecy?"

"You know that's not what I meant. If seeing him destroyed means you must become like him, then I would rather he lived a long and miserable life on the other side of the world."

"I am *nothing* like him." Sophia stood and walked to the window, gripped the sill and leaned heavily on it. Outside, carriages filled the street, which was wet and dirty from what was left of the last snowfall. No one looked up. No one ever thought to look up, to see what was there around them beyond the limits of their vision.

"No, you are not," Cecy said gently, "but you might become so."

"If he is not dead, he will simply return when the term of his transportation is up and find new ways to torment me!"

"They could make his transportation permanent."

"But they will not. It is not *justice*, Cecy."

"And? You don't want justice. You want revenge."

"And it seems I will have neither," Sophia said. She flung herself away from the window and out the door, down the stairs and into the foyer before remembering she held both the fob and the ring clutched in a fold of her skirt. She stood in the tall, narrow room, feeling the hard angles of one and the soft curves of the other through the muslin, then slid the ring over her finger and let herself be encompassed by Vision. Mr. Rutledge was outdoors, standing beside a barn, possibly, some large structure anyway; she knew little of agrarian life. He was talking to a younger man. It was all extremely boring. She removed the ring and traded it for the fob.

Lord Endicott was in a coach now, probably a post-chaise, though it was difficult to tell from the inside. It was passing through a town; all these little towns surrounding London looked the same to her, the same ancient Tudor framing, the same little inns bearing the same—

Sophia looked again. No, it didn't look the same, it *was* the same. Lord Endicott had turned around and was returning to London. He had tricked her *again*, had taken the road to Portsmouth just long enough to convince her of his destination, waited until he was certain she would have sent the law there to arrest him, and now was turning back on his trail. Oh, he was cunning, but she would not be so easily deterred. *Where* was Daphne? She needed to get word of this to Mr. Rutledge immediately.

No. That was foolish. Lord Endicott might change his direction again and again and leave them trailing after him like puppies after a crafty old fox. She needed more information. She ran back upstairs and into her room, tossed the ring and the fob into the drawer, and flung herself onto her bed to Dream. He would not escape her. He might be able to taunt her in Vision, but he had no defense against Dream.

She found only one door waiting for her when she dropped into Dream. That was either a good sign, or a terrible warning; if events were funneling into a single future, it meant something was coming that would be almost impossible to avoid. She laid her hand on the door and was drawn into Dream. Even before the Dream fully enveloped her, she heard the roar of applause, but found herself on a pebbly shore, watching the tide as it slammed into the cliff side. It was Dover. Toy boats bobbed on the soapy grey stone of the water; the painted white circle of the sun hovered low above the horizon; men and women like sticks with arms and legs passed around her, ignoring her.

Lord Endicott appeared, standing between her and the shore. He was the only other recognizably human figure in the Dream. He disappeared, then popped back into existence as if he were a Bounder rather than a Shaper, vanished and appeared again. He had his back to her and was looking out over the ocean—no, he was looking at the boats as if trying to choose which one to embark on.

A heavy weight dragged at each of her hands. In one hand, she held Mr. Rutledge's ring, which had grown large enough for her to wear as a bracelet. In the other, a long-barreled pistol weighed her down. It was beautiful, with gold inlay and a shining barrel that looked oiled, it gleamed so. She raised the pistol, pointed it at Lord Endicott's back, and hesitated—and the Dream came apart, and she was back in her room, on her bed, sweating and shaking from the intensity of the Dream. This was what events were leading to. Lord Endicott would Bound to Dover, where she would be waiting, and he would not know to flee her. And she would have her revenge. All the paths of Dream led to this.

She lay, still shuddering, making her plans. It was tempting to run through the streets, looking for a Bounder who could take her to Dover, but the Dream was incontrovertible; she would be in Dover at the right time, which meant Daphne would return exactly when she was needed. That gave Sophia enough time for one more crucial errand.

When she once again had control of herself, she went back to the drawing room, where Cecy was staring into the fireplace, her sewing forgotten on the seat beside her. "I am going out for a while," she said.

"Please don't be angry with me," Cecy said. Sophia realized she had been crying. She went to her knees in front of her friend and put her arms around her.

"I am not angry with you, Cecy, and you are right," Sophia said. Lying became easier the more you did it. "But I need some time to let go of my anger at Lord Endicott, do you understand that?"

Cecy nodded. "Mr. Rutledge will capture him soon," she said. "I know he would want you to See it."

"I will not be gone long." She squeezed Cecy once more, then went downstairs to summon the carriage, gripping the fob as she waited. The Vision still showed the interior of the carriage; Lord Endicott had not yet arrived at his destination. When Peter pulled up to the door, she told him where to go, and glared at him when he seemed about to question her decision to travel unescorted into Whitechapel. But it was the only pawnshop she knew, and she dared not stop to Dream of one closer to home. Besides, the proprietor owed her a debt, even though she did not intend to identify herself in order to collect on it.

The pawnshop owner was disinclined to tell the eccentric woman she could not have what she wanted, when it turned out she had hard coin to spend. Sophia had left off the red gloves for this excursion to protect her identity, and there was a moment when she picked up the pistol and was overwhelmed by the images of death associated with it. That moment shook her resolve; could she shoot a man? *If it is Lord Endicott, I can do anything,* she thought, and gripped the pistol's hilt more firmly.

She walked out of the shop with her new purchase in a drawstring bag it was undoubtedly not meant to be carried in. It was not the long-barreled beauty of her Dream, but a more practical, smaller pistol the pawnbroker nevertheless assured her would be perfect "for madam to defend herself with." She also had powder, shot, and wadding, and five minutes' instruction in loading the thing. More than enough. She would only need to use it once.

She returned to the house and smuggled the pistol up to her room, then retrieved her gloves and, after a few moments' thought, Mr. Rutledge's ring, and returned to the drawing room to find it empty. Cecy must have felt unwell again. Fortunate for both of them, since Sophia was tired of having to lie to the people she cared about. She drew off one glove, tried the fob again—still the carriage—then, after a moment's hesitation, picked up the ring and located Mr. Rutledge's Vision. He was alone now, standing behind the same barn, occasionally looking up the empty road. One more person to lie to, though in his case it was a lie of omission. She would send Daphne back for him once she had got what she wanted. Where was Daphne, anyway? Surely she was done running errands for Mr. Rutledge by now.

As if her thoughts summoned her, Daphne appeared in the middle of the room. She looked more windblown than usual and the tip of her nose as well as her cheeks was red. "Is Cecy not well?" she said. "I apologize for taking so long—"

"Never mind that," Sophia said. "I need you to take me to Dover. Right now."

CHAPTER 31

IN WHICH SOPHIA MAKES A
DECISION

"Dover?" Daphne said. "Why Dover?" Her eyes went wide. "Sophia, did you—you would not have lied to us about—he will escape, Sophia, how could you think—"

"I never lie about my Sight," Sophia said. "Lord Endicott has tricked me. He made it seem he was going to Portsmouth, but he is on his way to Dover. I have Seen where he will be and I am the only one who can stop him in time. Please, Daphne, we cannot delay any longer."

"But, Sophia, he cannot possibly reach Dover faster than I can fetch Mr. Rutledge. It's a long journey."

"He's not going there directly. He knows where he can find a Bounder to take him there," Sophia said. "Please, Daphne. He is still traveling, but at any moment he could reach this Bounder, and then it will be too late."

"I don't know—"

"*Please.* If he escapes...."

Daphne still looked troubled. "You can fetch Mr. Rutledge after you have taken me there," Sophia said.

"All right," Daphne said, "but you will wait for me to find Mr.

Rutledge and not go tearing off after Lord Endicott by yourself, agreed?"

"Agreed," Sophia lied. "Wait while I fetch my cloak."

She ran to her bedroom for her largest cloak, picked up the drawstring bag and concealed it in the heavy velvet folds, then ran back to the drawing room. "I need not ask if you are able to lift me," she said, though the joke sounded dull to her. Daphne smiled in a way that told Sophia she did not think it was very funny either. She put her arms around Sophia, heaved, and with a flicker of insubstantiality, they were in a tiny chamber with an angular symbol painted on the wall in short, broad strokes of black.

"It's—I should accompany you, Mr. Wallis will not know what to make of you," Daphne said. She pushed the door open with some effort because it stuck. It gave out a loud *crack* when it was finally freed of the frame.

The room beyond was dimmer than the chamber, lit by a few low-burning candle stubs, had been. Half a dozen men looked up from their drinks to regard them with a kind of dull non-interest. The man behind the bar, by contrast, gave them both a very keen look. "Lady Daphne," he said. "Who's your friend then?"

"It doesn't matter, Mr. Wallis, she has the money," Daphne said. Sophia, startled, shook her head at Daphne, and Daphne rolled her eyes and dug a few coins out of the pouch strapped across her chest. "There," she said. "My friend is going to wait here, and I'm bringing through a lot of other people, so be polite to her and you'll profit by it, understand?"

"I ain't stupid," Mr. Wallis said. "Care for a drink, Lady Daphne's friend? On the house."

"No, thank you," Sophia said.

"Now, *stay here*," Daphne said. "It may take me a little while, because he's outdoors and I'll have to Skip there from Portsmouth, and it's a long way—well, longish way—but we'll be in time, I know we will." She vanished. Sophia immediately went for the door.

"I thought you was staying here," Mr. Wallis said.

"So did Daphne," said Sophia, and emerged blinking into the late afternoon light. She had been to Dover only once before, and that many years ago, and she had forgotten how crowded the town was. Carriages of all sizes rumbled past in both directions, passing carts laden with crates and bundles ready to ship out on the next tide. When was the next tide? Though she knew in her bones she would be at their rendezvous on time, she could not help feeling fear that she was wrong, that Lord Endicott would be able to Bound into whatever location his Bounder knew the signature of, stroll through the city, and step onto the right boat just as it was casting off.

Sophia found a quiet corner, took off her glove, and felt around in the drawstring bag for the fob. Her hand fell first on Mr. Rutledge's ring, and she had enough time to See him still staring down the same empty road before she thrust it away. Then the fob was in her hands, and she Saw a town, not Dover, thank God, and a sign with no writing on it, just the five-spiked sun that meant a public Bounder transportation company. She dropped the fob back into the bag and ran, tugging her glove on as she went.

She had no idea where she was going, had not seen any of Dover in Dream except that one fatal spot where Lord Endicott would be, and she had to stop and ask directions to the harbor more than once. The men she spoke to, one an elegantly dressed gentleman, the other a sailor with blue tattoos on his wrists, eyed the red gloves without comment. What did they make of her, wild-eyed and imperfectly concealing her agitation? She had no time to care what other people thought. She ran on, pushing people out of her way, wishing she could See through Lord Endicott's eyes as she ran.

She skidded around a corner, ran down a street lined with blank-eyed buildings of stone, ricocheted off a woman bundled up against the cold, and realized she was within sight of the harbor. In the distance, the famous white cliffs rose tall against the grey sky. Another storm was coming in. It might prevent the ships from sailing out, which would prevent Lord Endicott from leaving—but she had forgotten, *she* would be the one stopping him.

She walked more slowly now, casting about for anything familiar. This was definitely the street, and she had been standing on the right-hand side. She turned to put her back to the buildings on that side and began walking sideways, glancing quickly to either side to keep from running into anyone. Other pedestrians gave her looks that said they thought she was mad.

As if she were seeing the shops overlaid on their Dream counterparts, her real vision and her memory of Sight slid together, matching her Dream exactly. She stopped to look around. Behind her was a gap in the row of shops where an alley cut between two buildings, leading she could not tell where. It was more of a crevice than an alley. She looked at the sky. The light was not right, and the sun had not yet reached the right place. Sophia took several steps down the alley until she was concealed from the passing bystanders, then removed the pistol from its bag and began loading it. She spilled a few grains of powder in her haste and made herself slow down. There was no hurry. Everything was coming together as she had Dreamed.

She went back to the mouth of the alley, the pistol concealed in her cloak, and settled in to wait, watching the crowds for her prey to come into view. No one looked her way. She began to feel as if this were the Dream, in which she passed invisibly through the crowds her Dreaming mind conjured. Some of them would witness Lord Endicott's death. They would be able to tell the world the truth.

The truth. Sophia looked at her red-gloved hand. Would they know the truth, though? That she had been forced to seek revenge because the world would not give her justice? She needed a plan for when this was all over. She would not be able to return home immediately, because Sir Arthur would want to arrest her, even though her only crime would be executing a madman and a criminal. She might need to take ship to France for a while. Cecy would be devastated. Sophia's hand began to tremble. Cecy would just have to understand, that was all. None of them were safe while Lord Endicott lived.

She looked up the street again, then at the sky. Still not time yet. She had left her watch at home and had no idea what the actual time was. The pistol was growing heavy, but she didn't dare put it away in case Lord Endicott came and she fumbled getting it out.

Someone cleared his throat, very nearby. Sophia brought the pistol up and swung around fast in the direction of the harbor. "Please don't shoot me," Mr. Rutledge said, stepping out from around the far side of the next building.

Sophia lowered the pistol. "How did you get past me?"

"I didn't. I went down to the harbor by a different road and was returning this way, hoping I would find you before it was too late."

"Do not interfere. This is where Dream has led me. Lord Endicott will not escape me."

"No, he will not. Rowley's men are coming into Dover as we speak. They will capture him, I promise you. Go home, Mrs. Westlake."

"You understand *nothing*," Sophia said, bringing the weapon up as she spoke and forcing Mr. Rutledge back two steps. "He is charming, and noble, and he will not face death, and that is unacceptable to me!"

"His evil will be exposed for everyone to see. You will be vindicated. He will never be able to torment you again. Why is that not enough for you?"

"Because it is not!" Sophia realized where the pistol's muzzle was pointed and lowered it. "He will find some way around whatever meager punishment the courts hand down! This is the only way I can protect myself, and Cecy and her baby, and everyone I love."

Mr. Rutledge wrested the pistol from her hand as easily as plucking an apple from a tree. "That is not the reason," he said, low and intense. "Don't lie to me, Mrs. Westlake. You want revenge. Endicott hurt your pride and made you look the fool, and you can't bear that."

She felt as if he'd shot her in the chest. "That's not true," she began.

"It *is* true. I know you. You are strong, and brilliant, and you know the use of your talent better than anyone alive. But you're also proud, and you cannot endure being made mock of. You need Endicott dead because alive he is a constant reminder of how you were betrayed."

"That's not true," she repeated, but faintly, feeling as if her voice had been stolen away. "He—it is justice—"

"It's revenge," Mr. Rutledge said. He looked at the pistol in his hand, then offered it to her; she took it automatically, clutching it tightly because her fingers were numb. "If you will only be satisfied with his death," he went on, "I won't stop you killing him. Then I will take you into custody, and hand you over to Rowley's men. You will go to prison, and you will be tried, and when they discover you used your talent in killing Endicott, you will hang. *And you will deserve it.*"

She gasped. "You can't mean that."

"I do mean it. This is not who you are, Mrs. Westlake. The woman I know would never hurt her friends by destroying her life so thoroughly. If you kill Endicott, you become a stranger to me and to everyone you know. And I think you will be a stranger to yourself."

"But—" she said, and could not think of a way to end that sentence. She looked at the pistol she held. Its oiled barrel gleamed. "But he will win," she said, quietly, and tears came to her eyes.

"He lost the moment he tried to bury your name with the War Office," Mr. Rutledge said. "Every attack he has brought against you has failed. You simply haven't been able to see it." He put his hand on her arm. "Please, Sophia. Remember who you are. Let this Dream of vengeance go."

His hand was warm, even through all the layers of sleeve and cloak and glove. She looked up at him, at those dark, intent eyes, and the hard knot of pain at the center of her chest began to loosen. He was right. She had already won. "I can't," she said, then closed her mouth on whatever foolish words might try to escape her lips. "Mr. Rutledge, how foolish have I been?"

"Not foolish. Desperate. And I believe you have forgotten how many people care about you and will not leave you defenseless against your enemy. Think of Mrs. Barham and Lady Daphne."

"They have gone to great lengths to support me. I have used them shamefully ill." Sophia wiped her eyes with her free hand. "I hope they will forgive me."

"I believe they will."

"They are not my only friends. Mr. Rutledge, I owe you a debt."

Mr. Rutledge smiled. "You can set it against the debt I owe *you*, for forgiving me my inability to believe the truth of your words. I deserved your anger."

"No, you did not, and I..." She became conscious again of his hand on her arm and blushed. Could she tell him she thought of him as much more than a friend? No, the streets of Dover were not the place for such a declaration. She felt as if she were waking from a long, oppressive Dream in which nothing made any sense. "I want to go home."

"Lady Daphne is around the corner, waiting. Do you still have my ring? I will tell you when Endicott is captured."

"Thank you," she said, stepping past him into the street, "but I don't care anymore." She turned right to join Daphne—and saw Lord Endicott not twenty paces away.

Sophia gasped, and took half a step back. Lord Endicott looked as startled as she did. Then everything happened at once:

Lord Endicott brought his pistol to bear on her

Mr. Rutledge grabbed her arm and slung her roughly behind him

A clap of thunder, high and sharp and very nearby, rang out

and Mr. Rutledge grunted and stumbled backward, knocking her down.

CHAPTER 32
IN WHICH IT IS UNCERTAIN WHO
IS HUNTER, AND WHO IS PREY

S ophia screamed, lending her voice to the chorus of screams the gunshot had elicited, and staggered to her feet, still clutching her pistol. Lord Endicott bowed low to her, a courtier's bow, then took off running toward the docks. She screamed again and ran after him, but he was Shaping himself as he ran and becoming as fleet-footed as a deer. She stopped and brought her pistol to bear on him, her hands shaking. There were too many people, but she could just see him, at the limit of her range—

"Sophia, help!" Daphne cried. "Help me—he's bleeding—I can't do it, Sophia! Help him!"

Her words struck Sophia like the bolt of lightning that surely should have preceded that thunderclap. She turned to see Mr. Rutledge lying too still on the ground and Daphne crouched a few feet away, her head between her knees. No one was approaching their little tableau; almost everyone stood frozen, or was looking about in confusion as if Lord Endicott had not taken his shot mere feet from where they stood.

Sophia threw the pistol away and ran as hard as she could back to Mr. Rutledge's side, falling to her knees and grabbing the front of his coat as if that would make him stand. Blood was spreading across his ugly brown waistcoat and pooling beneath him. Sophia pulled up her skirt, not caring who saw, yanked at the seams of her shift until most of it tore free, and wadded the fabric up and pressed it hard against his chest. Mr. Rutledge moved then, reaching toward her, and she said, "Hold still. Daphne. *Daphne*. Stop being a self-indulgent child and get help."

"But I don't know—who do I get, what do I *do*, Sophia?"

Sophia tried to steady her breathing. She would have to be the sensible one, no matter how much she wanted to fling herself across Mr. Rutledge and sob. "Dr. Garland," she said, but realized she did not know where the doctor was. With Cecy? Was she ill enough for Lewis to call Dr. Garland for help? There was no time for Daphne to Bound all over London, looking for an Extraordinary Shaper. "Wait a moment," Sophia said, thought *Show her to me*, and dropped into Dream like a stone into a pool, barely registering her body's collapse across Mr. Rutledge before the doors of Dream opened up before her, all of them bearing the doctor's face.

She threw herself into the nearest one, and Saw Dr. Garland as a two-dimensional painting, frozen in the act of speaking to someone not represented in the Dream. Panting, she looked wildly around for a door to the outside, a window, anything, and Saw nothing but blank white walls, smooth and shiny like pearls. She rose out of Dream as rapidly as she had dropped into it, gasping as if she were rising out of the ocean's depths, and found that Mr. Rutledge had put his large, bloodstained hand over hers where it lay on the front of his coat. The touch of his hand made her want to weep.

"No," she cried, and dove back into Dream and the doors with the doctor's face overlaid upon them. "*No!*" she shouted again, and the doors shivered, and shattered, and then only one remained, and she let it pull her into another Dream of shining white walls and a flat drawing of Dr. Garland—and a single tiny window, one glass pane too thick to see through.

She could feel time sliding away from her, and for half a moment she imagined herself waking from Dream to discover she was clutching a corpse. She screamed and struck the glass with all the strength that was in her. Her fist passed through empty air, and the glass splintered and melted away, leaving a hole she could barely fit her head and shoulders through. In the non-light of Dream, she saw a street, carriages like black turtles creeping along the street, a familiar stair—and relief shook her sleeping body so that she woke before she could bring herself out of Dream. "Go to Cecy," she gasped, "and bring the doctor here, and *hurry*."

Daphne vanished. Sophia removed her hand from Mr. Rutledge's limp one and bent over his face, and her terror faded a little when she felt warm air sighing out of his mouth, though his eyes were closed and he was still motionless. She went back to leaning hard on the wound. Blood had soaked through the cloth and was turning her red gloves redder, filling the air with its sharp hot coppery smell.

She realized she had an audience, men and women crowded around murmuring, carriages stopped where the crush of people blocked the road, and she shrieked at them, *"Stay back!"* They moved back, but only a short distance, and Sophia wished she could leap to her feet and pummel them until they fled, gore-crows that they were. She looked at Mr. Rutledge's face again; he was far too pale, and his eyes were still closed, but his lips were moving. "Don't try to talk," she said.

"… not… your friend…" he said, his deep voice almost inaudible.

Sophia again felt as if she were the one who had been shot. "I promise I don't want vengeance anymore," she said. She shook her head to dash away the tears she had no hands for wiping. "Please do not hold it against me that it took so long. I cherish our friendship."

He shook his head, slowly, making it flop back and forth. "…stay with me…"

"I'm not leaving."

Mr. Rutledge smiled, then coughed. Blood flecked his lips. He shook his head again. "…want you to marry me…" he said.

Sophia gasped, then began to laugh. "You know I could never marry anyone but you," she said, crying harder now through her laughter. "Now stop talking, or I might change my mind."

He smiled again, then lay still. Sophia looked around, though it was hard to see through her tears. Where was Daphne? How long could it possibly take her to Bound to Cecy's drawing room and Bound back to that tiny room in the tavern and then Skip... oh, it was too far. They would be too late. She had killed him.

She pressed harder and did not look at Mr. Rutledge's face, afraid of what she might see there, remembering how empty Richard's face had been at the end, how vacant, and the thought of seeing that emptiness again on the face of the man she loved tore at her heart. *I hope Lord Endicott is gone*, she thought, and laughed again. She sounded hysterical. The last thing she needed was her nemesis coming back, armed and ready to kill her now that her protector was—*not dead, he's not dead, he can't be dead*—

"Move aside, Mrs. Westlake," Dr. Garland said, following that command up by shoving Sophia away from Mr. Rutledge so she sprawled on the paved sidewalk. Daphne came to help her stand, though she was still shaking.

"Forgive me, Sophia," she sobbed, "I didn't know—how will they use me on the battlefield if I can't bear the sight of blood—oh, *no*." She turned away and knelt, pressing her face against the hard-packed earth of the road. Sophia ignored her, her eyes fixed on the doctor and her patient, who lay far too still.

Dr. Garland slung her satchel on the ground and unrolled it, taking a large pair of shears from it and cutting through Mr. Rutledge's ugly waistcoat and his shirt to reveal the expanse of his stomach and chest. Blood still flowed from the rough, round hole. Dr. Garland put her hand over it and sat in the attitude of someone listening to a distant sound.

"All of you, move back or I'll give you hives," she said in a loud but pleasant voice, and the crowd moved as they had not for Sophia. "Mrs. Westlake, I don't want to lie to you," she said more quietly. "This doesn't look good."

"He's dead," Sophia said, and sat down because she was afraid she might collapse if she did not.

Dr. Garland shook her head. "But the treatment could kill him. Just —don't panic, whatever you see." She put both her bare palms on Mr. Rutledge's chest, framing the wound, and he began convulsing so hard Sophia could hear his head striking the hard stones. Without thinking, she slid to put her hands beneath his head, cushioning it, and thought

I am getting blood in his hair, but it is his blood, perhaps he will not mind so much and had to bite back another hysterical laugh.

The convulsions went on for so long. She felt as if she had been holding his head for hours. Mr. Rutledge's face grew even paler, and his lips were tinged blue as if he were not breathing, though he was thrashing so hard she could not tell if that were true. She wished she could put her arms around him, stop the awful jerking motions that were such a contrast to his still, unmoving face, but all she could do was hold his head still and pray a series of unconnected, fragmentary pleas.

Then he bucked hard once, jerking his head from between her hands, and lay unmoving once again. Sophia held her breath. "Doctor," she began, but her voice was too faint, and the doctor ignored her—or was it that she did not want to tell Sophia the truth?

Then the little hole in Mr. Rutledge's chest quivered, and a deformed ball of lead popped out of the wound and slid a little way down his bloody chest. Dr. Garland spread her hand over the wound again, and pressed down with her palm, gently, then slid her hand away, revealing skin that was bloody but unmarked. There was not even a scar to show where he had been shot.

Sophia breathed out, feeling dizzy, then breathed in more deeply as Mr. Rutledge exhaled, shallowly, the movement of his chest barely visible, but steady. Dr. Garland picked up the ball and held it out to Sophia. "Hold onto it," she said. "Some men like to keep them." Sophia turned it over in her hand, grateful for the gloves that prevented her from Seeing anything associated with it. She hoped he would not want to keep it.

"Is he... will he be perfectly well, doctor?" she said, her voice still unsteady. "He looks...."

"You saw how the Healing affected him," Dr. Garland said. She looked exhausted, grey-faced, but her voice was strong. "He won't wake for an hour or so, and it will take him a few days to be fully recovered, but since he survived the Healing, I see no reason he should suffer any lasting damage. Good thing he's so solidly built, or there might have been complications—but you don't need to hear my war stories. I imagine you've Seen enough of your own."

Dr. Garland wiped her shears on the sleeve of Mr. Rutledge's bloody coat and stowed them away. "Lady Daphne, do you know the signature of St. Margaret's Hospital?"

Daphne stood, wiping her forehead. "Yes, Dr. Garland. And I can manage to get him there. Please forgive me."

"Happens to a lot of people. It's nothing to be ashamed of."

Daphne nodded, closed her eyes against the sight of Mr. Rutledge's gory chest, and crouched, worming her arms under his shoulders and knees. She grunted, and heaved, and was gone. The watching crowd, who had taken advantage of the doctor's distraction to gradually move closer, let out a collective sigh of admiration. The doctor stood, stretching until her joints popped. "Plenty of rest, a lot of tea, and he should be back to normal in a day or so," she told Sophia.

"But I... you should tell that to... I do not know who will care for him when he leaves the hospital," Sophia stammered.

Dr. Garland's eyebrows went up. "Not you? My mistake."

Sophia blushed. Now that Mr. Rutledge was gone, she began to doubt what she had heard. He had been barely clinging to consciousness; probably he did not remember saying anything to her, or if he did, thought it was a dream. "We are friends," she said. She hoped it was still true, whatever else might happen. Whatever else she might feel for him.

A blur in the distance turned into Daphne, Skipping toward them. "Shall I take you next, Dr. Garland, or Sophia?"

"The doctor, please, and... to the hospital?" Sophia said. Dr. Garland nodded, put her arms around Daphne, and then they were gone, and Sophia was left alone. The onlookers, who seemed not to realize her gloves were red from more than Mr. Rutledge's blood, seemed also not to know what they should do with her.

"I am perfectly well, please do not trouble yourselves," she said to those few who made as if to approach her. She pulled her cloak tight around herself to conceal the bloody mess her gown had become and began walking back in the direction of the tavern. Behind her, the crowd began to disperse, and soon there were only a few people standing there, telling, from what little Sophia could hear, exaggerated stories of what had transpired there. She tried to summon revulsion at their gruesome eagerness, but was too weary to be properly outraged on Mr. Rutledge's behalf.

She peeled off her blood-soaked gloves and dropped them on the ground, then remembered the pistol and retraced her steps, looking for it. It was gone. Good. Someone else would put it to better use than she nearly had.

The empty bag lay nearby, still within the shadow of the narrow alley—but it wasn't empty, was it? She picked it up and felt for the outlines of the ring and the watch fob. It might be too overwhelming for her to touch the ring right now, since Mr. Rutledge had owned it for so long it could have absorbed the horror and shock of the attack despite not being on his body at the time, but...

She reached inside and pulled out the watch fob, and steadied herself against the whirl of images, seeking out Lord Endicott's current Vision. The other Visions, both static and moving, were so familiar they were easy for her to ignore, but it still took her several moments to locate the one she wanted. Passersby must think she was a madwoman, staring at nothing like that. She drew in the correct Vision, settled herself to See through her enemy's eyes, and had a moment's terror at seeing her own face looking back at her.

She dropped the fob into the bag and blinked as the Visions faded. Lord Endicott stood across the street, his body occasionally obscured by passing traffic. He was smiling at her with that pleasant, happy smile that concealed who knew what kind of madness. He did not appear to be armed.

Sophia stood there watching him, her mind a blank slate waiting for instructions she was helpless to provide. There was nothing she could do to stop him escaping justice, but then he did not appear to be trying to flee. She felt as if there were something she ought to say, or do. Before she could stop herself, she was crossing the street, weaving between the carriages until she stood before him.

"I can't remember which of us was the hunter, and which the prey," he said, conversationally, and held out his hand as if inviting her to dance. She ignored it.

"I thought I was the hunter," she said, "but your trap nearly caught me."

"I only want you to think well of me."

"I don't intend to think of you at all, from this time on."

The smile vanished. "At first you were an obstacle," he said, "an impediment to my affairs. Then you were an adversary. Now you are nothing but an annoyance. That fat bastard stopped me putting an end to you, but I see he's not here now. I suppose it's too much to hope he's dead?"

Silver flashed in his right hand, and now his smile was that of the predator he had claimed to be. Sophia took a step backward, then to the side, unable to look away from the knife but also very conscious of the carriages passing behind her, blocking her escape. "Time enough to kill you, then take—"

A blur struck him. He flung up his arms, and then he was simply gone, with nothing more than a *pop* to indicate he had ever been there. Sophia, stunned, looked up the street, then toward the harbor. He had vanished. The knife lay on the ground in front of her; she thought about picking it up, then kicked it away, thinking in her confusion that it might carry Lord Endicott's madness on it.

She looked around again. No one seemed to have noticed anything was wrong, but in the distance she saw someone she recognized. She met Benjamin Vane halfway up the street; he was breathing heavily from running. "Did you find Endicott? Where's Rutledge?" he said. Then he said, "Good Lord, Mrs. Westlake, you're covered in blood! Are you all right?"

Sophia opened her mouth to answer and realized it was all too complicated to explain. "Did you send a Bounder here?" she said.

"All our Bounders are busy bringing men in to capture Endicott," Vane said. "Where is he?"

"I don't know," Sophia said.

"He's at Bow Street," Daphne said, Skipping to a halt beside them. "I don't know what you were saying to him, Sophia, but he was preoccupied enough I could snatch him—do you know no one's ever done that before, Skip and grab someone and Bound away? I believe I've redeemed myself." She dropped into a crouch and bent her head, breathing heavily. "I'm so *tired*, Sophia, I had to carry Mr. Rutledge twice in the last hour, that's four times in all today, and I wish I hadn't bragged because he is *heavy*."

"Oh, *Daphne!*" Sophia exclaimed, and fell to her knees before her friend, clasping her around the shoulders and drawing her close. "Such heroics!"

"I guess that means we can all go home," Vane said. "Is any of that blood yours, Mrs. Westlake? Then you should clean yourself up afore anyone draws the wrong conclusions. Lady Daphne, can you take Mrs. Westlake home?"

"Just... give me a minute," Daphne wheezed.

"Thank you for everything, Mr. Vane," Sophia said, almost extending her hand to shake his before remembering that it, like the rest of her, was covered in Mr. Rutledge's blood.

"I'm not sure I did aught, but I can tell you I'm grateful I didn't have to arrest you today," Vane said with an uncharacteristic grin. Daphne stood up, then shuddered and looked away from Sophia.

"This is so embarrassing," she said, "it's only blood, everyone has it inside them, it's just when it's on the outside—" She glanced at Sophia and squeezed her eyes shut, then opened them again. "I can do this." She put her arms around Sophia's waist, and in a blink they were in Cecy's drawing room.

"Oh, Sophy, I am—*Sophia!*" Cecy's face went as white as Mr. Rutledge's, and Sophia had to leap forward to catch her as she fainted.

Sophia laid her carefully on the chaise longue and began chafing her wrists, saying, "Daphne, I believe there are smelling salts—no, never mind, she is waking up. I beg your pardon, Cecy, I forgot how I look, but I assure you I am quite well—none of this blood is mine."

Cecy gasped, then began to cry. "You killed him, Sophia, why did you do that, they will hang you now!"

"No, Cecy, Lord Endicott is alive, this is Mr. Rutledge's blood, Lord Endicott shot him—*no*, Cecy, he is alive, you know Daphne fetched Dr. Garland for him. Everything is all right."

"I do *not* know any of that! All I know is that Daphne came running into my bedroom, crying out that Dr. Garland must come now, and I thought—oh, I do not know what I thought!" Cecy sat up and threw her arms around Sophia. "Where is Lord Endicott?"

"Bow Street. Daphne captured him."

Cecy looked at Daphne in astonishment. "You?" Then she began to laugh. "I believe the War Office will regret not taking you on earlier. Imagine what you might do to Napoleon's forces."

"Oh, I have no regrets," Daphne said. "I would never have had cause to learn these things in the War Office. Just as *you* owe Lord Endicott a debt for forcing you to expand your talent, Sophia."

Sophia buried her face in Cecy's shoulder. "I owe him for a great deal more than that," she said.

CHAPTER 33
IN WHICH THERE IS, AFTER SOME ARGUMENT, A HAPPY ENDING

I t took a message from Sir Arthur, thanking her for her part in bringing Lord Endicott to justice, to finally persuade Sophia it was all over. She had been so obsessed with hunting down her prey that everything else seemed unreal.

Now, scrubbed clean and dressed in fresh, untorn clothing and gloves that were red only from cochineal dye, she sat at the dinner table and nibbled her food and could not quite believe she would not settle into Dream that night, searching for a way to defeat her nemesis. Had it been only five hours? She replied to something Cecy said without really hearing her, and then was startled to hear her friend laugh.

"I believe Lady Ormerod is a lovely woman, but I would hardly call her 'delicious,' " she said. "Come now, Sophy, you should be celebrating."

"I will, soon," Sophia said, "but for now I still cannot believe Lord Endicott is in prison."

"I can," Lewis said, "and I'm just as happy we no longer have to worry that he will send anyone after us."

"What did you do with the watch fob, Sophy?" Cecy asked.

"I had Daphne throw it in the Thames. Right into the center

where it's deepest." She had watched from the shore as Daphne had Skipped overhead and the speck of silver had plummeted into the icy water. She had no desire to See anything related to Lord Endicott again.

"You should return Mr. Rutledge's ring to him," Cecy said. "I hope he recovers quickly."

"Dr. Garland thought he would," Sophia said. She took a large bite of fish to give herself an excuse not to speak further. Surely he had regained consciousness by now. Did he remember what he had said to her? Did he *want* to remember? Why on earth would he say such a thing, if they were nothing but friends? *Be honest. It is a long time since you thought of him as only a friend.* She took another large mouthful of fish, as if she could stop her inner voice speaking as easily as she could her lips.

She excused herself after dinner, pleading tiredness, which was true as far as it went. Dressed for sleep, she lay in her bed, still wearing her gloves, and turned the ring over and over in her fingers. He had given her permission to use his eyes, yes, but she did not think that permission extended past the exigencies of the moment, when they were searching for Lord Endicott. And she did not imagine he would want her prying into his past, much as she wanted to see more of his many adventures. What she wanted was to see *him* again, to ask him if he truly meant what he'd said, and handling his ring was a poor substitute for that. She put the ring away in her drawer, removed her gloves, and tried for the next two hours to fall asleep.

The next day began with a message from Sir Arthur, asking Sophia to come to Bow Street to swear out an affidavit against Lord Endicott, since as an Extraordinary she was not required to testify personally in court. From there everything was a blur of questions in which Sophia repeated her story—her whole story, from her first Dream of Lord Endicott down to Daphne's spectacular capture—to Sir Arthur and Benjamin Vane and several other people until it seemed to have happened to someone else. By noon she had become impatient, and by one o'clock she remembered she was an Extraordinary and did not have to put up with that kind of treatment.

Sir Arthur, in a last attempt to exert his authority over her, warned her that as an Extraordinary she would have to make one more statement, this one to the Crown, and it was then she realized Lord Endicott's attempt on her life was a capital crime for which there could be no commutation. He would hang for trying to kill her. The idea gave her no satisfaction. She went home and sat in the drawing room, staring at nothing. Mr. Rutledge did not come.

Word reached the newspapers sometime late that day, and the next morning the house was plagued by eager men wanting Sophia's story. Lewis tossed a few of them into the street, and the rest dispersed. "They will probably make things up to sell their papers," he warned Sophia.

"I find I am no longer disturbed by anything they might write," she said. "This will pass, and some other excitement will draw their attention, and everyone will forget about me and Lord Endicott."

"If that's what you want," Lewis said, and went back to his study.

Mr. Rutledge still did not come.

That night Sophia once again lay wakeful, conscious of the ring in her drawer the way she might be aware of an open flame threatening to set her bed afire. Perhaps she needed to call on him. Though he might not be well enough to receive callers. Or was he regretting his delirious words, and hoping never to see her again? Unless he thought she had only accepted his offer to humor him, to keep him from being agitated in his wounded condition, in which case she ought to go to him and reassure him of her affection for him. Her love for him.

It is so strange, she thought, *I truly intended never to marry again because I did not believe I would find anything like what I had with Richard again. It never occurred to me to look for something different.* Five times she opened the drawer and held her hand over the ring, five times she closed it and went back to staring at the high, invisible ceiling.

She woke groggy and exhausted the next morning, and dressed slowly, aching as if she had spent the night in Dream. *I do not know why I bother sleeping at all.* She settled herself in the drawing room with a book she had no interest in reading. Someone would likely come this morning to escort her to Whitehall, to make her statement yet again.

Representatives from the War Office would be there as well, ostensibly to give her support, but Sophia was certain they would face intense questioning about the War Office's role in everything that had ensued from Sophia's first Dream of Lord Endicott's crimes. It gave her a feeling of wicked pleasure at their discomfort and an even better feeling at having the chance to look her former superiors in the eye and watch them cringe in embarrassment at how wrong they had been. Mr. Rutledge had said she had grounds for suing them, though she was not sure it was possible to sue the government. She only wanted them to grovel for her forgiveness so she could be patronizingly gracious at them.

Simon opened the door. "You have a caller, ma'am. Shall I say you are at home?"

"Who is it?"

"Mr. Rutledge, ma'am."

It was as if thinking of him had made him appear. How strange that Simon did not react to the sound of her heart trying to Skip out of her chest. "Please show him up," she said, probably too loudly, but her ears were filled with a low hum that made everything else seem very far away. She took a seat in the uncomfortable chair—or should she be standing when he entered? She stood, paced, sat down again, and was in the process of rising when the door opened and Mr. Rutledge came in.

He showed no sign he had ever been injured. On the contrary, he looked very good—better than good, because he was wearing a well-cut suit with a handsome waistcoat and a cravat that, while not the height of fashion, at least looked as if he had spent some time on tying it properly. She had never seen him dressed so well, and for one mad moment she thought *He is here to propose again, properly*, but his expression was closed off, severe, and not that of a man on such a happy errand.

He shut the door behind him but did not approach her. "Mrs. Westlake," he said.

"Mr. Rutledge," she replied.

"I understand," he said after a brief pause, "that I owe you my life. Thank you."

She couldn't think of anything to say to that, since he had saved her life first, so she only nodded. What *should* she say? If he did not remember asking her to marry him, or had changed his mind, she would look like such a fool if she brought the subject up. But they could not simply stand there in silence. They were, if nothing else, still friends. She hoped. Why could she not simply speak her heart?

"Will you sit?" she said, waving her hand in the general direction of the chairs.

"I should not stay long, I have a statement to make at Bow Street," he said.

"I have already given mine. Sir Arthur is disappointed in me."

"How is that?"

"He believes I should be willing to repeat myself half a dozen times, as if I might change my mind about what happened at some point."

"I'm afraid I won't be very useful to him. I have insisted my involvement remain confidential. And I don't remember much of anything except being shot."

Of course he didn't. To think she had been so eager to see him. Now she only wanted him to leave so she could go to her room and weep. "You look entirely recovered," she managed.

"I feel very well," he said. "There is not even a mark to show where the ball entered."

"I know," she said, then wished she could take the words back, pretend she had not seen him so exposed, and stammered, "that is, I was... I saw Dr. Garland Heal you, the ball—I put it somewhere but I cannot remember now, if you wish—Dr. Garland said you might want it..." Her voice trailed off as her mind began shrieking at her to stop speaking before she made even more a fool of herself.

Mr. Rutledge nodded, though she had no idea which part of her babbling speech he was acknowledging. He shifted his weight, and looked toward the fireplace, where the fire was burning low. No point in building it up when they would both be quitting the room soon. "I do remember," he said, "that is, it is a very blurry memory, but I remember asking you to marry me."

Her heart began trying to leap out of her chest again. "You did," she said.

"And I also remember," he added, "that you accepted me." He

turned his gaze on her, that direct, uncomfortable, unsmiling gaze. He did not look like he thought it was a pleasant memory.

"I did," she said. She did not know what else to say. Did he love her, or not?

He looked toward the fire again. "It occurred to me," he said after a very long moment in which Sophia thought she might scream, "that you might have felt some obligation to me, for being wounded in your stead. That your answer might have been influenced by that sense of obligation. So I am here to tell you that you need not feel bound by your answer. I will not hold you to it."

Sophia blinked at him. Obligation? Could he have misunderstood her so completely? A hundred different responses welled up within her, but what came out was, "Oh?"

"I consider you a true friend, Mrs. Westlake," Mr. Rutledge said, "but I cannot help thinking—I am thirteen years your senior, and while that may not be such a difference in the eyes of society, I am also quite set in my bachelor ways and I do not—I believe I am an unlikely choice to make you happy. If you consider marrying again, it should be someone more your contemporary, someone you can meet as an equal. I hope you will still call me friend."

"Oh," Sophia said again. Everything seemed to be happening at a remove. She managed to look into his eyes without bursting into tears. So, they were to be friends. Such a pale substitute for what she wanted. But—

She examined him more closely. His formal, measured words were at odds with his face, which bore a tangle of emotions, pain, sorrow, uncertainty. He looked exactly like a man who was doing a very painful duty and expected to be shown the door at any moment. What was it he had once said—that he was doing the world a favor by not entering into a state of matrimony? Set in his bachelor ways, indeed. It seemed he was as bad at speaking his heart as she was. She longed to throw her arms around him and kiss his troubles away. But perhaps another ploy might be more effective.

She turned away and picked up the poker, jabbed at the fire. "Then I suppose I'm free to marry Lord Chumleigh."

She heard him take in an astonished breath. "Chumleigh?"

"Well, yes. I believe he is quite devoted to me in his own right and not only as Lord Endicott's proxy, and he *is* nearly my age, which according to you is crucial to marital happiness. I'm sure, now that he isn't influenced by Lord Endicott, I will be able to break him of his gambling habit. And I imagine I'll become accustomed to the smell of tobacco, with time.

"Though... Mr. Hawley does pay me the most particular attention; do you believe I might be happier with him? That laugh of his might become endearing if one heard it often enough, I suppose. And I do consider him my equal, in every sense, except for his lack of interest in current events, and his inability to understand my jokes, and—I suppose I *don't* consider him my equal, after all. Now, Mr. Spencer—"

"Mrs. Westlake," Mr. Rutledge said in a rather strangled voice, "what are you *thinking?*"

"At the moment, I am thinking tormenting you is rather enjoyable," Sophia said. She dropped the poker and rounded on him. "How dare you determine what will make me happy? As if your age were enough to outweigh everything else you are to me? If you are concerned that I accepted your proposal out of gratitude, then I suggest you ask me again, right now, and see how I respond when you are not dying on the ground in front of me!"

She took a deep breath, and added, "And if you do *not* ask me again, right now, I will find Lord Chumleigh, and drag him to the nearest church, and you will have to suffer in the knowledge that your wife is married to someone else!"

Mr. Rutledge sank onto the nearest chair and covered his eyes with his hand. "Sophia," he said, "if I ask you to marry me, will you leave off filling my head with nightmares?"

"I might, if it is a sincere enough proposal," she said.

He slid off the seat to drop to one knee before her. Even kneeling, he was surprisingly tall. "Sophia, my love," he said, taking both her hands in his, "I cannot imagine living without you, and if you consent to marry me, I will do everything in my power to make you happy."

"You already have," she said, and leaned down to kiss him.

ACKNOWLEDGMENTS

This book would not have been possible without the generous feed-back of Jana Brown, Hallie O'Donovan, and Jacob Proffitt, the last of whose insights into romance in fiction were much appreciated. Sherwood Smith kindly read this novel in draft and provided many useful facts about British usage and period accuracy; any remaining mistakes are entirely mine.

The Bow Street Runners have been represented in popular fiction frequently in recent years. For an excellent text on the fact behind the fiction, I recommend *The First English Detectives* by J.M. Beattie. Not easy to find, but well worth reading.

THE TALENTS

THE CORPOREAL TALENTS: Mover, Shaper, Scorcher, Bounder

MOVER (Greek τελεκινεσις): Capable of moving things without physically touching them. While originally this talent was believed to be connected to one's bodily strength, female Movers able to lift far more than their male counterparts have disproven this theory in recent years. Depending on skill, training, and practice, Movers may be able to lift and manipulate multiple objects at once, pick locks, and manipulate anything the human hand can manage. Movers can Move other people so long as they don't resist, and some are capable of Moving an unwilling target if the Mover is strong enough.

An EXTRAORDINARY MOVER, in addition to all these things, is capable of flight. Aside from this, an Extraordinary Mover is not guaranteed to be better skilled or stronger than an ordinary Mover; Helen Garrity, England's highest-rated Mover (at upwards of 12,000 pounds lifting capacity), was an ordinary Mover.

SHAPER (Greek μπιοκινεσις): Capable of manipulating their own bodies. Shapers can alter their own flesh, including healing wounds. Most Shapers use their ability only to make themselves more attractive, though that sort of beauty is always obvious as Shaped. More subtle uses include disguising oneself, and many Shapers have also been spies. It usually takes time for a Shaper to alter herself because Shaping is painful, and the faster one does it, the more painful it is. Under extreme duress, Shapers can alter their bodies rapidly, but this results in great pain and longer-term muscle and joint pain.

Shapers can mend bone, heal cuts or abrasions, repair physical damage to organs as from a knife wound, etc., make hair and nails grow, improve their physical condition (for example, enhance lung efficiency), and change their skin color. They cannot restore lost limbs or organs, cure diseases (though they can repair the physical damage done by disease), change hair or eye color, or regenerate nerves.

An EXTRAORDINARY SHAPER is capable of turning a Shaper's talent on another person with skin-to-skin contact. Extraordinary Shapers are sometimes called Healers as a result. While most Extraordinary Shapers use their talent to help others, there is nothing to stop them from causing injury or even death instead.

SCORCHER (Greek πιροκινεσις): Capable of igniting fire by the power of thought. The fire is natural and will cause ordinary flammable objects to catch on fire. If there aren't any such objects handy, the fire will burn briefly and then go out. A Scorcher must be able to see the place he or she is starting the fire. Scorcher talent has four dimensions: power, range, distance, and stamina. Power refers to how large and hot a fire the Scorcher can create; range is how far the Scorcher can fling a fire before it goes out; distance is how far away a Scorcher can ignite a fire; and stamina refers to how often the Scorcher can use his or her power before becoming exhausted. The hottest ordinary fire any Scorcher has ever created could melt brass (approximately 1700 degrees F). When she gave herself over to the fire, Elinor Pembroke was able to melt iron (over 2200 degrees F).

Scorchers are rare because they manifest by igniting fire unconsciously in their sleep. About 10-20% of Scorchers survive manifestation.

EXTRAORDINARY SCORCHERS are capable of controlling and mentally extinguishing fires. As their talent develops,

Extraordinary Scorchers become immune to fire, and their control over it increases.

BOUNDER (Greek τελεταχύς): Capable of moving from one point to another without passing through the intervening space. Bounders can move themselves anywhere they can see clearly within a certain range that varies according to the Bounder; this is called Skipping. They can also Bound to any location marked with a Bounder symbol, known as a signature. The location must be closed to the outdoors and empty of people and objects. Bounders refer to the "simplicity" of a space, meaning how free of "clutter" (objects, people, etc.) it is. Spaces that are too cluttered are impossible to Bound to, as are outdoor locations, which are full of constant movement. It is possible to keep a Bounder out of somewhere if you alter the place by defacing the Bounding chamber or putting some object or person into it.

An EXTRAORDINARY BOUNDER lacks most of the limitations an ordinary Bounder operates under. An Extraordinary Bounder's range is line of sight, which can allow them to Skip many miles' distance. Extraordinary Bounders do not require Bounding signatures, instead using what they refer to as "essence" to identify a space they Bound to. Essence comprises the essential nature of a space and is impossible to explain to non-Bounders; human beings have an essence which differs from that of a place and allows an Extraordinary Bounder to identify people without seeing them. While Extraordinary Bounders are still incapable of Bounding to an outdoor location, they can Bound to places too cluttered for an ordinary Bounder, as well as ones that contain people.

THE ETHEREAL TALENTS: Seer, Speaker, Discerner, Coercer

SEER (Greek προφητεία): Capable of seeing a short distance into the future through Dreams. Seers experience lucid Dreams in which they see future events as if they were present as an invisible observer. In order to recognize the people or places involved, Seers tend to be very well informed about people and events and are socially active. Their Dreams are not inevitable and there is no problem with altering the timeline; they see things that are the natural consequence of the current situation/circumstances, and altering those things alters the foreseen event. Just their knowledge of the event is not sufficient to alter it.

No one knows how a Seer's brain produces Dream, only that Dreams come in response to what the Seer meditates on. Seers therefore study current events in depth and read up on things they might be asked to Dream about. Seers have high social status and are very popular, with many of them making a living from Dream commissions.

An EXTRAORDINARY SEER, in addition to Dreaming, is capable of touching an object and perceiving events and people associated with it. These Visions allow them not only to see the past of the person most closely connected to the object, but occasionally to have glimpses of the future. They can also find a Vision linked to what the object's owner is seeing at the moment and "see" through their eyes. Most recently, the Extraordinary Seer Sophia Westlake discovered how to use Visions attached to one object to perceive related objects, leading to the defeat of the Caribbean pirates led by Rhys Evans.

SPEAKER (Greek τελεπάθεια): Capable of communicating by thought with any other Speaker. Speakers can mentally communicate with any Speaker within range of sight. They can also communicate with any Speaker they know well. The definition of "know well" has meaning only to a Speaker, but in general it means someone they have spoken verbally or mentally with on several occasions. A Speaker's circle of Speaker friends is called a reticulum, and a reticulum might contain several hundred members depending on the Speaker. Speakers easily distinguish between the different "voices" of their Speaker friends, though Speaking is not auditory. A Speaker can send images as well as words if she is proficient enough. Speakers cannot Speak to non-Speakers, and they are incapable of reading minds.

An EXTRAORDINARY SPEAKER has all the abilities of an ordinary Speaker, but is also capable of sending thoughts and images into the minds of anyone, Speaker or not. Additionally, an Extraordinary Speaker can Speak to multiple people at a time, though all will receive the same message. Extraordinary Speakers can send a "burst" of noise that startles or wakes the recipient. Rumors that Extraordinary Speakers can read minds are universally denied by Speakers, but the rumors persist.

DISCERNER (Greek ενσυναίσθηση): Able to experience other people's feelings as if they were their own. Discerners require touch to be able to do this (though not skin-to-skin contact), and much of learning to control the skill involves learning to distinguish one's own emotions from those of the other person. Discerners can detect lies, sense motives, read other people's emotional states, and identify Coercers. Discerners are immune to the talent of a Coercer, though they can be overwhelmed by anyone capable of projecting strong emotions.

An EXTRAORDINARY DISCERNER can do all these things without the need for touch. Extraordinary Discerners are always aware of the emotions of those near them, though the range at which they are aware varies according to the Extraordinary Discerner. Nearly three-quarters of all Extraordinary Discerners go mad because of their talent.

COERCER (Greek τελενσυναίσθηση): Capable of influencing the emotions of others with a touch. Coercers are viewed with great suspicion since their ability is a kind of mind control. Those altered are not aware that their mood has been artificially changed and are extremely suggestible while the Coercer is in direct contact with them. By altering someone's emotions, a Coercer can influence their behavior or change his or her attitude toward the Coercer.

Coercers do not feel others' emotions the way Discerners do, but can tell what they are and how they're changing. Many Coercers have sociopathic tendencies as a result. Unlike Discerners, Coercers have to work hard at being able to use their talent, which in its untrained state is erratic. However, Coercers always know when they've altered someone's mood. Coercers do not "broadcast" their emotions, appearing as a blank to Discerners. Because Coercion is viewed with suspicion (for good reason), Coercers keep their ability secret even if they don't use it maliciously.

An EXTRAORDINARY COERCER does not need a physical connection to influence someone's emotions. Extraordinary Coercers are capable of turning their talent on several people at a time, and the most powerful Extraordinary Coercers can control mobs. The most powerful Extraordinary Coercer known to date is Napoleon Bonaparte.

ABOUT THE AUTHOR

In addition to The Extraordinaries series, Melissa McShane is the author of more than twenty fantasy novels, including the novels of Tremontane, the first of which is *Servant of the Crown; Company of Strangers*, first in the series of the same name; and *The Book of Secrets,* first book in The Last Oracle series. She lives in the shelter of the mountains out West with her husband, four children and a niece, and three very needy cats. She wrote reviews and critical essays for many years before turning to fiction, which is much more fun than anyone ought to be allowed to have. You can visit her at her website **www. melissamcshanewrites.com** for more information on other books and upcoming releases.

For news on upcoming releases, bonus material, and other fun stuff, sign up for Melissa's newsletter at http://eepurl.com/brannP

Made in the USA
Coppell, TX
14 April 2022

76507207R00184